A French Affair

CATHERINE DALY

POOLBEG

Published 2006
by Poolbeg Press Ltd
123 Grange Hill, Baldoyle
Dublin 13, Ireland
E-mail: poolbeg@poolbeg.com

Typesetting, layout, design © Poolbeg Press Ltd

1 3 5 7 9 10 8 6 4 2

A catalogue record for this book is available from the British Library.

ISBN 1-84223-228-2

Typeset by Type Design in Sabon MT 10.5/13.8 pt
Printed by
Litografia Roses, Spain

www.poolbeg.com

ABOUT THE AUTHOR

Catherine was born in Dublin and spent her childhood in Belgium and Ireland. After qualifying as a pharmacist from Trinity College, she worked in a hospital in Chichester in the South of England for five years. She returned to Ireland in 1996 and lives in Dublin with her husband and two children.

This is her third novel with Poolbeg and her previous novels are *All Shook Up* and *Charlotte's Way*.

She is the creator of the website www.writeon-irishgirls.com, an online resource for writers and readers, and welcomes readers and writers from all over the globe to participate in the chat.

For more information, or to contact Catherine, visit her official website at: www.catherinedaly.com

She loves to get feedback by e-mail: info@catherinedaly.com

ALSO BY CATHERINE DALY

Charlotte's Way

All Shook Up

ACKNOWLEDGEMENTS

Thank you to readers everywhere, without whom there would be no books and no need for writers. And of course special thanks to those who read *All Shook Up* and *Charlotte's Way*. Many of you even took the time to contact me and let me know what you thought – without feedback like that it wouldn't be nearly as much fun to write. So keep getting in touch!

Thanks to Denis, Lorcan and Clíodhna who put up with more than usual to get this book onto the shelves. Thanks as ever for your love and patience. And to Lorcan and Clíodhna – now that the book's finished, I'm back in charge of the television remote control!

To all the friends I've made through writing – far too numerous to mention, you know who you are!

Thanks finally to everyone at Poolbeg, especially Gaye Shortland my editor, and to Ali and everyone at Curtis Brown.

For Denis, Lorcan and Clíodhna

Chapter 1

As Evie took five wide rollers out of the top of her hair, pulled a brush through the ends and blasted her whole head with a few bursts of a glossing spray, she watched her daughter playing happily with her own make-up in front of a play-sized dressing-table.

You have no idea, sweetheart, Evie thought nervously, that our lives could be about to change forever. Because the week ahead, originally planned to be Evie's first childless holiday since Holly was born, had suddenly developed the potential to bring her past rushing up to confront her.

Evie was in a hurry, having pressed her snooze button once too often after only four and a half hours' sleep. But her colleague's hen night the night before had been worth it – one of Evie's best nights out in years – so good, it

1

almost made her look back fondly at the days before Holly was born. The days when she was able to go straight from work to the pub, from there to a nightclub, sometimes on to a party, and, on occasion, straight back in to work the next morning. Now, as she struggled to keep her eyes open, she wondered where all her energy had gone.

"Yes, that's right, good girl, Holly!" Evie smiled at her daughter who was smoothing the Velcro fastening on her shoe. "Now the other one."

As she watched, she again marvelled at the wonders of genetics, which had given her a daughter who looked so unlike her. Evie was tall, strong-featured and had straight, mousey-brown hair (admittedly coloured an expensive glossy chestnut), while Holly was tiny, with fine elfin features and dark brown, almost black hair which tumbled in unruly curls around her face. Evie's eyes were blue and no amount of mascara gave her more than a few sad, stubby eyelashes, whereas Holly's brown eyes were set off perfectly by long, sweeping, doe-like lashes, which made Evie think of Arabian princesses in children's storybooks.

"Can't find my other shoe," Holly said. "It's aaaaaall gone!"

"Like my energy," Evie muttered, then out loud she added: "You had it earlier …" She took a deep breath. Please, she prayed silently, not this morning. We're running late and I have a flight to catch. "Have another look, sweetheart, maybe it's under the bed."

Deciding to abandon her make-up – she could do it in

the airport later – Evie diverted her all energy into finding Holly's shoe.

Together they searched the living-room, the hall, the kitchen and the sparkly pink wonderland that was Holly's bedroom. Evie retraced both their steps but it was no good. The small, size-eight, pink runner had vanished. Temporarily left this planet. It happened at least once a week – just as Holly and Evie were ready to depart for Holly's crèche, one of her shoes or socks, her hair-band or some other item of (pink) apparel would disappear.

"Perhaps," Evie suggested finally in a conspiratorial tone when it was clear that the pink runner was not going to reappear, "perhaps, just this once, I'll let you wear your party shoes to school."

Holly looked at her mother suspiciously. Her party shoes were her most precious possessions. Bought by Granny Marian (in BT2 and Evie went into a cold sweat every time she tried to imagine how much they cost), they were bright and sparkly, patent ruby-red – just like Dorothy's slippers in *The Wizard of Oz*. When Holly wore them she felt like a grown-up and she walked slowly and carefully, like a "princess" with her toes pointed. In fact, as she had once confided to her beloved Granny, her party shoes were so pretty they could be called "jools for feet".

And now Mummy was suggesting that she be allowed to wear them to school!

"I s'ppose I could," the little girl offered, careful not to appear *too* enthusiastic, "but I'll have to tell Miss Amy that I have to wear my wellies in the garden. Even if it's *not* raining."

Holly stood up and, with the care and grace of a prima ballerina, stepped regally into her bedroom and waited for her mother to take the shoebox down from the top shelf. She waited until she was presented with the glittering treasures, then pointed at the chest of drawers.

"And white socks, Mummy. These pink ones don't 'go'."

Suddenly, Evie felt all trace of impatience and worry at being late for her flight vanish. They disappeared in a puff of smoke worthy of the best efforts of Good Witch Glenda.

"Let me see you!" she ordered when Holly was finally ready, white socks and all. "Do a twirl!"

Her daughter obliged and then stumbled happily into her mother's waiting arms in a well-rehearsed move.

"Who's the luckiest mummy in all the world?" Evie asked, breathless with adoration.

"*You* are!"

"And who's the bestest, most beautifulest, most wonderfulest girl in the whole wide world, and all the universe as well?"

"Holly is!" And as she smoothed down her dress, pointed one toe and admired her shoes, the little girl repeated with even more conviction and gravitas than usual: "Holly is." And Evie felt that her heart would burst with love.

♡   ♡   ♡

Soon Holly was safely fastened into her car-seat, and they were en route to Rainbowland.

"Don't forget Granny will be collecting you today for your big sleepover," Evie reminded her daughter, as she swallowed a lump the size of a small grapefruit in her own throat. "I'll phone you every night I'm away and I'll bring you back a really good present from France."

She glanced in the rear-view mirror to see how Holly was taking this reminder of her absence, but the red shoes took up most of the little girl's attention and she merely muttered, "'Kay. I'll have fun in Granny's."

Evie dropped her daughter off with a minimum of fuss. She had warned the crèche staff that Holly might be more clingy than usual this morning, but she sensed they thought she was being over-protective. And of course, they were right – Holly skipped off happily, babbling about her red shoes, while her teacher was left holding out a box of tissues to Evie. Although she had planned her holiday months ago, it was only now that the reality sank in. A whole week without Holly? She swallowed again, apologised to Holly's teacher and took refuge in the car to wipe up her tears.

On the way to the airport Evie counted up the reasons she was leaving her baby behind.

Firstly, Evie's mother Marian was really looking forward to having Holly to herself for a whole week. Since Evie's brother, his wife and their two boys had moved to New Zealand, Marian felt her recent widowhood all the more keenly. So Evie knew it would do her good to spend some time with her youngest grandchild – to take her mind off the fact that her two grandsons were on the other side of the world.

Secondly, it would do Holly good to spend some time away from Evie. Although she was a confident and unclingy child who had never had reason to doubt that her mother would always be there for her, Holly would be off to "big school" in just over a year's time, and although she had settled well into playschool, it would do her good to learn to rely on her own inner resources.

And finally, it was a long time since Evie had spent time with her best friend, Monique, without Holly being there too. They needed a proper, child-free holiday. They had been promising it to themselves, after all, since before Holly was born. This fantasy holiday had of course involved long-haul flights and tropical cocktails – but as they were both low on funds, Evie's first Holly-less holiday was going to be the rather less exotic option of a week in Monique's house.

Monique had moved to France over five years ago, and since then Evie had taken advantage of cheap flights to visit her a few times a year. Raising a child on her own meant cutting back on other holidays, so Evie was doubly glad to have Monique to visit. But it also meant that she never got to go away entirely on her own.

And that was another reason this holiday was so important. Since going back to work full-time a year ago, she could feel the pressure build up inside as she tried to cope with job, house and child all on her own. She would be no use to anyone, least of all Holly, if she collapsed into a little heap of nervous exhaustion. So this week of not having to get up at sunrise, or cook and clean for the world's tiniest mess-monster, promised to be something of a break for Evie.

Or rather it *had* promised to be, until Monique broke some rather earth-shattering news a week ago.

"Evie, I wasn't going to tell you about this at all," she said on the phone. "To be honest, I was hoping it, or rather *he*, would go away . . . but, Evie, Alex Ryder has been looking at property in my neck of the woods, and he's only gone and settled on a place just down the road from me."

Monique went quiet then, as though she was waiting for Evie to explode. Because Alex was Evie's old boss. The owner of a small computer software company, he had let her go not long before his company went public. If Evie had been working for him when the company floated, she would have been in line for a payout in the form of shares. Evie had refused to talk about it since then, but Monique knew she was very bitter.

"How on earth? Alex in France, near you . . . but why?"

"The Bristol flight into Bergerac," Monique replied simply. "He chose this part of France because he could get back and forward to Bristol easily. He chose our estate agency because he knew a few other people in Bristol who had used us. And of course, not all agencies have someone who speaks English."

Evie was tempted to call off her holiday. The thought of running into him when she wasn't expecting to …

But Monique read her mind: "You don't have to meet

him, Evie. I know his place is down the road from me, but he may not be in France at the same time as you. And anyway, all that's in the past, isn't it? If necessary, just let the air out of his tyres one day, and then forget about him."

But forgetting about Alex wasn't going to be easy – Monique didn't know the full story.

Chapter 2

Y ou are one sad excuse for a twenty-seven-year-old, Evie scolded herself a few hours later as she changed terminals in Stansted. She hadn't shaken off her depression at leaving Holly.

You are going on holidays, she told herself. Ho-li-days! Drink, dance and debauchery in the company of your best friend.

But Holly had seemed so happy this morning despite saying goodbye that, although Evie knew she didn't really have a concept of how long a week was (seven "big sleeps" being more sleeps than you can count on one hand), she couldn't help feeling just a tad unwanted and unloved.

It would be different if she were leaving Holly with her father, Evie imagined. Then she would walk away like most other mothers she knew – with a large measure of relief and a little smidgin of mischievous schadenfreude at leaving the other half to cope for a change. But Holly had never met her father and so far Evie had fielded all questions about him with vague mutterings of being "Mummy and Daddy all rolled into one". She could never decide when would be the right time to explain it properly to Holly. Just as she had never decided when she should tell Holly's dad.

♡　　♡　　♡

Monique sat in the small outdoor café at the edge of the runway in Bergerac airport and waited for the flight from Stansted. She was sipping a small black coffee and scribbling the odd note into a blue folder open on the table in front of her. A few firemen were cleaning a fire truck outside a hangar on the edge of the runway, only a few hundred feet from where she sat. But in heavy suits their enthusiasm for their work was limited in this early summer heat. Like Monique they kept looking up to scan the sky for any sign of the incoming plane. A gust of wind blew across the tarmac and disturbed her papers. It was all the excuse Monique needed to tidy away the trappings of work, stretch out her bare legs to absorb the hot French sunshine and declare her holiday officially started.

It had taken the five years Monique had lived in France for her grandmother's French genes to finally gain dominance over her Anglo-Saxon ones, but she had finally achieved the separation between work and leisure that the French regard as vital to civilised living. She switched off her phone at lunch hour and used her one-and-a-half-hour lunch break to eat, relax and meet friends rather than to scurry around shopping or to follow up on clients. And she rarely, if ever, worked during her time off.

She also *looked* more French than she had five years ago. Her small manicured hands flew about in animation whenever she spoke and her heart-shaped face was more expressive when she talked in her grandmother's tongue than when she spoke English. But it was her hair and her clothes that set her apart from her English compatriots in the small airport. Monique's shiny bob skimmed her jaw-line with laser-like accuracy – it was clearly a hairstyle that could only be maintained by regular fortnightly visits to the *coiffeuse*. Her knee-length skirt and tailored silk blouse were *just* the right cut to flatter and look stylish without making her into a fashion victim.

Monique smiled at the middle-aged couple who came and sat at the table next to hers. They were overdressed for the early summer heat; they looked flustered and hot and were surrounded by plastic bags full of bottle-shaped parcels. They were clients of hers – an English couple who had spent the past week touring the area with her, looking at run-down properties to buy and renovate with a view to eventually semi-retiring to France to run a guesthouse. They had spotted the perfect farm complex, but it was above their budget so they were returning home to see if they could raise the necessary finance.

Monique hoped, as much for their sake as for her own, that they succeeded. She had shown them several houses, from ready-to-go businesses with established reputations, to ruins that were little more than four tumbledown walls, and she had recognised the gleam in their eyes when she led them around the farmhouse near the quaint medieval town of Issigeac. Situated in the middle of several acres of fields (which luckily for Monique were planted with sunflowers this year), the farmhouse had already been restored, but there were several barns and a stunning dovecote (a typical Périgordian *pigeonnier*) waiting to be transformed into really special holiday accommodation. The couple had fallen in love with the place; it was now their gold standard, and if they didn't manage to buy it, everything else would be a compromise.

Monique loved matching people to properties. Since moving to the Dordogne, she had worked with three estate agents, but her current job was her favourite. The other two had been too hard-sell for her. Ironically, the small local company she worked for now ended up making far more sales. And Monique made more commission.

The distant roar of a jet engine announced the arrival of the flight from Stansted and about half the customers in the café got to their feet – either moving closer to the glass barrier separating them from the runway, or going outside to watch for the arrivals who would soon be emerging onto the steps already being rolled into place. Monique's couple, far too early for their Bristol flight, stayed where they were. Monique waited until she spotted Evie – one of the first passengers to emerge, blinking, into the sunshine. Then she went out to wait outside the baggage collection hall.

The two women met outside after Evie had collected her bags.

"Don't bother looking for a trolley," Monique said, taking the heavier of her friend's two bags. "We're just over here."

Straight across from them, parked on the edge of a small grass verge, was "The Bug": Monique's beloved Citroen 2CV, painted to resemble a ladybird – shiny red all over with black spots the size of large dinner-plates scattered across the bonnet and doors. The soft top was folded back and the sight finally put Evie into a holiday mood. She began to relax as she threw her bags in the back, and she even managed to smile when Monique asked after Holly.

"She's going to be spoiled rotten. And don't worry – she'll love it," Monique reassured her when Evie went quiet after saying how much she was going to miss Holly and how she didn't seem at all bothered by her mother's absence. "Of course she'll miss you, but she's got the prospect of a super holiday to distract her. A week's sleepover with Granny Marian? Hell, a week of your mum's pampering would be *my* idea of a luxury break!"

They both went quiet as they remembered when Monique had last been in Dublin. Her engagement with long-term boyfriend Tom had just ended and she needed to get away from anyone who knew him to lick her wounds. France was out because he had met everyone over there so his permanent absence would leave a big hole in conversations. And besides, Monique knew that most of her French friends would be far from heartbroken to see the back of him. Bristol was where the two of them had grown up and they had too many friends in common. So Monique had fled to Dublin for a week. Evie had just started back at work but Holly hadn't got her crèche place yet so Marian was minding her during the day. Monique joined her godchild on the couch and the two of them watched *Teletubbies* until the little girl dropped off to sleep and then the two women drank tea and watched daytime television together. Marian was still reeling from the loss of Joe, Evie's dad, so they took turns looking after each other.

"Don't I sound terribly self-centred, wishing misery and sadness on a little girl, just so that I can feel more wanted?" Evie finally managed to grin, diverting conversation safely away from that depressing time. "I only hope you have enough planned to keep me distracted from missing her!" And from worrying about meeting Alex, Evie added silently, amazed that she had managed to resist raising his name. "You were able to take the week off, weren't you?"

Used to having to negotiate every last hour of leave months in advance, Evie couldn't get used to Monique's cavalier attitude to her employer.

"Of course I was able to take holidays. French law is really strict on the subject of holidays for us, the proletariat. In fact, Céline," Monique referred to her employer, the owner of the agency, "is relieved that I'm taking a week now. I've so much time owed to me that theoretically I could leave her high and dry for weeks on end, just when all the English holidaymakers are over here falling in love with the area."

Evie smiled – Céline's English was book-perfect, but her accent was appalling, and her tolerance of some of her more eccentric English clients was low.

"The only thing I have to do while you're here," Monique continued, as she veered wildly onto the other side of the road, onto the grass verge and almost into an orchard to overtake a tractor, "is to let a surveyor in to re-inspect a property. Don't worry," she added, mistaking the reason for Evie's pursed lips and look of alarm as the car returned to its own side of the road, "I'm letting him in at eight thirty tomorrow morning, so you'll probably still be eating breakfast by the time I get back."

"Breakfast?" Evie said weakly, checking her seatbelt and wondering if Monique would take offence if she closed her eyes for the rest of the trip. "Hell, I won't even be out of bed at that time! I hope to be suffering mild after-effects of an obscene amount of the local produce." She waved her hand in the direction of a vineyard to make herself doubly clear. She'd been working too hard lately and needed to seriously let her hair down. It might take a few days to switch out of "Mommy mode", but Evie had long ago decided that this week she was going to rediscover her mad, pre-Holly self. The Evie who didn't think twice about staying up till dawn and who, in college, had been the undefeated champion of almost any drinking game her fellow students had challenged her to.

The friends chatted and gossiped during the drive from the airport. They had been best friends for nearly ten years, since college. Evie had been studying in Bristol University, and Monique, whose parents had helped her buy a small house near the university, had been her housemate as well as her landlady. So they swapped news of college friends, many of whom, like Evie, were Irish and had moved back to Dublin; of work colleagues from a brief time when the two had worked together in London; and of friends they had met since splitting up – Monique having moved "temporarily" to France to improve her evening-class French.

Soon they arrived at Monique's old farmhouse on the edge of the small village of Ste Anne. Stepping through the front door was like stepping back in time; into a long salon that took up most of the ground floor. French windows at the back of the house led from the kitchen to a patio and a large garden. It was mostly laid to lawn but Monique's interest in gardening was evident in several shrubs, a rose bed and a few flower-filled borders. Two smaller windows at the front of the house looked down over the other houses in the village, built mainly of sandstone with red tiled roofs. Beyond the village, fields were planted with sunflowers or with ripening wheat dotted with brilliant red poppies. The hillside on the other side of the valley was clothed mainly in lush vines.

The big room was comfortably furnished and

decorated with an eclectic mixture of second-hand and antique furniture and ornaments, which reflected Monique's magpie-like interest in *Brocante* shops and flea-markets. The only obvious intrusions from the twenty-first century were a small yellow microwave in the kitchen end of the room and a laptop plugged in beside the huge sandstone fireplace at the other. In the kitchen end of the room most of the space was taken up by a heavy oak refectory table covered in a yellow and blue flower-patterned oilcloth. On it were some coloured files in a pile and several loose photos of properties, which were scattered across its surface.

Evie wandered over and flicked through some of the pictures. Every time she visited, she would look longingly at the houses on offer and fantasise about moving to France. She and Monique had spent many a wine-lubricated hour discussing it. There was a lovely little village school crying out for pupils, so Holly would be sure of a warm welcome. Property prices in this part of France, although rising rapidly, were only a fraction of those in Dublin – so Evie could sell her house at home, pay off her mortgage and be left with enough to buy something almost loan-free in the Dordogne. The climate was so much more pleasant and the country air was sure to help Holly's asthma.

Evie's fantasy was predictable – she would picture Holly skipping happily into the small school and growing up to be bilingual. She could imagine leaving her job in Dublin and going back to working freelance, with the millstone of a mortgage gone from around her neck. She would learn to cook wholesome, imaginative meals with the wonderful local ingredients purchased during a friendly walk through the local market. And she might even take in bed-and-breakfast customers in summer to generate a little extra cash. (Evie was addicted to "new life in the sun" television programmes!)

But then being Evie, reliable and realistic, she would take a reality-check. She would ask how she could possibly cope on her own without her mum to baby-sit in emergencies. She would have no backup other than Monique, and although her friend was the best in the world, she wasn't family.

"So! See any houses you fancy?" Monique teased when she saw what Evie was doing. She looked over her friend's shoulder and saw that she was looking at the aerial photo of a large converted barn with several ramshackle outbuildings surrounding it. She took it back casually and handed Evie another pile to leaf through. "That house is way too big for you – if you're going to play fantasy *Place in the Sun* you may as well be realistic! I'll let you have a look at the properties I was loading onto the computer – I've some really nice ones at the moment. They'd nearly tempt me to move. And talking of computers – can you take a look at mine while you're here? I know you set it up last time so that I could access the files straight off the server at work, but I seem to have screwed it up again."

"Yeah, no problem," Evie answered. She would be able to fix that in her sleep. "Just so long as I don't have to go into the office and set up the whole system in there again!"

Monique blushed. She had been showing her friend around the estate agent's office when she had started working there, and Céline had asked her to take a look at their new website – they were having teething problems. Between language difficulties and the ancient system they were using, it had taken Evie the best part of a day to sort out some obvious problems, but she had refused to give up.

"No, don't worry," Monique said. "The system in the office is working fine."

Evie flicked her way through another few photos, while Monique took the one with the large barn complex and slipped it discreetly back into a manila folder.

"Give me that!" Evie snatched the file from Monique. She stared at it. Stared at the label which carried a series of letters and numbers followed by a pencilled-in name: *Alex Ryder*.

"Sorry," Monique apologised. "I thought I'd put that file away …" She paused. "You may as well have a look at it now. I have to say he has taste, your ex-boss. I brought him around I don't know how many other places in the hope of getting rid of him. Most of them cheaper, and all of them nice and far away from here, but Céline had already shown him this one and he came right back to it."

Evie nodded dumbly and flicked through the other pictures. It was time to tell Monique why the prospect of seeing Alex again was so terrifying, but she couldn't find the words.

"Well …?" Monique prompted after a minute or so of silence. She seemed to have guessed what was on Evie's mind. "It's a long time ago, Evie. There's more to the story than just losing a great job and a bonus, isn't there? Did you and Ryder have a thing together?"

"Forget it." Evie picked up her bags and made for the open stairs in the corner of the room. "And forget him. I'm here to enjoy myself. Sod him!"

She put her foot on the first step, then turned around.

"Oh, hell. I may as well tell you now. You're bound to find out, or at least work it out for yourself eventually … You may even have guessed now that you've met him. Yes, I did have a 'thing' with Alex and we had … I mean … he …"

"He's Holly's father?"

"Yes. And he doesn't even know she exists."

Chapter 3

"I know I told you Holly was the result of a one-night stand," Evie said later that night over dinner. She had avoided talking about it for the rest of the afternoon, and she was grateful that Monique didn't push her. "And, I suppose, I was fairly wild then. You and me both! Or rather you were if Tom wasn't round. He was your 'stabilising' influence, your sensible older boyfriend. Well, a while after I started working for Alex, he became my stabilising influence! And it certainly wasn't a one-night stand. It built up slowly, very slowly actually, over a few weeks and months. It was after you'd gone to France, so I guess I was feeling lonely. It started with some working lunches together. I kidded myself at first that he was 'mentoring' me and I really liked him. In fact, I fancied him like you wouldn't believe, but I couldn't imagine him ever being really interested in me. Then he invited me to a couple of films – he was big into Arthouse cinema and he said he'd love the company, and he didn't know anyone else interested. Then we might go for a drink afterwards, and I began to realise that we were 'dating', or whatever you want to call it. I was afraid of what everyone at work would say – Rydercom was still quite a small company at the time, so it would have been impossible to keep it quiet. I mean, it was a great place to work: everyone got on so well together, and we all went drinking together – Alex included. But he was still the boss, and I was the last person to join the company."

Evie stopped and looked round; she looked as though she was studying her surroundings. The wooden riverside terrace, built on stilts over the edge of the water, amongst trailing willow branches. The yellow and blue *Ricard* sunshades, folded up now that it was evening. The redchecked paper tablecloths fastened over the white cotton cloths below with steel clips. But Evie had eaten here often and was only looking round because Monique's scrutiny was making her uncomfortable.

"And Alex was married," she continued after a while. "Separated, but not divorced. And he had three children."

This last sentence came out more bitterly than Evie had intended, making Monique realise that Holly's missing father weighed more on Evie's mind than she had ever admitted.

"Everything made me cautious. So when Alex said he wanted to introduce me to everybody as his girlfriend, I said, no, we should wait, that he was moving too fast."

The restaurant owner arrived with a dessert wine, interrupting Evie. She made a big ceremony of opening the bottle at the table, chatting to Monique in French as she did so. Out of politeness, she translated her first few remarks into English for Evie's benefit, but soon realised Monique's guest had retreated into a world of her own.

"So how did you get from 'dating' to … Holly?" Monique asked when she finally got rid of the Frenchwoman.

Evie smiled as she remembered. "Like I said, I really liked Alex, and I fancied him rotten. And he was … well, to put it mildly, he was bloody good in bed! Made me appreciate why a woman might be interested in an older man." Evie grinned at that. When they were seventeen and starting first year, she had been shocked that Monique's boyfriend, Tom, was so much older and an experienced soldier when the rest of them were barely out of school. But as the years passed and the age gap "narrowed" she had just teased her friend about her "older man". "Soon I began to realise that I loved him," Evie continued. "So I began to feel silly about keeping him a secret from everyone. I felt that I was building the differences between us into something huge. Something they weren't. So what if he had children by a former marriage? If I was going to exclude a man on that basis, I could forget a large proportion of the British male population. And I persuaded myself that twelve years was hardly a *huge* age gap between us. And if I didn't want to go out with the boss – I was confident enough to think that a new job would be very easily come by. A lot easier than another man like Alex. I was just getting ready to tell him all this; I was waiting for the right time when …"

"When what? What happened? What went wrong?" Monique was impatient to find out how Evie had gone from moving her relationship with Alex up a notch to fleeing the country on the next Dublin-bound flight.

"He went back to his wife," Evie spat. "We'd been 'seeing each other' a year. Sleeping together for six or seven months. I thought I was about to 'do him a favour' by agreeing to go more public with our relationship, and he decided to go back to his wife. 'For the sake of the children.' And he as good as fired me at the same time. Scrap that – he did fire me. Or rather he got his wife to fire me – she was a 'partner' in the business."

Monique's mouth dropped open. "But … I mean," she shook her head in bewilderment, "they couldn't have just fired you. Aren't there laws against that kind of thing? And if you were pregnant by him …"

"If I wanted to invoke the law, yes, I suppose I could have crucified him. Or rather *them*, him and his wife. But it would have been too humiliating. Picture it – the young graduate falls for her suave older boss. She believes him when he says he and his wife are separated for good. His wife didn't *understand* him, he said – he'd told me that they only got married because she was pregnant. And then, when he goes back to his wife and she takes him back despite everything – the mistress tries to play the pregnancy card. It was too sordid to even contemplate going public with it." Evie shuddered, but didn't admit that one of the main reasons she didn't go after him was that he had begged her not to. "So when I discovered I was expecting Holly, I didn't tell him. I took their generous severance pay, hightailed it home to Ireland, put a deposit on a house and swore I'd never, ever go near him again."

"So Ryder doesn't even know about Holly? You never told him in all these years?" Monique repeated, just to be sure. She didn't know whether to be shocked at Evie keeping it from him or proud of her friend for standing her ground. "Have you never wondered …?"

"Of course I've wondered how they'd get on. She looks like him – now you've met him, you can see what I mean." Evie seemed to be talking to herself now. "They've the same hair, the same eyes – those lovely warm brown buttons. Same upturned nose. And when she giggles – you know those gorgeous dimples Holly gets? Pure Alex!"

Evie was smiling so fondly that for the first time Monique understood some of what she had felt for Alex before he dumped her.

"It didn't work out," she said carefully. Very gently, as if she were afraid of startling Evie. "Alex going back to his wife, I mean. They got divorced. Because of French inheritance law we had to have copies of his divorce papers before he could proceed with the sale. Despite leaving you to rescue his marriage, Alex and his wife got divorced anyway."

♡   ♡   ♡

That night, Evie couldn't sleep. The knowledge that Monique had met Alex, and had been talking to him less than a week ago, was killing her. Monique had probably treated him just like any other client. Like any of the hundreds who arrived in her little corner of France to find their place in the sun. Monique would have been polite to him, friendly even. She had no doubt joked and chatted as they travelled around the Dordogne countryside together. She had laughed at his jokes. She had done her best to get to know him so that she could find the right house for him. And she had obviously succeeded because Alex wouldn't be buying the house at the other end of the village unless he loved it.

When Monique told her about Alex buying the house, it hadn't hit her just *how* close he was going to be. Just over a mile away. Twenty minutes' brisk walk. How on earth could she go on visiting Monique when she ran the risk of running into Alex at any moment? In the village shop. In the café. In any one of the weekly markets she loved to stroll through when she was in France. She had always thought that one day she would go to Alex, to tell him about Holly. She would sweep into his life like some sort of avenging angel and wreak all sorts of havoc. She would arrive from the safety of elsewhere – somewhere she could retreat back to. It had never occurred to her that he would find his way back into her life first, riding on something as banal as coincidence. Or was it fate?

Because as far as Evie was concerned it *was* the wildest of coincidences. No matter how Monique tried to dress it up.

"I myself chose this part of France so I could fly back and forth to Bristol easily," Monique had explained, "to see my folks and my friends." And Tom, although she didn't mention him. "Alex must have thought along the same lines. He can drive to Bristol Airport, hop on a plane and be in his house in France in less time than it would take him to drive to London."

But that didn't explain why he had ended up in Monique's estate agency, buying a house in her village.

"He probably tried everywhere else as well," Monique suggested lamely. "Or he could have got our name from any number of solicitors in Bristol. We've sold to loads of people there since the direct flight went in – and we're so *brilliant* that of course everyone recommends us to their friends."

Evie decided to stop thinking about how Alex had come to be in Ste Anne and concentrated instead on how she felt about it.

Did she want to see him again?

Should she try to contact him to tell him about Holly before she ran into him accidentally?

How did she feel about his divorce?

Would she still fancy him?

To her surprise, she answered the last question with a resounding "yes". If Alex was anything like she remembered him, he would still fill all the criteria of her ideal man. He was taller than she was (at five foot nine

Evie appreciated tall men). He was attractive in a masculine way without being too good-looking, or requiring high maintenance (Evie didn't believe in having to compete for bathroom time). He was fun to be with. They shared the same sense of humour. He was amazing in bed. Not that Evie had much to compare him with – a few fumbling college romances and then, after Holly was born, long periods of abstinence broken by the occasional mad fling with princes who turned into toads. Wearing the rosy spectacles of hindsight, Alex seemed like quite the hero.

Then a flush swept through Evie's body. She was so hot that she had to get out from under the covers and stand by the open window to cool off. She poured herself a fresh glass of water from the bottle Monique had left on the dressing-table and she sipped from it slowly. She couldn't believe the way her mind was taking her. Instead of fantasising about humiliating Alex in a sweet act of delayed revenge, she was remembering what he was like in bed. And wondering if he was still as good.

♡   ♡   ♡

Monique finished laying the table for breakfast, scribbled a note to Evie and slipped out of the house quietly for an early morning walk. It was just after eight and the village was just waking up. The bread had already been delivered so she popped her head around the shop door and asked them to keep her a couple of croissants and *pains chocolat* as well as her usual baguette and promised to pick them up on her way back.

She had heard her friend padding about the room next to hers in the middle of the night and guessed that she hadn't slept well. She wondered if Evie was interested in Alex again, now he was divorced, and tried to imagine them together. To her surprise it wasn't difficult. Especially if she included Holly in the picture. Monique decided to tread very carefully over the next few days – and avoid giving Evie any advice whatsoever about Alex. If she wanted to talk, fine, Monique would listen. But Evie might be better off not talking about Alex until she was used to the idea of seeing him again. Otherwise she might say something she regretted and then refuse to back down out of stubborn pride. Monique needed to keep Evie's mind off Alex for the next twenty-four hours at least. And she knew just the person to help her with that. She took out her mobile and phoned her boss at home.

When Céline had heard Evie was coming to France, she had offered the services of her son Laurent and his best friend Joël as tour guides. Without Holly, the girls should make the most of the region, she insisted, and that meant visiting the vineyards to sample the produce and long boozy lunches without worrying about the drive home. Joël had a convertible car that he was more than keen to show off – so he and Laurent could share the driving. When Céline made the suggestion, Monique had avoided giving her a definite answer because she knew that Céline was matchmaking. She wanted Monique to get together with Joël now that Tom was out of the picture.

But Laurent would be the ideal "distraction" for Evie and, what the hell, Monique wasn't about to turn down the opportunity of a couple of days being squired about by a couple of good-looking men.

"*Céline, salut, c'est moi, Monique*," she said when the other woman answered. She continued to speak in French. "Is Laurent still available?" Then she laughed. "Yes, of course. Joël as well." They spoke for a little while longer, Monique frowning at a mention of Alex Ryder, then she wound up the call by saying, "Alright, Céline, I'll call Laurent at home. I just didn't want to put him on the spot, in case he'd made other plans."

♡   ♡   ♡

When Monique arrived back at the house a drowsy Evie, still in her pyjamas, was filling the kettle. Monique waved the bag of bread and croissants in her direction.

"Go and have a shower if you like, and get dressed. I'll make breakfast. We'll have it outside." Monique went around opening the last of the shutters and then opened the windows to let in the day.

Suddenly Evie was wide awake and a grin spread across her face. "Croissants and coffee in the garden? I think I can cope with that!" She knocked back her orange juice and skipped towards the stairs. "Give me ten minutes."

Monique heard the electric shower hum to life above her head and smiled as she heard Evie burst into tuneless song. Then she frowned and wondered whether to tell her the piece of news she'd just heard from Céline: Alex was flying into Bergerac tomorrow to complete on the sale of his house.

When Evie came back down, she found Monique on the patio with a map of the area spread between the plates and cups.

"How about St Émilion?" Monique asked, clearing a space. "Touristy, but not too bad at this time of year, and anyway, you've never been there, so you have to do it at least once!"

"Can we visit a château? Buy some obscenely cheap wine?"

"We'll definitely do a château. And buy some wine. But don't forget you're flying, so you can't take much home with you!"

"That's true – guess I'll have to drink it so!"

"Do you remember Laurent, Céline's son?" Monique asked as she poured coffee.

"Remember him?" Evie laughed. "How could I forget him? We drooled over him for a whole week when he was painting your office. I've never seen you show such enthusiasm for DIY as you did then! What's he up to? He must be nearly finished college by now. Will he stay in Paris or move home do you think?"

"Evie, darling," Monique held out the breadbasket and Evie's hand hovered before choosing a *pain chocolat*, "Laurent finished his PhD a year ago. He's actually a few years older than us. We felt all grown up because we'd started real jobs while Laurent was still 'at school' – but you forget that at the time he was a qualified architect, and he was doing his doctorate in the environmental impact of modern materials. And yes, he has moved 'home', but not to Céline's place. He's bought himself a house on the outskirts of Bergerac."

"Oh!" Evie tried to imagine a more mature Laurent, but it was no good. All she could see was a tanned, muscular, paint-splattered hunk laughing as he threatened to splash Evie and Monique with his brushes. A very pleasing image. "What about Laurent, anyway?" Evie asked, reaching out for a croissant while Monique topped up her coffee.

"Laurent and his friend Joël are going to chauffeur us around today."

"Oh goody! I bags Laurent! You get Joël."

Monique went pink, and Evie resisted the temptation to tease her. She had met Joël a few times and liked him. Maybe he'd made some progress with Monique since last time she'd asked her! About time too, Evie reckoned. It was all very well going into decline after breaking up with your fiancé, but a girl has to have some outside interests. And Monique had never gone out with anyone apart from Tom.

But if Monique and Joël were going to get anywhere, the relationship needed to be hot-housed; so if her friend wanted to double date, Evie was happy to go along with it. And from her point of view, if you had to double date, you could do a lot worse than Laurent. After getting hot and bothered thinking about Alex last night, Evie reckoned that maybe a quick holiday fling would do her the world of good. She'd been celibate for *waaay* too long.

Chapter 4

If Monique's idea had been for the two couples to pair off, she couldn't have planned it better, Evie reflected as they sat eating lunch in a small square in St Émilion.

Joël's English was good, but he could get lost if they spoke too quickly, while Laurent spoke English fluently. Evie's French was good enough to understand most of what Monique said, but she wasn't confident enough to speak the language, and she hadn't a hope of understanding the guys if they spoke too fast. So Evie and Laurent spoke English, Joël and Monique spoke French and Monique and Laurent hopped between both languages and translated if necessary. Complicated, but fun, and you rarely missed anything because most of it was repeated at least twice if not three or four times. And because Laurent made a point of speaking more English than French, it made Evie feel picked out for special treatment. She hoped Joël felt the same about Monique, because she could see he obviously was smitten.

Monique had explained firmly that she and Joël were good friends, but since her break-up with Tom they had grown closer. She emphasised "friends" and refused to discuss romance. From the look of Joël, Evie would be willing to bet her mortgage that they had never slept together – and that he desperately wanted to. Evie could sense that Monique was interested in Joël but thought maybe that she just didn't want to rush into anything on the rebound. If it could be called rebound a whole year later. But Monique was touchy, very touchy, on the subject of Tom, and worse on the subject of "moving on". Evie couldn't understand it because she felt Tom and Monique had been moving in completely different directions long before they split up.

"So, remind me." Evie turned to Laurent, determined not to waste time thinking about things she could do nothing about. "What's the name of this château we're visiting this afternoon?"

She studied him with as much attention and appreciation as she would a work of art. He wasn't over-handsome – Evie was suspicious of too-good-looking men – but he was what her mother would have called "easy on the eye". Like Céline, he had black hair, but his owed nothing to a bottle. It was wavy and cut in layers and just a little too long to be fashionable. On a less masculine man, the style would have been a definite turn-off, but it made Evie long to tangle her fingers up in it.

He was tanned, which made the teeth in his slightly crooked smile look all the whiter, and he had the bluest eyes she had ever seen.

"It's Château Bécard," he answered, interrupting her musings. "One of my favourite St Émilions. They have fabulous cellars underground – it will give you a chance to cool off." He smiled at her. The others had been wearing jackets, or in Monique's case a heavy cotton cardigan, all morning, but Evie had abandoned hers within a couple of minutes of leaving the car. According to them, it was only slightly warmer than usual for this time of year, but Evie had come from cold, wet Dublin. So Laurent had been carrying her canvas jacket all morning, and he kept checking she was coping with the heat and offering her water.

"And cheap wine? You all promised me cheap wine to bring home!" Evie pouted. So far they hadn't let her put a foot inside any of the wonderful-looking wine shops they had passed, claiming they were all charging tourist prices.

"Not at the château, but later, I promise you, we'll stop at a great place I know on the way back to Bergerac, and you can buy as much wine as you like. Or rather, as much as you can carry back on the plane."

Laurent said it quietly and gently, as if he were sharing some secret with her, and the intensity in his eyes made Evie shiver with pleasure. She knew that if she were to hand him the phone directory and get him to read it out loud to her, and to her alone, in some secluded place, within half an hour she would be a gibbering mass of desire.

♡　　♡　　♡

"I suppose we'd better get going then," Monique said with some reluctance. She was enjoying her long leisurely lunch and had just finished her second glass of wine. But the sun would be shining directly onto their table in a few minutes and it would probably get too hot for Evie. She was also aware of the chemistry between Evie and Laurent and wasn't sure where it left her and Joël.

She had always thought of him as just a good friend, but now, as she watched Evie studying Laurent so intently she began to look at Joël with new eyes. She liked the way his blond hair flopped down to frame his face. It wasn't quite surfer-length, but at least it wasn't army-regulation short like it had been when she first met him and he had just finished his compulsory military service. His eyes were probably best described as greenish-brown, although they had little specks of gold in them, which sparkled when he was animated. Unlike Laurent, Joël had left college straight after his business degree, and since then he had been very much hands-on in the family wine business. He pruned and weeded the vines, lugged about heavy equipment and tractor attachments and spent a fair amount of time outdoors. The fresh air and physical labour suited Joël. All in all, Monique decided, not a man you'd kick out of bed for eating biscuits.

And she wasn't flattering herself when she reckoned he felt the same about her. The space between them had shrunk perceptibly in the past couple of hours – not that anyone else would notice, but enough that if Joël stepped away from her for any reason, Monique was suddenly aware of his absence.

But it was happening too fast for her and she was confused. It was all very well for Evie. Everyone knew where she stood. In a few days' time she would hop on a flight home to her daughter in Dublin and what happened in France would stay in France. A holiday romance between Evie and Laurent was a brilliant idea. He was a bit of a womaniser, serious about his work as an architect, serious about rugby and not serious about much else. So he wasn't going to get hurt. Joël was a different matter. In the five years she had known him, he had never been seriously involved with anyone. Céline had joked once that her godson only had eyes for Monique, and at the time Monique just laughed it off uncomfortably. She was with Tom at the time and felt so lucky to have him that she couldn't imagine anyone else looking at her twice. But now she had to admit Joël had always been more than attentive.

And as usual, when Tom entered her head, Monique felt uneasy. As if just thinking about another man made her unfaithful to him. And that he would know.

"Come on, you lot!" She hurried the others along. "We haven't got all day."

♡   ♡   ♡

As they wandered back through the shuttered streets of the small town, they fell into two couples again, with

Evie and Laurent taking up the rear as he pointed out features of interest to her. She laughed that having an architect showing her around was like having her own personal tour guide.

"It must be great being an architect in an area like this where the buildings are all so beautiful. Even the small ones, they all have their own character – the different metalwork on the shutters, carved stone around the windows ..." She named some of the features he had drawn her attention to earlier.

Laurent just shrugged. "It can be difficult too, very difficult sometimes. It is hard to do something different. A mayor won't make a decision, so he sends it up along the line and it can take forever to get planning permission." He frowned, maybe thinking about some project he was having just those difficulties with. "Usually, in the practice I work with, we end up compromising. Everyone is a little bit happy and no one is really happy."

"But it's important – surely you don't want to risk losing your heritage." Evie had heard her father complain over and over about the destruction of Dublin. Her mother said he had almost cried when he and the other protestors were finally evicted from the Viking site at Wood Quay. And up to the day he died, he would detour halfway around the city rather than drive past the Civic Offices built on the site. "I mean, you have so much still intact here. Why would you want to knock it down?"

"I'm not talking about knocking things down, Evie, but what about the 'heritage' of today? Why can't our

38

generation leave a legacy behind for our great grandchildren to consider worth protecting?"

"But you do! Look at Paris, the Pompidou centre, the Louvre Pyramid …" Evie didn't want to argue, but she felt he was driving her to it, that he wanted to have his say.

"They are all institutional buildings. In cities. But look at these houses." He waved his arm about, not actually realising that they were out of the town now and that he was waving at the ramparts. "Ordinary people need to have houses of their time too. Five centuries ago, no city official would have dared tell their citizens that they had to build with mud and wood, just because that is what was used on the same site many centuries before. But around here, most homes are built to look like houses of the past, not like today. Modern materials are used and then covered up in a strange pastiche of the past. That is much more ugly than anything I would build of glass and steel. But the ugliness is hidden, so nobody cares. It's just like politics."

They had arrived back at the car, and Joël had switched on the engine, with the roof still on, to allow the air conditioning to kick in. Laurent's voice had got louder, and the other three were standing in a line beside the car like an audience.

Finally Joël applauded and said in his heavily accented English: "Bravo! I did not understand it all, but bravo! Laurent spoke with *passion*," he used the French pronunciation, "and that is what is important."

Joël got into the driver's seat, Laurent slipped in

quickly behind him and, after a moment's confusion, Monique sat into the passenger seat, leaving Evie in the back with Laurent. Earlier, on the drive into St Émilion, the two guys had been in the front because they had been sitting there when they arrived to pick Evie and Monique up. Now it looked as though, for the moment at least, the split into couples was complete.

♡   ♡   ♡

When they arrived at Château Bécard, they had just missed an organised tour, but as Laurent had phoned ahead to tell the owners they would be coming, the owner's daughter arrived down from the main house to show them around herself. She greeted the group enthusiastically; although Evie noted most of her enthusiasm was directed at Laurent.

"I was at school with Émilie," he explained quickly.

Too quickly, it seemed to Evie, and she looked at Émilie and saw amusement on her face. Then Émilie's eyes darted between Monique and Evie, apparently approving of both as she raised a congratulatory eyebrow at Laurent before diverting her attention to the group as a whole.

"We will start in the vineyards, I think," she announced. "I will tell you a little about how we grow the grapes, and look after the vines, and then we will come inside to where we make the wine."

They stepped back outside into the bright sunlight and Evie pushed her sunglasses down over her eyes. Joël moved up to walk beside Émilie and waited until she had finished explaining how each vine was examined, how leaves were plucked by hand to allow the sunlight reach the grapes and how only a few bunches of grapes were left on each vine. Then he began speaking to her in French about specific techniques. Evie tuned out – they were going into a lot more detail than she was interested in and in complicated technical French. Although the care given these little berries, still only green and the size of orange pips, went some way towards explaining the astronomical cost of the château's first growth.

"It's amazing," she told Laurent. "I never realised so much work went into it! And it's all done by hand, by experts."

"Joël's vineyard isn't like this," Laurent said, "much to his chagrin, it must be added. His wines, although his land is in the Bergerac region, in the Pécharmant even, would never command prices high enough to justify this kind of work. His pruning and harvesting is done largely by machine, although he does hand-prune one field of vines for his prestige wine. And that is really growing in reputation. You will taste it tonight – the restaurant we are taking you to has it on its menu."

Evie hadn't been aware of any plans for dinner and she exchanged a quick glance with Monique who just shrugged. But Evie was glad to be spending more time with Laurent, so she grinned and shrugged back, as if to say "Let's just go with the flow".

Joël and their hostess were still deeply involved in the technicalities of vine-tending when they went into the cellars where the wine was stored. A long underground gallery stretched out into the darkness. It was dug out of the stone and reinforced in places with arched brickwork. Evie was just beginning to make out the shape of wooden barrels in the centre of the gallery when Émilie snapped on a light, leaving them all blinking for a few seconds.

"The temperature down here is a constant thirteen or fourteen degrees, summer and winter," she told them. "These cellars, dug out before the present house or 'château' was built, have been in my family for over two hundred years. The barrels you see are a mixture of 70% new and 30% one-year-old oak. We only use French oak, and the wine is stored in the barrels for eighteen months."

She reeled off some more statistics – the numbers of bottles per vine, per hectare, per barrel – but Evie couldn't concentrate. Laurent was standing closer to her than he had stood all day. He was just behind her, looking at Émilie over her left shoulder, and although he seemed to be concentrating on what the Frenchwoman was saying, it seemed more than a little of his attention was straying Evie's way. Every third or fourth breath, his exhalation seemed to change direction subtly to disturb the hair around Evie's left ear. She decided to raise the stakes a little and coughed gently, then leaned forward, taking her head just out of the reach of his breath. Laurent followed her, moving forward himself by shuffling his feet about, as though he was getting tired of standing still. When the whispery breath in her ear resumed, now more insistent and making Evie shiver pleasurably, she leaned back again while Laurent stayed where he was. Their bodies weren't touching, but felt only molecules apart. Evie tried to concentrate on Émilie's explanation of the first fermentation of the grape juice, but all she could think about was how the wafer-thin layer of air between her and Laurent had warmed up to well above fourteen degrees.

"Now, we go and taste some wine," Émilie announced, causing Evie to start with surprise. As they moved towards the ramp up to the outside world, she stumbled against Laurent and he caught her elbow to stop her from falling.

"The ramp was for rolling barrels before we had machines to pull them up," Émilie explained.

She looked at Laurent, who was still holding Evie's arm although she had well regained her balance. Émilie looked amused, but rather than get embarrassed or defensive as an Irishman might have, Laurent moved closer to Evie. Although he removed his hand, his air of possession was unmistakable. Evie asked herself why she wasn't annoyed, then decided they were all playing a game, and although Émilie had probably been in this territory before, Evie was now the lady of Laurent's manor. She decided to stake her claim more decisively.

"Ooh, wait!" She stopped halfway across the gravel drive and lifted one foot, hopping. "Stone in my shoe!" she explained, smiling flirtatiously.

Monique rolled her eyes up to heaven, but to Evie's delight Laurent knelt down and removed her sandal with one hand, holding her calf firmly with the other. She held onto his shoulder, placing her fingers as close to his neck as she dared, "for balance". He shook out the offending article of footwear and placed it firmly but gently back onto her foot. Then still holding her leg he looked up at her, like Prince Charming claiming his Cinderella, and asked: "Is that good?"

"It's perfect, thank you!"

Evie knew she was grinning like the Cheshire Cat but she couldn't help it. She was having way too much fun. She hadn't played a man like this since she was a teenager. Anyone who said the chase was better that the catch knew nothing. *This* was the best bit. The seduction, or catch, was complete (although Evie wasn't quite sure who had seduced whom) and from now on, each move in the game took them closer to consummation. Now it was time, Evie decided, to step back and let Laurent make all the moves. She liked being wooed, and he was on home territory, so it was up to him to surprise her.

She had a feeling Laurent would prove to be exceptionally talented when it came to surprises.

♡   ♡   ♡

The drive home was uneventful from Evie's point of view. They stopped, as promised, at an unspectacular-looking wine shop, but inside she found a real Aladdin's cave, a wine-lover's treasure trove. Every region of France seemed to be represented on crowded shelves and in open wooden cases, stacked perilously on every square inch of available floor space. It made Evie totally confused as to what she should buy. In the end, on Joël's advice, she chose some local wines, and he promised her a bottle of his own wine as a present. Monique bought a few half-cases of her favourite white Bordeaux for the house and then the guys dropped them off.

"My God! You are such a t-a-r-t!" Monique laughed once they were out of earshot. "I was afraid you were going to throw him over a barrel in that cellar and ravish him right there!"

"Now … why didn't I think of that? I must be slipping!"

"Don't flatter yourself, kiddo! This is me, remember. I know how long it is since – "

"Let's not lower the tone please, Monique!" Evie flounced towards the front door. "I am in a mood for being seriously romanced! I'd better go and *tart* myself up before the lads get back to pick us up for the evening." Then she added quickly, remembering that Monique hadn't known about the dinner plan: "You don't mind about the guys just assuming we'd be available for dinner, do you? You hadn't anything else planned?"

Evie looked so nervous that Monique couldn't help laughing. "Don't worry, I'm not about to spoil your fun. And no, I had nothing planned. *I* don't plan every move months in advance like some people I know."

Evie narrowed her eyes and pouted. "That's right – gloat! Just because you don't have to organise a baby-sitter every time you poke your nose out the front door. One day you'll be in the same boat – and I'll laugh louder than anyone else!"

"Not for a long time yet, sweetie!"

But Monique's grin was strained and Evie realised that if she hadn't broken up with Tom, they'd be married by now. She wondered if children had been on the agenda and decided that now wasn't the time to tease Monique about Joël.

♡   ♡   ♡

The restaurant Joël had chosen was about a twenty-minute drive away. When they turned off the main road and began to climb a hilly track, Monique asked him if he was sure he knew where he was going. The track was bumpy, with a ridge of grass along the middle of it, and there wasn't a building in sight. Eventually they reached the top of the hill, and just as Joël began to drive down the other side, they saw it.

An unremarkable two-storey stone building clung onto the side of the hill. There was a sign saying "*Auberge de la Crépuscule*" tacked onto the front door.

"That sound like it's something to do with toads," Evie said cautiously as they walked from the car.

Laurent roared laughing. "You're thinking of *crapaud*," he said. "Crépuscule means … early night time …"

"Dusk!" Monique supplied, trying not to laugh herself. Evie worked really hard on her French and could be touchy about it.

Laurent picked up on this. "Easy mistake to make," he said, throwing an arm across Evie's shoulder and giving a comforting squeeze. "Besides … listen …" He put a finger to his lips.

When they stopped talking, the silence was filled by a chorus of several hundred toads from some pond or lake down in the valley.

"I was right!" Evie nudged Laurent. "There *was* something to do with toads!"

His arm dropped from her shoulder to her waist where it stayed until they went into the restaurant and Joël confirmed their booking. Then Evie and Monique saw where the restaurant got its name.

On the other side of the dining room the wall was made almost entirely of glass and the hill fell away beneath it, facing west. The sun wasn't yet setting, but it was low in the sky and, given the few puffy clouds and the hills in the distance, it promised a spectacular sunset.

They were led to a table beside the window.

For a few minutes they were quiet, just looking out at the scenery, taking in details of the countryside, which they recognised, but which looked different from up here.

"Are those the woods …?" Monique pointed away to her right, to a ridge from which a dense blanket of green spilled downwards, until it met a yellow field of rapeseed marking the start of the cultivated area. "The woods that start behind the village, the woods that I've got at the end of my garden?"

"Yes, well done," Joël said. "I thought I had completely lost you on the drive. You have a good sense of direction."

"The direction of the sun helped," Monique admitted, but she was still obviously pleased to have got it right. "And the spire. It's too far away, but I thought it might be Ste Anne's."

Sure enough, poking up from the middle of the cushion of forest was a tiny spire. Evie wouldn't have noticed it unless it was pointed out.

They turned their attention back to the serious matter of considering the menu.

Laurent ordered champagne to begin with, while Joël asked for a bottle of his own red to be opened and brought to the table.

"Even if we all order fish, it will go with the cheese, and you're not leaving without trying it," he warned Evie.

"Hey, don't worry about me. I'm on holidays. You pour and I'll drink. As long as it's got alcohol in it – bring it on!" She hadn't felt this relaxed in years.

Monique and Joël ordered scallops to start, followed by sea-bream for Joël and lamb for Monique. Evie allowed herself to be persuaded to try the foie gras, followed by a seafood platter, which she would share with Laurent. She liked the idea of them stretching out their hands to eat from the same dish.

The champagne arrived and Laurent insisted on opening it himself. He allowed the creamy foam to run down his fingers as he lifted Evie's glass, filled it and handed it to her. When the others were served, Laurent looked straight at her as he raised a toast: "*Aux crapauds!* To the toads!"

They all laughed and tipped their glasses together, then drank. Laurent raised his left hand to his mouth and licked some of the spilled champagne off his fingers.

Evie's breath caught as she realised that the champagne she was drinking had run across those same fingers. Laurent's eyes were still locked into hers. She felt heat rise through her body and then he looked away and pointed out the window: "From the toads to the ... what was the word? Dusk. *Des crapauds à la crepuscule.*"

Sure enough, the pink sky of a few minutes ago was giving way to deep purple, and the sun, a brilliant ball of molten copper, was half submerged beneath the ocean of woodland on a hill due west of them.

Evie was almost overcome by beauty. She knew this feeling of total bliss was temporary but she was determined to make the most of it. A night of it.

Chapter 5

Joël seemed more than aware of what was going on between Evie and Laurent, and although he joined in conversations with them, he spent most of his time talking to Monique. And as Monique watched the two of them flirt, she wished she could just relax and give in to the same impulses as Evie.

Joël was very attractive, he was fun to be with and, Monique had no doubt, wouldn't need to be invited twice into her bed. But he was also a good friend and Monique was terrified of screwing that up. Always a bit of a loner, it wasn't as if she had friends to spare.

Up to now, Joël had always struck her as fairly easy-going. He was relaxed about most things, and his laid-back attitude to life appealed to her – it was so different to her own. But today she had seen him get serious.

Talking to Émilie about wine he was animated, concentrated and passionate. And it was a side to him Monique found she liked. For the first time, she began to seriously consider someone other than Tom as having potential as a boyfriend. It was a strange feeling for Monique, and somewhat scary. She wasn't ready for it.

"Have you ever eaten here before?" Joël asked her. "I was hoping to surprise you."

He was speaking French now, so it was obvious that he had chosen the restaurant for Monique, not her guest.

"No. And I've never heard of it. There are no ads anywhere. Not even a sign up from the main road."

"There is a sign, but it's hidden in the undergrowth. This place doesn't need to advertise. It's booked up months in advance."

"So how did you get a table at such short notice?"

"Oh, I just pulled some strings, called in some favours. Céline helped," Joël said casually. But he went red, and Monique suspected he had put a lot of effort into the evening. It gave her a warm feeling, despite Céline's obvious hand in things again.

Céline couldn't understand how Monique had gone this long since Tom's desertion without replacing him. To Céline a good sex life was as necessary as good food and good wine to enjoy life.

But what she didn't realise was that Monique hadn't been entirely celibate for the past year. Her good friend and employee had played with fire and had got herself badly burnt. But that's all over now, Monique repeated to herself. It's all over and it's in the past.

♡   ♡   ♡

"I suppose this is the kind of architecture Laurent approves of?" Evie said to the whole table during a lull in the conversation. She waved her hand around the restaurant, pointing at stripped stone walls and at the overhead beams way above their heads. Though from the side they had approached it the building looked conventional enough, inside it was predominantly glass and steel.

Joël smiled and was about to answer but Laurent cut him off.

"This is one of the places where I learnt what is possible."

He explained that he had taken a year out, halfway through his architecture course, and had looked for a job with an architecture firm just to make sure it was really what he wanted to do.

"They were working on this building at the time and I loved it. I went back to work for them full-time when I finished."

He explained how one side of the old house, the downhill side, had been dangerously unstable when the firm had assessed it. As they ate their desserts, he took them through the arguments and discussions, the plans proposed and rejected before finally one of the partners had suggested simply stripping off the damaged wall, supporting the whole building with steel drilled into the rock below, leaving them free to do what they liked with the rest.

"It must have cost a fortune!" Monique, ever the estate agent, objected. "Far more than pulling the whole thing down and starting from scratch."

"Three or four times the amount," Laurent boasted with pride. "But the owner had vision. He knew he hadn't just bought a house, or even a spectacular site." He waved dismissively at the view. "He was investing in one of the most brilliant buildings in the area."

Laurent's voice had grown louder as he told the story, and when he ran out of words diners at other tables looked away suddenly as if embarrassed to be caught listening. He suddenly grew bashful. He topped up all their glasses to cover his confusion and then ordered coffees all round.

"This restaurant has won a host of awards," the headwaiter told them with pride when he brought them a *digéstif* on the house with their coffees. He had been listening in, and had recognised Laurent. "It has been featured in journals – some of them international architectural journals."

When he left them to enjoy their drinks, Evie turned to Laurent. "So what other brilliant buildings around here have you been involved in, Laurent? What else do you have to show me?" She loved the fiercely passionate look in his eyes when he talked about architecture.

"If I may, I will show you one tonight. On our way home?" Laurent looked across to Monique for permission.

"Where are you thinking of, Laurent?" Monique asked cautiously, not wanting to be dragged halfway round the country in the middle of the night.

"*La Maison des Oies*, of course. It's nearly finished. You and Joël have already seen it, but I can show Evie. Before the new owner takes possession."

Evie saw Monique's momentary look of dismay before she rearranged her expression to one of neutrality. She was sure the others hadn't noticed.

"Where's *La Maison des Oies*, Monique?" she asked casually.

"In the village, in Sté Anne. Well, just outside it really; at the opposite end to me. We haven't driven past it yet while you've been here —"

"That sounds easy enough!" Evie interrupted. "We can walk down there after Joël drives us home."

"It's a house the agency is selling," Monique continued carefully. She wondered how much more she would have to say before Evie copped on. She wanted her to get the information subtly. Evie had had a fair bit to drink and Monique wasn't sure how well she'd be able to hide her feelings. "Remember? A house on the other end of the village? You saw the brochure yesterday, just after you arrived?"

Alex's house. Or rather the house Alex was in the process of buying. Monique saw the precise moment that Evie realised what she meant, and to her relief she didn't seem to react — at least not to the extent that Joël or Laurent would notice. But there was a strange gleam in her eyes. A dangerous gleam.

"Maybe it would be better to wait until tomorrow, Laurent?" Monique suggested without much hope of success.

Evie and Laurent spoke at exactly the same time.

"No, I'd love to see it tonight!"

"No time like the present!"

Then they laughed and locked eyes.

"Will you two join us?" Laurent asked, without looking away from Evie.

Monique and Joël looked at each other and Joël shrugged his shoulders, saying what he knew was expected of him: "I have an early start in the morning. I think I will go home when I have dropped you all to Monique's place. You can walk up to the house, can't you?"

Monique wondered how often he had played this role in one of Laurent's seductions. If Evie was aware of it, she obviously didn't care. In fact she looked as though she was enjoying the sheer drama of it. So Monique took her cue and spoke her line too.

"I'm too tired to go traipsing round at this time of night. And I've seen the house often enough in the past six months – I've lost count of the number of German, Dutch and English property hunters I've dragged through it." Then she smiled wickedly, unable to resist adding: "I presume I can leave Evie in your capable hands, Laurent?"

Chapter 6

Evie felt like she was walking on air as she and Laurent strolled along the middle of the road through the deserted village. Although she could hardly wait to get to the house and see what Laurent had planned for her, the delicious anticipation made her feel so alive that she wished the road would last forever. They walked apart, about a foot between them, and hadn't said a word since leaving Monique's.

As they left the restaurant, Joël and Monique had stayed back to talk to someone and Evie found herself outside on her own with Laurent. They walked towards the car, and as they turned the corner into the car park, he pulled her towards him and kissed her. He seemed to put his whole soul into the kiss although only their lips and hands were touching. Evie took a step closer, desperate to feel the full length of his body against hers. Then the door of the restaurant opened, a brief burst of chatter disturbed the night air and Evie heard Monique say: "They're probably waiting for us back at the car."

Laurent moved away from Evie, leaving her to step into the space where he had been standing only a fraction of a second earlier. She almost gasped with frustration.

"Sssh!" He placed the tip of his finger against the lips that were still tingling from the touch of his mouth. He smiled, took her hand and led her the rest of the way to the car.

She couldn't remember any of the journey home. There had been a conversation about what she and Monique planned to do the next day. She might even have taken part in that conversation, but if she had, she had no idea what she might or might not have said. The four of them then stood around awkwardly outside Monique's as Joël refused an invitation to come in. Monique opened the front door and took a spare key off her key-ring to give to Evie.

"I won't wait up!" she whispered.

"Wise decision," Evie agreed.

Evie was glad that a brilliant moon lit up the night sky. It had only just occurred to her that going to examine an enlightened piece of architecture in the middle of the night was a somewhat poor excuse to slip away. Now that they were nearing the end of the village, and as she saw the pavements give way to grass verges ahead, her heart began to beat faster. In a few minutes she would be walking around Alex's house. She would walk through rooms he had wandered through, appraising them before deciding to buy the house. He would have tapped the walls, in that absent-minded way he had when he was concentrating. He would have looked through the windows to admire the view that was soon to be his. He would have asked to have the swimming-pool cover pulled back, so that he could see if it was in good condition.

Who had shown him around the first time, Evie wondered. Monique or Céline? How many times had he visited the house before he decided it was the right one for him? Or did he know from the moment he set eyes on it? Evie decided that was the most likely scenario.

Alex knew what he wanted, he went after it and more often than not he got it. Once he had wanted her, he had pursued her with patient determination until finally he had got her. And then he changed his mind.

Tonight Evie would make love with another man in Alex's house. Before he had slept a single night in it himself.

"Here we are."

Evie had been so caught up in her own thoughts that she hadn't noticed that they had walked a few hundred yards past the last house in the village and were standing in front of a hard-packed pale sandstone drive. It sloped gently upwards and, having been newly laid, gleamed brightly in the dark. Evie followed it with her eyes, but it curved to the left past some trees so she couldn't quite see the house.

"Shall we?" Laurent held out his hand, sensing her hesitation. "We can just take a quick look if that's all you want."

Evie took the hand he was offering and grasped it firmly in her own. She stood up straight and breathed in deeply to give her confidence.

"Lead on – and I want the full tour."

They walked up the drive together and Laurent put his arm around her. Although hard-packed, the gravel was uneven in places and not the ideal surface for the high heels she had chosen to show off her long, toned legs. As the house came into view, she strained to remember what she could of the property brochure. She had only looked at one photo of the front of the house and then at a site-plan. The original stone house was fairly traditional. There were large windows at first floor level (it was a converted barn) and smaller ones with wide stone sills on either side of the front door.

Behind the house and stretching away from it was a courtyard framed on both sides by a collection of outbuildings. The pool, if she could remember correctly from the plan, was at the far end of this courtyard.

When they finally reached it, Evie was glad to discover that the house was smaller than she expected. It had looked very "grand" in the photos, and not the kind of place she could imagine Alex buying. His flat in Bristol had been tiny, despite all his money. So small in fact, that on the weekends he had the kids, he usually took them away somewhere, or else baby-sat in the family home while his ex-wife went shopping in London, or Paris, or wherever. While his *wife* went shopping, Evie reminded herself firmly. She was still his wife then.

"So, how did you get involved in renovating this house?" Evie asked. "Was it because your mother was the selling agent?" From what she had seen so far, and from what she knew of Laurent's artistic sensibilities, she imagined that restoring an old stone farmhouse would not have been his project of choice. It must be a bread and butter job.

"Actually, it was the other way around. I got her the job of selling it. The original owner employed us, and then, long before we'd finished it, he said he was selling."

"How come?"

"He didn't go into details. Maybe he ran out of money. Although all our bills were paid on time. Maybe he just wasn't able to spend as much time here as he had hoped. Or maybe he just wanted to make a quick profit." Laurent shrugged his shoulders. As long as he could complete his work, he obviously didn't care who owned the finished building. "Come on, I want to show you around." His face lit up in the moonlight like a child's on Christmas Eve.

Inside, when the lights were switched on, they stepped from the hall into a room that looked more or less as Evie had imagined it. Like in Monique's, there was a fireplace at one end and a kitchen area at the other. But unlike Monique's, this room was bigger and had a door leading out of it at either end. Because of its size a large dining table fit comfortably at one end, with a black leather three-piece suite settled around the fireplace at the other.

In the middle of the room was a large set of French windows, which Laurent walked across to, picking up something from a shelf recessed into the wall. The room was so brightly lit that it looked pitch black outside, and Evie could see their reflections in the glass. Laurent opened the windows fully and stepped onto a patio outside. A gust of air entered the room and Evie realised that it was warmer outside than in. Like in many of those old French houses, the thick stone walls kept the house cool in summer. She joined Laurent but as her eyes hadn't adjusted to the dark, she saw nothing.

"Close your eyes," Laurent ordered and she obeyed. He lifted her hair and kissed the back of her neck and Evie shivered. He stood behind her, resting his left hand on her left shoulder, touching her neck.

"Now, open them," he whispered, leaning closer.

The courtyard was lit up by recessed spotlights laid in a cobbled path around a central lawn. The outbuildings Evie had seen in the plan were nothing like she had imagined. Although the roofs, and presumably the outside walls, matched the main house, the sides facing the courtyard were made almost entirely of glass.

Laurent pressed a series of buttons on a remote control in his hand and, one by one, more lights came on.

Evie clapped her hands in delight. "It's gorgeous, magical!"

Displayed on either side of the courtyard, like in an open-fronted dolls' house, were the remaining rooms of the house. Another living room, larger and more formally laid out than the one Evie had already been in, was furnished with modern, sculptural furniture. There was a dining room in a similar style. She could see two bedrooms and two more empty rooms with boxes and decorators' paraphernalia stored in them.

Next Laurent pointed the remote control at the gap between the buildings at the end of the courtyard space.

A rectangular swimming-pool lit up and the cover began to slide off, rolling away from them.

Evie walked across the patio and onto the lawn. Her heels got stuck in the grass and she bent down to take off her shoes. But before she could reach them, Laurent was on his knees in front of her, unbuckling the fine leather straps. Evie left the shoes where they fell and walked across the grass towards the pool. The grass was soft underfoot, bliss on her feet just released from torturing shoes, but not as cool as she expected. The cobbled path between the grass and the pool was cold though, so when she stepped onto a shallow Roman step, the water felt warm.

"Do you want to swim?" Laurent asked.

"I haven't any swimwear," Evie answered.

Laurent smiled and raised his eyebrows in an unspoken question, but Evie wasn't ready to undress in front of him.

"I want to see the whole house," she told him instead. "Everything."

They re-entered the house through a dressing room beside the pool, which in turn led to a corridor with the living and dining rooms off it. Evie walked through them in a dreamlike state and Laurent pointed out particular features like hidden speakers, which he demonstrated by filling the house with music, and floor-level lighting, which shone upwards throwing the stripped stone walls into relief. Evie was unable to resist trailing her hands across things, touching leather, glass, wood and stone, enjoying the sensation of the different textures. Soon they were back at the central part of the house again, and Evie's pulse quickened as she knew that next they would be taking a tour of the bedrooms. In the kitchen, Laurent stopped long enough to take glasses and a bottle of champagne from the fridge, and without saying anything he opened the door to the rooms on the opposite side of the courtyard.

They stopped in the first bedroom, the bigger of the two Evie had seen through the windows. Laurent dimmed the lights so that they could see everything outside. Now most of the light in the room seemed to come from the courtyard and the lit pool. A breeze caused the surface of the water to ripple, throwing shimmering blue light onto the white ceiling. The sheets on the bed were folded back, like in a top-class hotel. Like in a dream.

"Who owns all this ... stuff?" Evie asked, unwilling to break the spell, but still needing to know.

"The current owner brought in a designer. But he's selling it exactly the way you see it, fully furnished," Laurent said. "All this will belong to the new owner. An Englishman."

Evie stood at the end of what she now knew to be Alex's bed, looking at Laurent.

He stepped closer, stood behind her and put his arms

around her. "What are you thinking?" he whispered into her ear.

To Laurent's surprise, he really wanted to know. This night was turning out exactly as he had planned – but it was nothing like he expected.

At first, he hadn't put too much thought into today. Joël liked Monique and Joël was his best friend. So if Joël needed him to make up numbers so he could spend time with Monique, it was no different than his friend had done countless times for him. But then Laurent met Evie. When it became obvious she was interested in him, Laurent had performed a series of well-rehearsed moves that had taken them to this moment. And although he thought he knew exactly what he was doing, suddenly he realised he was way out of his depth.

"What are you thinking?" he repeated when Evie showed no sign of answering, but just took his whispering as an invitation to stretch her neck backwards, presenting the soft skin of her throat to his mouth.

"I'm not thinking," she answered at last when he didn't move. "Or rather, I was thinking I'd love some of that champagne."

He broke away, opened the bottle and took a mouthful from its foaming neck. He kissed her and they shared the fizzing liquid, swallowing it as they seemed to want to swallow each other.

Laurent's fingers trembled as he eased the straps of Evie's dress down over her shoulders and she purred, kitten-like, allowing him to slip it down her body, past her hips, until it slid to the floor.

Chapter 7

Monique didn't sleep well. Although she hated to admit it, she was jealous of Evie. Jealous that Evie was making love to a gorgeous man while she was in bed, with nothing to hug but her pillow. She was jealous that Evie could so easily switch off from her life at home and turn into the sexy temptress she was tonight. It was a long time since Monique had seen Evie like this. She thought motherhood had tamed her. Whereas Monique, who had none of the responsibilities her friend had, who had no one to please but herself, had allowed her adventurous, hedonistic side to be killed off.

Joël lingered a few minutes after Evie and Laurent floated down the road towards Alex Ryder's house. He was waiting for a repeat invitation to come in, Monique knew – having only turned down the first because that's what Laurent expected. Now that it was just the two of them, she knew she should ask him in again. He wasn't standing there discussing Château Bécard's vineyards because he thought Monique was fascinated enough to want to discuss them in the moonlight. But although Monique longed to dispense with words and just take his hand to pull him inside, instead she muttered something about his "early start" tomorrow and not wanting to be responsible for his bleary eyes.

Joël kissed her goodnight then, with his hand on her arm, holding it, rather than just laid on it, and with his thumb pressing insistently on the soft skin of her forearm. His kiss told her that he understood and that he was willing to wait for her. It made Monique feel like howling with loneliness, because she understood nothing herself.

♡   ♡   ♡

But Joël was beginning to lose patience. When she was with Tom, he could tolerate being kept at arm's length. He was happy just to be her friend. But after they broke up, she had pushed Joël away further for a while and it hurt and confused him. At first he thought Monique just wasn't interested in him and he had nearly come to accept that there was no future for them together. But little things, like the way she began always calling him when she got back from England to tell him she was back and to catch up on news, or the way he was always her standby man if she needed a partner at a social event, kept Joël hanging on.

The official story of their break-up was that Tom refused to contemplate moving away from his home and family business in Bristol, while Monique wouldn't give up her house and job in France. They had commuted between the two countries for five of the ten years of their relationship, and Monique had decided enough was enough and called it off. Joël had no reason to doubt this story, but he wondered if it was as simple as that. Perhaps she regretted her decision. Or perhaps she was hoping Tom might come to regret his and change his mind. They had certainly stayed in touch since the split – Tom had been seen in France, although Monique never mentioned his visits, and Monique had continued her regular visits to Bristol until about four months ago. Joël didn't know what had happened on that last trip, but when she came back, she complained of flu picked up while she was over there and stayed at home for a week refusing to see anyone. If she hadn't emerged looking so ill and depressed, Joël might have taken it as a good sign – that it really was over.

Joël couldn't understand why Tom still had such a hold over Monique so long after she broke it off with him. He had met the other man a number of times but he hadn't spent any significant amount of time with him. Tom's arrival in France was usually a signal to Monique's French friends that she would be out of touch for a few days. And to be honest no one really minded. Tom spoke no French and was arrogantly determined not to learn any. Joël had tried to speak English with him, for

Monique's sake, but there was something about Tom that rendered him tongue-tied and made him forget all his carefully studied vocabulary. Joël wasn't sure how he managed it, but Tom always managed to make him feel embarrassed, in France, for only being able to speak French.

But there was nothing extraordinary about the man. If it weren't for his connection to Monique, Joël could have met Tom ten times and would have had trouble remembering the smallest detail about him. If points were to be handed out for being unremarkable, Tom's outstanding achievement would be his high score. He was about five foot ten, of average build, with muddy brown hair and a wholly forgettable, bland, featureless face. He was older than Monique, by about seven or eight years, but although he was protective of her, he never came across as more mature, or more experienced. Partly because any time she was around Tom, Monique always seemed to act younger than she really was, unsure of what she wanted and happy to let him make all the decisions. It was so totally different from the go-ahead, confident Monique Joël was used to seeing the rest of the time. But in the past four months that uncertainty seemed to have seeped into the rest of her life. She went to work, she came home, she ate and she slept. But she didn't seem to know what else to do with herself. Monique, who used to be so full of energy, with such a long list of all the things she wanted to do with her life, didn't seem to be able to decide what she wanted to do with the next twenty minutes. So she took the easy option and did nothing.

Until this week.

Evie was good for Monique, Joël had discovered. Maybe it was because Evie had no idea what was going on, and Monique had to put on an act. Or maybe because Evie's obvious delight to be here had rubbed off on Monique. But whatever it was, Joël loved seeing Monique sparkle for the first time in months. He even thought she was going to ask him in tonight, when the romance between Laurent and Evie had filled the air with a feeling of anything being possible.

And yet Joël wasn't sure how he would have reacted if Monique had invited him into her bed tonight. He wanted her so desperately it hurt. She was all he thought about at night when he couldn't sleep. But he needed her to want him in the same way. He didn't just want to be the Band-Aid she applied to whatever wounds Tom had inflicted.

♡　　♡　　♡

Laurent walked quickly along a dusty right-of-way though the fields. He had just left Evie back at Monique's, and this shortcut, along with a quick walk along the main road, would take him to his mother's house in just over half an hour. He had left his car there earlier, and he would probably spend what remained of the night in his old bedroom, before going back to the Englishman's house in the morning to clear up.

The sleeve of his shirt was damp, but drying quickly

in the warm air as he walked. It was damp from her hair, from where he had draped his arm about her shoulders as they walked back through the village. After making love, they had walked naked across the grass to the pool and had swum there to cool off. Then they made love again before Evie insisted on being walked home. Laurent was disappointed she wanted to leave, although he hadn't shown it for fear of scaring her off. And because he didn't understand his own reaction. More than anything in the world he wanted to wake up beside Evie, and he didn't know why. She had sucked part of his soul into those deep eyes of hers, and he didn't think he'd ever get it back. He didn't want to. To his surprise he was more than willing to entrust his soul to her, if she'd only share some of hers with him.

Laurent had never been in love. He had had a few "long-term" relationships, one lasting as long as eighteen months, but he had always been careful not to get too involved. He never made promises, and he didn't expect any in return.

His mother, Céline, was twice divorced. She divorced Laurent's father when Laurent was six, after a string of affairs. Laurent's stepfather, whom as a boy he had adored for making his mother smile again, had in turn left her when Laurent was nineteen. Twice he had seen his mother brought to her knees by losing a man she loved, and he deplored the power it implied a man could hold over a woman who loved him. He didn't want that kind of responsibility. He didn't want a woman to love him so much that her happiness depended on him. He was sure he would fail her because that's what the men in his family did: His father, then the man he had loved like a father and whose example Laurent had followed in everything. Even his grandfather, Céline's father, was on his fourth wife, a woman not much older than Laurent himself.

♡　　♡　　♡

Evie was on the phone to Holly when Monique poked her head around the door the next morning. Feeling guilty, because she had phoned too late last night and Holly was already asleep, she had set an alarm this morning. She wanted to catch her daughter at that lovely sleepy, babyish time of the day, when they could speak nonsense to each other and before the mundane daily routine of getting up, dressed and ready for the day got in the way. At home, this time of the morning would be spent in Evie's bed. On weekends they often chatted until Holly grew drowsy again in her mother's warmth and fell asleep, snuggling up, and leaving Evie to wallow in the closeness and baby smell of her.

"Two minutes!" Evie mouthed at Monique, who was about to go out again when she saw Evie on the phone.

Holly was barely tolerating her mother's conversation, because on waking she had been promised a trip to the zoo and all this chat was delaying things.

"She was coughing a bit last night," Marian said when Holly abandoned the phone to her. "I just gave her an extra puff of her inhaler, and it seemed to do the trick."

"That's exactly what I'd have done," Evie reassured her.

"She's still a bit sniffly though."

"Just remember to bring it with you today. What's the weather like over there?"

Glad that it was a warm, dry day, and that Holly wouldn't get wet or cold, Evie left her mother to the task of entertaining her until they could leave for the zoo. It was just after half eight in France, half seven in Ireland, so it would be a while before the gates opened to the public.

"Do you want to walk down with me to get bread for breakfast?" Monique asked, sitting on the edge of Evie's bed. "I'm dying to hear all the gory details of last night. And to hear what you thought of the house. It's amazing, isn't it? I would have shown it to you myself except that I thought, well ... because of the whole Alex thing ..."

"Stop, stop, stop ... I'm not listening. Let me throw on a pair of shorts and a T-shirt, and I'll meet you downstairs. We need coffee to do any discussion of yesterday full credit!" Evie bounded out of bed, full of energy despite her late night. And full of the joys of life because of it.

♡   ♡   ♡

Evie's croissant crumbled in her hand as she tried to spread jam on it. Eventually she gave up and just took mouthfuls of the warm dough and scooped up the crumbs with her fingers between mouthfuls of strong coffee.

"Even when I take this coffee home with me, it never tastes this good," she complained half-heartedly, pouring herself another mug of it. "Is it something to do with the water over here or is it just because I'm nearly always in a hurry and stressed out when I drink coffee at home?"

"Some people swear it's the UHT milk makes it taste different," Monique said. "But I don't take milk, so I wouldn't know." She pointed to her black brew. "But now that you've satisfied that astounding appetite of yours – all the more amazing when you consider the amount you ate for dinner – you can tell me *about last night*!"

Evie giggled apologetically and snaffled the last croissant, her third. "I seem to have built up something of an appetite alright. Wonder why? Must have been that late night swim!"

"I won't ask where you got swimming togs from," Monique snorted. "I guess by the time you got round to swimming, you probably didn't need them."

"You guess correctly!"

Evie put her croissant down, put her elbows on the table and her chin on her hands. "Seriously though, Monique, I had one of the most, no – *the* most romantic night of my life. It was like a fairytale. You're right – the house really is amazing. When he switched on the lights in the courtyard, and then all the rooms around it lit up, and then the swimming pool …"

"I've seen the house," Monique reminded her, without mentioning the context in which she had seen it. "Just tell me about how it went."

"Brilliantly! Better than I could have dreamed. Right

down to the chilled champagne, crisp white linen sheets, moonlight swim … I have to hand it to you, Monique – when you lay on the holiday entertainment, you know how to do it in style!"

"Champagne and fresh sheets!" Monique spluttered. "No wonder he hot-footed it out of here so fast yesterday after dropping us off. He had a lot to prepare for his big seduction."

Evie stuck her fingers in her ears: "I'm not listening, I'm not listening. It was romantic, I don't want to think about the nuts and bolts!"

"He'd bloody better have tidied up after himself," Monique muttered under her breath, but then she smiled. "So … what next?"

Evie looked at her cautiously. "What do you mean?"

"Any plans? Are you going to see him again? Have you fallen in love? Is he flying over to Ireland to meet the family? You don't think I want details of the sweating and grinding, do you? Give me romance, girl! Real romance."

"Well … I think that was it … I mean, I am on holidays …" Evie looked crestfallen. It hadn't occurred to her that Laurent hadn't asked when, or even if, he could see her again. And up to this moment it hadn't bothered her. "I wasn't expecting anything else …"

"But it would be nice to see him again?"

"It would have been, I suppose, yes. I mean definitely. But we didn't make any plans so I suppose last night was all it was …" Her voice drifted off. "Trust you, Monique!" she said then with more vehemence. "I was in great form until –"

"Close your eyes, tap your heels together and spin around three times!" Monique ordered. "You shall go to the ball!"

"Monique …" Evie looked warily at her. "What are you up to?"

"Nothing. That is … I forgot to tell you … well, I deliberately didn't tell you because I wasn't sure if you'd be exactly thrilled …" Monique paused for effect. "We're going to Céline's annual drinks party this evening. And her darling son will most definitely be there."

A small smile flitted across Evie's face before she thought to ask: "And Joël, will he be there too?"

"I'm sure he will." Monique stood up to clear the table. "Laurent's bound to have invited him. Why?"

"You know very well why!" Evie pretended to be indignant. "He fancies the pants off you – that's why! How long are you going to keep the poor boy waiting?"

"It's not that simple, Evie, okay?" Monique turned and walked quickly towards the house.

Evie gathered up what remained of the breakfast things and followed her into the kitchen.

"Monique, what's wrong? It's over a year since you broke up with Tom …"

"I know it is," Monique agreed tonelessly.

"So surely …?" Evie looked closely at her. "You've got to move on. Okay, maybe not with Joël, but …"

"Joël's fine. I mean he's nice, I like him. But it's nothing to do with him … I mean it's not his fault that I … Look, forget it, Evie. You don't understand."

"No," Evie admitted, "I don't. And I never will if you don't try to explain it to me."

"There's nothing *to* explain, alright," Monique said wearily. "Let's just say I'm not over Tom yet, and leave it at that. I'm not ready to move on."

"If you say so."

Evie looked hurt and Monique hated lying to her. But then, she reasoned, it wasn't really a lie. She wasn't over Tom, and she had no idea if she ever would be. She had no idea how to even begin to get over him.

"By the way," she said. "I'm not trying to change the subject … but there's something else I need to tell you."

"What's that?" Evie asked.

Monique hesitated.

"What is it?" Evie asked. "I have to say you've got me worried with that serious face you've got on."

Monique took a deep breath. "Alex Ryder's in France."

Evie, who had been drying dishes as Monique washed them, stopped dead. She went pale. "When, I mean, since when? Where?"

"Since about now. Céline told me yesterday. She said Alex was flying in this morning to complete on the sale of his house. It was supposed to be next week, but then everything went through faster than expected."

Evie sat down with a bump on one of the chairs at the table. "Why didn't you tell me? He could have come in … I mean … when I was with Laurent …" Evie tried to shut off the images in her head. "Jeez, Monique! What were you thinking of?"

"Relax, Evie –"

"Relax!" Evie gasped. "Monique, have you any idea –",

"Evie, calm down for a second. Credit me with at least some intelligence, would you?"

They glared at each other, until Evie dropped her gaze.

"Sorry," she said.

"I knew the earliest he could possibly get here was about ten o'clock," Monique began to explain. "And that was assuming he came straight here to Ste Anne. But because he's completing on the sale today, he'll probably go straight to the Notaire's office in Bergerac. I also guessed you wouldn't stay out the whole night. And if you weren't back, I'd have gone and got you myself. Anyway, Laurent knew Alex was coming, so he was hardly going to –"

"Laurent – knew that Alex – how?" Evie stopped for a moment to let the implications settle in. "Monique … does Laurent know Alex?"

"He *works* for him, Evie. Or rather, he does now that Alex has bought the house. So of course they've spoken. Laurent's the main architect on the project. You knew that, Evie!"

Had she known? Evie wasn't sure. Last night was long on images, warm fuzzy feelings and delightful sensations, but precious short on practical details. She had absorbed the fact that Laurent's company was doing the work on the house that Alex was buying. But she hadn't let herself join the dots.

"So they've met?"

Monique nodded.

"Did they … you know …get on? Did they like each other?"

"Evie," Monique said carefully. "Until two days ago, Alex was just a client – admittedly I knew you and he had 'history' but I thought it was all work history. And Laurent was just Céline's son, not the man you were planning on hopping into bed with at the first opportunity." Monique winced at Evie's frown as she said this – she hadn't meant to sound flippant. "To be honest, it never really occurred to me to be interested in how Alex got on with Laurent, unless it screwed up the sale on us."

"I suppose," Evie conceded after a long silence. "But you still should have told me."

Monique only shrugged, not willing to concede the point. Evie had enough information to make the connection. She knew the house Laurent was taking her to last night was Alex's, and she knew Laurent was renovating it. If Monique had stated the obvious, Evie might have felt obliged to back out of her flirtation with Laurent, if only for the sake of some propriety Monique didn't give a shit about. And to be honest, she didn't see why Alex should be allowed get between Evie and any man.

"Anyway, there's more …" Monique went on.

"More? You mean more than having to look around everywhere I go for the next few days, ducking behind hedges, so that I don't run into Alex?" Evie threw her hands in the air in mock surrender. "Shoot – it can't get any worse."

Monique hesitated. "Céline's party," she said slowly. "She throws this party every year – and as well as friends and family, she invites business associates, clients, potential clients. I *have* to go to this party, Evie. And …" she paused, hoping Evie would guess what she was going to say, "and Alex Ryder is probably going to be there tonight."

Chapter 8

"No way, Monique!" Evie gasped indignantly, when she realised that her friend wasn't going to back down. "Wild horses wouldn't drag me to that party. I don't want to see him."

"You have to, Evie. Sooner or later, you're going to have to meet him. Forget Holly for a moment, and forget that you always planned to tell him eventually …" Monique ignored Evie's dumbfounded expression. It wasn't rocket science, or even particularly clever psychology. Evie was always going to tell Alex about Holly, because Holly deserved to know and Evie was too decent to keep it from her. "Forget the whole Holly situation for a moment," Monique continued – although "the Holly situation" was not the way she would have worded it if she'd had more time to think, "but you're my best friend, you love this part of France and I love having you here to visit. You can't let him scare you away."

"Not now though, Monique. I'm not ready to see him yet. I need some time to prepare. Next time maybe …"

"If you don't meet him this evening, there won't be a next time, will there? Be honest with yourself. It'll build up into something huge, and you'll put off coming over, until the mere fact that you've put it off will become huge, and then –"

"Okay, okay, I get the picture!" Evie was honest enough to recognise that Monique was right. "I'll go. I might even acknowledge Alex's presence if he's there, but don't, please, expect me to talk to him. Even less to be polite to him. Not just yet."

"Okay. And don't worry, I'll be with you every step of the way. I'll stick to you like glue. And don't forget, it's not quite as big a deal for him as it is for you. He doesn't know about Holly. And he probably managed to persuade himself at the time that he was doing the decent thing in going back to his wife!"

♡   ♡   ♡

Evie felt sick as she checked her reflection one last time before setting out for the party.

I want to look good because I'm seeing Laurent again, she told herself. This has nothing to do with Alex.

Although she was glad that Monique had promised not to let her out of her sight all evening, the prospect of seeing Laurent again *was* an attractive one. Since

Monique had asked her whether she and Laurent had made any plans to see each other again, Evie kept asking herself why they hadn't.

Maybe it was because he knew about the party and he guessed that Monique would bring Evie along to it.

Or maybe he was reluctant to butt in again on their girls' week without a definite invitation.

Or maybe he just wasn't interested.

Round and round the theories went until Evie felt like a teenager waiting for the phone to ring.

And so, as she got ready to go out, she checked her reflection one last time in the mirror.

♡　　♡　　♡

Since his mother started her estate agent's business when he was in his teens, Laurent had always dreaded "the summer party". When he was younger, he had been on best behaviour at this networking event designed to help Céline's fledgling business along. Then as he grew older, and used to help her out in the office at weekends and holidays, he knew many of the clients personally. He knew who was thinking of selling up and knew which of the English clients had tenants, friends or relations thinking of buying in the region. And now that he was working in a forward-looking architectural firm, and hoping to make partner before too long, the contacts he made at his mother's parties were valuable to him personally.

But he still dreaded them. He was tired of the way the

formal bonhomie broke into drunken familiarity as the night went on. He hated the huge feat of organisation. He hated the way the caterers deferred to him because Céline was too busy entertaining. And he hated having to be polite to so many people he had nothing in common with.

Until this year. This year Laurent changed outfits three times before the party. To his mother's amusement, he arrived early, bearing flowers, and kissed her with more enthusiasm than usual. He asked her if she knew who was coming for definite and if anyone called off at the last minute. He kept looking at his watch, starting at half three, although the first guests were unlikely to arrive before six, and even the caterers weren't expected until five. So to keep himself busy he decided to take a look around the house and garden one more time to make sure everything was in place.

Céline's house (she had bought it since her divorce from Laurent's stepfather so he had never considered it home) looked quite different to most of the houses in the area. It was of a formal, more northern style with huge glass windows and ornate wooden shutters. The roof was made of bluish slate rather than the tiles used on most farmhouses and the house gave off a comfortable air of prosperous gentility. In fact it looked like a small château. It had once stood at the centre of a wine estate in the nineteenth century, but since the Phylloxera blight, the vines had never been replanted. It was reached by a wide gravelled drive that ran from the road and which continued around the side of the house. The driveway had plenty of parking for this evening's guests and Laurent checked again that the gates were open and that all of his mother's antique planting urns had been pulled well back out of danger. Then he walked around the house to a large limestone-paved terrace at the back. Two interconnecting reception rooms had several pairs of French doors opening onto this terrace, but they were closed at the moment to keep the inside of the house cool till later.

The large lawn had plenty of shade trees around the edges, and at the end of the garden a long table had been set up under an awning to act as a second bar for those guests who felt a trek to the house was too arduous in the heat. At this table, Laurent saw two uniformed waiters laying out glasses. He recognised one of them but merely waved in greeting rather than going down to say hello. He could hear the sound of a radio, on which the two men were obviously following the football, and besides, he wasn't in a mood for small talk right now.

He couldn't get Evie out of his head and it was driving him crazy. How was she doing this to him? He went back over every moment of the previous twenty-four hours to try and spot the precise moment when his interest in Evie as a challenge, or as a potential conquest, had turned into this obsession. He couldn't spot the difference between her and any other woman he had met and seduced in the same manner. She had flirted with him; he loved flirting and she was easily his match. Physically, she was good-looking, attractive but not spectacularly so – Laurent had bedded more beautiful women than Evie. And while their lovemaking was intense, Evie was far from being the most skilled woman he had ever slept with. She responded to him with a touching naïvety – sharp indrawn breaths as he undressed her, a kitten-like moan when his lips found her breasts and tugged gently at the nipples and a joyous laugh when they came together at last. And the whole time, she kept her eyes open – cataloguing each touch, each change in his expression, storing them in some hidden part of her psyche. He had never felt so much the centre of a woman's attention, and yet that wasn't the fascination either. Because for the first time in his life, he wanted to focus all the attention back onto the woman; he wanted to break down a barrier she didn't even know was there.

Laurent had the bug bad, and he didn't know what to call it. He refused to call it love, because he didn't believe in love at first sight. He believed love was something that developed as you got to know someone, which was why he had been careful never to let any woman get too close. Lust implied his interest was solely physical. Even obsession was too strong a word, because obsession implied long-term, implied a need to know every detail, be permanently close to the object of the obsession, and right now Laurent felt as though he would be satisfied just to be in the same room as Evie for a few more minutes, to catch another glimpse of her, to exchange even a few words with her.

The party got off to a frustratingly slow start. Céline had accidentally chosen the date of a French international soccer match, and even the most courteous of guests knew they would be forgiven for not arriving until after the final whistle. Which meant that Laurent was stuck talking to Céline's prize client of the moment – the rich Englishman who also happened to be Laurent's client. And they should have been celebrating, because Monsieur Ryder had signed on the dotted line that morning. His nice fat cheque was sitting in the bank and Céline's commission with it.

The English clients were Laurent's responsibility until Monique arrived, his mother had reminded him as she opened the door to the first of them. Laurent hoped Monique wouldn't be much longer. The first couple, who spoke good French and regarded France as their home, had gravitated towards the kitchen where the caterers had set up a portable television set to monitor French progress on the pitch. So Laurent was left alone with Alex Ryder, who was embarrassed to have been invited to the party, had obviously only turned up out of politeness and was horrified to see how few other people had arrived, because he couldn't make a discreet escape. He spoke no French, so Laurent couldn't palm him off on anyone else, but he had managed to steer him out onto the lawn at the side of the house so that he could watch both the driveway and the terrace.

"I believe you and Monique are from the same part of England," Laurent said, trying to prevent a conversational silence. If he didn't keep talking,

Monsieur Ryder ("Please, call me Alex") might want to talk about his house and Laurent felt uncomfortable doing that. (After all, he *was* watching over the man's shoulder for the woman he had sex with there last night.)

"That's right, we both hail from Bristol," Alex confirmed. "But we didn't meet until I came to France. Small world, eh?"

"Very small," Laurent agreed, fishing around in his memory for some other conversational titbit of information. "My mother, Céline, says you are thinking of getting more heavily involved in the French property market. I thought your business was computers?"

"It was," Alex answered, "but I just sold the business. It was time to get out – I wasn't competing as well as I had been with the big guys and they wanted to buy me out." He shrugged. "I always dreamed of living in France, but ..." he frowned, "well, let's say, the timing's right. I haven't looked seriously into the whole property thing, but it interests me. And I need something to keep me interested now that I've sold the company."

"Expensive hobby – property!" Laurent said with a smile.

Alex laughed in agreement. "My hobby's sculpture, actually. But I've never had much time to practise it."

"Hence the studio?" Laurent had been asked to submit suggestions on how to incorporate a large studio into Alex's house without compromising the original design. He got the impression that if he had failed Alex might have pulled out of the sale.

Laurent was about to ask him what kind of sculpture

– under any other circumstances he suspected he might actually enjoy talking to Alex Ryder – when he spotted Monique's car pull in off the road.

"Can I get you another drink?" Laurent pointed to his companion's half-empty glass. His own was full, as he felt too nervous even to sip at it.

"No thanks, this will do me. I can't stay long, I have to …" Ryder let the sentence fade away.

Monique and Evie had stepped onto the lawn and Laurent found he was holding his breath, afraid that Evie would get her heel stuck in the grass as she had last night. Then he breathed out again when he saw that she had anticipated the problem and was wearing a pair of wedge heels.

Both men watched as Céline greeted the girls and directed them round the side of the house. Neither man seemed aware that each was staring as intently as the other. They watched as Evie and Monique made their way to the table set up as a bar, and they seemed mesmerised by the women's very action of choosing a drink.

Laurent recovered first. "Of course, you know Monique …" He signalled frantically to her to come over. He desperately wanted to unload this guest onto her so that he could greet Evie.

But Evie was the first to spot the waving and Laurent felt a strange sense of detachment as he watched her smile freeze and she turned to whisper something to Monique. Monique didn't turn to look towards Laurent but, with an exaggerated gesture, greeted someone inside the house and led Evie inside to meet them.

"Monique, the estate agent." Laurent heard the words as though from a distance, although the speaker, Alex, was still beside him. "Yes, of course I know Monique … we've met on a number of occasions … she's from Bristol … but we didn't meet until I came to France …"

Laurent thought that the Englishman's voice sounded slightly strangled and that he was repeating himself, but he was too blown away by Evie's reaction to try to process the information.

If he were anywhere other than at his mother's party he would leave now, before he made a fool of himself. But he couldn't leave. And if he didn't drag his attention back to Alex Ryder, he would make a fool of himself without Evie's help.

"Are you alright?" To Laurent's surprise, Monsieur Ryder had knocked back the remains of his drink in one gulp and was looking around – whether for another drink or for somewhere to put the empty glass wasn't clear. He had gone pale and the hand holding his empty glass was shaking.

"I'm fine. It's the heat. I should go …"

"Come inside. It's cooler. I'll get you some water."

Glad of any excuse to move in the same direction as Evie, Laurent crossed the lawn towards the door he had seen her vanish through.

But Alex didn't follow him. Instead he made for the front of the house, to where his car was parked.

"Monsieur Ryder!" Céline stopped her guest in his tracks with a vice-like grip on his arm. "Monsieur Ryder, let me introduce you to the mayor of Ste Anne. Colette Deschamps – this is one of your new citizens: Alex Ryder."

She introduced him to an attractive woman in her fifties, who extended a perfectly manicured hand in his direction.

♡   ♡   ♡

Monique and Evie were talking to an English couple about the vagaries of budget airlines' schedules, when, out of the corner of her eye, Evie spotted Laurent making his way rapidly towards the house. To her relief, Alex didn't seem to be with him.

She was about to make her apologies to the people she was talking to, so as to move towards him, but he ignored her completely and barely acknowledged Monique with a tiny nod of his head.

By now a professional networker at this kind of event, Monique didn't flinch and merely observed Laurent in an ornate gilt mirror over the fireplace. "Don't stare," she warned Evie, as the English couple wandered off to stand nearer a fan.

"Where's Alex?" Evie asked, unable to move off the one spot. She could just about see Laurent's reflection in the mirror, but she was terrified to turn her head and find Alex looking at her. Or worse still, standing nearby. Then she would be forced to acknowledge him.

"He's in the garden, talking to the Lady Mayor," Monique said. "Or rather, being talked *at* by the Lady Mayor."

Now that she knew she was safe from Alex for at least the next minute or so, Evie allowed herself the luxury of wondering what the hell had got into Laurent.

"Evie, let me introduce you to …" Monique was saying.

The name didn't register with Evie, but she pasted on a smile and tried to look interested as the German woman explained how difficult it was to navigate around French inheritance law. She and her partner were not married, the woman explained, but both had children by former relationships, and really, the legal minefield they faced now …

Evie however was reliving the moment Laurent had come indoors. She might as well not have been there the way he looked right past her …

Suddenly she felt she was being watched and she turned a fraction, just in time to see Laurent turn away. He reddened – something which Evie, although she was annoyed at his behaviour, found endearing.

Then over his shoulder she spotted Céline heading towards the house with a reluctant Alex in tow. Panicking, Evie saw Laurent go out the set of French doors furthest from Céline and Alex so she followed him. She was only vaguely aware that she had just left the German woman mid-sentence, in the middle of a description of a yoga centre in the Vosges mountains.

"Laurent." She laid her hand briefly on his arm to slow his progress, then removed it fast, as though it was burnt. "Laurent … I … ehm … hi!"

"Evie," he answered simply, and then he took a step

back and waited to hear what she had to say.

They stared at each other. Evie couldn't help glancing over her shoulder to check on Alex's location, and that's when it hit her that Laurent had been standing with Alex when she arrived at the party – he had waved to her and Monique. He would have seen her panic-stricken look and her flight indoors. She had been in such a state of shock on seeing Alex that Laurent's presence beside him had barely registered.

He thinks it was him *I was avoiding,* she realised. *That's why he ignored me earlier. He doesn't know about me and Alex … and how can I explain it to him* now *… after last night in Alex's house?*

"Your glass is empty, let me get you another drink," Laurent said grimly.

Before she had a chance to react, her glass was gone, with Laurent, across the lawn towards the bar and she was left standing on her own feeling foolish, especially now that the party had really got going and everyone else seemed to be chatting, interrupting and laughing in little groups all around her.

"Evie."

Her heart responded to the familiar voice by somersaulting several times in quick succession. *Too extreme a response,* Evie scolded it, *given the number of years that have passed.* She turned slowly, praying that the owner of the voice was with someone else.

He was alone. The two of them faced each other like lions in an arena.

He hasn't changed, Evie thought, as she looked him

up and down. She couldn't tear her eyes away from him although, to her surprise, she resented his presence not because of their past but because he was confusing things between her and Laurent. His hair hasn't even started receding, she noticed. And then, barely even realising she was doing it, she began to look for traces of Holly. There it was: her daughter's turned-up nose, present in a more grown-up, stronger version on Alex. Both of them had brown eyes and dark brown hair, but his eyes didn't sparkle as brightly and his hair wasn't as shiny or as tightly curled as Holly's. Alex was tall, so Evie had always wondered where Holly's miniature stature had come from, but now that she looked at him with new eyes, she realised that Alex was actually quite fine-featured for a man. And he had lost weight in the past five years, so although he didn't look skinny, he was certainly far from being brawny.

"Alex," she said at last, "fancy meeting you here!"

"Yes," he agreed sarcastically, "fancy! How are you?"

"Fine, and you?"

"Fine."

"And your wife?" Evie couldn't help adding coldly. "Is she *fine*?"

"My ex-wife you mean. Yes, she's fine too."

"Your ex-wife? *Ex*-wife? That's a shame. And a bit of a waste, wouldn't you agree?" Evie longed to ask him how long his marriage had lasted after he left her. She wanted to know if he thought sacrificing their relationship had been worth it in the end, but she was afraid she would get emotional and that she would lose the eerie calm that had descended on her.

Alex just stood there with his mouth open, in shocked amazement.

Then, to her relief, Evie saw Monique hurrying towards them. Thinking that she had just come to rescue her from an embarrassing encounter, she was alarmed to see a panicked expression on her friend's face.

"Evie," Monique said, completely ignoring Alex. "Your phone, is it switched on? Your mother's just sent me a text message. She's been trying to reach you."

"I left my phone in my bag. It's in the car!" Evie held her hands out for the keys and then ran towards the car. Monique followed her, but her heels slowed her progress across the grass.

Alex felt winded and it was as though he had been dropped head-first into some sort of altered reality. He was watching his estate agent run across the lawn chasing the only woman he had ever really loved.

Then someone appeared at his side. It was the architect fellow, Laurent, holding two drinks. One looked like sparkling water. An earlier memory of this bizarre evening flashed into his head. A memory featuring Laurent offering him a glass of water. Better late than never, Alex thought.

"Thanks," he said, taking the glass from Laurent's unresisting fingers.

He downed two large mouthfuls before realising it was a gin and tonic. Another memory, a much older one, emerged. Gin and tonic was Evie's tipple. Laurent had been talking to Evie before Alex approached her, and

Alex realised with a strange frisson that he had just knocked back Evie's drink.

"I thought it was water," he apologised, spluttering. He saw a trace of lipstick on the glass and was torn between two equally strong desires – to touch the glass to his lips again or to hurl it from him with as much force as he could muster.

From where they were standing, the two men could see Evie opening the boot of Monique's car and reaching inside it. Then she slammed it shut again and turned her back on them.

Monique had reached her, but kept her distance until it looked as if Evie had got through on the phone and was talking rapidly. Then she put a hand on Evie's arm, and then an arm around her shoulder. When she finally stopped talking, Evie looked shaken and pale – the two men could see it even from where they were standing – and she was looking around, as though trying to figure out what to do next. Alex longed to comfort her, but he knew that it was an impulse that belonged in the past and that his presence would only make things worse. The two women hugged, and then Monique led her friend back into the house.

"Please excuse me," Laurent said, making Alex jump. "I have to …" He gestured in the general direction of the door the two women had gone through. "I must …"

"Of course, go," Alex said. "Tell Evie I hope …" He didn't know what he hoped for Evie, and anyway Laurent was already walking away from him. "Tell Evie …" He sighed, reached into his trouser pocket for his own car keys and made his way to where his car was parked. This time nobody got in his way and he escaped the party.

♡   ♡   ♡

"Evie's daughter has had an asthma attack," Céline told Laurent quickly in French, when he finally found them all in his mother's bedroom. She had just put down the phone, and then she turned to Evie and began speaking in English. "There's a seat on the plane, but you need to leave now. Laurent will drive you." She held up a hand at Monique's protest. "You've been drinking, it's Friday evening and the gendarmes could be about."

Laurent thanked God he hadn't drunk more than a few sips of wine.

"Are you okay, Evie?" he asked, and then cursed himself silently. How could she be okay? She was barely holding together. The last thing she needed now was a display of sympathy or kindness.

Fortunately Laurent's mother began speaking again in a business-like tone before Evie had time to respond.

"Holly's fine now, but she's being kept overnight in hospital to be on the safe side. Evie needs to get on that London flight. She should have no trouble connecting from there to Dublin *as long as she makes that flight*." Céline emphasised the last few words with a glare at Laurent.

He looked at his watch and realised they would be cutting it fine. But he didn't want to panic Evie. "We'd better go. Now."

Monique made to follow them, but Céline held her back. "Let them go, Laurent will be quicker on his own, and anyway that ridiculous car of his has only two seats."

♡   ♡   ♡

They drove in silence until they got to the main road, then Laurent put his foot down.

"You will need to be quick in Monique's house," he warned her. "Grab your things and go. Just make sure you have your passport."

"Thanks for this, Laurent."

"It's no problem."

He waited in the car while she ran into the house. Was it just because she was upset and worried that she was so distant, he wondered, or was she embarrassed to be forcing her company on a man who was only ever meant to be a one-night stand? He cursed the fate that meant she would be boarding a plane and flying away from him in under an hour. And in such circumstances. When he walked past her earlier, it had been out of a childish desire to punish her for avoiding him when she arrived. To show her that he didn't give a toss. But at the time he assumed he'd have all night to find out where things really stood between them.

When she emerged from the house her eyes were red-rimmed. Without wanting to intrude on her privacy – she had made an effort to conceal her crying from him – he still wanted to give her some comfort.

"Has your daughter – Holly – has she ever had an

attack like this before?"

"No … I mean I don't know." Evie shook her head in confusion and Laurent wondered had he done the right thing in asking her. Then she tried a half smile, as she realised it would probably help to talk, to put her fears into proportion. "Not like this. She's had spells of breathlessness before, but never bad enough to need to go to hospital. But then, it might just be that Mum panicked – maybe she wasn't that bad at all." She swallowed a laughing sob. "I spoke to Mum again just now, in the house, to let her know I got a flight. She says Holly's sitting up in bed, giving the doctors hell!"

"She sounds like her mother!" Laurent smiled. "Is her father at the hospital with her?"

He knew Evie didn't live with Holly's father, but that was as much as he knew. To be honest he was fishing for information. It was a mistake.

"No, he isn't. He's not around," Evie said. "He's not a part of Holly's life."

She didn't say "mind your own business", but she might as well have, as she lapsed back into stony silence.

They were within sight of Bergerac Airport before Laurent plucked up the courage to say anything else.

"I admire you, you know."

"What?" Evie, who had been staring out the window, turned towards him again.

"I admire you," he repeated. "Bringing up your daughter on your own. You work full time; you own your own house …"

"Mum helps out a lot." Evie sounded like she didn't

want to take credit for being a good parent – not when she was on holiday and her baby was in hospital.

"But it's still hard," Laurent insisted.

"Yeah, it's hard," Evie agreed finally after a long silence. "But it's great too. More than great." She was smiling as they pulled into the airport.

"It's not your fault –" Laurent started.

"What isn't?" Evie interrupted.

"She could have had this attack while you were in Dublin, while you were at work or out visiting a client with your phone switched off …"

"But she didn't. She had her first bad asthma attack while I was away on holiday."

There was nothing Laurent could say to argue with that.

"You go sort out your ticket and check in," he said instead. "I'll park and bring your bag round."

By the time he joined her, Evie was queuing for security. Laurent knew he only had a few minutes left, but he had no idea what he wanted to say to her. He decided to bring up the subject of earlier and see what happened.

"That guy I was talking to when you arrived at the party …" he began.

"Ye-es?" Evie replied cautiously.

"You were talking to him too," Laurent went on. "Alex, Alex Ryder his name is." He took a deep breath. "He's the one who's buying the house … *La Maison des Oies*, where we …"

"I know," Evie interrupted, before he could say anything about last night. "Look, Laurent, when I arrived at your mother's party, it wasn't you I was avoiding. It was Alex. I used to work for him when I lived in Bristol …"

"What is it about Bristol?" Laurent joked, playing for time. "Everyone in England seems to come from there. Am I the only fool who thinks London is the capital?"

To his relief Evie smiled. "I went to college there. That's where I met Monique. And I worked there for a while until –" She stopped dead.

"Until …?" Laurent prompted. She was near the top of the line and soon she would disappear.

"Until I went back to Ireland."

Now he understood. "Evie …" He wasn't sure how to put it. "Evie, you said you worked for Alex. Was that all or were you …?"

"Yes." She smiled at his embarrassment. "Alex is an ex. It was strange seeing him there."

She had reached the top of the queue. She emptied her pockets and put her handbag and keys into a plastic tray in front of her. Laurent laid her bag on the rollers in front of the X-ray machine. The guard invited her to pass through the metal detector.

"Evie …" There was no time left to think. "Evie …"

He pulled her towards him and kissed her. At first she resisted, but then she melted into him and kissed him back. Harder if anything than he was kissing her. The guard looked on, amused, and invited the next person in the queue to pass through ahead of Evie.

They broke apart and spoke at once.

"I'd better …"

"Can I …"

"Madame?" The guard indicated the metal detector again.

"I'd better go through."

She walked through without sounding any alarms and didn't look back until she was about to vanish behind the screen leading to the departure area.

"Thank you," she mimed at him then. "Thank you!" Then she blew him a small kiss.

♡　　♡　　♡

In Stansted Evie phoned her mother again. Holly was fine. She was asleep, and she would definitely be allowed home tomorrow. Evie hid in the toilets until she had stopped crying. Then she phoned Monique and told her to pass on the news.

"Give Holly my love," Monique ordered. "And buy her a Get Well teddy on my behalf while you're waiting for your plane."

"I will," Evie promised, then looked sheepishly at the bagful of get-well presents on the floor beside her. Guilt offerings supposed to compensate for not being there. "I'd better get going," she said, afraid she was going to cry again. "I won't phone again till the morning – it'll be too hectic later."

"Take care!" Monique blew a kiss down the phone before she hung up. She had a feeling it was going to be a long night for Evie.

It was a good thing Monique had no idea just how long a night it would be for her too.

Chapter 9

It was nearly midnight by the time Evie finally made it to Holly's bedside. Her mother, who had been reading beside her granddaughter's bed, had fallen asleep with the book on her lap. Evie watched them both for a few moments and then burst into tears again.

"Sweetheart," her mother said, waking up. She whispered and tried to shush Evie's noisy crying. "Sweetheart, she's fine, Holly's fine. It wasn't a severe attack. I overreacted, I think. She's going to be okay."

But the more reassurance Evie heard, the harder she cried. "I should have been here," she sobbed finally when she was able to get the words out. "I should have been here."

"You're here now." Marian pointed to Holly who was opening her eyes, wondering at the commotion.

"Mummy?" she asked. "Mummy, I went in an 'amby-lance' ..."

"Yes, Holly – I know, sweetheart. You can tell me all about it in the morning. I'm here now. So you go back to sleep now." Evie lay down on the bed next to her little girl and watched her drift off to sleep again. She listened to the precious breaths raise and lower her baby's chest. "I'm here now."

Alex was staying in a riverside hotel in the nearby town of Lalinde. He had booked in for four nights, as he hadn't planned to return to England until Monday evening. The "foreign property expert", a Bristol-based solicitor he had employed to help him through the French bureaucracy, had warned that a Friday appointment to sign the papers didn't necessarily mean the papers would get signed on Friday. In the event, the whole meeting had gone far more smoothly and quickly than expected, and Alex was left with three days to kill and no idea what to do with himself. Although he was booked in for a meal in the hotel dining room, he had no appetite left.

He had been totally unprepared for his reaction to seeing Evie again. When he left the party his hands were shaking as he put his key into the ignition of the rental car, and he pulled out of Céline's driveway straight onto the wrong side of the road. Fortunately he didn't meet any other cars and when he reached the main road, the road signs reminded him of where he was. He pulled into a gateway to compose himself.

He still loved her. Four and a half years of wondering where she was, four and a half years of trying to persuade himself that he hated her for running off like that, four and a half years of getting used to the idea that he would never see her again, had all disappeared in a single moment when he saw her step out of a car onto a gravelled driveway in rural France.

What the hell was she doing here? She was smart, he had to give her that – the only place he would have thought to look was in Ireland. When she finally left Bristol for good, Evie had covered her tracks well. She must have been a better computer operator than Alex had given her credit for, because although he thought his personnel files were reasonably secure, she had hacked her way in and removed every trace of herself. All her previous addresses, the details of her next of kin, her social security records, tax and pension records, all wiped. It was as though she had never existed. At the time he made the difficult decision that if she really wanted to get away from him that badly, he might be better off not finding her. But now he was desperate to see her again.

He had been about to turn his car around, to go back to the party and confront her, but as he pulled out cautiously, a black sports car sped towards him and he reversed back quickly into the safety of the gateway. He had watched from there as Evie flew past in Laurent's car, far too fast for him to contemplate following them.

Alex stood at the window of his hotel room and

watched the Dordogne flowing sluggishly past below him. He wondered what to do next. Two swans floated by, moving against the current, dipping their heads below the surface from time to time to dig at weeds hidden beneath. Swans mated for life, he thought bitterly. How were they so good at choosing the right partner? Biology and instinct were obviously better guides than emotion and brains, because humans seemed to make an unholy mess of their own mating habits. First time round, Alex married his childhood sweetheart. They had a baby on the way, and they were in love. What a mess that had turned out to be! Not only had he lost his wife, he'd come very close to losing his company to her. Second time, he hadn't even made it as far as the altar before he was ditched, fleeced and left hanging out to dry. And second time round it had hurt a lot more because he hadn't fallen out of love with Evie.

He had to find her. If only to find out what he had done wrong and to convince himself that he hadn't screwed up completely and that she was at least partly to blame. He also needed to know that there wasn't the remotest chance of their getting back together again and then he would be able to get on with his life.

He recovered his car keys from the bedside locker, grabbed the map so that he wouldn't get lost on the small country roads in the dark and headed out the door to Ste Anne. He might not know where Evie was, but he was damned sure Monique would. And he knew where to find Monique.

Chapter 10

Joël held the door open for Monique and she collapsed gratefully into the passenger seat of his car. He had arrived at the party shortly after Evie's drama, and although he had offered to drive Monique home straight away, she insisted on staying. At least until Laurent got back, she said. In the end, after a call from Evie in Stansted saying that Holly was fine, Joël and Monique had stayed on at Céline's party until nearly midnight, and Monique had drunk a lot more than she intended to. She even flirted with Joël as he got in beside her and told her to fasten her seatbelt in a mock teacher-like voice. She laid her head on his shoulder and told him she was far too drunk to find the buckle and would he mind doing it for her.

He did, and as he stretched across her he couldn't

resist planting a small kiss on her lips. To his relief, she didn't look horrified.

"You're nice, Joël," she said sleepily. "You're far too nice for me, that's your problem. But I'm glad I've got a friend like you."

"And you're drunk, far too drunk to be making sweeping statements like that," he replied as he started the engine. But the description "nice" and the word "friend" hurt him more than he had thought possible, so when they got back to Monique's he refused her invitation to come in. Two days ago he would have given anything to have her offer him a coffee or a drink this late at night, but he meant it when he said she was too drunk – if she made a decision about him, he wanted it to be a real one.

So he waited in the car for her to open her front door, but didn't wait for her to turn around and wave a last goodnight. If she made another attempt to invite him in, he wasn't sure he'd be able to resist.

♡   ♡   ♡

"Tell me what happened," Evie begged her mother in a whisper. "Everything, from the beginning, and don't leave anything out."

Holly had fallen back to sleep and Marian had called a taxi, but at this time on a Friday night it was going to be at least another hour before one arrived.

"Holly was fine when we left the zoo," Marian said. "At least I think she was. She was still a bit sniffly, but that was all. I had taken the buggy with me, because I knew that running all over the zoo would wear her out, and we had taken the bus in. As a treat. After the zoo, the weather was still warm, so rather than go straight home I thought I'd take her for a walk in the buggy. Along the quays to McDonald's on O'Connell Street."

"That was some walk," Evie said.

"To be honest, she was so tired, I thought she'd have a little sleep in the buggy, then have something to eat, and she'd enjoy the trip home in the bus all the more."

"That sounds like a good idea." Evie didn't want to rush her mother, but she felt that all these details were getting her nowhere. "So when did ..."

"She fell asleep almost as soon as I started walking," Marian continued. "I put the sun-shade up although it wasn't very sunny, but it was warm, muggy, and I thought that would keep her cool. The doctor said that might have contributed to it ..." Marian's eyes filled with tears. "I thought I was doing the right thing ... keeping the sun off her ... but the traffic was so heavy along the quays, there were so many exhaust fumes ... they were belching out of cars just at the level of Holly's face and the hood of the buggy was keeping them all trapped in around her little head. I didn't even notice how bad it was, because ... well, I'm used to walking along there. And I'm tall, I suppose ..."

"It's not your fault." Evie listened in horror. It would never have occurred to her either. She and Holly drove everywhere, or if they walked it was only short distances and Holly refused to get in the buggy.

"Apparently diesel fumes can trigger asthma, the doctor said," Marian continued. "And the mugginess of the day didn't help ... the air quality in the city centre was really bad ..."

The nurse interrupted to say the taxi had arrived, and Evie was left to her own thoughts.

Car exhausts? She had never really thought of them as real source of danger to Holly. Their house was floored with wood, tiles and lino so as to give dust mites nowhere to hide. Their small garden was planted up carefully with plants which produced no pollen, although Evie had had Holly tested for every allergen under the sun and she didn't react to anything in particular. So when she had managed to keep her daughter's asthma under control, she felt she was on top of the problem.

She had seen air quality reports on weather forecasts, but she hadn't really thought they applied to her. She lived in a leafy suburb, with plenty of fresh air, or so she thought. But she was also only a few hundred yards from a main road. Could this happen to Holly in their own back garden?

It was too much for Evie to absorb right now. She curled up in the chair beside Holly's bed and tried to get some sleep. She tried not to wonder how on earth she was ever going to keep her little girl safe.

♡　　♡　　♡

There was something bothering Laurent. Something buzzing away in his subconscious all the time he was back

109

at the party, talking to his mother's guests. He couldn't put Evie out of his mind. His last memory of her as she disappeared into the departure lounge had been of her smiling back at him, and of the small kiss she had blown. It seemed to land on his lips, still moist from hers, making them tingle again.

All night he tried to think what it was that was bothering him. What had seemed wrong or out of place about anything she had said. But nothing came to him.

When he finally got home, in the early hours of the morning, he found the stuff he had dumped there earlier in the day, after tidying it out of Alex's house.

The sheets he and Evie had made love on.

The glasses they had finally made of use of after they went swimming.

The empty champagne bottle.

He had taken them all out of Alex's house this morning.

Alex's house.

Evie had screwed him in Alex's house. In Alex's bed. And all the time, she knew what she was doing.

"You bitch!" he cried, throwing her lipstick-stained glass at the fireplace. "You were using me!"

He pulled the sheets towards him and buried his face in them. They smelled of last night.

"Oh Evie!" he moaned. "How could you have?"

But even in the depths of his unfamiliar despair, Laurent realised that she had done nothing to deceive him; and that he had himself set out that morning with seduction and a one-night stand in mind. But the honesty did nothing to help him and bitterness was much easier to stomach.

"You bitch!" he repeated to his memory of her. "I hope I never meet you again, you fucking bitch!"

♡　　♡　　♡

Monique closed the front door behind her and found her way to the kitchen with just the streetlights filtering through the window to guide her. She switched on the light in the cooker-hood and took a glass from the draining board by the sink. She filled it with tap water and emptied half of it in three big gulps. But it was too warm. The mains pipe ran close to the surface, and Monique knew she could run the water for ages before it would run cool. So she poured out the remainder and turned to the fridge for bottled water.

She saw a figure stand up out of the tall armchair at the far end of the room.

"So, Monique, it's just the two of us now. I've been waiting for you," a man's voice said menacingly in English. "And, Monique, it's time we had a little talk."

She dropped the glass and screamed.

Chapter 11

"Please, sit down." Monique's uninvited guest waved at the chair on the other side of the fireplace. "You look a little shaky. Did I frighten you? I'm sure I didn't mean to."

"How did you get in?" Monique stayed where she was, leaving the kitchen counter between her and the man who had stepped into the light now, so she could see him more clearly.

"Too easy, really. Remember your estate-agent sales patter? 'This area is sooooo safe! So friendly ... I've lost count of the times I've forgotten to lock my back door, and nothing bad's *ever* come of it!'" He spoke in a high-pitched voice, mimicking her.

"I think you should leave." Monique was feeling panicky.

"And I think you should sit down, Monique," he repeated his invitation. "It's time we had a little talk, wouldn't you agree? Cleared the air a little?"

"I don't know what you're talking about."

"Oh, I think you do. And I don't like being lied to, Monique."

"I'm not lying. I have no idea what you're talking about."

"Please," he said, stepping closer to her. "Please sit down and we can behave like civilised human beings."

"I think you should leave," Monique repeated, trying to keep the hysteria from her voice.

"I'm not leaving until I get what I came for. Information, Monique, and the truth. That's all I want. That shouldn't be too difficult, should it?" He was in the kitchen now and she could smell him. He'd been drinking. A lot. And it smelled like whisky. She could see the shadowy outline of a bottle and a glass in the fireplace, and she wondered how long he'd been waiting for her. What kind of a state he'd built himself up to.

"We can talk in the morning. I'm tired. Just leave now and we'll talk in the morning," she pleaded.

"Tired? Then why don't you sit down?" He stood back to let her past the counter and pointed at the sofa by the fireplace. "We'll both sit down and have a nice chat, will we?"

Monique edged her way past the kitchen counter and then made a run for the door.

She felt a stinging slap to the side of her face, and then she fell, hitting her head on the press with a loud crash.

She could taste blood in her mouth – her lip had split, either from being hit or from biting it as she fell.

"Silly, silly, silly Monique. I thought we could do this the easy way, but obviously not."

Monique played dead. The sound of her head against the press would hopefully convince him that she'd fallen harder than she had.

Unfortunately he was too impatient to notice.

Her scalp burst into a million little sparks of pain and she screamed again, as he picked her up by the hair and dragged her across the floor.

"Let's start again, Monique. First question – what happened to my child?"

"I told you, I –"

He lifted her higher, then dropped her back onto the tiled floor and she felt something crack in the side of her face.

"Wrong answer!"

He picked her up by the hair again and began to drag her past the front door, towards the other end of the room.

"Let's try again, shall we? What happened to the child, Monique?"

The door opened as Monique felt herself fall to the floor again.

"*Leave her alone!*" came a man's voice.

Monique could vaguely make out a figure in the doorway, lit from behind by the streetlights.

"Well, well, well! What have we here?" said her attacker.

The door slammed shut, rendering the newcomer invisible. Instinctively, Monique rolled back towards the kitchen and curled into a ball beside the fridge, shielding her battered face with her arms. Then she ran out of strength and out of willpower. Now it was between the two men who had entered her home without invitation to fight it out between them. There was nothing more she could do.

♡   ♡   ♡

Alex launched himself at the other man, and they both went down. He pinned the man's shoulders to the floor.

"Who the fuck do you think you are to – oof!"

Somehow, a knee had worked its way loose from the writhing mass beneath him and made contact with the most vulnerable part of his anatomy.

He doubled up in agony, only vaguely aware of a figure lurching past him towards the kitchen, to where Monique was. He flung out his leg, and a body came crashing down on top of him. Pain exploded in his chest.

Bloody hell! There goes a rib, he thought.

This time the other man was slower to get up, but Alex was still winded. He tried to get up too but fell over as the figure struggled with him to get to the door. He let him go, then dragged himself towards the door, shut it by throwing himself at it and looked for some kind of catch to lock it with. In the end, he just slid down and sat with his back to it.

"Monique!" he called out hoarsely when he had recovered enough breath. "Monique, he's gone! Are you alright?"

Nothing.

"Monique!" he called out, more frantically now. "Monique, where are you?"

He heard scuffling behind the kitchen counter and then the sound of sweaty bare feet crossing a tiled floor.

"Monique, it's me, Alex. Alex Ryder. Are you alright?" He tried to get to his feet, but something in his ankle gave out and he collapsed with a moan.

He heard footsteps on the wooden staircase, then heard a door slam over his head and the unmistakable sound of a key turning in a lock.

As the adrenalin drained from his body, the pain took over and Alex tried to assess his situation.

He had at least one cracked rib, and his left ankle was seriously screwed up. He was lying against the door of a strange house, trying to prevent a dangerous maniac from coming back. He had no idea how many other open doors and windows there were. There was a woman he knew very little about locked upstairs. She had been beaten up, but he had no idea how seriously. The attacker had hopefully left the scene, but Alex had no idea who he was or even what he looked like. He was in a foreign country, and like the arrogant bastard he was, it had never occurred to him to learn a single word of the language.

"What the *fuck* do you think you're playing at, Ryder?" he moaned.

♡   ♡   ♡

Laurent was tempted to leave the phone ring out, but it was so rare for anyone to phone him this late at night, especially on the phone he only used for work, that his curiosity was roused.

"*Allo? Ici Laurent Toussaint.*"

He wasn't quite with it, and it took him a couple of moments to recognise that the voice on the other end was speaking in English. Gabbling in English might be a better word. And making very little sense. Suddenly Laurent realised that he was talking to Alex, from Monique's house, and that Monique might be in some kind of danger.

"Don't move," he ordered. "I'm coming."

He phoned Joël from the car. It would take him at least twenty minutes to get to Monique's but Joël could make it in five. Probably less if he thought Monique needed him.

When Laurent arrived, Alex was sitting on the sofa with his leg raised on a chair and a bag of frozen vegetables draped over his ankle. He was holding a cloth filled with ice against his forehead. A few bloodstained tissues were lying on the floor, and he seemed to have some sort of cut on his forehead, which had stopped bleeding now. He was very pale and his breathing was laboured.

"I'm fine," he lied, holding up a hand to forestall Laurent's enquiry. "Monique's upstairs. Joël called a doctor and they're both trying to persuade her to open the door."

Laurent took the steps two at a time.

The doctor and Joël swung around. The doctor took a step back, away from Laurent, unconsciously putting Joël between herself and this new arrival. She was in her forties, looked as if she had been roused from her bed by this late-night alert and was still unsure what was happening.

"Laurent!" Joël said, relieved. "She won't let us in."

"But she's conscious?"

"We can hear her crying."

"We don't have time for this," Laurent said. "She could be seriously hurt – there was blood on the floor downstairs." It had looked to him as if someone had been dragged, bleeding, across the living room. "Monique!" he called out gently, but firmly. "We need to get in. I know you're hurting and you're scared. Joël is here, and there's a doctor here, a woman. Alex is downstairs. Whoever it was who attacked you is gone. Now if you don't open the door, I'm going to have to break it down. Do you understand, Monique?"

They waited for an answer from inside, then heard her cross the room and turn the key in the lock before crossing the room back to where she had come from.

Joël put his hand out to open the door, but Laurent stopped him. He nodded at the doctor to go in first.

"Monique," the doctor said gently as she turned the door knob, "I'm coming in, alright?"

She pushed open the door and Laurent could see

Monique sitting on the bed, her knees clutched to her chest, her back to the door. She was rocking slowly.

A blue light flashed outside the window of the house.

"Joël," Laurent took charge, "Joël, you go down and see to the ambulance. Explain what's happening and translate for Monsieur Ryder."

The doctor had reached Monique, and Laurent was glad that Joël missed the look of horrified shock on her face when she saw her patient. Monique must be bad. His own stomach contracted with fear.

"Have the gendarmes been called?" the doctor wanted to know.

Laurent didn't know, but his priority right now was Monique. He moved into the room. "Will you treat her here," he asked the doctor, "or transfer her straight to the hospital?"

The doctor had called an ambulance for Alex, but now she could see that Monique would need one too. And soon. On the other hand, she didn't want to leave Alex waiting with a possible broken rib – the last thing the man needed was a punctured lung.

"Wait," she told Monique, putting a hand on her shoulder.

Then she stepped away and Laurent saw Monique for the first time. One side of her face looked twice its normal size and her eye was swollen shut. The other side was grazed and bleeding, and already ugly purple bruises were starting to form.

The doctor cleared her throat to attract Laurent's attention. He walked trance-like to where she was standing by the door.

"There's no chance that the man downstairs is her attacker, is there?"

Laurent's eyes shot open. He hadn't considered that. After all, there was so sign of anyone else.– they only had Alex's word that … No, Alex was the one who had called them. There was no reason for him to have done that before making his escape.

"He wasn't the attacker," Laurent told her. "We don't know who was, but not him."

"In that case, they can share an ambulance … neither of them is in any immediate danger, but I'd rather get them seen sooner rather than later."

Chapter 12

By lunchtime the next day, Alex was fit to be released from hospital. He had correctly self-diagnosed his fractured rib, but strapping and painkillers made it bearable. His ankle wasn't broken but he had done damage to the ligaments when he used it to trip up his opponent. He would be on crutches for a few weeks.

"And the other guy got to *run* away," he said with bitter humour to Laurent when he came to collect him.

"Yeah, the other guy," Laurent said carefully as he helped Alex into the car. "We need to talk about that."

"I didn't get a good look at him. Sorry, I already gave the police all I could. He was taller than I am. Heavier, I think, but anyone would have felt heavy the way they landed on me. It was dark, but I'd swear he had darkish hair ..."

"Monique says she has no idea who attacked her. The doctors think she's in a state of shock. The gendarmes … well, they're worried that she's protecting someone. Someone she's afraid of …"

Laurent's expression was wary and Alex felt a chill down his spine. He'd been told this morning, in quite formal terms, not to leave the area without telling the police. At the time he'd managed to persuade himself that it was a *request*, because he was a witness, and that he was being oversensitive to imagine hostility behind the formal tones, but now he allowed himself to imagine the other possibility.

"I'm not a suspect? They don't think I could have …"

"They don't know what to think."

"But I was the one who called you! You can tell them that. Jesus! How could I be a suspect? I saved her. I walked in while she was being attacked and …" Suddenly Alex realised how the police were thinking. What was he doing just "dropping by" to "save" Monique from an "attacker" whom no one but the two of them had seen? He joined the dots. "They think this is a domestic. That Monique and I are lovers, that we had a fight and that she's protecting me by not saying anything. The fact that we're both English … oh God, we're both from the same city! This is just too easy for them, isn't it?"

"They haven't said anything …" But Laurent didn't deny it. He had seen quite clearly the direction the gendarmes' questions were taking them.

He drove Alex back to his hotel and helped him up the stairs to his room.

122

Alex changed out of his bloodstained clothes into a loose T-shirt and a pair of jogging pants, which he could pull past the plaster on his leg.

"We should get something to eat," Laurent said. He felt uncomfortable spending too much time in another man's hotel room. "Can you drink on those painkillers?"

"They didn't tell me *not* to. In my book, that's permission."

"And if you pass out, I'm getting used to carrying you around," Laurent joked. "I'd rather not make a habit of it though– people might talk."

Alex laughed, then moaned with pain and wrapped his arms around his chest. He went pale.

"Are you alright?" Laurent had visions of calling another ambulance.

"Just don't make me laugh, alright?" Alex muttered between clenched teeth as soon as the worst had past.

"Okay," Laurent promised, grinning mischievously. "Rugby's a forbidden topic then? Specifically English rugby."

"What?"

"No talking about English rugby – you said no jokes. I mean that laughable performance of your team against ..."

Laurent dodged and threw up his hands in surrender as the other man threw a mock punch in his direction.

"Ouch, you bastard!" Alex groaned, clutching his ribs again. "Come on. You mentioned something a moment ago about alcohol and passing out. Let's go – I like the sound of both of those right now."

They had lunch in a small restaurant near Bergerac hospital because they wanted to get back in to see Monique as soon as they were allowed. She had a hairline fracture on her cheekbone, but most of her other injuries looked a lot worse than they were. Everyone's main concern now was her state of mind

"About the attack – is there anything else you can think of?" Laurent asked Alex. "Anything at all?"

He was desperate to identify Monique's attacker. During the night it had occurred to him that maybe this was something to do with the business and, if it was, his mother could be the next target.

Alex swirled his wine around. He had played it safe, with only one glass, but even so it was making him delightfully woozy, and the pain was receding nicely. He replayed what he could remember of the events of the previous night in his head and he repeated to Laurent everything he had already told the police.

"You think her attacker was English?" Laurent asked, jumping on the one detail he hadn't heard before.

"Yes, definitely," Alex said. "There was an open window – that was how I heard Monique scream as I got out of the car. As I was running up the path, he was saying something about a child. And he was accusing Monique of lying. And he spoke English to me too, when I came in. He was definitely English, Laurent."

"Or spoke good English?"

"No!" Alex shook his head violently in emphasis and grimaced. "Ooh shit! That hurt. Okay, so that's no jokes, and no contradicting me, please."

"Yes, Mummy!"

"I'm warning you! You still haven't seen the other guy. I might have done more damage to him than I remember!"

"So – the other guy," said Laurent, returning to the point. "You're sure he was English?"

"Definitely. What he said was idiomatic – something like 'What have we here then?' and the accent was perfect."

It didn't get them any closer to working out who it had been.

"Don't take this the wrong way," Laurent said after a while, "but –"

"What was I doing in Monique's in the first place?" Alex finished his sentence for him. "I was wondering when we'd get around to that." Although Alex wished he didn't have to answer. He still didn't know what the relationship between Evie and Laurent was. But he decided not to beat around the bush. "I went to see Monique because I wanted to ask her how to find Evie."

"And she wouldn't tell you so you beat her up?"

"That's not even remotely funny, Laurent."

"Sorry."

The atmosphere between the two men went from warm to glacial in the space of a second.

"So why did you say it?" asked Alex.

"To get it out in the open, because I know you thought it crossed my mind. And maybe I needed to hear you deny it. And besides, it's made you angry at being under suspicion instead of just scared. Doesn't that feel better?"

They stared at each other with guarded hostility.

"Well, do you … did you … think I did it? Even for a second?" Alex asked at last.

"No. The doctor last night asked me the same question. But I trust you."

They were silent for a few moments, then: "Thanks," Alex muttered gruffly. He was embarrassed. He was touched by Laurent's faith in him, but he wasn't used to showing emotion, especially around men. He was far more comfortable trading English rugby jokes.

"So why are you looking for Evie?" Laurent decided to press home his advantage. He had pushed his anger towards Evie to the back of his mind for the past few hours, but it was coming out again. If he understood a bit more about her and Alex, and what might have driven her to the other night, it might hurt less.

"I …"

Laurent could see that Alex was trying to decide how much to tell him. This new friend who trusted him.

"We were together, once," Alex said eventually. "A long time ago. We split up and I never fully understood why. I need to understand."

Laurent could hardly argue with that.

He jumped when the phone in his pocket rang. He looked around apologetically at the other customers and went outside to take the call.

"That was my mother," he told Alex when he came back in. "From the hospital. Monique's awake and she's doing okay. She's allowed visitors now."

He ordered the bill and won the struggle to pay.

♡   ♡   ♡

"So where is she?" Alex asked Laurent on the way back to the hospital. "Evie, I mean."

"Would Monique have told you, do you think?" Laurent asked

Alex struggled with his conscience. "I don't know," he admitted. "You know where she is though, don't you? Is there something between you?"

"We're friends. And don't ask me to tell you where she is, because I don't know enough of what went on between you."

"Sorry, fair enough."

As it happened, Alex was confused. In all the panic last night, no one had mentioned calling Evie. And she hadn't been at the hospital this morning. Maybe he was wrong – maybe she and Monique weren't as close as he thought, but they had certainly looked it when Monique was comforting her at the party. And yet, it was Laurent she left with ... so maybe he was the reason she was in France.

Alex's head was hurting.

Stop trying to think so hard, you idiot, he told himself.

♡   ♡   ♡

Monique looked worse, if anything, than she had the previous night. Although a lot of the swelling had gone down, the bruising was worse and in a hospital gown she looked small and helpless. But the blank stare on her face was the most frightening thing of all.

She was fully aware of what was going on around her, she answered questions to do with her care with single syllables, yes, or no, but the moment anyone tried to ask what happened, her eyes glazed over and she looked away.

"Did you manage to contact her parents?" Laurent asked his mother.

"They're on holidays. They spoke to her on the phone and she told them not to come home." Céline shook her head with concern. "It's the only time I've seen her get in any way animated at all. She was adamant that they not come to France. She wouldn't let me talk to them and talked down all her injuries. She even tried to make a joke of them. She said she surprised a burglar. Certainly, it sounds like the only reasonable explanation I can think of."

Laurent shook his head and told her what he had heard from Alex.

"Do you think we should call Evie?" he said. "I know she has her own problems at the moment, but …"

"There's no way Monique would allow that," Joël said, joining in the end of the conversation. He was carrying two little plastic cups of strong black coffee and he looked wretched. Since last night he'd told Laurent that he had dropped Monique off only a few minutes before the attack. Her attacker had been waiting in the house for her and Joël must be agonising over how different the outcome would have been if only he'd gone in with her.

"I'm not sure we can take too much notice of what Monique does or doesn't want at the moment," Céline said firmly, knocking back one of the coffees in a single mouthful. "She's not going back to that house on her own. But on the other hand, if she doesn't go back to her own home, she may never feel safe there again."

Chapter 13

"She certainly doesn't look like there's much wrong with her now," Marian said, smiling, as Holly chatted up the airport policeman and asked him was his gun real.

Evie just nodded; she was completely dazed. She was in Stansted airport for the second time in three days. Last time she was phoning Monique to give her an update on Holly; this time she was flying out with her mother and Holly to take care of Monique. She was glad her mother had offered to come with her – she didn't want to leave Holly behind, but she wasn't sure what she was going out to France to face. She didn't fully understand what had happened over there. Céline said that Monique claimed to have surprised a burglar who then attacked her, but everyone else seemed to think something more sinister had happened. Alex was involved – he had rescued her – but Evie recognised some hesitation in Céline's voice as she passed on this final detail.

But what upset Evie most was that Monique was attacked on the night she had returned to Dublin. No one had ever suggested that she shouldn't rush home to Holly. No one had tried to tell her that Holly would be fine. Could wait another day. But if Evie had even missed her flight, and had to postpone until the next morning, Monique wouldn't have come home alone that night. It was no use telling herself that Monique lived alone and had come home alone on countless nights. On Friday night she was supposed to have had Evie with her and she hadn't.

"Evie, love," her mother said gently, mistaking the reason for her daughter's tense expression, "stop worrying about Holly. She's fine – they wouldn't have let her travel unless they were absolutely certain. You know they said they wouldn't have even kept her overnight except that it was her first asthma attack and you were away."

At first, Evie wasn't sure at all about the trip to France and she tried to persuade Céline to bundle Monique onto a plane to Dublin. But when the doctors said that there was no reason Holly couldn't travel, and that warm country air would in fact probably do her the world of good, she had agreed that the best place for Monique to recover would be in her own home.

"I know, Mum, thanks. But actually I'm worried about what we're going to find when we get to France.

Theoretically I only have this week off …"

Evie's explanation faded away. She couldn't even begin to explain how short the next five days seemed when she had so much to deal with. Monique needed her and might need her beyond this week. She would see Laurent again and she hadn't had time to try and work out where she hoped that was going. And most of all, Evie worried about Alex. The moment he laid eyes on Holly he was bound recognise her for who she was. But it was too late to change her mind.

Holly was coming to France and that was that.

♡   ♡   ♡

At that moment Alex was being dropped back to his hotel to collect the last of his things and to settle the bill. With a fully furnished house to move into, it seemed stupid to go on paying for his, admittedly luxurious, hotel room. He joked that he'd changed his mind about going back to England, because his experience in Bergerac hospital was so good that he might as well stick with them to see out his treatment. But to be honest, Alex was afraid of walking into the Gendarmerie to tell them he was leaving France because he was afraid they might ask him not to.

So when he walked into the hotel lobby and saw the police inspector sitting in one of the armchairs, although his heart sank he wasn't completely surprised. The atmosphere towards him had cooled somewhat in the hotel and, more alarmingly, in the hospital. Even Céline seemed to be over-compensating. She was being *too* nice to him, as though she felt guilty for not being one hundred per cent convinced of his innocence.

"Monsieur Ryder!" The man stood up out of his chair, folded up a copy of *Sud Ouest* and handed it back to the receptionist with a smile. She, Alex noted, avoided looking at him directly and merely put his room key on the counter without a word.

"Could we go upstairs, monsieur? To your bedroom?"

"I'm just checking out. Perhaps you'd like to call out to Ste Anne. I have a house there and I've decided to make a start at moving in."

Alex thought it would be a good idea to establish the fact that he was moving to France, that he would soon be a part of the community, a taxpayer, and not just a foreigner any more.

"I am aware of your latest purchase, monsieur, but I won't take up much of your time. Shall we?" The way he indicated the stairs left Alex under no illusions – it was an order, not an invitation, and he hobbled upstairs cursing under his breath.

He unlocked his room, uncomfortably aware that the policeman seemed to be watching his every move, as though he suspected Alex was about to make a mad dash for freedom.

"I have a problem, Monsieur Ryder." The policeman took the chair at the small writing desk near the bed, leaving Alex to sit in one of the armchairs by the window. It left Alex in the uncomfortable position of having to look up at the policeman. "I have a young lady who was attacked and she seems unaware of the identity of her attacker."

"It wasn't me! Monique has told you that. How many more times does she have to tell you?"

"And it was a burglar who attacked her. Yes of course, she told us. A burglar that only the two of you seem to have seen," he said sarcastically. "She is unable to give us a description, and your description … well, let us say … it lacks detail."

The policeman went silent, and Alex sat it out. Maybe if he was guilty, he would begin to babble contradictory details now, but he was just exhausted. And he had no more details to give. But he had to admit that the silence was an effective tool. It made him want to break it. To say anything at all.

The phone by his bedside rang, making him jump. The inspector merely turned his head slowly and looked at it.

"You may answer it."

Alex felt like saying he'd damned well do whatever he liked in his own hotel room but he just hobbled across the floor and picked it up.

"It's for you!" He hobbled back to his chair by the window, leaving the receiver on the nightstand for the policeman to pick up.

"*Oui!*" the inspector barked into the phone. Then he spoke French quickly, much too quickly for Alex to catch a single word, and angrily. He slammed down the phone and glared at Alex. "I had told the receptionist I was not to be disturbed, but it seems that your friend is coming upstairs anyway!"

Laurent came in without knocking.

"Bonjour, monsieur," he said to the inspector, and then he turned to Alex. "The girl downstairs said you had a guest and didn't want to be disturbed, but when I heard who the 'guest' was, I was sure you wouldn't mind my interrupting. It's not as if you've anything to hide, is it?" He kept smiling and began to speak in French to the policeman, whose face tightened in anger before he turned to Alex.

"Very well, I have just a few more ... problems ... that maybe you can 'help' me with, Monsieur Ryder."

"Fire ahead!" Alex was relieved to have Laurent there. And he was bloody glad that Laurent was holding firm. Even Joël seemed to be wavering. His English had deteriorated markedly in the past twelve hours, and Alex couldn't help thinking that it was to avoid talking to the foreign devil.

"Monsieur Ryder, perhaps you could tell me how long you've known Mademoiselle Saunders?"

Alex tried to calculate mentally. "A few months ... three, four?"

"Perhaps you could be a little more precise?"

"Very well." Alex did his best not to sound exasperated. "I came to France with my two younger children for the mid-term ... Then they went back to school ... I started looking for a property that week, so it would have been early March. Madame Lesauvage – Céline – introduced me to Monique about a week later ... we're in June now ... so that's three months; like I said."

"Madame Lesauvage said you came straight to her agency? That you hadn't been to any others?"

"She was recommended to me. A solicitor, some business contacts in Bristol. Why do you ask?"

"And you *say* you never met Mademoiselle Saunders before Mme Lesauvage introduced you? Are you certain? You'd never have met her in Bristol, for example? Think carefully, it's a big city I know, but …"

"I met Monique, 'Mademoiselle Saunders', for the first time, in France, in March," Alex repeated, now beginning to lose his patience. He made as if to get to his feet – he was going to show this man to the door. He caught Laurent's cautionary gesture out of the corner of his eye, but ignored it. "Now if you have no more questions …"

"Please sit down, Monsieur Ryder. I can see you are in some discomfort and I will show myself out in a moment. But first, would you mind telling me, just to satisfy my curiosity, where you spent the first weekend in February?"

Laurent got to his feet and looked as if he was about to interrupt.

"It's okay, Laurent," Alex said, waving him back. "I remember very well where I was in early February. The sale of my business was going through so I was in Bristol. And I have any number of people who can vouch for that if necessary." He allowed himself a small smile of victory. "Why? Did your 'burglar' strike in February too? Some other woman?"

"Non, monsieur, our 'burglar' did not strike back on

the first weekend of February. But that was when Mademoiselle Saunders presented to Bergerac hospital in the late stages of a miscarriage. She had come straight from the airport, in an ambulance, having begun to haemorrhage during a flight from Bristol. The miscarriage was brought on, it seems, by 'falling down the stairs' during her time there."

Chapter 14

Evie phoned Céline to tell her that the plane would be delayed.

"Don't worry, just let me know when you board and Laurent will be waiting for you at the airport."

They had agreed that Evie would use Monique's car while she was over, so she needed a lift from the airport.

"How is she?" Evie asked.

"Much the same. She's not saying much. She still insists she disturbed a burglar." Céline's tone took on an even more bitter note than Evie had noted earlier that day and she wondered what she wasn't being told.

"Why are you all convinced it wasn't a burglar?" she asked. "And why do you think Monique would lie?"

"I know nothing, I am just an old woman," Céline said, her voice dripping with sarcasm. "But you are her closest friend: maybe she will talk to you, and we will get to the bottom of all this."

"Céline." Evie was getting worried now. "Céline, what are you not telling me?" She tried to sound firm rather than scared. "I am bringing my mother and daughter over to stay in Monique's house. If you believe we're going to be in any danger, I want to know about it!"

"I'm sure you won't be in any danger," Céline assured her, and Evie thought she heard an emphasis on *"you"*, "but to make absolutely certain, either Joël or Laurent will sleep on the sofa until … well, until we know what's going on."

Oh, great! Evie thought, Laurent on the sofa, and Alex down the road.

"How's Alex Ryder, by the way?" she asked as casually as she could manage. "I believe he was hurt too? Is he still in France?"

"Monsieur Ryder is fine, considering. And he is still in France … I think he may be moving over here sooner than he planned."

♡   ♡   ♡

Laurent stood up after the inspector delivered his bombshell, not sure what he planned to do or say, but the shock made it impossible for him to stay seated.

"You see my difficulty, Monsieur Ryder," the policeman went on, obviously forgetting that he had said he was about to leave. "There are just too many coincidences."

"Coincidences?"

Alex had gone pale again, and Laurent wasn't entirely sure that it was because of the pain in his ribs.

"Yes, Monsieur Ryder, coincidences. Let me count them up for you. One – you happen to arrive at Mademoiselle Saunders' house just as she is being attacked by a burglar –"

"I can explain that," Alex objected. "I called –"

"Two – Mademoiselle Saunders and yourself both sustain injuries consistent with a violent struggle, but there is no sign of an intruder." He left unsaid the fact that he hadn't looked very hard for a third person he clearly didn't believe existed.

"Three – you and Mademoiselle Saunders are both from the same city. I have ascertained that her parents' home is less than a half a mile from your apartment. It is not impossible that you could have met in a night-club or a pub."

"I don't get out much to pubs and I can't remember the last time I was in a night-club."

"A good-looking divorced man like you – such a shame, monsieur!"

Laurent felt that the man was badgering Alex. After all, a coincidence was a coincidence. And since the flight went in, there were plenty of people from the Bristol area who had met for the first time in the Dordogne. It was the same all over France as the airlines opened up more and more routes. Half of England seemed to be emigrating. He wondered should he intervene to help Alex out, but he wasn't sure what kind of legal footing they were on. If the inspector didn't have anything solid he probably wouldn't take Alex in for more formal questioning, whereas for Laurent to object too strongly, or to insist that Alex got a lawyer, might make things look worse for him. And, although he hardly admitted it to himself, Laurent felt that there was more to come, and he wanted to hear it.

"And finally, shortly after Mademoiselle Saunders suffers her miscarriage, caused by an unfortunate 'accident' in Bristol (on a weekend you admit you were in the city), you show up here. Of all the areas in France, you choose the Dordogne – no crime there, of course, it is the best part of France!" He swelled with pride and laughed at his own joke, but Laurent couldn't help notice his first use of the word "crime". "Of all the estate agents in France you choose the one Mademoiselle Saunders works in. Of all the properties she shows you, you buy one so close to her house?"

"I've had enough of this!" Alex shouted. "Tell me exactly what you believe I've done, and then get out!"

"Monsieur?" The policeman got to his feet. His face was a caricature of wounded feelings. "Monsieur Ryder, have I said I suspected you of anything? I have merely shared my information with you. *I* believe that Mademoiselle Saunders is protecting someone. And whoever it is is not the kind of person I want in my community. *You* are about to join our community so I am quite sure that you wish to ensure that there will be no repeat whatsoever of this kind of behaviour?"

♡   ♡   ♡

Laurent drove Alex to Ste Anne in silence. He helped him with his crutches getting out of the car but let him open the front door himself, while he went to get the suitcases from the boot.

"Where will I put these?" he asked when he followed Alex into the house.

"Leave them!" Alex snapped.

"Don't be silly, how are you going to move them? I'll put them in the main bedroom."

"Okay, thanks," Alex said grudgingly. "It's out there, second door –"

"I know," Laurent said. "I built it, remember?"

Laurent left the bags in Alex's bedroom. The bed was already made up, as Céline had sent her housekeeper to give the place the once over before Alex moved in. Then Laurent went and checked the fridge. There was enough in it to keep Alex going for a day or two.

Alex had settled on his leather couch and had his leg raised on the cushion beside him. Laurent had seen him take painkillers after the policeman left his hotel room, but they didn't seem to have taken effect. The Englishman's face was grey.

Laurent took a bottle of Joël's wine from the cupboard. Alex's "care package" had been made up yesterday, before the inspector's questioning, and it contained evidence of how grateful everyone was that Alex had intervened to save Monique. Laurent wondered whether it would have been so bountiful if they had all contributed to it today.

"Come on, let's drink to your new house before I have to go and collect Evie. No champagne I'm afraid, but I can guarantee you'll enjoy this! A present from Joël."

"I've got off to a great start in France, haven't I?" Alex looked awful.

Suddenly Laurent regretted mentioning drink. Maybe he should call a doctor.

"The gendarmes have nothing on you," he said instead. "If they had, they'd have taken you in by now."

"Right. That makes me feel *so* much better! Cheers!" Alex knocked back his glass of Joël's prestige 1996 Cuvée without tasting it. He held out his glass for a refill.

"Are you sure?" Laurent asked. "The tablets?"

"Don't refuse me a fucking drink in my own home, man. I'll get plastered if I damn well want to."

Laurent poured, but Alex put the drink on the edge of the fireplace without taking another mouthful.

"C'mon, Laurent. Out with it!"

"What?" Laurent sat on the other side of the fireplace.

"Do you still believe me?"

Laurent had been hoping he wouldn't ask. "I believe you," he said as convincingly as he could. Because deep down he probably did, although he still had a few more questions he needed answered.

"And the others? My new friends? My future 'community'?" Alex asked. It hadn't escaped him that not only was the police inspector convinced he was guilty, but he had also received a none too subtle warning from the man.

"I don't know what they think," Laurent said honestly. "We haven't really talked about it."

In fact there seemed to be a stunned embargo on any discussion of what had really happened to Monique. No one seemed to want to challenge her story in front of the others. Laurent didn't know if it was out of loyalty to her, or because they just didn't want to contemplate the alternative. Joël had come the closest to pointing the finger at Alex. When Laurent said he had cancelled his flight home and would be staying in the village, Joël suggested that he and Laurent draw up a roster for sleeping on Monique's couch. Although of course he never actually linked the two facts.

Chapter 15

Evie wished that it was anyone other than Laurent coming to pick her up. But Céline had her hands full with seeing Monique's clients as well as her own, and Joël was taking care of Monique until Evie arrived to take over. They reclaimed their luggage, exited the building and Evie looked around for Laurent. She couldn't believe the way her life had changed beyond recognition since she had last stood here. On the flight, Holly had fallen asleep, and Marian, who was a nervous flyer, had buried herself in her book, so Evie had been left with time to think for the first time since the whole chain of events had been set in motion.

The hard-won security she had built for herself and Holly felt like a distant dream. She had been fooling herself if she thought she had any control over their lives.

And it wasn't just the danger Holly and Monique had found themselves in which had changed everything. Totally unexpectedly, Evie had met a man whom she just might be capable of falling in love with, but he lived here in France, a world away from her life in Ireland. And another man, the very one who had taught her not to trust herself when it came to love, had re-entered her life. Her child's father, Alex. Who had helped her create this special and unique person beside her and who had had such an unexpected effect on her when she saw him again. Because to Evie's surprise, any time she managed to steal a few minutes' sleep, it was long-suppressed memories of Alex that filled her dreams. But when she was awake, if she wanted to think of something that would make her smile, it was her time with Laurent that she replayed in her mind.

♡   ♡   ♡

Laurent was sitting in his mother's car, across from the small terminal building, waiting for Evie to emerge. He wanted to watch her for a minute or two before going to greet her, to see how he felt about seeing her again. Walking around Alex's house earlier, he had seen Evie in everything he looked at. And his anger came back, as hot and as bitter as when he realised why she slept with him. But everything was so much more complicated now. Alex was no longer just Evie's former lover or Laurent's employer – he had become a friend of sorts.

Laurent groaned and rested his head on the steering

wheel. He longed to close his eyes and to catch up on some of the sleep he had missed out on in the past couple of days, as if that would make it easier to sort out the mess inside his head. Instead, he stepped reluctantly out of the car and walked towards where Evie and her mother were waiting. A little girl in a yellow dress was picking daisies under the tree they had piled their luggage against. As Laurent caught Evie's eye and waved, the little girl looked up to see who her mother was waving at.

Holly and Laurent's eyes met, and Laurent realised that everything was about to get a lot more complicated.

$$\heartsuit \qquad \heartsuit \qquad \heartsuit$$

Monique wished they would all just leave her alone to deal with this her own way. She was glad she hadn't been left alone in the house since she came back, but she didn't see why they all insisted on *talking* all the time. Her head hurt, and it wasn't just the bruises that were to blame.

The implications of what had happened to her were too difficult for Monique to face right now, so she concentrated instead on the fact that Evie was coming soon. Evie's holiday had come to an abrupt ending on Friday, and although that was the one thing that *wasn't* Monique's fault, she was looking forward to making it up to her. She knew that Evie needed a proper break, and she had so much more she planned to do with her. Holly being here this time made it more difficult, of course, but Evie and Monique had managed to enjoy themselves in the past with Holly around, so they'd manage again.

Besides, Marian had offered to come as well, so she could baby-sit. Monique was racking her brains for a way of throwing Laurent and Evie together again as well – another night with him would do Evie the world of good.

Monique examined her face in the bathroom mirror and grimaced. Then she wished she hadn't as pain shot up the side of her head and her eyes filled with tears. She didn't know how long it had been since she took the last dose of painkillers, but … what the hell: she popped two more from the blister pack and swallowed them gingerly. She was not a pretty sight. Even after several carefully applied layers of make-up, the bruise on her cheek was still visible. The graze on her forehead was beginning to heal, but it was still weeping small amounts of fluid, so make-up just slid off it.

"This time, you stupid prick, you went too far," she muttered under her breath.

But then as quickly as the thought crossed her mind, she drove it away again. It was the drink, she reminded herself, and concentrated on making herself more presentable.

She brushed her hair forward, but it did nothing to improve her appearance. Oh well, she thought, what were big sunglasses and broad-brimmed hats invented for, if not for emergencies like this?

Then she flushed the toilet and opened the bathroom door loudly, coughing before she came downstairs. She wanted to give them plenty of warning to stop talking about her.

Joël looked up and switched off the television when

she came down.

"Hi," he said shyly. "Feeling any better?"

"Where is everyone?" she asked. The house was eerily quiet and she wished Joël hadn't switched off the television. She looked about. Someone had cleaned the house while she was in hospital, and there was no trace of Friday night. Which was good, she thought. It would help everyone forget it.

"Céline's showing properties and Laurent's gone to collect Evie," Joël said.

"Already?" Monique's watch had got broken on Friday, and her wrist was bruised and uncomfortable, so she hadn't dug out her other one.

"You were asleep quite a while," he smiled. "Can I get you something? Sit down."

"No." Monique remembered just in time not to shake her head. "Let me. What would you like, a drink? Coffee? Something to eat?"

"Monique," Joël said firmly, getting to his feet and guiding her to the sofa, "sit down. Relax, let us help you."

She hadn't the strength to argue, although she wanted to keep active. It was so unfair; her mind was ready to move on but her body was slowing her down. It needed rest to heal and she needed painkillers to banish the pain. And the painkillers were contributing to the drowsiness.

"So what will it be?" Joël asked from the kitchen. "I make a good omelette."

"I'm not hungry," Monique said.

"I know you're not. You haven't been hungry since ...

Anyway, you have to eat."

He cut some bread, put some cheeses on a plate, laid out some cold meats and brought them over to the table. He laid glasses and then went over to get Monique.

"I can do it!" she said irritably as he was about to help her to her feet. She would go over to the table, she decided, and play with the food till Evie arrived. Then Holly would fly about the house like the little whirlwind she was and hopefully distract attention from her.

Evie's stomach flipped when she spotted Laurent. She wanted, more than anything on earth right now, for him to put his arms around her and hold her tight, until he managed to convince her that her world could be a safe, uncomplicated place again. But she was unprepared for the sheer force of her reaction when she saw him – she could hardly breathe with nerves.

"Is that Laurent?" her mother asked, following the direction of Evie's glance. "Nice! I approve," she added mischievously. It hadn't escaped her notice over the past day or so that Evie had a tendency to escape into a pleasant-looking trance at the mention of his name. But as Laurent approached, Evie realised he didn't seem to have any interest in her at all. He couldn't take his eyes off Holly. And Holly, having established that the stranger approaching them was the one Mummy was waiting for, was staring right back.

Oh my God, Evie realised as she saw the expression

on Laurent's face. He knows. One look at Holly and he's worked it out.

There was a resemblance certainly, but Evie hadn't realised it was that strong. Then she remembered Laurent knew about her and Alex, so she hoped he'd just done the maths. She wanted to be able to tell Alex in her own time and not have someone else drop her in it.

Fortunately Laurent had recovered enough by the time he reached them.

"Evie." He held her at arm's length while kissing her very formally on each cheek. "Welcome back to France." He turned to her mother. "Madame Kinsella?" He took the hand she held out to him, then surprised her by kissing her on each cheek too. "And this must be Holly?"

Finally Laurent's eyes met Evie's and she couldn't believe the hurt, bewildered look she saw in them. But she hadn't time to think of anything except to silently beg him with her own eyes not to say anything yet. He must have understood, because he nodded imperceptibly, then reached down to pick up their cases.

"The car's over here," he said. "I rang a few people to try and borrow a booster seat for Holly, but I didn't have any luck. I have a cushion –"

"It's alright, I packed the one I keep in my car!" Evie's mother said brightly, glad to be able to add something. She didn't know what was going on between her daughter and this good-looking Frenchman, but he seemed to be *a lot* more than a friend. She had a feeling she was in for an interesting few days.

On the drive back to the house, Laurent managed to

drop Alex's name casually into conversation at least three times. Evie thought she would scream if she heard him repeat the words "Alex Ryder, Monique's client from Bristol" one more time. She knew what he was trying to do of course, but she couldn't tell whether or not he was surprised that the name didn't seem to mean anything to Marian.

"I need to talk to you," she hissed at him as they were getting out of the car. "Alone, I need to explain something."

"I think, somehow, Evie," he whispered back wryly, when he was sure Marian wasn't listening, "I think that you have a lot of explaining to do, and not just to me."

Evie closed her eyes and groaned as she realised just how right he was. When she looked at him again, he was smiling. But it wasn't a very pleasant smile.

"*Courage!*" he said in French. "It could have been worse – Alex could have been here to greet you. But don't worry, he's only down the street, so you'll see him again soon!"

He was laughing at her and enjoying her obvious discomfort. Yet the cold, angry look in his eyes made her shiver.

♡   ♡   ♡

"Monique!" Evie tried not to look shocked when she saw her friend. Although her imagination had painted a much worse picture of the injuries, she wasn't prepared for actually seeing them in the flesh. Monique had been busy with the make-up, and the mere thought of her in front of the mirror, trying to hide what she could of her injuries, filled Evie's eyes with tears.

They hugged and everyone went quiet around them, until Marian bustled into motion, made loads of noise and shooed the two of them upstairs for some privacy.

"Oh Monique," Evie said when they closed the door of her bedroom behind them, "I should have been here."

"Don't be silly – you had to go home to Holly. How is she?"

"Holly's fine but what about you? What happened? Are you able to talk about it at all?"

"Of course I am, I've done nothing but talk about it; I'm getting very sick of talking about it. He was waiting for me when I came in –"

"Who?"

"He, the burglar, whoever." Monique looked away and went to open Evie's wardrobe, then realised that all the bags were still downstairs, so she closed it again. Without looking directly at Evie she went on: "He attacked me. Alex heard me scream, ran in and rescued me. End of story."

"And you have no idea who it was?"

"It was dark; I saw nothing. It was all over so fast …"

Evie knew Monique was lying. Suddenly she understood Céline's frustration on the phone and Laurent's caution in the car. She was scared of whatever Monique had got herself into, but she knew that whatever she said right now would be the wrong thing, and she didn't want to drive her friend away before she had a chance to help her.

"Poor you," she said instead and hugged Monique. "I wish I'd been here for you."

♡   ♡   ♡

Later that night, when she was sure Monique was asleep and when Marian had settled into the attic room with Holly, Evie came back downstairs. Laurent was on "guard duty" tonight and he stood up when he heard her on the stairs. It was obviously time to have that chat.

But when she saw a stern, almost sneering look on his face, the day and all the horrors of the previous days caught up with her and she burst into tears.

"I'm sorry," she sobbed, running to the kitchen end of the room to get away from him. "I'm sorry, I'm sorry, I'm sorry." She swiped at her face ineffectually with a screwed-up ball of kitchen paper. "I don't know what's wrong with me. I'll be alright in a minute, I'm sorry."

But she wasn't alright. The tears kept coming and coming and huge violent sobs shook her body. She began to shiver although the house was hot – stiflingly hot, as no one wanted to suggest opening windows or doors.

"I'm sorry," she kept saying, "I'm alright, I'm sorry, I don't know what's wrong with me, I'm sorry."

Then Laurent was standing there with a glass in his hand.

"You're in shock," he said, and the tenderness in his voice made her cry harder. "You've been through a lot.

Drink this."

She took a sip and made a face. It was brandy, a particularly harsh brandy, probably the bottle Monique kept beside the cooker for sauces.

"All of it," Laurent insisted, and when she had obeyed, he took the glass, put it in the sink and led her to the sofa where he had been sitting.

As the brandy began to work, Evie's sobs began to subside, but she still couldn't see from tears. Laurent pulled a chenille throw off one of the armchairs and placed it gently over her shoulders.

"You poor thing," he said, wrapping his arms around her like a child. "You poor little thing. You don't have to be strong all the time. My poor little Evie. It's okay, now, it's okay."

And soon she began to believe him. She stopped crying and fell into a dreamless sleep in his arms.

Chapter 16

Evie woke with a start. She thought she had heard a thud, or a crash, but wasn't sure if she had dreamed it.

"Ssh!" Laurent unwrapped his arms from around her and placed a finger on his lips. He straightened up stiffly, making Evie wonder how long she had been asleep, and walked slowly to the front door. He opened it carefully, then pulled it open all the way and ran down the steps to the street.

Evie went to the door and looked out. There was something in a white plastic bag on the doorstep, and a fist-size rock on the bottom step. Laurent was standing in the middle of the road looking up and down the deserted village.

"*Merde!*" *Shit*, he said under his breath as he came

back towards the house. "He could have thrown that rock from anywhere."

Evie bent down to pick up the bag.

"Don't touch that!" Laurent cried, but it was too late – Evie had already picked it up.

It was warm, and she dropped it again, throwing it away from her. When it landed, they could both see the blood pooling in the bottom of the bag.

"Go inside and lock the door," Laurent ordered. "I'll be back in a minute."

She stepped inside and waited, shivering.

"What was it?" she asked him when he finally joined her.

"A baby rabbit. Skinned," he answered. "I took care of it."

"It was still warm," she remembered with a shudder.

"Are you okay?" he asked.

She nodded dumbly, although she couldn't really remember what okay felt like.

"I know this isn't the best time, but I need to ask you some questions, Evie."

She nodded again and they sat down.

"How long was I asleep?" she asked.

"Just over an hour." The tenderness crept back into Laurent's voice. "You didn't move a muscle – you must have been really exhausted."

"It's been a mad few days," Evie agreed. She was embarrassed at her behaviour earlier, and she couldn't believe that Laurent hadn't moved or taken his arms from around her in all that time.

"Where do you want to start?" Evie asked.

"I'm sorry, I know you're exhausted, but ..." he nodded his head in the direction of the front door, "well, what just happened makes it all the more urgent."

"I'm okay now. And anyway I'm not sure I could go straight to sleep after that. Where do you want to start?"

"With Alex."

"What about Alex?" she asked cautiously. There was just so much about Alex he might want to know that she didn't know where to start.

"He doesn't know about Holly?"

She shook her head, not able to meet his eyes.

"Why didn't you tell him?"

"It's a long story, but it ended just about the time I discovered I was pregnant."

"How would he have reacted, do you think?"

She shook her head in confusion. "I don't understand where you're going with this ..."

"Okay ..." He scratched his head. "Let me put it another way ... you didn't leave him *because* you were pregnant?"

"*What?*"

"Evie, this is important, but was Alex ever, in any way ..." Laurent hesitated. Evie had obviously loved Alex, was still haunted by him all these years later ... she could hate him for what he was about to say. "Evie, was Alex ever violent towards you?"

"No, no way." Evie was shaking her head violently as she pulled away from Laurent, who, without either of them being aware of it, had taken her hands in his. "No, this is crazy. Laurent, tell me what's going on. Right now!"

It took him a couple of minutes to fill her in and he watched Evie's face grow hostile as he spoke.

"You think I ran away from Alex because I was pregnant, because I was afraid of what he would do," Evie said slowly when he'd finished. "You think he caused Monique's miscarriage and that he's some kind of crazy stalker who's followed her to France. That he attacked her and that she's protecting him. You are one sick individual, Laurent Lesauvage! For your information Alex Ryder wouldn't hurt a fly, let alone a child, unborn or otherwise. If you must know, he left me because he couldn't bear what our relationship was doing to his *children*. He loved me, at least I think he did, and yet when his wife begged him to go back for the sake of his *children*, he dumped me with about as much ceremony as binning last week's porridge."

Evie stood up and stalked towards the stairs.

"Wait, Evie!" he pleaded. "Just give me two more minutes, please!"

She crossed her arms as she stood at the bottom of the stairs and looked at him.

"Go on," she said, begrudgingly.

"Firstly, up to now, I've been the only one defending Alex. Everyone else has jumped to the conclusion that he's the attacker. Secondly," he came over and stood so close to her that she could feel the heat from his body, "secondly, I had to say all that because I was afraid for you, Evie. Although I like Alex and I trust him, I could have been wrong about him."

"And …?" Evie knew there was more to come.

"And thirdly – Monique is definitely protecting someone. Random burglars don't come back to leave skinned rabbits on your doorstep."

"Although at least the rabbit puts Alex in the clear," Evie said as she sat down again.

"Why?"

"You said he was on crutches. I don't think he could have got up to the door quietly enough to leave the rabbit, throw the stone so we'd find it straight away and then run off."

Laurent had to admit that was true. But he wished he knew which Alex Evie was defending – Holly's father or her former lover.

"But you're right about Monique," Evie admitted at last, when they had been sitting in silence for a while. "She's hiding something, something important. She's just too 'cheerful' about the whole thing and pretending none of it has really happened. It's all a big act. I can only remember seeing her like this once before – when her father died. We were in first year in college at the time. It was strange, at the time – we were all so young, and no one was really sure how to react around her – none of the rest of us had lost parents. But it didn't matter, because she came back after the funeral and was straight back to being our madcap Monique. Partying harder than ever before, as though nothing had happened. And yet there was this curtain that had come down behind her eyes, which she didn't want any of us to see past. Admittedly, none of us really tried too hard."

"Her father?" Laurent asked, looking confused. "Then who was that she was talking to on the phone the other day? She said her parents were on holidays, and she wouldn't let them cut their holiday short because of what had happened to her."

"Her father left home when she was quite young. I think, reading between the lines, that he drank, and that's what killed him in the end. But Monique doesn't talk about him. And I mean not at all. I'm not even sure what age she was when her mother remarried. When she says Dad, she means her stepfather. He adopted her, and she took his name."

"You're tired, Evie," Laurent said suddenly. "You should get some sleep."

"No, I couldn't, not yet," she said quickly. "I'd start thinking about this whole thing too much. I'd like to stay up for a while longer and talk about something completely different if you don't mind. Unless … oh, God, sorry, Laurent, that was probably just your polite way of saying 'Get the hell off my bed!'" She patted the sofa cushion beside her. "You must be exhausted too."

She stretched and was about to stand up.

"Stay!" Laurent ordered, laying a hand on her arm and smiling. "I'd love to talk about something else for a while. My mind's going round in circles too. Wine?"

Without waiting for her answer he went to the fridge, took out a bottle of white wine, and poured two glasses.

"*Santé*," she toasted, touching her glass to his before they took their first sip.

"*Sláinte*," he said back with a grin.

"Talk to me about your job," Evie suggested.

"What about it?"

"Anything. About the buildings you've worked on, about what you believe in. Anything. I like listening to you talk about architecture." Evie remembered the first day they had spent a lot of time together, the day of the trip to St Émilion, and how she thought she could have listened to him reciting the phone directory, with that deep, accented voice of his. Was that only a few days ago?

Laurent talked for a while, and then suddenly he went quiet just as he began to describe how his firm had tendered for the job on Alex's house. Although it wasn't his house then.

"What is it, Laurent?" Evie asked, her heart suddenly beating faster. She suspected that deep down this was why she had asked him to talk about work.

"Why did you make love to me in *Alex's* house, Evie?"

"Because that's where you brought me, Laurent."

It was true and she made it sound so simple that Laurent felt some of his anger and confusion drain away. He looked into her eyes and tried to read something there, anything at all. She was a fine one to talk about curtains pulled down inside eyes, he thought.

"Why did you bring me there, Laurent?"

"Because it's beautiful. Because you're beautiful. Because I created it and I wanted you to see what I could do. What I was capable of … I suppose I wanted to show off!" he admitted sheepishly. "And I wanted it to be special."

162

"It was special, Laurent. Do you know what I told Monique the next morning? I told her it was the most romantic night of my life."

Laurent felt himself blush. He had never been one to brag about conquests, although he knew men who did, but he had always wondered what women told each other, "after". To be told that was both wonderfully flattering and exquisitely embarrassing.

"And the fact that it was Alex's house, Alex's bed?" He held her face in his hands so she couldn't turn away from him. "Did that matter to you?"

"I won't try to lie to you, Laurent."

"Was it revenge?"

"No ... I don't know, I don't think so. It was just ... something. Maybe I was looking for proper closure? And it was exciting, Laurent. Unbelievably, passionately, exciting. I have no idea how much of that was down to knowing it was Alex's house and how much was purely down to you. But you excited me long before I knew where you were going to take me. You know that. We both knew how that night was going to end."

Laurent could feel the pulse in Evie's neck quicken. Her lips didn't close when she finished speaking, her voice had thickened and her pupils widened. He knew she wanted him as much as he wanted her.

"Kiss me, Laurent," she pleaded. "Please, just kiss me."

It would be so easy. Their faces were only inches apart. And they both knew it wouldn't stop at kissing.

"I can't," he said simply.

"Oh, my God!" Evie closed her eyes and tried to turn her face away from him to hide her humiliation. "I'm sorry, I've made a complete fool –"

"Evie, open your eyes," he ordered. He held her face in a vice-like grip. "Look at me," he told her. "This isn't just about you and me any more, is it?"

"What do you mean? I'm single … I can choose whoever I like to –"

"But the man you used to love, the father of your child, has just re-entered your life."

Evie wished she could say that Alex didn't matter any more, but she couldn't lie to him. And she was slightly ashamed of what she had just tried to do. Getting involved with Laurent would have saved her from having to think too hard about how she felt about Alex, and that was the coward's way out.

Chapter 17

By next morning, after tossing and turning most of the night, Evie had made a decision. She was beginning to have an idea of what might be going on, but if she was right, she wanted Holly and her mother out of there.

"I'm sorry to have dragged you over here, Mum, but I'm going to have to send you home again. And I want you to take Holly with you."

Marian had heard about the rabbit, so she couldn't argue, but she tried to persuade Evie that she and Monique should come too.

"Monique's not moving, Mum. She can be stubborn as a mule when she wants to be, and I can't leave her here on her own. But I promise you, we're not in any danger – we're not going to be left on our own for so much as a minute. Besides, I also have some things to sort out myself."

"I don't suppose one of those things would be a good-looking Frenchman by the name of Laurent, would it?" Marian said, after a long silence. She seemed to recognise that Evie wasn't going to budge, so there was no point in adding to her worries by creating a fuss.

"Stop fishing, Mum." But she was happy enough to leave her mum to speculate about Laurent. Especially as it now looked as if she was going to get her out of the country before she had a chance to meet Alex.

By the time Evie had got Holly dressed and lathered in industrial strength sun-cream, got herself showered and dressed and found her way downstairs, the others had gathered and the gathering had a feeling of a war-conference about it. Marian had taken Holly for "a walk" and Laurent shot Evie a warning look so she said nothing until she had some idea of what was going on.

Céline, who had stopped by on her way to work, and Joël, who looked about to move in, judging from the amount of bags dumped inside the front door, were arguing quietly in French.

Monique was the only one behaving in any way "normally".

"Coffee, Evie?" she asked brightly from behind a pair of Jackie Onassis sunglasses. "It's freshly made. No croissants, I'm afraid – no one's got around to going down to the shop. Would you like some toasted brioche?" She pointed to a loaf wrapped in yellow plastic.

"That would be lovely, thanks. Can I give you a hand?"

"No, you go and sit down, I'm fine."

"Come on out to the garden," Laurent suggested.

"We can lay the table there."

"And you can talk without 'upsetting the children'," Monique snapped sarcastically.

"Monique –" Evie began, but Laurent just shook his head and she got the impression that this argument had been fought several times already this morning. She followed him outside

"I told the others about last night," he explained. "Everyone's pretty upset with Monique for not telling us what's really going on. Now that it's pretty obvious it's not random."

"I'll try and talk to her again today," Evie promised. "Did you tell the police?"

"Yes, but they don't seem that interested. They more or less implied that if Monique won't help herself, there's not much they can do for her."

Fair enough point, Evie had to concede, but she wouldn't say it out loud for fear of sounding disloyal.

"They didn't even want to have a look at it – the rabbit," he continued. "So, I got rid of it properly this morning. You're sending your mother home?"

"Yes, after last night … the rabbit thing … after that, I thought it would be safer. And I'll be able to concentrate on Monique."

"I think you're doing the right thing. But I want you to be careful too – do you promise me?"

"Are you staying again tonight?" she asked.

"No, Joël will be here tonight. I have to go to Périgeux on a job." He glanced at his watch. "I'm leaving in about an hour's time and I have to stay there tonight. Possibly tomorrow night too." His heart jumped when he saw her look of disappointment. "I'll try to get back tomorrow if I can," he promised, squeezing her hand gently before standing up. "Monique said something about taking you to see Sarlat tomorrow, after your mum's gone."

"Oh, for God's sake!" Evie said irritably. "What's she playing at?"

"It's not such a bad idea," Laurent said. "It's a couple of hours' drive away, so you might get talking. And it'll be good and crowded when you get there."

"I s'pose," Evie agreed reluctantly.

"And today you'll spend most of the day driving back and forth to Bordeaux," he grinned. "My mother said she couldn't book tickets for Marian and Holly out of Bergerac, but I suspect she didn't try too hard. Besides, a direct flight to Dublin will be easier for your mum rather than having to switch in London."

"What were Céline and Joël arguing about?" Evie asked suddenly.

"He wanted to go with you and Monique to Bordeaux but Monique insisted that she'd rather it was just the two of you. My mother agreed with Monique. I'm sure she believes that throwing the two of you together as much as possible is the best way of getting Monique to tell us if she needs help."

"Poor Joël," Evie said. "He feels awful about this whole thing, doesn't he? About being the one who dropped her home on Friday."

"And he's the one she's pushed furthest away since it happened."

A French Affair

♡   ♡   ♡

The rest of the day passed in a blur of packing up again, driving to the airport, getting Holly (who was delighted to be going on another flight) and Marian (who was trying not to look too worried) onto their plane.

Monique was glad of all the activity, although she dreaded the drive home from Bordeaux and the inevitable interrogation from Evie. When no one was looking, she had made a phone call, so she knew it wasn't over yet. But instead of feeling afraid, she was relieved. She needed to finish things properly this time – the sooner the better. She knew she wasn't in any danger because she was never alone and public confrontations weren't Tom's style. But she knew it was vital to keep the others off the trail until she sorted things out properly. If Tom thought someone had set the French police on him, he would really flip and Monique was afraid to guess at how that would end. And, to be honest, she didn't really want to see him get in trouble. She just wanted to finish it.

"Let's go shopping!" she said brightly to Evie as she led the way back across the airport car park. It was phase one of Monique's distraction plan. "You've got a face on you as long as a wet bank-holiday Monday, and you could do with some retail therapy."

"Shopping? Monique, what's got into you?" Evie was close to tears. The reality of sending Holly back to Dublin hadn't hit until she arrived at the airport. Sending her off through the security barrier without chasing after

169

her, grabbing her and taking her back to Ste Anne was the hardest thing she had ever had to do. It was only knowing that the unknown danger in France seemed greater than the tiny risk of another asthma attack in Dublin that had held her back. And now Monique was behaving as though the only reason Evie was staying in France was to resume her interrupted holiday.

"Grow up, Monique!" she snapped as they got back to the car. "I'm driving," she said when Monique put her hand out for the keys. "And before you tell me to stop treating you like a child, you can bloody well stop behaving like one."

She got into the car, tears flowing down her cheeks now.

"Holly, the only real child around here, is on a plane out of here," she said. "And you, the person we're all trying to protect, are behaving like there's nothing wrong. Like this is all some big game. Someone tried to kill you, Monique."

"No one tried to kill me, Evie!" Monique snapped. "Don't be so bloody melodramatic!"

"Someone broke into your house. He beat you up, and God knows what he'd have done if Alex hadn't arrived." Evie paused to see if Monique reacted to Alex's name. But she was staring blankly ahead. "Then he came back, and he left a dead, skinned rabbit on your doorstep. I was there, dammit, I saw it. He might have been standing there watching me. Dramatic? I'll give you that, but don't go accusing me of melodrama."

"Okay, let's go home, if that's what you want to do,"

Monique said sulkily.

"The only thing I want right now, Monique, is for you to cut the bullshit!" Evie's anger began to boil over. "In fact, we're not going anywhere until we've talked this out. Get out of the car!"

Monique didn't move.

"Fine! I'll be in the terminal building, having a coffee. You can find me there when you're ready."

Evie stormed across the car park.

"Hey, you haven't locked the car!" Monique called after her.

"Well, you'd better talk fast then," Evie shouted back without turning around. She ignored the amazed looks of other passengers. Let everyone think they were a pair of madwomen. At least one of them was.

She was shaking with anger by the time she found a snack concession that had a free table, so she decided against ordering coffee, afraid that the jolt of caffeine would only make her worse.

"*Une Orangina, s'il vous plaît,*" she ordered instead, feeling the need for a sugar rush and the comfort of the sweet orangey taste that would always remind her of childhood holidays.

"*Deux, s'il vous plaît,*" she heard Monique say behind her.

They sat at a table in the corner and stared at each other until the waiter brought their drinks.

"Do you really think I'd have let you bring Holly and Marian over here – do you think I'd have let you come over yourself, if I thought there was any danger? To any of you?" Monique asked when he had left.

"The Monique I used to know wouldn't have, no," Evie snapped. "But that Monique's gone AWOL. She went missing some time between Friday night and Saturday morning."

"There's no danger, Evie. I promise you the situation's under control."

Evie saw that Monique believed what she was saying, but it didn't make her any less scared. There was a dangerous gleam in her friend's eyes just visible through the sunglasses, an almost manic certainty in her expression that made Evie worry for a second that the shock had unhinged her in some way.

"So tell me what's going on, then," she pleaded. "If it's all under control, surely you can trust me, let me help."

"Sorry," Monique's face clouded over again, "I can't tell you. You wouldn't understand. But you've got to trust me – it's going to be okay."

"You know they think it's Alex who attacked you?" Evie said, trying another tack – to appeal to Monique's conscience. "From what Laurent says, they're this close," she held up her finger and thumb a couple of millimetres apart, "to arresting him."

"It's not Alex and they know it." Monique waved her hand dismissively. "They also know that they can't arrest him without any evidence, and they won't find any, because it wasn't him."

"Well, it's not just the police, Monique. Alex has moved into the area, and he hasn't been able to stick his nose out the front door. Everyone thinks he's some kind of thug."

"Look, I'm really sorry for Alex's troubles, but they're not my fault. If he was really worried, he'd have gone back to England to wait till all this blew over."

"But you could sort it all out in a flash, couldn't you? Don't forget he was the one who rescued you."

"And I'm grateful …"

"But you had it all under control?" Evie mimicked.

Before Monique could react, she leaned across the table and snatched Monique's hat and sunglasses. She pinched on the bruise under Monique's eye with her thumb and forefinger. "That far but no further – was that how well you had it under control?"

A security guard edged closer to their table so Evie stood up and threw the hat and glasses back at Monique.

"I'm only trying to help, Monique," she said and walked back to the car before she burst into tears again. She couldn't believe what she'd just done. She'd pinched and hurt her best friend deliberately because she'd lost control of her own fear and frustration. But the worst thing was how placidly Monique had accepted the treatment.

Monique stood up shakily, put her hat back on and hid behind her sunglasses. As she walked through the terminal building, she could feel her eye, where Evie had pinched her, throbbing. That far and no further, Evie had said. Monique would like to be able to say yes, but she couldn't be one hundred per cent certain – she had seen the whisky bottle on the fireplace.

But the next time she would make sure there was no whisky. No possibility of things getting out of hand.

"Monique," Evie asked carefully before starting up the car, "please, I just have to ask you this. Is this someone you're involved with … you know … romantically? Someone new you haven't told us about?"

"Oh please, Evie!" Monique answered, glad she had rehearsed it several times in front of a mirror. "Now you really *are* getting melodramatic!"

Evie wanted to ask then if it was Tom. Not because she really thought he was capable of behaving like that, but because she wanted to hear Monique say no. She couldn't bear the thought that for as long as she had known Monique she was with someone violent, and that she hadn't known, hadn't helped. Or that Monique had never trusted her enough to tell her.

But she couldn't ask Monique outright. Because last night, when Laurent asked her if Alex had ever been violent towards her, she felt sick. Her skin had crawled with revulsion. His question made her feel ashamed – almost dirty. Laurent assumed her instinctive horror was in defence of Alex; but it wasn't. What Evie had really felt was tainted. Disgusted by his suggestion that she could have loved someone who was violent towards her.

So how could she put the same question, the same suspicion, to her best friend?

Chapter 18

"I'm going for a walk," Evie announced after a hurried, uncomfortable dinner. Joël looked as if he was about to object to her plan so she promised: "I'll just walk around the village. I won't go far."

But twenty minutes took her the whole way around the few streets before she found herself back outside the little shop just down the road from Monique's. Reluctant to return to the house, she went in and bought a copy of *Sud Ouest* with the intention of taking it along the street to Antoine's café and practising her French reading over a cold beer.

As she came out of the shop, a small red car pulled up alongside her.

"Evie, I heard you were back in France." Laurent had finally told Alex that Evie lived in Ireland full-time but was coming over to France to Monique.

"Alex," Evie said, suppressing her desire to run in the opposite direction, "I thought you were housebound."

"I was," he said, rolling down the window all the way, "until I persuaded the rental company to swap my car for an automatic."

"Good idea," Evie said. And then, hating herself for even thinking of it, she asked: "And when did you get your new car?"

"Don't talk to me!" Alex muttered. "You have no idea how much bloody red tape ... They said they'd bring it at one o'clock, but I should have known better. It was four before I saw it. Lunch must have got in the way."

"Four o'clock today?" Evie asked casually.

"Yes, this is my first trip out."

They looked at each other awkwardly and Evie could see that he wished he had overcome his instinctive good manners and had driven past without greeting her. They were on their own here, without the social buffer of other people around them, and neither was sure if they had anything left to say to the other. Or rather Evie was sure that this was neither the time nor the place for what she had to say.

"Can I offer you a lift back to Monique's?" Alex asked lamely, although they both knew she could walk the distance in not much longer than it would take him to turn the car around and drive her there.

"No thanks." She pointed her newspaper in the direction of the café. "There's a cold *pression* with my name on it down there, and I'm not going to keep it waiting a second longer."

She found it strange she could sound so casual. But she was over the shock of finding him again, and the night with Laurent had put her in a stronger position emotionally. Besides, she was amongst friends in Ste Anne while Alex was the outsider.

"*Pression?*" Alex repeated, looking puzzled.

"Draught," Evie translated helpfully. "As in beer." Her mouth was already watering.

"I don't suppose ..." Alex's voice trailed off, and he looked so pathetic that Evie couldn't stop herself.

"Why don't you join me?" she asked automatically, then cursed under her breath all the way down the road when Alex accepted and went to park. She suspected she had issued the invitation to prove something to herself.

"So!" Alex said as he sat down, having bumped into virtually every other customer on his progress between the tables.

"So!" Evie agreed and wished she were anywhere else on earth. "You need to get a bit more practice in with those crutches."

"Yeah, you're right!" Alex agreed, giving way to another long silence. "How's Monique?"

"Fine, considering," Evie answered. She had got out of the house to get away from Monique and she wasn't about to start discussing her with Alex. "But thanks for ... well, you know ... rescuing her."

Alex shrugged.

Their beers arrived, and they drank thirstily.

The past sat between them uncomfortably, like a

badly behaved child they had both agreed to ignore.

"Two more, please," Alex ordered from the waiter, as he put down his half-empty glass. "Aah! I needed that."

"You'd want to watch it if you're going to drive home again. And I can't see you getting up that driveway of yours on crutches," Evie warned. It had been hard enough in high heels.

"You've seen my house?" Alex asked with almost childish pride. He looked relieved that they had found something neutral to talk about. "It's fantastic, isn't it? If I'd been involved in the plans from the very beginning I wouldn't have done it any differently. Laurent's very talented, isn't he?"

"I suppose so," Evie agreed. She didn't want to discuss Laurent with Alex.

"I've got a swimming-pool, you know. I can't use it until they take this thing off …" He pointed to his plaster. Evie knew what he was about to suggest – he had always been effortlessly polite, the very soul of hospitality. "But you and Monique are welcome to come up for a swim. And did I hear someone say you were bringing your little daughter over with you? I'm sure she'd love –"

"She's gone home again," Evie interrupted quickly. And then, although she had hoped to avoid talking about it, she told him about the rabbit. She'd have said anything to take the subject off Holly. It was impossible to talk about kids without asking about their age or about their father. And Alex might be a lot of things, but he wasn't stupid.

As Evie described the events of last night, Alex went

very quiet. Then, in a small, nervous voice, he said: "I take it from the fact that you agreed to have a drink with me that you're not in the 'Alex is a woman-beater' camp?"

"No, Alex, I would never have suspected you of *that*." And before he could get a chance to ask her what crimes she might hold him guilty of, to try to raise the subject of their shared past, she added brightly: "Besides, you couldn't have been involved in last night. You wouldn't have been able to run away fast enough after throwing that stone."

Alex frowned and he looked at her coldly. "And of course I couldn't have *driven* away," he said. "Because, as you so carefully established earlier, I didn't get my new car till this afternoon."

He pulled himself awkwardly to his feet.

"Alex, wait!"

"I thought it was a good sign that we could at least talk civilly to each other. But I was mistaken – we weren't chatting: you were interrogating me. Checking out my alibi. Goodbye, Evie. See you round."

He left money on the table to cover the beers and struggled his way back onto the street.

"Oh sod you anyway!" Evie muttered under her breath. "I don't owe you anything."

But then she cheered up. Now she was alone, with a beer and a newspaper, on a warm evening in a roadside café in France. It was as good as being on holidays.

When she couldn't concentrate on her newspaper, Evie just sipped her beer slowly and watched the village around her. The early heat wave had run its course and temperatures were more normal for this time in June. But the carefully tended window-boxes and gardens along Ste Anne's main street had benefited from the sun. Red-hot geraniums, azaleas, roses and clumps of lavender provided splashes of colour and plenty of work for the last of the day's bees. One garden, sloping right down to the edge of the road a few gates short of Monique's, had a swathe of evening primrose, which had grown denser than ever this year. Evie watched, knowing that as the temperature dropped the flowers were opening one by one, and the yellow patch grew more luminous as the daylight faded.

It's so bloody beautiful here, she thought. It was the last place on earth you would have expected the goings-on of the past few days.

Once again she allowed herself to imagine moving here. She had done the maths so often that she skipped right past that and instead tried to think about the other implications. Evie had been reluctant to really consider moving anywhere because of Holly. With no father, Evie imagined her daughter needed another constant presence in her life and up to now that had been Marian. But Alex living in France changed all that.

Sooner rather than later, Evie was going to have to tell him about Holly, and she was fairly certain that he was going to insist on being involved in her life. She knew Alex was a good father, or at least he had been five years ago – that was one of the reasons he had left her.

But what if Evie and Alex were unable to settle their

differences and at the very least become cordial with each other? Then Evie would definitely be better off staying in Dublin. She wasn't going to expose Holly to being caught between two warring parents.

Laurent was another unknown and Evie smiled as she thought about him. A few days ago she might have persuaded herself that she was falling for him. But she recognised that he was the first man to pay her so much attention since Alex, and he was also solid, safe in the current crisis. So she didn't trust her emotions any more. And yet she couldn't forget that he had called her beautiful, and meant it. Was she vain enough to let that influence her?

Evie was confident that she could support herself and Holly in France. Her skills were totally portable. She could write web content and design websites no matter where she was in the world – all she needed was a high-speed line and a computer. But she had worked freelance before and wasn't sure she was ready to go back to it. Being self-employed had its own problems – Evie had got herself a regular job because of them. Her current job gave her fixed working hours and a guaranteed sum of money in her bank account each month. When Evie was self-employed, she had always been busy. But because she was terrified it wouldn't last, she had never been able to turn down work and she found it difficult to separate her working life from her home life. And when a child has only one parent, that's a crucial separation to make.

Which of course brought her right round in a circle back to Alex. If she moved to France, and assuming Alex wasn't too freaked out by a new, nearly four-year-old daughter, Holly would have two parents near at hand. And one of them, from the sounds of things, would be as good as retired.

Interesting times. Wasn't that the traditional Chinese proverb? "May you live in interesting times."

Or was it a traditional Chinese curse?

Chapter 19

Because it had already been planned, and because Evie couldn't think of a better way to keep a close eye on Monique, they went to visit Sarlat the next day.

"Evie, I'm sorry we argued yesterday," Monique said when they were a few miles out from Ste Anne. "Any chance we could just pretend it never happened?"

More than anything else in the world, Evie wanted to go back to where they were last week, although she wasn't sure they could if Monique continued not to trust her. But she told herself that if she were ever going to get Monique to open up to her, she had to at least leave the door open.

"Okay, Monique. It's behind us. Although I won't pretend to be happy you won't trust me. But I'm here if you want to talk, no matter what it's about."

Monique disappeared into guilty silence for a while after that, but soon she was pointing out landmarks and tentatively drawing Evie into conversation. They stayed on safe subjects all the way to the medieval town and by the time they got there, Evie was almost able to persuade herself that this is what it would have been like if she were on her original, uninterrupted holiday. They wandered up and down the narrow streets of Sarlat and admired the sandstone buildings whose half-timbered upper floors leaned towards each other like lovers trying to embrace over the heads of people scurrying below: people who loved their town enough to have planted flowers everywhere – in window-boxes, troughs, old fountains and even buckets. Evie took enough photos to make her feel like a real tourist, and then they sat down in a small square for lunch.

"I wish you lived in France too," Monique said in a small voice after they ordered. "Don't get me wrong, I love being here. I mean look at it – what's not to love?" She waved her arm about expressively. "But well, sometimes I wish I had someone as close as you near at hand."

Evie held her breath – was this it, was Monique about to confide in her? "You know I'm only a phone-call away," she said. "And anyway, you have friends here, haven't you?" But even as she said it, Evie realised that Monique didn't have as many friends as she would have expected, given how long she had lived here.

"Well, yes, of course, but most of them are …" She searched for a description. "They're just not as close …"

Monique's house was full of get-well cards, and Evie knew there had been plenty of visitors to the hospital, but it only now struck her as odd that none of her friends had visited her at home. Monique had always been an intensely private person. In college she had rented out rooms in the house her parents had helped her buy, because she couldn't afford not to. But as soon as she was working Monique paid the whole mortgage herself. She hadn't even wanted to share with Evie.

"Have you ever thought about moving back to Bristol?" Evie asked carefully. Monique had never sold the house, there were tenants paying the mortgage, so it was a reasonable question.

"Ugh, no!" Monique shuddered. "I couldn't go back to that weather. Or the food! No, I really do love living in France, it's just that … I dunno." She shrugged, and Evie's heart went out to her. She looked so isolated and sad and lonely.

Their meals arrived and they picked at them, pretending to have a better appetite than they did. Evie tried to analyse what her friend had just told her. She contemplated telling her that she *had* been thinking about moving to France, or rather fantasising more seriously about it, but Monique looked too vulnerable right now, and Evie didn't want to raise her hopes if nothing came of it. Besides, if Monique were going to stay in Ste Anne, she needed to invest emotionally in putting down roots in the community there, not hold out for some future hope of imported company.

And that's when it hit Evie – Monique was living in

France, but it wasn't really her "home". Not in the same way as Dublin was to Evie. Not even in the same way as Evie had imagined Ste Anne could be if she moved here. To Monique, where she lived was about a house, the weather, how she was going to earn her living, how easy it was to go on holidays. To Evie these were just the nuts and bolts, the details that allowed you to make a home where you wanted to be. To Evie, home would always be about the people who came in and out of her life each day.

♡　　♡　　♡

Later that evening, Evie and Joël were in the garden after an early dinner. Monique had just finished clearing up the table and announced she was going to take a long bath.

"Anyone want to use the bathroom?" she asked brightly. "Because when I say long, I mean really long!"

Evie had noticed that she was moving more stiffly this evening so guessed that her less serious injuries, the bruising to her legs, chest and back, were beginning to bother her. But she didn't dare ask about it or offer sympathy because they had just enjoyed a reasonably relaxed meal, and she didn't want to introduce any note of tension.

"I'm glad you're here," Joël said after Monique had gone upstairs. "She hardly says a word to me. I feel so …"

"Stop, Joël. Don't. She just needs time, that's all. Sooner or later we'll find out what's behind all this, and we'll sort it out."

Like Evie he looked restless, and he cast his eyes around the garden as if searching for something to keep himself occupied. But Monique spent time each day pottering out here, and there was very little to do. The heat and drought of the last few weeks meant that even the grass didn't need to be cut. Eventually he unwound a hose and gave a long drink to the bed of roses Monique had carefully cultivated in the sunniest part of the garden. The damp air he stirred up as he watered and pulled a few tiny weeds carried the sweet scent of tea-rose towards Evie but instead of making her relax and remember all the good times she had spent in this garden, it made her angry, wondering was it all a lie.

"I can't take much more of this!" she said out loud.

Joël looked up, in surprise.

"She's going to have to tell me!" she said.

"You think you know?"

Evie thought it sounded more like a statement than a question, so she wondered had he been thinking along the same lines.

"Tom?" he asked carefully.

"It's the only person I can think of … but, no. It's just too far-fetched. They were together nearly ten years. And there was never … I'm sure I'd have known …" Evie's voice trailed off. How could she be so sure? In college, fair enough, she had shared a house with Monique. But since then she and Monique had lived apart. For most of that time they had even lived in different countries. Monique might just have put on a good act when they were together. Still, it didn't feel right to Evie. She couldn't imagine Monique keeping something like that from her for so long. She couldn't imagine Monique putting up with something like that for so long.

"No," she repeated. "I just can't imagine it. It makes no sense. Unless there's something we know nothing about ..."

"The miscarriage?"

"Stop it!" Evie said. "We don't know. We're just going round in circles here. I'm going to open a bottle of wine – any preferences?" Because they'd eaten so early, and it was a curry, they'd just had water with their meal

"I'm not fussy ..."

"Well, I am. I want something good. I'll be back!"

Evie knew Monique had a few bottles of Joël's wine in the cupboard under the stairs – she had seen them when she was putting the wine away last week – and she decided to look for one of those. She hadn't seen Joël smile in three days, so she was going to see if she could get him talking about his beloved vines.

She fetched glasses and a corkscrew and put them on the garden table – she was going to get Joël to open the wine when she found it. Then she took out some cheese and bread to have with it.

But when she opened the large cupboard under the stairs she stopped dead. There, in front of a few half-full bottles of spirits, was a bottle of whisky. Nearly empty. She took it outside.

"Joël," she said shakily, "Joël, did Tom come to visit Monique after she got hurt?" It was the only explanation that made any sense to her. The only explanation she wanted to believe, even though she knew already that it wasn't true.

Joël shook his head.

Evie held up the bottle with a distinctive garishly coloured label.

"This wasn't here last week," she said shakily. "I'm certain of it. I had to reorganise the cupboard to fit Monique's wine in. And I only know one person who drinks this stuff – it's poison. Really harsh and really cheap. He developed a taste for it in the army."

She paused. She hated what she was about to say.

"Tom's been in this house, Joël. And it could only have been on Friday night."

Chapter 20

Evie had secretly been praying that she was wrong, but when she finally confronted her, Monique didn't try to deny that Tom had been there. He'd been the one waiting for her on Friday night.

"But it was a misunderstanding …"

"A misunderstanding?" Evie cried. She was trying to keep calm – in the time she was waiting for Monique to finish her bath, all the while she'd been trying to calm Joël down, the pressure inside her had built up to exploding point.

"No, Monique, a misunderstanding is when you stand someone up on a Saturday, because you thought they said Sunday. A misunderstanding is when one of you is waiting under Clery's clock and the other is standing outside Bewley's. This is … this is …"

They were in Monique's bedroom. Monique was sitting on the bed with her back to the wall and her knees hugged to her chest.

"I don't believe this," Evie said. She walked to the window and looked out. It was getting dark, and the darkness felt unsafe. She reached out the window, pulled across the shutters and bolted them. Then she felt foolish, but she didn't open them again. Instead she went and sat in the half-darkness beside Monique. They were both sitting with their backs to the wall and staring straight ahead.

"Was it the first time, Monique?" Evie was hoping harder than she could imagine that Monique would nod, or answer in the affirmative, but instead she looked ahead in silence.

"The miscarriage in February …" Evie said gently.

Monique's head turned savagely. "How did you …?" Then she slumped in resignation and shrugged her shoulders. It didn't matter any more. Nothing mattered.

"Is that why you broke up?" Evie continued. "Did you end it with Tom because …"

"No!" Monique surprised her by denying it vehemently. "No, it was nothing to do –" She stopped and fished around in her head for the right words. Then she spoke slowly and carefully. "Tom and I split up because he wouldn't move to France and I wouldn't move back to Bristol. Everything else … this …" she flapped her hands as though the words she was looking for were fluttering in front of her, just out of reach, "this stuff … it started afterwards. After we broke up."

"Monique, I don't understand. Why didn't you tell someone? Why didn't you tell me?"

"I'm not sure. I think maybe I nearly did, a few times. On the phone, or that time just before Christmas, when you were over. But I didn't know how to. It was too unreal. So far from anything ... it just didn't belong in your world, Evie. In our world. I thought I could handle it. And each time ... each time, I was sure it was the last."

Evie was about to get up and turn on the light. Although it wasn't late, with the shutters closed the room was getting darker and she could only just about see Monique's face. Then she thought it might be better like this. It might be easier to talk in the dark. So she did nothing, just waited until Monique was ready to go on.

"I never thought he'd be so opposed to the idea of living in France," Monique said at last. "I always thought he'd come around. But when we began to talk about it seriously, it was like I was talking to another person altogether."

"Go on," Evie encouraged.

"It was ... last year ... when we broke up – remember? I'd gone to England to try to get him to commit to a date to get married. We'd already chosen a hotel – near home. We'd all but agreed on what kind of ceremony we wanted; we'd virtually agreed a guest list! Then he asked me had I started looking for a job yet. A job in England he meant. And it all went downhill from there. He ranted at me. Told me I was being stubborn refusing to move 'home'. He acted like I was just some stupid woman who needed to be told my own mind. The subject of kids came up. I can't remember how it came up, but it got really ugly from there. I think he brought it up as a way of proving to me that I couldn't go on living in France. He said – as if it was fact, as if I couldn't possibly argue with him – he said that I couldn't bring up an English child in France." Monique remembered how unshakeable he was, and she tried to convey to Evie the sheer force of Tom's argument. "He'd been to Bosnia, he said. With the army. He said he'd seen what happens when you try to force two cultures to live together." Monique looked confused and lost again. She seemed to be pleading with Evie to understand. "He was like a different person, Evie. He was spouting all this National Front rubbish about not mixing races. That our child would always be an outsider in France. Wouldn't understand its English heritage. Wouldn't be brought up to be proud of his Englishness. It was scary. It wasn't the Tom I thought I knew, so I decided it was the drink. We'd had a few beers with dinner, and he was still drinking. Not too much but … Anyway, I told him to calm down. That we'd talk about it in the morning … when he was sober. He flipped when I said he'd drunk too much. He started calling me all sorts of names. I got up to leave, he tried to stop me and …" She stopped.

"He hit you?" Evie asked at last when the silence had stretched longer than she could bear.

"Yes. Well, not exactly. I went to open the front door, and he pushed me. Hard. Against it. He held me there and told me I wasn't going anywhere until he said I could. Then he said he was sorry. And he thought we should just go to bed and talk about it in the morning. I thought it would be okay in the morning … so I stayed. The next morning he acted as if nothing had happened." Monique had picked up a pillow, which she laid on her knees. She was twisting a corner between her fingers. "He was really sweet. He brought me breakfast in bed. He brought me arnica cream for the bruise on my jaw and rubbed it in gently. He asked me if it hurt, but made no reference at all to how it had happened. Then he said he had to go in to work, that I was to wait there and that we'd talk in the evening. I told him I wasn't waiting, that I was leaving. He told me not to be silly, that he loved me and that we'd talk in the evening. It went on like that for a few minutes. Me saying that I was going, him saying that I was staying. All the time he was getting gentler and nicer, as though I was a child. A sick child. So I let him go."

"And then you left?"

"Yes. Although I felt like I was sleepwalking. All I knew was that I had to get away … not because I was afraid of him. I knew that what had happened was … I don't know how to say it … too extreme to be real. He had been pushed to the limit and pushed back."

Evie fought to hold in an angry gasp – it sounded as though Monique was blaming herself – but Monique continued as if she hadn't heard.

"The reason I had to get away was because I needed time to think. Tom had as good as told me he didn't want me unless I gave up living in France and moved to England. And I needed to get my head around that.

France, and being a quarter French, has become an important part of me in the past few years – and he was rejecting it out of hand. It was as though he didn't really want me for who I was. What he wanted was a wife, a particular kind of wife, and I was lucky enough to have been offered the job. But it had to be accepted on his terms only."

In Monique's mind it all came down, Evie realised, to Tom rejecting her. Not to Tom being a mad, fascist, racist bastard.

"What did you do?" she asked. She needed to understand how it could have gone on so long.

"I phoned him at work. I told him I was leaving him."

"Did you mean it?"

"Yes, I did. I mean I really thought I did. But I think a little bit of me wanted him to apologise, to say it was all a big mistake. Make some acknowledgement of what had really happened. But he just said he understood I was upset. That I was right to think we needed to take a break and that he'd get in touch when I'd had time to calm down and come to my senses.

"So I flipped. I told him it was all off between us, that I never wanted to see him again as long as I lived and that I thought he was sick. I told him to go and get help. I told him he'd pushed me because he was drunk. And that next time it might be a lot worse. I said for his own sake he needed to see someone."

"How did he react?" Evie asked.

"He didn't." Monique shrugged. "He just said as calmly as ever that I was overwrought. That I was upset.

He said he was calling off the wedding because it seemed to have put me under so much stress and because I obviously wasn't ready to start a family. And then he hung up."

"He tried to make it sound as if he'd broken up with you?" Either he was deluded or very, very clever, Evie thought. Did he hope Monique would want to prove him wrong?

"I didn't really think about it at the time. I was too upset. You don't just stop loving someone because they've decided not to marry you. I still had a few days' holidays left, and I didn't want to go back to France. I'd told Céline that I was taking time off to organise the wedding – I couldn't face telling her it was all off, not yet. Anyway, I hopped on a flight to Dublin and came to stay with you and your mum."

Evie remembered how she had comforted Monique the best she could over her broken engagement, but she had been unwilling to say anything against Tom in case the pair of them made up their differences. If she had known the whole truth, could she have found the right words to stop the course of events that had brought them to this?

"I wish you'd told us the whole story," she said.

Monique sighed. "Not then, I couldn't have. I didn't know what the whole story was! I thought I'd just broken up with my fiancé because we couldn't agree on where to live once we got married – but who knew what his reasons were?"

"Monique, listen to me. This is important. You broke

up with Tom because he was violent towards you and because you realised he wasn't the kind of man you thought he was. He didn't reject you. I don't want to hear you say that again, alright? You left *him*."

Monique nodded, but it was an automatic response and Evie knew she was being humoured. So she said: "It wasn't over yet, was it?"

Monique looked exhausted, drained and so pale that Evie worried that the stress might be too much for her. But then she reasoned she'd lived with this inside her for a year, and this is what it had led to. No matter what it took, Evie was going to get the full story tonight. She heard the front door open downstairs and felt a momentary jolt of alarm. Then she recognised Laurent's voice and realised Joël would have phoned him about Tom and the whisky bottle. She wondered if Laurent had finished in Périgueux or if he'd made the trip down because of the call.

Monique didn't react at all to the voices. It was as though she'd finally abdicated all responsibility to others. She must be so tired, Evie thought.

"He turned up on my doorstep, here in France, nearly two months later," Monique continued. "With flowers of course. Tom was always one for romantic gestures. Remember that?"

Evie remembered. Not only was Tom older than the guys in college, and earning a salary already, but he believed in romantic gestures. His periods of leave from the army always seemed so short, and he lived them to the full. But unlike the other squaddies, he didn't spend his leave in the pub or social club on prolonged boozing sessions. He insisted on spending the time with Monique. Flowers, candlelit dinners, country hotels in the backend of nowhere. The girls in their class thought he was the most romantic thing since Prince Charming; the boys thought he was just a tiny bit weird. In time, Evie began to wonder too – had he no friends, no one but Monique to spend time with? And could he only communicate with her by buying her things? By following the Hollywood rulebook of romance? She realised even then that he was very untypical for the army, and she wasn't surprised when Tom finally bought his way out early to join his father's insurance business.

"He'd brought me a rosebush," Monique was saying. "Pale pink, my favourite colour, and the scent was amazing."

Evie remembered how the scent of roses had made her feel earlier and she wondered was it some kind of premonition. She shivered and then shook her head to clear it of such a fanciful notion.

"I didn't know what to say, so I just stood there," Monique continued. "He got the spade, dug a huge hole and mixed in some compost from my compost heap. Then he planted the rose, filled in the hole and watered it. I remember thinking, 'He really knows what he's doing,' and I was surprised because it was a side of him I'd never seen before. Then he cut off one of the roses and gave it to me. He put his arm around me, and told me he didn't want to lose me as a friend."

Monique stood up and began to pace in the darkness.

She was rubbing her hands up and down her arms so hard that she must be almost hurting herself. Evie longed to beg her to stop, but she was spellbound, unable to move.

"This is the crazy bit, Evie. Then we began to talk about our time together, and he began to kiss me. I went to jelly. He knew just how to get to me. He bloody should have: we'd been together since I was seventeen ... and I missed him and I still wanted him. And it's scary being on your own when you've always had someone ... Anyway, we ended up in bed. The next morning I realised I'd made a huge mistake, so I told him it was just for old times' sake and that I didn't want us to get back together. He said okay, but he didn't see how that should affect us being friends. That we had a lot of friends in common – all of them in England of course – and he didn't want me to lose contact with people just because of him. It made sense, so I agreed. But when I dropped him to the airport, he said something really strange. He said he hadn't told anyone we'd split up for good, just that we wanted to cool things a bit. I tried to say that I considered our relationship over, and he just said it hadn't felt like that last night. He smiled, and then he was gone. And the more I thought about it, the more I thought maybe it was a good thing. Maybe he would come around ... To be honest, I didn't know what I thought, except I knew it wasn't over, and part of me was glad ...

"For the next few months, I didn't see him. He sent cards, soppy ones, with pictures of puppies, kittens and all that. Saying that he was sorry he was so tied up in work and couldn't come and visit me. Then one weekend that I was in Bristol I agreed to meet him for a drink. To prove that we could still be friends. That was when he asked me to come back to him. He kept going on about how perfect we were for each other. How we'd been going out for so long. That I'd never really had any other boyfriend before him, so what did I know of the world? Then he'd drop little things into the conversation like how living in France for so long, amongst foreigners, had changed me. But that was okay, he understood, and he'd look after me. And before I had a chance to react, he'd be off on a completely different subject, leaving me wondering was I imagining things.

"He knew I couldn't cause a scene, not in public. So when he asked me to come back to his house to talk some more, I agreed. The first thing I said as we walked through the door was that I hadn't changed my mind and that I wasn't leaving France. But before I had a chance to say I didn't want to be more than friends, he asked me how I was getting on in France. Was there anyone else? And when I said there was no one, he made a pass at me. So I told him no, that I hadn't changed my mind. He seemed to accept that and we had another drink – at least I think it was only one. Things got a bit hazy ... he began to rub my feet ... and we talked some more. He made another pass at me. I told him that I couldn't, that I'd come off the pill ..."

Evie could imagine what was coming next.

"We used condoms ... but somehow ... Anyway, in the morning he was different. He said he'd just proved to me that I couldn't live without him. That there was never going to be anyone else, because I still loved him. That I was used to him and that I'd never really be able to sleep with another man after him. He told me he'd keep waiting for me, but that his patience was running out …

"When I realised I was pregnant, I didn't know what to do. For a while I ignored it and I tried to pretend it wasn't happening. But I wanted a child so badly. Maybe that's what kept me coming back to Tom, the fear of not finding someone else. So the thought of an abortion never even crossed my mind. Eventually I decided I'd talk to a solicitor in England, just to see what the position was about letting Tom have some access to the child without making any firm commitment to him. After all, I didn't want to cut my child's father out completely … and I knew he wanted kids as much as I did…

"I planned to just pop in and out of the country in one day without telling anyone I was there. I'd arranged an appointment with the lawyer. But Tom was at the airport. He was delighted. What a wonderful coincidence, he said – he'd just dropped off a client. He invited me to lunch, and when I refused he said coffee. When I turned that down, he said he'd give me a lift wherever I was going. So I agreed to the coffee. Just to get rid of him, so he wouldn't know where I was going. But he took me to his house, told me to come in while he changed his shirt – he showed me where a biro had leaked all over it. When I hesitated, he looked at me strangely and asked me was I okay – I looked 'different'. To distract him, and because I was afraid he'd notice I was pregnant, I came in."

Evie could guess what the only outcome of a meeting like that could be.

"I couldn't believe I'd been so stupid, Evie ... Years ago he set up my computer to collect my e-mails, and I never changed the password. All that time he'd been reading all my e-mails. So he had my flight details, he had copies of my e-mails to the family law centre, everything. All laid out on the kitchen table.

"So he said now we definitely had to get married – no child of his was going to end up a bastard, and there was no need to worry about solicitors. He'd even let me work in France until a month before the baby was born, to give me time to sort out selling the house and to give Céline notice ...

"I began to scream at him, 'It's over, it's over! Can't you understand it's over? and he hit me across the face. Then he apologised and said it was because I was getting hysterical. He gave me a drink and told me to calm down. He had a drink too, a couple. But I think he'd probably had a few in the airport already because he got really drunk really fast. He was going on and on about how we were going to get married, and we'd live in his house until I sold the French house and then we could afford to buy another, bigger house. Because of course we'd have loads more kids ...

"I got up to leave and he slammed me really hard against the door. The door handle was quite low ... and it felt ... that was probably what ..." Monique couldn't say it. She closed her eyes and tensed up at the remembered pain.

"That was what caused the miscarriage," said Evie.

The tears came then and Monique collapsed on the bed beside Evie who put her arms around her and held her while she sobbed.

"He wasn't thinking, Evie. There was no way he'd have done anything to hurt his baby if he'd been thinking straight. Those whiskys went straight to his head. He doesn't eat breakfast, so they were on an empty stomach …"

Evie wanted to scream at her to stop defending him, but she wasn't sure it would really help Monique to believe she had loved a monster and had gone on loving him long past the point of reason. Besides, defending Tom and convincing herself that it was an accident was probably Monique's way of distracting herself from the loss of her baby.

"I began to cry and told him I was sorry, and I'd think about marrying him, but that I couldn't think about it properly until after the baby was born. That seemed to satisfy him for the moment. I told him not to say anything yet, because if I told Céline too soon, she mightn't help me sell the house and I wouldn't get the best price for it. I was trying to think of a way of persuading him to let me out and go back to France. I was terrified that the baby was hurt, but I was afraid to say anything, because he'd have blamed me and he might have flipped even further.

"He kept me there until it was time for my flight back. We 'agreed' that he'd leave me to think about everything until closer to the birth and that he'd let me handle things my end.

"But on the flight I began to bleed. I was in hospital for three days in Bergerac, and in that time he'd phoned the house at least five times, but then nothing after I came home. I didn't know what to think. I kept expecting him to call me, and then I'd tell him about the miscarriage, but he never did. I wrote to him eventually, but he never wrote back. Soon I began to believe that maybe it was over at last. But he obviously didn't believe me about the miscarriage. He must have thought I made that up to get rid of him. When he came to France, he probably planned to confront me again. He expected to find me over eight months pregnant; tired, exhausted and closer to facing life as a single parent. He may have intended to wear down my protests. Who knows? And when he found me, I wasn't pregnant. There was no baby. He must have thought I had an abortion to finally get rid of him."

Evie began to understand what had been going through Monique's head these past few days. "Monique, even if he did believe that, and you don't know it for certain, it doesn't justify what he did to you."

"But you can understand why I can't just turn him over to the police?"

Her question was a plea to be forgiven for lying to her rather than a real question, so Evie was tempted to agree. But she didn't understand. Not really. If it had been the first time Tom was violent … maybe you could write it off to being upset at losing his child … No! Even if it had been the first time, what he did to Monique was just too far off the scale. But the past wasn't her main worry right now. She needed to keep Monique safe.

"What now?" she asked carefully.

"I have to tell him … I can show him the hospital notes …"

"Monique, you're not planning on meeting him again, are you?"

"I'm not planning anything. I don't know where he is. He hasn't gone back to England, though. I do know that. I've phoned there a few times. So then I phoned his mobile and got a French dial-tone."

Evie stood up and turned on the light.

"Look at me, Monique," she ordered. "Tom's dangerous."

"He was upset …"

"And it was a misunderstanding, I know." Evie felt like she was humouring a truculent child. "But just in case … will you promise me not to meet him on your own? If he's still in France, he's coming back. That trick with the rabbit was probably only the tip of the … oh my God!"

Evie retched and ran to the bathroom as she suddenly realised what the skinned and bloody baby rabbit, curled up in its plastic bag, was designed to look like.

Chapter 21

"Are you okay, Evie?" Evie had vomited until there was nothing left in her stomach and then dry-retched until she had no strength left.

At some point Laurent had come into the bathroom and held her hair back and mopped her face. Now he was kneeling on the floor beside her and was rubbing her back.

"No," she answered honestly. She couldn't imagine ever being okay again.

"What happened?"

She told him a shortened version.

"Can you come with me, Evie? Joël's seeing to Monique and he's going to insist she takes a sleeping tablet. But I need to talk to you, away from here."

"Where do you want to go?"

"Antoine's."

Evie just stood up and followed him – it wasn't as if anything she said or did now was going to make the slightest bit of difference to anything.

But Laurent had made a good decision. He obviously hadn't brought her down to the bar just so they could talk out of Monique's hearing. Although there were only a few other customers, it was bright, even a bit smoky, in the bar and there was music playing. Evie began to realise that the world hadn't just ended.

"Cognac?" Laurent offered.

"Oh, God, do I look that bad?" Evie tried to smile but knew she failed miserably. She shook her head. "Beer's fine. Or wine. Yes, that's it, red wine, please."

Laurent went to the counter and came back with a medium *pichet* and two glasses.

They drank for a while without saying anything. Soon the warmth of the wine and the sheer mundane normality of the bar took effect and Evie began to feel more normal too. She had drunk many a pre-dinner *pastis* here, and Holly had played, there, on the floor, hiding under the pool table with the owner's little Shih-tzu. It didn't seem like a place that would ever change. No matter what happened in the next few hours or days, this bar, Antoine's, would open up, and the same faces would come in for a mid-morning coffee, a quick shot on the way home for dinner or a *digéstif* to help down the meal they had been served at home.

"Okay, Laurent. I'm ready. Out with it," Evie said.

"He's still here."

"In France? I know …" She told him about the French dial-tone on his mobile.

"No, here, right here. Somewhere near Ste Anne."

Evie looked around fearfully as if expecting to see Tom's lanky form greet her from some hidden corner of the room.

"That whisky bottle," Laurent said. "I saw one like it the day I went to dump the rabbit. In the big bins in the car park behind the shop. It meant nothing to me at the time, but it was right there, at the very top of the bin. I just automatically pulled it out to put it in the glass recycle bin instead, but it was in a plastic bag of other stuff. A shopping bag with empty food tins, a milk carton, I think. I'm not sure what else."

"So we can check the hotels, auberges …"

Laurent shook his head. "If he was staying somewhere like that he wouldn't need to have dumped stuff where he did. You say he was in the army before he took over his father's business … he'd have done survival training … so he's probably dug himself in somewhere, or he's on the move. Sleeping rough and dumping his rubbish to cover his tracks."

"Oh my god, Laurent, you've got to be joking!"

He just shook his head and waited for the logic to sink in.

"So why nothing … since Monday?" she asked.

Laurent hesitated. "He's waiting … watching …"

Evie put a hand up to her mouth. "The woods! Oh my God, Laurent, he could have been as close as the end of Monique's garden!"

"Those woods stretch for miles, Evie, he could be anywhere …"

"And they run right along the back of the village. Any time he likes, he could get to within a few metres of the house without anyone seeing him … but he could see us …"

Evie tried to remember – had she ever changed with the lights on but the curtains open? Had she showered …?

"We've got to get Monique out of there, Laurent."

He shook his head. "No, at the moment he thinks he's in control. If we change anything we'll alert him, and we may never find him." Laurent avoided saying that he might also get more dangerous. "Right now, if he *is* watching, he thinks we've had dinner, a few drinks, a perfectly normal evening. He knows that either Joël or I have stayed since he attacked Monique, so it won't look odd that Joël hasn't left."

"Are you going to have to leave, then, to make it look …?"

"I'll stay, Evie, but if he's watching the house we have to make him think there's a good reason I'm staying." For the first time, Laurent lost his serious look and there was a glint in his eye. "I'm afraid, Evie, we're going to have to make it look like you've seduced me and stopped me from going home to my nice chaste bed."

"Somehow, Laurent, the words 'chaste' and 'bed' don't belong in the same sentence when you say them …" Evie tried to make a joke of it, but her laugh came out as a sob.

Laurent reached across the table, put a hand around

her face and used his thumb to wipe a tear from below her eye. Then he leaned over and kissed her gently on the lips.

"It's going to be okay, Evie, I promise."

Evie swallowed another sob, and nodded.

"Had we better rehearse that again?" she asked, leaning towards him.

"Outside," he growled, leading her to the door.

"This feels weird," Evie complained.

Laurent just put his hands to her face and kissed her again. But it was a stage kiss. Both of them could feel the window at the other side of the room. The window that gave onto the back garden and the woods beyond.

Laurent backed her towards the sofa, and lay her down on it. She was out of sight now, so she tried to relax.

"Stay there," Laurent ordered.

He walked across the room to the window, stripping off his shirt as he went. He tossed it carelessly over one of the dining chairs.

He stopped for a second at the window, as though he was trying to see out, but the lights in the room were on full, and Evie knew that he would see only blackness, his own reflection. She watched him, looked at his bare, tanned back and felt a jolt of desire. That was the back she had wrapped her arms around on Thursday night. She had run her fingers across those muscles, she had traced the shape of his neck, his shoulders, his waist. Her legs had wrapped themselves around his waist. She had dried that bare back with long strokes of a soft towel, when they both got out of the swimming-pool, naked, and ended up in the pool-house making love again. And she hated herself for thinking like that right now.

Laurent opened the window and pulled the shutters closed. He bolted them and closed the window again, then he pulled the curtains, making sure not a chink of light escaped. Then he turned round.

Evie was still on the sofa, suddenly unsure of what to do next. More than anything she wanted Laurent to join her and to take their performance to its conclusion, now that they'd lost their audience. There was something in the danger that made her want Laurent all the more. All her senses were heightened by fear and adrenalin pumped through her veins, driving up her pulse. But more than anything she didn't want to sleep alone.

"Goodnight, Laurent," she said suddenly, springing to her feet. She flew upstairs and shut the door before she made a fool of herself.

Chapter 22

At about half four in the morning, Laurent felt Joël shake his shoulder gently and he struggled to wake up fully. It was still dark in the house because Joël had bolted all the shutters before going to bed, but they both knew that the sun would be coming up soon.

Without talking, they got ready and left the house, locking it behind them again. Laurent stopped barely long enough to let Evie know what they were doing. A heavy dew had fallen overnight, as Joël had predicted, and it suited them. Anyone sleeping outside tonight would have needed shelter or got very wet. At this time of year, out of hunting season, game hides would provide the ideal place to take shelter, and there were three within half an hour's walk of the house. The two men were fairly certain that in one of them they would find their quarry.

The woodland smelled damp and mushroomy after the night's dew, and the air was the coolest it had been for over a week. The sky was brightening, but there was a heavy mist dipping down to meet the trees on the higher hills, and it helped muffle any sounds they made on their passage between the trees. They knew these woods like the back of their hands and moved quickly from one hide to the second, having made hardly a sound. But when they were about forty minutes out from the house and the world was beginning to wake up, Laurent sent a pheasant crashing out of some undergrowth, squawking with indignation as its breakfast was disturbed.

As the sun began to burn off the mist, the air was beginning to heat up. Joël signalled to his friend to slow down. There was only one hide left to try. Neither man voiced the fear that they might be wrong, and that Tom might have chosen a hide further from the village, leaving them with ten or twelve to search, or that he was somewhere else altogether and merely driving in each night to hike through the woods.

The third hide came into view at the top of a hill. It was like a corrugated iron builders' hut suspended amongst the branches on stilts, and it was reached by a long, rickety-looking ladder. Joël had often come here with his father to shoot pigeons. The two men crouched down for a few minutes to listen.

And then they heard it. The faint but unmistakable sound of a snore.

They began to move up the hill, Joël ahead of Laurent, hoping that Tom was sleeping off the effects of a heavy night's whisky-drinking and wouldn't be easily alerted. Laurent wanted to reach him before Joël, afraid of what his friend might do, so he speeded up and in his haste stepped on a dry branch. It sounded loud as a gunshot. Joël turned in exasperation for a second, then began to sprint to the top, Laurent close behind.

But before they got there, they saw a figure drop the last couple of metres from the hide onto the ground, roll and disappear from sight. By the time they reached the top, there was no one there.

"*Merde!*" Laurent cursed.

Joël crouched down to look at the ground, then stood up and looked in the direction he reckoned Tom had fled. A particularly dense clump of brambles indicated a dip in the ground and he pointed to it.

As they approached it, a lanky figure broke cover and began to run towards them. He aimed at Laurent and rugby-tackled him, knocking him hard against a tree.

Laurent came to a few moments later, with Joël leaning over him.

"I'm fine!" he shouted, although he was far from sure he was. "Go after him, *now*!"

Joël suddenly come to the same conclusion as Laurent and panicked. He got to his feet, stumbling the first few steps before getting into his stride as he ran off down the hill.

In the seconds when Tom had charged towards him, Laurent had seen his face. Filled with fury and hatred, it was the face of a man with nothing left to lose.

♡   ♡   ♡

Alex was dreaming. Evie was in his swimming-pool and there was an alarm going off that he ought to attend to. But he didn't want to drag himself away from watching her swim lengths, up and down, with strong fluid strokes. The alarm grew louder and he began to realise that he was dreaming about Evie while the alarm was in the real world. He resisted its power, desperate to go on enjoying this stolen time with Evie, but it was no good. The dream dissolved, the sound of the alarm changed subtly and Alex realised that it was the phone on his bedside locker.

"Hello!" he barked, and it sounded more like a curse than a greeting. "Laurent, slow down," he said as he listened to the voice on the other end. "I can't make out a word you're saying." He listened again.

Suddenly he was wide awake. He swung his legs over the side of the bed and felt around with his good foot for his crutches. He tried to ignore the pain in his ribs, as they adjusted too quickly to this new position, and pulled on a pair of shorts discarded on the floor the night before.

He muttered a prayer of thanks that his keys were still in his pocket and that he had saved a few vital seconds. Then he stood up, and pain shot up his leg, blurring his vision, when he put too much weight on his left ankle.

Cursing, he made his way out to the front of the house and into the car. Vaguely he was aware that it was

early, not even six, much too early for this kind of
dramatics. He fumbled with the ignition, then
remembered he was in an automatic. He eased the car
down the driveway.

Joël ran in a straight line towards the village, and
within three or four minutes he had Tom in view. There
was no doubting where he was headed. Joël was fit, and
he knew the terrain, but the other man seemed to be
drawing on superhuman resources and kept far enough
ahead. In fact he seemed to have widened the gap. When
the village, and then Monique's house, came into clear
view, Joël somehow found it within himself to put on a
burst of speed, and he changed his direction to try and
force the other man to veer away.

Then Joël saw where Tom was heading. The road on
the far side of the village turned sharply uphill, and when
Tom reached it he would be able to sprint along the
smooth surface to reach the front of the house before Joël
could clear the rough ground of the woods. So whichever
way Joël chose to run, Tom would still have at least a
minute or two on him. Joël hoped to God that Monique
and Evie were still asleep and hadn't opened any of the
doors or windows he had locked so carefully last night.
He stayed on the same course, then out of the corner of
his eye he saw a red car enter the village, from the
opposite end to Monique's, and speed along the middle
of the road. It was Alex, Joël realised with relief,

although he wasn't sure what the Englishman would be able to do on crutches.

Tom disappeared over a grass bank, and Joël knew he was on the road now. He had lost sight of Alex but he could still hear the engine of the small car, straining to keep accelerating at the rate its driver was holding down the pedal. Then Joël heard another noise, the grumbling of a much heavier engine pulling a heavy load up the hill. Lorries often drove this road early in the morning, turning off halfway through Ste Anne to join the old route to Spain and avoid tolls on the motorway.

The next few seconds seemed to pass in slow motion. The truck gunned its engine to climb the last hundred metres or so into Ste Anne. Alex's red car came into sight for a moment as it passed a gap in the houses and Joël realised he was driving on the left-hand side of the road. He heard the sound of tyres skidding, followed by the sound of metal and glass colliding with stone. The truck's brakes began to screech and almost drowned out the sounds Joël knew he would remember for the rest of his life – a long-drawn-out scream followed by the sickening thud of a body hitting a metal grille. The truck's brakes continued to screech for another few seconds, then it came to a stop and everything fell silent.

Chapter 23

Evie instinctively went to take hold of Monique, sure that she was about to rush out onto the road. But the scream seemed to have used up every last ounce of her energy and she sank to her knees on the damp gravel. Later they would discover that Tom had probably died before his body even hit the ground, and Evie would always wonder how Monique could have known. What instinct had informed her that he was beyond help or even comfort?

The tableau remained frozen for what seemed like minutes but was probably only a couple of seconds. Then birds, reassured that this human drama was of no danger to them, broke the silence. Never in Evie's life had she been so glad to hear the dawn chorus. It seemed to break the malevolent spell they were all under and allowed them to move again.

The first thing she did was to look around, to try to figure out what had happened. Moments before, she had been inside the house with Monique, trying to persuade her not to go out looking for Laurent and Joël. Monique wanted to be with them when they found Tom. Evie was trying to persuade her that Joël and Laurent knew what they were doing – that they would find Tom and deal with him safely. She had also been trying to quell Monique's fury at the plan that had been hatched behind her back.

And now there was a lorry in the middle of the street. Its front grille was distorted and smoking. Black rubber tyre-tracks on the road showed how the driver had attempted to steer or stop his vehicle. He was still in his cab and seemed unhurt, but he was staring straight ahead and breathing rapidly.

A red car that Evie recognised as Alex's rental was embedded in a garden wall. Its bonnet was open and smoking, its front windscreen was completely smashed out and there was no sign of a driver.

Tom was lying where he had landed – motionless and with no sign of any visible injury except for the grossly distorted way his body was lying. He was like a puppet whose strings had been cut and who had been thrown violently against the ground.

A door opened further down the street and a man emerged. He was speaking rapidly into a phone even as he made his way towards them. This first human sound since Monique's scream galvanised Evie into action. She ran towards Alex's car while the newcomer wrenched open the lorry's cab door and spoke to the driver.

"There's no one here," she screamed. "There's no one in the car!"

She looked back at Monique who hadn't moved from where she was kneeling in front of the house. More people had arrived now, and a small circle formed around Tom. The first man was helping the lorry driver down from inside his cab.

"Where's Alex?" Evie screamed, running back to where the others were. "Was he driving the car? I can't find him." But her French deserted her and she screamed over and over in English and failed to make an impression on the villagers who seemed unaware that there might be another victim of the accident.

Suddenly Joël was beside her. "Where's …?"

But before he could finish his question, Evie threw herself at him. "Monique's fine, Tom's …" She pointed at the small huddle of people and shook her head, looking away.

Joël took a step in the direction she had pointed.

"No!" she shouted. "Tell me, was Alex in that car?"

Joël ran to the car. He looked about frantically, then stood back, looked back along the road in the direction he'd seen Alex driving and then back at the car. Then he cleared the garden wall with a single leap and moved forward, scanning the ground in front of him.

An ambulance, arriving with its sirens blaring, almost drowned out Joël's shout of *"Ici!"* Here!

Evie ran into the garden but the paramedics reached

Alex before her and one of them held her back. All she could see was the back of Alex's head. He was lying on his front, motionless. As she watched, the lead paramedic carried out a quick but thorough examination, then called for something. A fireman stepped forward with a bolt-cutter. As Evie stepped closer, she saw that a length of rusty metal, like the stub of a clothes-line pole, was sticking through the side of Alex's face, pinning him the ground. She suppressed a scream and held her breath as two of the ambulance staff held Alex firm while the fireman cut through the metal pole. Most of it now remained stuck in the ground with about an inch sticking out of Alex's face just below his eye.

They loaded him onto a stretcher. If he was breathing, Evie could see no sign of it. But he must have been alive, because a female paramedic was holding a dressing around the metal to staunch the bleeding. The leader of the group barked an order and the ambulance reversed towards him.

The gendarmes, who had by now reached the scene, held everyone back while Alex was loaded into the back of the red vehicle. No one was offered the opportunity to travel with him as they sped off.

Silence descended again as they all watched the ambulance leave the village, then another ambulance team, one Evie hadn't noticed arriving, called the police over. The lorry driver was strapped into a stretcher chair and lifted inside the back of a second ambulance. He was babbling, and tears were streaming down his face. He kept pointing in the direction of the now covered body on the road.

Evie saw Monique standing a little way from the group around Tom, her arms clasped about her body as if to prevent herself from shaking. Joël walked over to her and tried to make her come away, but it was like trying to plead with a pillar of stone.

An ambulance driver was standing guard over the body, waiting for the gendarmes to give him the okay to transfer it to the waiting stretcher. Evie saw him call the officer in charge over and speak quickly to him, pointing at the ground near the body. The officer barked an order and one of the motorbike policemen came forward. He went to the back of one of the cars, and took a metal case from it. Then he bent down near the body, almost in the gutter, opened the case and pulled on a pair of latex gloves. Then, with chalk, he drew a shape on the ground around the body. Again he reached inside the metal çase and this time he took out a plastic bag.

Before he stood up again, Joël managed to drag Monique away. Just in time, before she had a chance to see the contents of the bag.

The policeman had recovered a long, unsheathed hunting knife only inches from Tom's outstretched hand.

♡   ♡   ♡

It didn't take long for the police to take preliminary statements and check everyone's identity. Then they began to pack up and left just one man behind to tape off the scene. It was then Joël realised that Laurent still hadn't returned. But just as he was about to go looking for him, he appeared, limping slowly and holding his left arm rigidly against his body with his right hand. His left shoulder was hanging down at an odd angle, but he barked an angry retort at Joël who tried to attract the attention of one of the remaining paramedics.

Laurent took in the scene with a few quick glances. He saw the covered corpse still visible in the back of an open ambulance and receiving no more attention. Joël answered his silent enquiry with the single word "Tom". He saw a female paramedic wrap a blanket round Monique, while a doctor took her blood pressure and another man questioned Evie and wrote the answers on a form attached to a plastic clipboard.

Then Laurent looked at the smashed red car and asked "Alex?" in a weak voice. Joël frowned, shook his head and said a few words quietly in French. Laurent's face went blank, as though he couldn't quite take in what had happened; but then his eyes rolled back, he dropped his injured arm and fell forward into a faint. Joël only just managed to catch him before he hit the ground.

♡   ♡   ♡

"You should go home to your daughter," Céline told Evie gently. It was three days since the accident, and Monique had just left the house to fly to Bristol. Tom's body had been flown home and she wanted to go too. "There's nothing more you can do here," Céline insisted. "You should go home to Dublin. I know you plan to go to the funeral in England next week, but I really think you should go home first."

Evie knew deep down that Céline was right, but she was uncomfortable with the idea. It felt too much like fleeing the scene.

"What about Alex?" she asked, although she already knew the answer. He was in a coma, and his ex-wife had brought his daughter and sons to France to be with him. Evie no longer had any reason to be there.

"I'll let you know if there's any change," Céline promised, but she was unable to look at Evie as she said it, and Evie knew that she meant she'd let her know if things got any worse. "And Laurent is taking care of things for him."

Laurent's shoulder had been dislocated by his encounter with Tom, and he had suffered some damage to his ankle, but apart from that he was fine. He hadn't left Alex since the accident, only barely tolerating the medical attention he needed himself. He was acting as translator for the family and smoothing out any problems they encountered. Evie had met him only once briefly, shortly after his shoulder had been put back in place, but neither was comfortable in the other's presence and he immediately made some excuse about Joël waiting to drive him to the trauma centre to check on Alex.

So Evie gave in and packed the last of her things, accepting Céline's offer of a lift to the airport. She knew she had no choice but to get on with her life. Monique didn't want to talk to anyone, either about the accident or what had happened before it, and Laurent was a few hours away in the trauma centre with Alex. By staying in France, Evie would just be a burden on Céline who had her own business to run.

And Evie longed for Holly. Her longing was physical, a pain that reached into her very core. But she was unable to put it into words or even allow the thought to take shape in her own mind. Without realising it, she felt guilty that she still had Holly to go home to.

Chapter 24

From: Céline Lesauvage
To: Marian Kinsella
Sent: July 19th 10:44 AM
Re: Monique and Evie

Dear Marian,

It was good talking to you on the phone last night. And I agree with you that it is unhealthy the way Monique and Evie have tried to go on as if nothing has happened. It's as though in burying Tom, they could bury everything that has happened and just get back to "normal". But remember, it is only a few weeks since the funeral.

I will admit I was shocked that Evie told you so little about what happened. I am glad I was able to fill you in on what

I knew, but to be honest, I feel a little in the dark myself. Monique has insisted on going back to work – "to take her mind off things" – but she has hardly exchanged more than ten non-work-related words with me since she came back from Bristol. I thought it was just me, that Monique couldn't talk to me because I'm not family and because I didn't know Tom that well, so I admit it was a relief to hear that Evie has been behaving the same.

Some news I am not sure you have heard, and I never mentioned it last night, but Alex has been transferred to hospital in Bristol. He has still not regained consciousness but the signs are improving and surgeons are anxious to do some more exploratory work on his eye. His family were anxious that he be closer to home.

I have to admit I am relieved, for my son's sake, that Alex has been moved. Laurent has been spending virtually all his free time in the hospital, although it is obvious there is nothing he can do to help.

I have put a report of the accident, from our local newspaper, in the post for you. There is a photo of Alex included in the article as I remember you never met him. Maybe it will help you understand some of what Evie is going through.

Yours,
Céline

Céline and Marian were right: Evie had tried to get back to normal as soon as possible. Or rather she tried to put on a show of being "normal" because she felt that nothing in her life would ever be normal again. Since the events in France, she felt as though she were living in an unfamiliar world. She turned up every day to work, picked up Holly as she always had and managed to read with and amuse her daughter just like any dutiful parent should, but it was as though someone had inserted a screen between her and her life. As though she were observing herself from a distance, and that none of her life really impacted on her any more.

Her boss had no idea what had happened and Evie knew he was getting increasingly frustrated with her faraway look and her reluctance to get involved directly with clients. She knew she was in no danger of getting fired, because she was too good at what she did, but to Evie her work had become just that – work. A way of putting food on the table and paying the bills. And more importantly a way of getting her out of the house each morning to a busy in-tray and a list of tasks that she needed to complete before she went home. Otherwise she knew she would find it more and more difficult to get up in the morning to face the day. The less decisions she had to make from one minute to the next, the better.

Monique apparently was the same – although Evie had only spoken to her a handful of times since the funeral. And each time they spoke, it was a stilted and false conversation – mainly about the weather (good in France, middling in Ireland), clients of Monique's (madly snapping up properties all over the Dordogne) and colleagues of Evie's.

Monique would dutifully ask after Holly and Evie would oblige with a factual report. But she soon switched the subject off her daughter. She didn't know if she was uncomfortable talking about Holly because of the baby she now knew Monique had lost, or if she was jealously protecting the "Holly" part of her soul from any taint of the ugliness she and Monique had experienced. She was also aware that she had been able to send Holly away before the worst happened, a choice no one else had had.

Because they had never discussed the accident, Evie had no idea if Monique felt as hideously guilty as she did herself. She guessed she probably did. The other possibility, and one that Evie only contemplated in the small hours of the morning when she couldn't sleep, was that Monique felt that much of the responsibility for Tom's death lay with Evie and that she was only keeping up communication for politeness or old times' sake. In time, their conversations would grow sporadic, and then they would cease. Monique would send a card for birthdays and Christmas until Holly was old enough to understand why her godmother had cut off contact.

Evie would never forgive herself for not going to the police with that whisky bottle. They should have been the ones to track Tom down and capture him. He would still be alive, Alex would be safe and none of the rest of them would have to live with such terrible stains on their consciences for the rest of their lives.

"How many times do I have to tell you, Evie – if we

haven't been paid to rewrite content, don't provide the service for free!"

Evie suddenly realised that her boss, Jamie, had been looking over her shoulder as she worked and was reading the words as she typed them onto the screen.

"He only paid us for web design," Jamie continued. "If he wants us to write copy for him, he can bloody well pay for it. Just fill in exactly the words he gave you, and leave it at that." He paused, waiting for Evie's inevitable challenge.

But he was disappointed. She just shrugged. "Sorry, it was automatic."

Evie had been writing Internet copy for so long now, and was so good at it, that she didn't have to think too hard about it. Normally she'd have complained that Jamie had over-sold design to this client when what this small hotel owner really needed was good site content to appeal to both customers and the search-engines. But she just couldn't be bothered. She knew that interactive 360-degree images of the breakfast room and flashing graphics weren't going to get Mr Johnston a single extra guest, but if that's the way Jamie wanted to run his business, it was up to him. And if he wanted to pay her obscene amounts of money to transcribe poorly written text, she wasn't going to argue with him.

"Why don't you call the client and arrange a meeting?" Jamie asked, in a more conciliatory tone. "You're right; that brochure he gave you sucks. And it's all wrong for the Internet. You could talk him into getting the job done properly, I know you could."

"I think I'll leave sales to you, Jamie. I'll just do what I do best, back here in the office," Evie answered, unable to look Jamie in the eye. She knew a lot more about the copy-writing and search-engine side of the Internet than he did, so if she were more involved in pushing her expertise they'd pull in twice as much business. But that was why she was working for someone else now and not for herself. She didn't want to have to worry about the bottom line. It might sound selfish, but if Jamie did badly, there were plenty of other companies who'd line up to take her on.

Evie could feel her boss watching her as she got back to work. She knew he just couldn't figure her out. Although she'd made it quite clear when he took her on that she had no ambitions beyond a nine-to-five job, he also knew she loved what she did and couldn't understand why she didn't want to do it as well as possible. Especially when he knew she could make him a heap-load of money in the process.

But eventually he took a deep breath and went to find someone else to torment. Evie knew she was too valuable to him to risk seriously upsetting her. She wondered how long it would be before she would be called into his office for another of his "if we're clever we can retire at forty" speeches. He just didn't seem to understand that retiring at forty, having missed all of Holly's childhood, was the kind of nightmare Evie only had on really bad nights.

Evie kept her head down for the rest of the afternoon, then stopped off in the gym before she collected Holly. As she pounded away the miles on the treadmill, she tried to imagine telling her mother the whole story about Alex. But she still hadn't come up with any way of saying it.

♡ ♡ ♡

From: Marian Kinsella
To: Céline Lesauvage
Sent: July 26th 11:22 PM
Re: Alex Ryder

Dear Céline,

Sorry for such a long silence, but I think you can probably guess the reason. I won't ask you if you knew what you were doing when you sent me that newspaper cutting, because it makes no difference. But thank you.

To answer the question implied by your action, although you are much too polite to actually ask it, I had no idea who Holly's father was.

The article describing Alex, his company and where he lived confirmed what anyone would have guessed from the photo. I haven't told Evie yet that I know. I have had the feeling over the last weeks that she was building up the courage to tell me something, so maybe I should wait for her to tell me herself.

How long have you known? Do you know if Alex knew?

Best wishes,
Marian

A French Affair

From: Céline Lesauvage
To: Marian Kinsella
Sent: July 27th 00:23 AM
Re: Alex Ryder

Marian,

You have no idea how relieved I was when I checked my computer on my way to bed and saw your e-mail. I was so worried about having sent that article to you and I really wasn't sure if I was doing the right thing. But through our telephone conversations and our e-mails, I think we are becoming friends and I would not feel comfortable knowing something as important as that without telling you.

So why the article? I suppose I could have told you outright about Alex, but sometimes people prefer not to know about such things. So leaving you to work it out for yourself gave you the opportunity to pretend it never happened, if that's what you wanted. I hope I did the right thing.

Believe it or not I never guessed about Holly and Alex until recently, and I'm fairly sure Alex knew nothing either. Laurent merely confirmed it for me when I asked him about it after the accident. Although I have seen Holly plenty of times over the past three years, and I have had Alex Ryder as a client for the past few months, I never noticed the resemblance. But then I never had any reason to look for it, as I didn't know of any connection between them. Laurent tells me *he* spotted it straight away – I wonder what that says about his feelings for Evie. Or about his friendship with Alex.

Laurent is in Bristol at the moment. He got the first available flight when he heard that Alex had regained consciousness. I hope this doesn't mean he plans to start torturing himself at Alex's bedside again. Luckily he is busy in work, which will limit the amount of time he can spend in England.

Did you know that Laurent and Evie haven't exchanged more than a few words since the accident?

Bisous *(kisses)*,
Céline

From: Marian Kinsella
To: Céline Lesauvage
Sent: July 27th 07:28 AM
Re: Alex Ryder

When did he regain consciousness? How is he? We have heard nothing over here.

I tried to phone you at home, but you must have already left for work – I had forgotten the time difference. I will try the office later, but please, please, if you see this e-mail before I get through to you, let me have any news you have so I can pass it on to Evie.

I hadn't realised that Evie and Laurent hadn't spoken. I'm afraid I can't throw any light on it. "Survivor's guilt" perhaps?

xx Marian

"Evie, I think we need to talk, don't you?"

Evie's heart stopped, then she saw her mother was smiling. They were in Evie's kitchen, Holly was asleep upstairs and Marian had just taken a photocopy out of her handbag. She passed it to Evie.

"She's the image of him, isn't she?" Marian said after she had given Evie a chance to skim through the article.

"I should have told you, Mum, sorry."

Marian shrugged. "Tell me now. What happened between you that you felt you couldn't let him have any contact with her?"

"He was my boss …"

"I worked that out from the article. Did he take advantage of you or something?"

"Mum! I was twenty-two, not twelve. No, we were together. It went on for nearly a year. But … well, to cut a long story short he went back to his wife. And his kids. They decided to give things another go."

"Pity he didn't try that sooner instead of seducing …" Marian bit her tongue rather than vent her feelings. She'd just remembered that the man had hung between life and death for the past four weeks. "I take it he didn't know you were pregnant?

Evie shook her head. "I couldn't tell him. For one thing it would have looked like a trick, a pathetic way of getting him back. And later, I never found the 'right' time. And now … now it's too late."

Evie began to cry – for the first time since the accident. Her mother let her empty out some of the pain and fear of the past month in huge racking sobs. She was glad to see her daughter finally admit that it wasn't all okay, that things had changed.

Finally, when Evie began to calm down she told her: "It's not too late, Evie. Alex woke up two days ago."

♡ ♡ ♡

From: Marian Kinsella
To: Laurent Lesauvage
Sent: July 27th 14:02 PM
Re: Alex Ryder

Dear Laurent,

It seems strange e-mailing you when we only met briefly in France, but I spoke to your mother on the phone this morning, and she gave me your e-mail address and mobile phone number. Maybe I should have phoned, but I'm afraid I chickened out.

I wanted to ask you to keep me informed about Alex's progress as I have just found out that he is my granddaughter's father. I hope Evie will find the courage to contact him herself, but at present she is afraid of upsetting him when he is in such a delicate state.

I don't know how much you know about how they parted, but I imagine it will come as a shock to him to discover he and Evie have a daughter together.

Please phone her. She is confused, and worried, and I am

afraid she is in no state to "take the first step".
Please tell Alex he's in my prayers and will continue to be. Wish him a speedy recovery.

Best wishes,
Marian

From: Marian Kinsella
To: Céline Lesauvage
Sent: July 27th 15:02 PM
Re: Laurent and Evie

Hi Céline,

It was good to talk to you earlier, and thanks for the update on Alex. The poor man. It sounds as if he'll almost be lucky to get away with just losing the sight in one eye. What a lot to wake up to. When will they take the bandages off his eyes, do you know?

Sorry, you probably haven't much more of an idea than I have. Hopefully Laurent will get in touch with me. How long is he staying in England?

As you suggested, I e-mailed him, asking him to phone Evie. Let me know if you hear anything. I'm afraid I chickened out of actually phoning him myself.

How is Monique doing? Any time I ask Evie her face blanks, and she just says Monique's doing fine, considering. Though what that's supposed to mean, I have no idea.

She still loved Tom despite everything, didn't she? She spent some time with me here in Ireland after their original break-up and she was completely devastated. What must she be feeling now that he's dead? Especially as she saw it happen. Any time I get frustrated with Evie's moods, I try to imagine what that must have been like for her. Waking up to find Monique already awake and trying to stop her going outside. And then the crash, right in front of them. Knowing Tom didn't stand a chance. Then seeing Alex's car buried in a wall and not being able to find him because he was tossed so far clear. Then finding him in that garden, with his face gouged by – Oh, God, I'm sorry. You don't need to read my nightmares. I'm sure you have plenty of your own.

I was going to erase that last paragraph, but I couldn't, it seemed disrespectful. No matter what Tom did, he was a human being. And there must have been some good in him, a lot of good in him in fact, if Monique loved him like that. We'll never know what happened inside his head, and it's not really for us to judge, is it?

Take care,
Marian

From: Céline Lesauvage
To: Marian Kinsella
Sent: July 28th 08:32 AM
Re: Tom

Dearest Marian,

I wish I had seen your e-mail last night as I would have

phoned you straight away. You sounded like you need to be cheered up. But I am on my way out the door now to meet a client, and it will be this evening before I get some privacy.

I admire your Christianity but I cannot be so forgiving of Tom. Any time I try to be, I see Monique's poor bruised face after he attacked her. And I remember the hospital in Bordeaux, when Alex's daughter Sophie was asked if she would like her father given Last Rites.

Oh, dear, that sounds condescending. As though I was suggesting that you couldn't understand because you weren't there. It's not what I meant to say at all. Maybe I just hate to think of you making yourself unhappy over him and I don't know how to say it better.

Monique *is* doing reasonably well "considering". She's back at work. I tried to get her to stay off longer, but she insisted she needed to be busy, and maybe she was right. She has to spend so much of her time "pretending" to be alright that maybe she will fool herself into believing it. I'm not sure, though, if that is a good or a bad thing. I hate to think what her nights are like. Sometimes she looks like she hasn't slept in a year. I know the doctor gave her sleeping tablets, but Laurent tells me that she refuses to take them.

My client has just pulled up outside, I must go. I will try to phone you tonight.

Bisous,
Céline

Chapter 25

Evie kept expecting to hear from Laurent. She had left a message on his phone asking him to let her know how Alex was, but that was days ago, and she'd heard nothing yet. All her news came second-or third-hand via her mother and Céline. Even Monique didn't seem to be that interested in Alex's progress. Evie wished she had the courage to get on a plane and go to the Bristol Infirmary to find out for herself, but she was afraid of what she might find. Alex was only just out of a coma, and probably still confused and upset. Apart from a host of broken bones, he had lost the sight in his right eye and he'd have a scar from lip to hairline to remind him of his encounter with the metal clothesline-pole he'd landed on. At this stage it was too soon to know if he'd regain any of the sight in his left eye.

She had also heard that his children spent a lot of time at the hospital, which meant that Sharon, his ex, must be there too. Tragedy had a strange way of bringing people together and Evie didn't want to be the one who screwed up Alex's hope of future happiness. If there were a chance of that, Evie would be the last person any of them would want to see. And anyway, Evie was fairly certain Alex wouldn't be laying out the red carpet for her after the last time they'd met – he had walked out on her in Antoine's bar, believing that the only reason she was talking to him at all was to check if he was physically capable of delivering a dead rabbit in the middle of the night.

♡ ♡ ♡

From: Laurent Lesauvage
To: Marian Kinsella
Sent: July 28th 07:28 PM
Re: Alex Ryder

Dear Mrs Kinsella,

Thank you for your e-mail.

Alex is physically stable, but emotionally he would not be able to cope with revelations about Holly. Please do not encourage Evie to tell him right now. He has still to come to terms with the loss of his right eye, and it is far from certain if he will regain much more sight in his left. At present all he can see is light and dark, and blurred outlines. He is due to have another operation on both eyes this afternoon, so if you believe in prayer, now would be a good time.

He has no memory of the events leading up to the accident, and indeed when he finally regained consciousness there was some possibility that he might have suffered permanent brain damage – he was confused and was confusing names of people he should have known well. His mind seems to have cleared now, however, and he performs well on most brain tests. But he is very depressed and suffers from mood swings. The doctors are unable to say yet whether this is as a reaction to his injuries or "organic" – in other words as a result of some physical damage.

Please pass this information on to Evie, as I have no e-mail address for her.

Yours truly,
Laurent Lesauvage

From: Marian Kinsella
To: Céline Lesauvage
Sent: July 29th 08:35 AM
Re: Laurent

Dear Céline

I don't think Laurent is very happy with me. I received quite a "formal" e-mail from him with an update on Alex's condition along with a strict order that he wasn't to be told

about Holly.
I don't think he'll be phoning Evie.

Hugs, Marian

From: Céline Lesauvage
To: Marian Kinsella
Sent: July 29th 18:23 PM
Re: Laurent

Dear Marian,

Don't worry about Laurent. It is me he is angry with, not you. He shouted at me on the telephone yesterday, saying I had no right to tell you about Holly – that it was up to Evie. I wasn't going to try to argue with him in a mood like that.

I asked him to phone Evie and bring her up to date, and he said he'd think about it. From the sounds of your e-mail he decided against it. It makes me sad. I think they would have been suited to each other. But you may be right about the "survivor's guilt" – Laurent was the one who phoned Alex to beg him to intercept Tom at the house.

Bisous,
Céline

Laurent knew that the English medical staff were somewhat baffled by his hovering presence at Alex's bedside. But he had discovered, after facilitating the transfer back to Bristol, that apart from his ex-wife Sharon and his children, Alex actually had few close friends or family in his native city. His brother flew in from Washington and stayed a few days, but he had his own family and work to get back to. And socially, after Alex's divorce, the work needed to keep his company profitable had stopped him from finding new social outlets when Sharon, his ex, "took custody" of most of their mutual friends. Their divorce had been messy and most of their friends had taken sides. Laurent began to understand why Alex had decided to move to France – a small village like Ste Anne must have offered him the chance of starting afresh away from a city in which he had alienated some friends during his divorce and neglected others due to pressures of work.

In his first week in hospital in England, former colleagues and associates visited Alex regularly. A few members of the film club had dropped by with DVDs of classic movies. The captain of the golf club even paid a duty call, but as Alex had never got around to playing much during his six-year membership, none of the other members put in an appearance. To Laurent's surprise Sharon's fiancé, Steve, came into the hospital more often than Sharon herself, but he said it was because he didn't like the boys to come in on their own, and Sharon had a lot of work to do to get their wedding organised.

But after a while the appeal of visiting first an unconscious patient, then a morosely depressed one, had worn off for most people, and Laurent felt duty bound to keep coming back. He had enjoyed Alex's company before the accident, and he was still working on his house. And most of all it was his fault that the man was here in the first place.

♡　　♡　　♡

From: Céline Lesauvage
To: Marian Kinsella
Sent: August 1st 09:02 AM
Re: Alex Ryder

Dearest Marian,

What a mad few days! Sorry I haven't been in touch (though I did try to phone you twice and got your machine). Laurent is back in France. He had to return for work, but he intends to go out to Bristol again very soon. He has just told me the strangest thing.

He and Alex were talking about Evie when Alex told Laurent that it was *Evie* who left *him*. He insisted that Evie changed her mind about their relationship, ran away and covered her tracks so that Alex wouldn't find her. He even implied that she had taken money from the company!

Needless to say Laurent couldn't believe Evie would do such a thing, and he is worried about Alex. What kind of things are going on in his head? Did he have some kind of dream while he was in a coma, and it feels real to him now? Maybe he can't remember, and his mind is "filling in the blanks"? Or could he have some kind of brain damage causing paranoid fantasies? I wish I knew more about this kind of thing. Please don't say anything to Evie. Laurent will try to find out more.

The gendarmes have returned Tom's belongings to his family, but despite all Joël's enquiries (he has a very good friend in the force) he can learn nothing new. He's just been told to wait for the inquest. Tom's car turned up parked at a hotel near Libourne (a town northwest of here – on the route from the ferry) and although he hadn't been there for a while, he was paid up to date and obviously meant to return there.

Bisous,
Céline

Laurent had done his research on the Internet before talking to Alex's doctors. He was worried that Alex's version of the past was so different from Evie's, and he had read enough to worry him that his friend might be suffering from some brain damage.

"It's not unheard of, certainly," the neurologist was saying. "It's called 'confabulation'. The mind is always making up stories, or dreams if you like, but with some injuries, the brain loses its ability to tell the real from the imagined. So a 'story' becomes the patient's reality. Did you say that Alex's version of the past is a 'rosier' version? Does it paint him in a better light than the version you've heard? Interesting ... it certainly could be indicative of further damage behind that left eye ..." He was scribbling furiously into the notes and Laurent could see a gleam of excitement in the young consultant's eyes.

"Well, I'm not completely sure …" Laurent didn't want Alex to suddenly become the doctor's next research paper. "You called it 'confabulation'. I take it that's to do with the story-building. But what about the actual damage? Is there any way you can test for that? Look for it on a scan or anything?"

The consultant put down his pen and smiled. Condescendingly. It made Laurent want to punch him.

"Mr Lesauvage … Laurent," he said. "The mind, or rather the brain, is a very complex organ. We take pictures, but we are a long way from understanding –"

"But in Alex's case," Laurent wanted to avoid the lecture and bring him back to the case in question, "what can we do to establish if he is suffering from some kind of damage and how will we know if it's permanent?"

The consultant shrugged his shoulders helplessly. "It's too soon to tell."

♡   ♡   ♡

A few days later, Joël and Laurent were spending a rare evening together. Rare since the accident, that is. Normally they ate together at least once or twice a week, or even more often when they were both single. In the end, worried that his friend was losing weight with the stress and all the travel, and more importantly losing his *joie de vivre*, Joël had been forced to play the guilt card.

He complained that he'd hardly seen him for weeks and asked if he needed to throw himself under a bus for Laurent to willingly spend any time with him.

"I've some news for you," he promised. "I've managed to get some information about Tom from the police at last." He knew this was the bait to definitely get Laurent to commit to meeting him.

"So what have you heard?" Laurent asked. They were eating in Joël's house – he brought a small roast chicken to the table and simply cut it in two, putting one half on each plate.

"Let's eat, then I'll tell you," Joël suggested, spooning potatoes, vegetables and gravy from the roasting dish. "How's Alex?"

He wanted to hear Laurent's news of Alex first, to see what kind of frame of mind his friend was in before deciding how much to tell him. He had pulled strings to gather the information – and strictly speaking, he shouldn't be sharing it. A few gendarmes had gone out on a limb to help him, and he didn't want to get them into trouble. But his main source, the inspector who had given Alex such a hard time, understood that Joël would pass on some of the information and he had been willing to take the risk. He still felt that if only he hadn't been so blinded by his own theory of Alex as lover-turned-sour, he might have protected Monique better. Although he couldn't officially approve of Joël and Laurent taking the law into their own hands, the consequences of their actions – a knife-wielding maniac killed in a tragic road-traffic accident – were far less damaging to his career than if Monique had been murdered in her bed by the same knife-wielding maniac. And so he shared some of Joël and Laurent's guilt over Alex.

"Alex is …" Laurent took a long slug of wine and sighed. "Alex is not doing as well as I thought he was doing." He told Joël the story of Alex's "confabulation" and how the consultant had explained it might be a sign of brain damage. "And if that's the case, there's a chance that his ability to distinguish between reality and things he's dreamed or imagined may be gone for ever …" Laurent didn't want to share the cases he had found on the Internet of patients in similar circumstances who had ended up in long-term institutional care precisely because of this inability to tell the real from the imagined.

"Any chance it's just some kind of misunderstanding?" Joël asked.

"Their stories are just too different. And I'm sure Evie wouldn't lie about something like that. She'd have no reason to. Besides, if she'd left him, for no good reason, or at best because he got too 'heavy', which Alex makes it sound like, would she not have got in touch at some stage, for Holly's sake? She stayed away because he had another family, and he made it clear he was leaving Evie for their sakes."

Joël thought about it for a few seconds, then he asked: "What does Alex say about this contradiction?"

"I haven't asked him. I don't know how to. Not without implying I think he's lying to me."

"And are there any other signs of this possible brain

damage? Any other stories or 'confabulations' that don't add up?"

Laurent shrugged his shoulders then screwed his face up in frustration. "That's the problem, I just don't know enough about his past. We talk mainly about France, you, Monique, Céline …"

"And Evie?" Joël added.

"And Evie," Laurent conceded uncomfortably. "He's so bitter towards her, and yet …"

"And yet what?"

Laurent sighed. "I think he's still in love with her. I think meeting her unexpectedly made him think he might get a second chance, and now … I wish to God I'd never called him that morning!"

This last statement exploded out of Laurent's mouth as though it had been trapped there under ever-building pressure.

"If I hadn't called him –" he added more slowly.

"The truck would have driven through the village without swerving …" Joël interrupted.

"Tom would still be alive …" Laurent went on.

"And he would have reached Monique at least a minute or two before I did. He would have –"

"We can't be certain he meant to harm them," Laurent said, trying to wipe Tom's murderous expression from his memory. "He was a soldier, sleeping rough, making his way in the forest. That hunting knife could have just been just that, a hunting knife. We both own several of them between us, Joël. Are we murderers? If you stopped either of us on a Sunday morning in hunting season we'd be armed to the teeth with knives and guns, but that doesn't mean …"

Tears were running down Laurent's face, and Joël realised that he'd been living with the guilt not only of Alex's injuries, but also of Tom's death. Laurent was fairly drunk by now – they'd finished dinner, and were just finishing their second bottle of wine. Nonetheless, he opened another bottle, poured two glasses and waited for Laurent's breathing to grow less jagged.

"He meant to kill her. Or at the very least seriously injure her," Joël said at last, when he was sure Laurent was listening. "And he wouldn't have let anything or anyone stand in his way. He'd have attacked Evie too, Laurent, and that's why you called Alex."

Laurent couldn't argue, but he didn't agree or even nod his assent: he just stared blankly ahead, waiting for whatever else Joël was going to say.

Thanks to his digging, Joël knew more about the gendarmes' discoveries than he had told Céline. A rather disturbing picture of Tom was emerging. The hotel bedroom he had pre-paid for and planned to return to was full of baby paraphernalia. Nappies, bottles and sterilisers. Baby blankets and a portable cot. His car, a recently purchased second-hand station wagon, was fitted with a baby seat and the boot was full of baby milk, more nappies and enough clothes to take an infant up to about six months old. Among his possessions were a false passport and two birth certificates – one for a boy and the other for a girl – and he was named, using the false name in the passport, as the father on both.

In the woods the police had found a weapons stash including several hunting knives, which they traced to shops in the Dordogne. So whatever Tom's plans had been when he arrived in France – probably just to abduct his child – they had changed when he realised Monique was no longer pregnant.

"There's no doubt in my mind, or in the minds of the police, what Tom intended to do that morning," Joël said. "It must have taken months of planning and preparation for him to get hold of those birth certs and his new passport. And he had gone out and chosen all the clothes for his baby. Everything was ready. Just imagine his state of mind … he was coming to France to get his child, and then there was no child. The man lost the plot, Laurent. He was furious and hurting and someone was going to pay. You feel guilty about Tom's death and about Alex's injuries and I feel guilty too. But I can't honestly regret the way things turned out now that I know what the alternative could have been – it could have been Monique and Evie instead." He topped up Laurent's glass yet again. "So drink yourself into oblivion tonight if you have to. Allow yourself that guilt for one more night. But when you get up tomorrow morning, I want you to put it behind you."

The only indication Laurent gave that he had taken in any of this was when he reached out shakily and drained his glass in two big mouthfuls and then laid his head on his arms on the table in front of him. Joël felt his heart break as his best friend began to sob like a child.

A French Affair

♡   ♡   ♡

From: Marian Kinsella
To: Celine Lesauvage
Sent: August 3rd 09:40 AM
Re: Evie and Alex

Dear Céline

Thanks for your last e-mail. It certainly gave me a lot to think about. I know I will just sound like a mother, but I really can't believe Alex's version of the story. And not just because I know that Evie would never steal money.

I am tempted to ask Evie if she has any idea what is going on, but I will follow your advice. If for no other reason than I suspect that she would storm over there and confront Alex, and that would be in no one's interests. So if you hear anything else, anything at all, please, please, tell me straight away. It is very worrying. Poor Holly – imagine if she is just about to find her father, only for him to be suffering from some kind of brain damage?

Hugs, Marian

From: Celine Lesauvage
To: Marian Kinsella
Sent: August 4th 07:58 AM
Re: Evie and Alex

Dear Marian,

I hope you didn't think that I believed Alex's story. Not even for a moment. There is something else at work here, and I hope we find out soon what it is. I pray that it is not brain damage.

Laurent will be in Bristol again next week and he is in daily contact with Alex's daughter Sophie.

Now that Alex is out of danger, his ex-wife Sharon has decided to go ahead with her wedding in the middle of September. (Apparently she is marrying a man Alex has a lot of respect for and is happy for his boys to live with.)

Monique refuses to see a counsellor. Both her mother and I have tried! Joël has tried to get her to talk to him, but she has been avoiding him. She said to me the other night that if Tom had been watching the house, he would have seen Joël drop her home a few times. And she kissed him. So of course it's her fault that Tom became a homicidal maniac!

Why do we women blame ourselves for every sin a man commits? If I could do one thing for the education of the next generation it would be to ban the teaching, publishing or reading of the story of Adam and Eve!

Bisous,
Céline

From: Marian Kinsella
To: Celine Lesauvage
Sent: Aug 4th 08:08 PM
Re: Adam and Eve not required

Dear Céline

Monique may have had a French grandmother, but her other granny was Irish. Guilt is in her genes!

Hugs, Marian

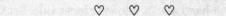

Monique was finding it harder and harder just to get out of bed in the morning. The job she used to love was now a desperate imposition on her time, and she hated having to smile and be polite all day. She was so exhausted by the time she got home in the evening that all she had the energy to do was to flop down in front of the television, or flick through the pages of a fashion magazine. She didn't even enjoy her garden any more. Whereas before she used to race against the fading daylight to steal a few more minutes to prune, weed or plant, it was weeks since she had bothered doing any work at all. The only reason she mowed her lawn was that Joël, driving past one day and seeing it getting long, had stopped and offered to do it the next day. Monique stayed out till after dark that night to get it finished. Because if she let Joël mow her lawn, she would have to invite him in afterwards for a cup of coffee or a drink and she couldn't bear to be in his company for more than a few seconds.

If she could have found the energy, she'd have left by now. She would be living somewhere completely different, preferably in a big, anonymous, bustling city, where she knew no one and where no one knew her. Where she wouldn't have to endure the sympathetic but curious glances every time she went shopping. She knew most people meant well, but she felt like a fraud who didn't deserve their sympathy. By not being more decisive, she had allowed Tom's dangerous obsession with her to grow out of hand and by allowing Joël to kiss her she had enraged him beyond reason. She should have followed up on her letter about the miscarriage by travelling to England with her medical notes. If he knew that he'd already killed his baby, then he would never have made the journey to France to ruin so many lives. Laurent and Joël would never forgive themselves for what had happened and Evie might never get a chance to tell Alex that he was Holly's father. And even if she did – what state was Alex in?

Laurent was surprised to discover that when he woke up in Joël's house, the morning after their discussion, he felt better. His mouth felt as if a small furry animal had crawled into it and died overnight and his head felt as if he had fought with a high-speed train and lost, but he had a newfound determination to look forward instead of back.

"Thanks," he told Joël over a breakfast which consisted solely of very strong coffee.

"Don't thank me, thank the wine," Joël answered, feeling awkward. "Hey, that could be a new marketing angle – '*Find the answers to all your problems at the bottom of a bottle of good French wine!*' – do you think it would catch on?"

Laurent snorted.

"So what are you going to do about Alex?" Joël asked. "Why don't you talk to his family? See if they can talk to him, bring up the past and see are any of his 'memories' different from theirs?"

"I can't." Laurent shook his head – gently and carefully – it was still a bit spinny. "To start with, I haven't given them any idea of what I'm worried about – I mean, brain damage is a huge thing to bring up if you're not sure. The doctors won't commit themselves one way or another – they say it's far too soon. And who would I ask? Sharon would be unlikely to have the full story of Evie and Alex's break-up, even if she were willing to rake up the past. And I can hardly ask his children to help me interrogate him. Sophie may act like she's all grown up, especially at the moment; but she's only fifteen. She's a kid with a kid's fears and worries, and there's no way I'm going to add to those."

"Well, then, you either leave it be, or you talk to Alex

about it," Joël said as if were the easiest choice in the world to make.

♡   ♡   ♡

"You don't believe me," Alex said when Laurent had finished talking a few days later. "Evie told you a different story and you believe her, you don't believe me." He spoke without emotion. This was just one more thing he would have to bear because there was nothing he could do about it. "I suppose you'd better go. Goodbye, Laurent. And thanks for all you've done for me since the accident. I suppose I should have said it before now, but I don't blame you. Maybe I did at first, but I don't any more. It was just bad luck. Or it was meant to be. Fate."

They were in Alex's hospital room. It was a private room, thickly carpeted and comfortably furnished with a desk that doubled as a dining table and two bucket-style armchairs by the window. Laurent was sitting in one of these chairs and Alex in the other. There was a low coffee table between them with a pile of magazines and a vase of wilted sunflowers on it.

Alex stood up stiffly and walked to the door.

"Goodbye, Laurent," he said again. "Be sure to send on the bill for your architectural work. Send it here to England – I'm not sure when I'll be in France again."

Now bitterness, or maybe sadness, had crept into his voice, and Laurent knew he had to be very careful with what he said next.

"I do believe you, Alex," he said, not moving from his

seat. "I believe that you're telling me the truth. Your truth."

"Don't humour me, Laurent. Treat me with a little bit of respect, and if you can't manage that, then get out."

Laurent noticed Alex's use of the word "if" and knew the other man hoped he'd find a way to stay.

"I've spoken to your doctors, Alex," he said. "They say that it's not uncommon in your kind of injury for the brain to –"

"You think I've lost it? That my mind's playing tricks on me? I remember, Laurent. I remember it as if it was today. I couldn't believe it ... I *wouldn't* have believed it if I didn't have the evidence in front of my eyes ... every day for months after she left ..."

His voice trailed off and Laurent heard the uncertainty creep in. He hated himself for what he was doing. His friend had suffered unimaginable damage to his body and now Laurent was as good as taking away his mind. His memories. The things that made him who he was.

"I remember, Laurent, it's real. It's not a dream, or my imagination, you've got to believe me ..." His voice cracked.

Laurent wished he could call back the words. It was too soon; he could see Alex's sense of reality dissolve in front of his eyes. He should never have confronted him with this until he was sure he was able to cope with it. But Laurent realised suddenly that it was his obsession with Evie that had pushed him forward. To protect his image of Evie he had been prepared to sacrifice his friend's sanity. As he watched Alex struggle to keep control, Laurent tried to imagine what it must be like. To be told that your memories might be false? That the events of your life might be no more than dreams?

Then something Alex had said caught his attention.

"Alex," he said urgently, "Alex, what did you mean by saying 'if I didn't have the evidence in front of my eyes – every day for months after she left'?"

"Her letter … I reread her letter, over and over …"

"There's a letter?" Laurent got up and went to stand in front of him.

"Did I not tell you?" Alex looked confused, obviously already doubting what he had or hadn't said. "She broke it off by letter …"

"No." Laurent was grinning now. "You didn't say anything about a letter. You still have it?" It was a rhetorical question; he knew Alex well enough to know there was no way he would have disposed of it. He had probably tortured himself with it regularly during the past five years.

"It's in my desk. In my apartment," Alex said. "It's a Victorian desk and there's one of those secret drawers at the back of the writing well …"

Laurent only waited long enough to get directions and the alarm code. In his excitement and his determination to prove that Alex wasn't after all suffering from brain damage, he completely forgot that if Alex was telling the truth Evie had a lot of explaining to do.

Chapter 26

Evie reread the photocopied letter in her hand. What a lovely thing to come home to, she thought bitterly.

She had just come back from a conference in Killarney – booked over six months ago, so she couldn't back out – at which she had spoken to other members of the industry and potential clients about the evolving nature of Internet marketing. The mid-week event had been busy and the schedule tightly packed, but Evie had still managed to find time to go for a couple of long walks on her own and she felt more relaxed than when she had left Dublin. (Of course three nights' sleep and being able to lie on until the unbelievably slothful time of eight thirty without being woken by a little girl had added to her sense of having had a holiday.)

She stopped off briefly at home before driving to her

mother's house to collect Holly, and found a pile of letters, mostly bills and circulars, waiting inside the front door. One, an envelope with unfamiliar handwriting and an English stamp, caught her attention as she tossed the rest onto the hall table.

In it were a photocopy and a brief note from Laurent. The photocopy was of a letter she had supposedly sent Alex when she "left him".

> *Dear Alex,*
>
> *I think you know that things can't work out between us – in fact this affair should never really have started. You're my boss and you're married.*
>
> *I really enjoyed my job, and it will be hard to find another I like as much. So if I take a "redundancy" payment as well as the holiday pay due to me, I'm sure you will understand. Continuing to work for you is impossible in the circumstances. I want this relationship to end, but you don't. Not the best basis for an employee/ employer relationship, as my chance of success within your company would be dependent on your goodwill.*
>
> *By the time you get back from your conference in Turkey, I will be gone and I think it would be best if you didn't try to find me – for your sake as much as mine.*
>
> *I'm sorry it had to come to this – we had some good times.*
>
> *Yours,*
> *Evie*

Her first reaction was fury at whoever had written it

and signed her name to it. Then disbelief that Alex could have fallen for it. It was typed, or rather printed off a word-processor, and while the signature at the end, simply "Evie" in purple ink, looked genuine, did he really think she'd have added her trademark little heart over the "i" on a letter like that? It was so formal, so horrible. And the veiled threat it contained, that she could twist their relationship to look like an older boss harassing a younger employee – how could Alex have believed she'd do that to him after the year they had spent together?

This was the letter of a woman who had screwed her way into her boss's heart for the sake of a promotion and then decided to take what she liked from the coffers. Not only had it destroyed their relationship, but it must have left Alex hating her and doubting that she had ever loved him.

She thought back to how he had behaved in France. At Céline's party he had greeted her coldly and then looked genuinely confused when Evie had been equally biting towards him. And when he stopped her in St Anne, and they had gone for a drink, he may have been hoping to delve deeper into the past only to have Evie confirm his earlier opinion of her by using the occasion to check his "alibi" for the night she and Laurent found the rabbit.

And thinking of Laurent, Evie took out the handwritten note sent with Alex's photocopied letter:

Dear Evie,
Having heard your version of how you and Alex split, and then a completely different story from him, I was

seriously worried that he had suffered brain damage. I found it hard to believe that you had left him as he claimed, with virtually no explanation, and even taking money from his company in the process. But then he directed me to this letter. Fortunately it clears up any worry about his mental state, but it leaves other questions unanswered.

Perhaps this letter is not what it seems, or perhaps it has been misinterpreted.

Best wishes,

Laurent

He had left it just vague enough, Evie realised, that he couldn't be accused of rejecting her story out of hand. But she had already seen how easily he jumped to conclusions – she remembered the night he had asked her why she had slept with him in Alex's house. He was so clear in his mind that she was using him to get back at Alex that he had forgotten it was he who had taken her there in the first place. Now that he had in his possession a letter that completely destroyed her character, had he stopped even for a moment to consider whether there was another explanation for it?

She discovered, without too much surprise, that she was more upset by Laurent's brief and to-the-point note than by the photocopy of a letter that was supposed to have come from her.

She lifted down a box from the top of her wardrobe. It was full of bank statements, payslips and other official papers from her time in the UK. She sorted her way into the bottom of the box and removed an envelope in Alex's handwriting. From it, she took the letter that had ended their relationship:

My dear Evie,

My wife has asked me to come home. Sophie was in trouble in school, and Sharon thinks it is because of our separation. She wants to give our marriage another try.

I have to put my children first as I'm sure you will understand. I'm sorry if I've hurt you, but you're young, and you'll find someone new. Someone better.

Sharon has agreed to break off all contact with Graham, the man she had the affair with, and I have to do the same with you. She is also a director of the company, as you are aware and it was her idea that you should leave RYDERCOM, but I beg of you not to make things more difficult for me. If you have any feelings for me at all.

I won't insult you by saying that the redundancy payment we propose is in some way a compensation for my leaving you, but hopefully it will give you time to find something else. You're very talented.

I will be leaving for the conference in Turkey tomorrow, and Sharon will handle all the details of your departure. I'm sorry. But I have no choice. It's for the best.

I will always remember you,

Alex

Evie read it again, looking for some clue by which she might have guessed that it wasn't from Alex. But this letter had been written by someone who knew him well. Someone who knew just the notes he would strike to appeal to Evie's conscience. "*I beg you not to make things more difficult for me*" – how could she have refused him that? "*You'll find someone better*" – Alex used to joke that he couldn't understand what she saw in an old fogey like him. And the "redundancy" payment had been so generous, so excessive almost, that it was just the kind of gesture that Alex, full of guilt, would have made. In fact, there was nothing that should have rung alarm bells with Evie. It may have hurt at the time, but when it looked as if Alex had had to choose between Evie's happiness and Sophie's it hadn't been at all difficult for her to imagine him choosing Sophie's. Especially if he'd been able to persuade himself that Evie "was young and would find someone new".

She folded the letter back into its envelope and placed it with what Laurent had sent her into a larger envelope. In her mind, Evie thought of all the things she wanted to say to Laurent. She wanted to ask him had she been completely wrong to believe they had shared something special. She wanted to know had she really come across as the lying, conniving bitch he seemed to believe her to be. She wanted to howl with the injustice of finally finding a man she thought she could fall in love with only to have him prove so fickle when it came to trusting her.

Instead, she took out a piece of notepaper and wrote a few lines to put in the envelope along with all the evidence of her destroyed happiness.

Laurent,

A French Affair

I received a letter too. I have enclosed it, along with the envelope it came in. I have sent the originals, because I don't care if I never see them again.

Whether the letters "are not what they seem" or a "misinterpretation", I leave for you to decide.

Evie

PS – You might find it useful to talk to Sharon Ryder.

She posted the letter on her way to collect Holly, and decided that in doing so, she had drawn a line under her relationship, or the potential of a relationship, with Laurent. Now she could concentrate all her mind on what to do about Alex.

But later that night when Holly was in bed, she switched on her computer to check her personal e-mails, and she discovered that life is never that simple. Laurent had sent her an e-mail. And it had been sent barely a day after his letter.

From: Laurent@immo-lesauvage.com
To: Evie Kinsella
Sent: September 5th 23:23
Re: Read this before opening my letter

Dear Evie,

You will get a letter from me in the next day or so. Please, please, please disregard the tone of the note I sent with it.

Within minutes of sending it I regretted it and I have been trying to phone you ever since. But I just get your machine.
I sent you a copy of a letter Alex received five years ago. The letter seemed to have come from you, and he sent me to fetch it when I told him I doubted the truth of his version of the past.

You see, I had been worried about his state of mind since the accident, as he kept telling me that *you* left *him*. But you had told me the opposite, *and I believed you,* *Evie.* So I began to be convinced that Alex was suffering from some kind of delusion. (Which is a documented side-effect of brain damage – especially to the part of the brain just behind the eyes. You can see why I was worried.)

The more unshakeable he became in his "memory" of how you left him, the more worried I became. Then he told me about the letter and I went to find it. You cannot imagine my relief that I was not the cause of permanent brain damage as well as all his other injuries. Without thinking, I had the letter photocopied, I wrote a poorly worded and ill-considered letter and I posted it to you. Within minutes I regretted it, but it was too late.

I now had a letter I couldn't believe in and your story about how Alex had left you. So I did what I should have done weeks ago and called Sharon Ryder. I had been protecting her and the children from my worries, but now I suspected that she might be behind the whole confusion.

When she heard why I was calling, she said she couldn't talk right now but that she would call me back. I am still waiting to hear from her. Alex keeps insisting that you left him and that the letter just proves it, but he is beginning to concede that maybe there was something unexplained behind your departure. To be honest, I think he is terrified to allow himself believe it for fear of having his hopes dashed.

Please believe me, Evie, when I say that it was because I trusted you that I confronted Sharon. I would hate to think that I had destroyed our friendship through a few careless words written in haste.

I know you will be in France next weekend for Monique's birthday. My mother has insisted that I come along too – so I will talk to you then. Hopefully the whole thing will be cleared up by then.

Your good friend,
Laurent

Evie wasn't sure why, but Laurent's e-mail left her feeling empty. Her anger had left her, but she didn't feel any sense of relief or any warmer towards him. Was it his use of the words "friend" and "friendship" that had disappointed her? They had never spoken of anything except friendship, so she could hardly expect an expression of his undying love. She also had a feeling that there was a subtext to Laurent's words, something she was missing completely. But she had no choice but to wait to see what Sharon had to say and how Alex, and Laurent, would react.

From: Laurent@immo-lesauvage.com
To: Evie Kinsella
Sent: September 5th 23:23
Forward: E-mail from Sharon Ryder.

Dear Evie,

As you will see from the below e-mail, the mystery is now solved. I have had to resist telling Alex myself because I am back in France and this is hardly news to be shared over the phone. Besides, Sharon wants to tell him herself.

I will talk to you at Monique's birthday party,

Best wishes
Laurent.

Original e-mail
From: Sharon Ryder.
To: Laurent@immo-lesauvage.com

Dear Laurent,

You were right to contact me, and I have spent days trying to find the best way of putting this. But there is no way around the truth.

I was the one who came between Alex and Evie five years ago. Alex and I had already broken up, and we were in the process of getting a divorce. We were also partners in the company and that had to be resolved as well, but Alex was being very reasonable. Too reasonable almost. I know I should have been glad, but a little bit of me probably felt that if he had really loved me, he would have been much more bitter when I had an affair. So when he found Evie, and was so transformed, I was jealous. I couldn't remember him ever having looked at me like that, and it felt like a betrayal.

I have to admit, I was also afraid that if he became more seriously involved with her, his reasonable attitude to the divorce might change because he needed to make a secure future for himself and Evie. And knowing that he was about to take the company public, I was terrified into believing that she would be made partner too.

So I don't know if it was jealousy or greed, but when the opportunity arose, I took it. The way I saw it I had nothing to lose and everything to gain.

Alex and some of the other senior staff were attending a conference in Turkey, so I had come in to work some extra days in the office. A letter arrived for Evie, addressed in Alex's handwriting, and it wasn't difficult to open it without tearing the envelope.

I went into a rage when I saw it. There was a plane ticket to Istanbul for after the conference and a brochure for a five-star hotel on the coast. It seemed so unfair to me. When Alex and I started out, a weekend in Blackpool was beyond our reach. I was working as a data-entry clerk for the county council and Alex was getting the business up and running. Every spare penny was going into that and we had a baby on the way.

That sounds like I am trying to justify what I did. And maybe in a way I am. But to myself I justified it by saying he was planning to spend money on his girlfriend. Money that he should have been spending on his children. And if he had a new family there was no way of knowing what would happen to our children, my children.

I substituted Alex's letter with the one you have already seen, and I tore up the tickets. Then I sent another letter to Alex, fired Evie and arranged for the "redundancy" payment, which I hoped would keep her out of the way. I took the precaution of removing all her details from our files and made it looked like they had been hacked out. I also did enough other damage to our systems to make him really angry with her and to keep him busy for a few days after he got back, so he wouldn't have time to go looking for her.

I'm not proud of what I did. And I'm not asking for any kind of "forgiveness".

I will go and tell Alex myself, face to face; I suppose I can't expect anyone else to do that for me. Since his condition has improved, I have been trying to persuade him to come to the wedding, but I doubt he will be able to face it after this. He seems so determined to move to France and I'm sure he'll want to put even more distance between us now.

I will try to tell him how sorry I am, but maybe you would repeat it again for me some time when his fury dies down.
Keep an eye on him for me.

Yours truly, Sharon.

Chapter 27

Evie clicked the mouse and opened her e-mail program one more time before finally switching off her computer. Her taxi for the airport would be arriving any moment now, so she tapped her fingers in frustration as the program seemed to take forever to spring to life. She had already printed off a copy of Sharon's forwarded e-mail, but she needed to look at it one more time on screen "live", as she had at least ten times since it came through the previous night. She also kept checking that Laurent hadn't sent another e-mail of his own. She thought he might have phoned her to see what her reaction was. She hoped he might have sent her an e-mail to give her some idea of what was going through his own head; but he was silent.

She knew Sharon would be telling Alex soon about

what she had done, in fact she might already have told him, but Evie had no way of knowing. She almost wished she wasn't going to France today – the thought of being stuck tens of thousands of feet in the air while Alex, or for that matter Laurent, might be trying to contact her was unbearable. But during an airline seat sale in February she had booked to come over for Monique's birthday, and given that she hadn't seen her since Tom's funeral, she could hardly cancel.

Evie lay awake all night, thinking of what she would say to Sharon if she ever had the misfortune to meet her again. It was like someone had flicked a switch in her brain, and she was able to feel again. The numbness cocooning her since the accident crumbled away, and the anger that had built up inside suddenly found an outlet. Sharon's attempts at self-justification or apology at the end of the letter only made things worse. The fact that she had so successfully put that time behind her was like a red rag to a bull. Sharon was getting married in a few weeks' time to a wonderful man even Alex approved of. He liked him enough to be happy for his sons to live with him. Whereas Evie had spent the intervening years as a single mum, unable to tell Holly about her father because she was afraid that her daughter would pick up on how she felt about him. And might think herself less loved as a result.

All Evie's memories of how Holly had come into being had been tainted by what Sharon had done. And Holly had lost nearly four years of knowing her father. No matter how Evie might come to feel in the future, she would never be able to forgive Sharon for that.

♥   ♥   ♥

Evie sat sipping a coffee as she waited for the call to board her flight. She was looking forward to seeing Monique again, but she felt guilty at how little they'd talked since Tom's funeral in Bristol. Evie had begged Monique to come to Dublin to recover, like she had the last time, but Monique was determined to go back to France. "I just want to go *home*," she said to Evie. "No one seems to realise that I'd be better off at home." And for the first time, when Evie heard Monique use the word "home", she felt as though Monique understood what the word meant. It was her safe place. Despite everything that had happened, she wanted to go back there and reclaim it for herself. But Evie didn't want to go back to Ste Anne. She didn't want to be reminded. She realised that if her flight hadn't already been booked long before any of this happened, she would have found excuse after excuse and never visited again. Never mind what it would have done to her friendship. Never mind that Monique wanted Evie to come to France so that they could face that morning together. Evie would have let it slide and slide until it was impossible to go.

Suddenly Evie's newfound anger directed itself elsewhere.

"Damn it," she muttered under her breath. "We can't let Tom continue to rule our lives from beyond the grave."

♡   ♡   ♡

In Bordeaux, Evie queued at the car rental desk and used her passport to fan herself. She had insisted on hiring her own car, not just to save Monique the drive to collect her, but also to give herself a sense of independence. Evie enjoyed driving in the French countryside. It was so different to Ireland, or rather Dublin, where Evie did ninety-five per cent of her driving. And today especially, Evie needed to be independent. She wanted to approach Ste Anne at her own pace. With her thoughts and memories uninterrupted. As little as a month ago, she would have been happy to be told she would never set eyes on the village again. But virtually every night since, she revisited it in her dreams. Her mother and Monique were right. She had to go back there, but she was damned if anyone else was going to set the agenda.

After driving carefully round the car park a couple of times to get used to the rented car's controls, Evie eased her way onto the *Rocade*, the ring-road, around Bordeaux. She had decided against the recently extended motorway and chose instead the national road that ran north of the River Dordogne. It meant adding about half an hour onto her journey, but the plane had made good time and Evie's bags had been first out so she knew she wouldn't be keeping Monique waiting. She found her exit easily enough, and once she left the busy ring-road behind, she rolled down the window and turned on the radio.

To her surprise, she began to smile.

Not the kind of smile she had got used to over the past couple of months, the kind of smile that was supposed to tell anyone looking at her that she was "alright", but a real smile. The kind of smile her face relaxed into unconsciously when she was having a good time. She had a two-hour drive ahead of her, through small towns and villages and along a road which wound its way past some of the most famous wine names in the world. French voices on the radio reminded her that she was a million miles from Dublin, and the radio was set on the undemanding *Nostalgie*, which played a mixture of French and foreign golden oldies.

Evie had no idea what the next few days, or even the next few hours, might bring, but it was out of her hands, so there was no point in worrying.

She made better time than she expected. Her flight had arrived in just before lunch so the roads cleared as everyone sat down to eat. Before she knew it, she was driving past Bergerac Airport and couldn't help remembering the day Laurent had dropped her there when Holly had her asthma attack. He had kissed her that day, and she had been absolutely certain that his kiss had been more than just a physical meeting of two mouths.

Evie's heart began to beat faster as she drove the last few kilometres to Ste Anne. She approached the village from the south-west and would drive past Alex's house first. When his roof came into sight, her heart was thumping so hard that she thought it was trying to jump right out of her throat. She slowed down as she drove up the hill.

Alex's house, and indeed the village beyond it, looked "normal". Sleepy even. The only sign of life was someone cutting Alex's lawn. Evie vaguely remembered hearing Céline say that a local man had looked after the gardens for the previous owner, so Alex had obviously kept him on. The gardener was naked to the waist, driving a ride-on mower, and his van, a battered white Citroën, was parked at the top of Alex's gravelled drive. Another man was pulling a thick, coiled white hose – it looked like swimming-pool equipment – from the back of the van, and as Evie drove past, she imagined Holly swimming in the pool he was about to clean. Suddenly Ste Anne wasn't so intimidating.

The village itself hadn't changed. There were two tourists sipping rosé at a table outside Antoine's, and the small shop, which sold everything from duck confit to newspapers, was just opening up after a long lunch break. The owner stopped to chat to a passer-by and held his hand up to shield his eyes as they both examined the sky and shook their heads ominously. Evie assumed they were discussing the chances of rain. For as long as she'd been visiting the Dordogne, rainfall was the local obsession. Too much or too little, and not everyone agreed on which it was, and when they would like to see it fall.

The wall Alex had crashed into had been rebuilt, the stones piled carefully on top of each other, and the only sign of what had happened was the new, sandy-yellow mortar holding them together. Across the road, just before the turning south, red paint from the lorry still stained a stone retaining wall.

Monique must have been looking out for her. As Evie finally turned her eyes towards her friend's house, she saw the front door open and Monique waving as she came to stand in the gravel driveway.

Evie hadn't realised that she'd been holding her breath, but she let it out slowly now with a huge grin. She'd driven through Ste Anne; she'd passed Alex's house and the scene of the accident. She'd arrived at Monique's, and nothing awful had happened.

"You got here!"

They looked at each other awkwardly before Monique opened her arms to give Evie a welcoming hug.

"I'm so glad you've come!"

"I'm sorry it took me so long."

"It's okay, I understand."

And suddenly the past two months disappeared.

By some unspoken agreement, neither of them mentioned anything important for the rest of the afternoon. They unpacked Evie's bags, then sat in the garden sipping first sparkling water, then a cool white wine while they caught up on everyday news.

Evie passed on a report of Holly's latest antics in playschool, and Monique chatted about local news. Evie heard that the weather had been so good all summer that Joël would be starting his *Vendange* or grape harvest soon, and Monique was brought up to date with Evie's latest frustrations at work.

By dinnertime they were ready to talk properly. Again without saying anything, they both knew they would talk about Evie's situation first. It would give them a less traumatic start

"Céline showed me Sharon's e-mail," Monique said.

She pulled apart a head of red frisée lettuce, tore the leaves into pieces and mixed them with a couple of handfuls of rocket and some lamb's lettuce from the salad box in the fridge. She handed the salad bowl to Evie to take outside.

"I can't believe Sharon could have done something like that," Evie said, gripping the bowl as thought it were a life raft. "I mean, what did I ever do to her? I wasn't the cause of the breakdown of her relationship with Alex."

"From the look of her e-mail, it wasn't you she was trying to hurt," Monique pointed out. "And to be fair —"

"Why bother?" Evie interrupted. "She certainly wasn't."

"To be fair," Monique continued, "she didn't know you were pregnant."

"What's that got to do with it? Do you think that would have made a difference to her?" Evie raged. "I mean, how long do you think she spent worrying about the consequences of what she was going to do? She saw an opportunity to screw up Alex's happiness and she took it. And in the process, she left Holly without a father for the past four years. I can't believe you'd even consider making excuses for her."

"So which bit are you most upset about?" Monique had deliberately got Evie riled up so she could put this question. "Holly, or the fact that she split you and Alex up?"

Evie went silent, and Monique watched as the reality of her situation caught hold of her again. "Oh, my God, Monique!" Evie put her head between her hands at the garden table. "This is such a mess."

Monique said nothing. She took cling film off a bowl of marinating chicken breasts and placed them on the barbecue grill. Then with a sharp knife, she began to slice a shiny purple aubergine and seasoned and garlicked the slices before sandwiching them in a fish griller to cook on the barbecue.

"How did you feel when you saw Alex at Céline's party?" Monique asked at last. "That was the first time you saw him."

"I dunno. Angry, I suppose. It brought up all my old anger at being dumped."

Her anger had continued right up until Sharon's e-mail, but it made her feel guilty, especially in the first few days after his accident. She knew that she should be worrying about whether Alex was going to live or die and not stewing over what he had done to her in the past. It was the guilt that had stopped her thinking about him at all, because she just couldn't get her head around it.

"And I was furious that he thought he could just come up and talk to me as if nothing untoward had happened between us. As if he hadn't dumped me." Evie paused and put her head in her hands. "Which of course he hadn't. Aaagh!! He probably thought he was being really brave, as the dumpee, coming up to confront me!"

"Did you fancy him?"

"What?" Evie nearly gave herself whiplash she lifted her head so fast.

"Okaaaay … *could* you have fancied him?" Monique asked. "He's a good-looking guy. Without your shared past, could you have fancied him?"

"I don't know what that's got to do with –"

"It's got everything to do with it," Monique insisted. "Like it or not, you and Alex are going to have to spend a fair bit of time together in the next few years. You have to introduce him to Holly and you have to get beyond what happened in the past. You have to admit, it would be very neat and tidy if you went back to where you left off – it would be a lovely way of clearing up the so-called 'mess' you've both been plunged into."

"Oh come on, Monique, I can't even begin to think like that …"

"Well, I think you should think about it and work out how you feel about it. Otherwise you might just fall into a relationship by mistake …"

Monique turned her back to attend to the cooking. The coals were sizzling and occasionally bursting into angry orange flames when chicken fat dripped onto them.

Evie tried to imagine herself and Alex as a couple. His voice at the party had undoubtedly made some forgotten part of her insides flip with desire before her brain caught up and reminded her to be mad with him. He *was* still good-looking. But in the past twenty-four hours, after she had pushed aside the hatred and anger, whenever she tried to think about him there was nothing left to fill the void.

"There's just nothing there," she tried to explain to Monique. "I can't make myself feel anything for him. Too much has happened."

"That's probably good," Monique said simply. She sat opposite Evie and smiled. "Start with a blank slate."

"How'd you get to be so wise?" Evie asked, although she was far from sure it could be so simple. She was fairly sure that her ambivalence towards Alex had an awful lot to do with his new "best friend" Laurent.

"I don't know about wise," her friend answered wryly. "I didn't do such a good job of sorting my own life out, did I?"

Chapter 28

Evie originally thought it was a horrible idea, but it turned out to be the best thing they could have done. Céline had booked a restaurant for the birthday lunch, and she had insisted that Laurent be there for it. Monique had also invited some other friends, bringing the group to ten people. The rest of the party knew about what had happened to Monique, but they weren't directly involved, so Evie expected an awkward gathering with plenty of long, embarrassed silences. But food and wine soon banished any uncomfortable feelings as they discussed the menu and argued over the wine list and soon they were talking and gossiping as if the events at the start of the summer had never happened.

Evie lost count of the number of bottles dispatched over lunch and she found her French improved with each glass of wine so by the end of the meal she was talking schools to Géraldine, the local primary school teacher who had been very helpful to Monique when she moved over first. Géraldine was very interested to hear all about Evie's daughter who was due to start school in another year.

"Of course in France Holly would start school this year, in the *maternelle*," she told Evie. "You should come and see the school. I take the youngest class, and I'd love to meet Holly."

"Watch it!" Joël warned from the other side of the table. "If you go anywhere near that school, Géraldine won't let you leave until you swear an oath to move to France and have three more children to fill her classroom."

"Hmph!" Géraldine snorted. "Just because I can't rely on the locals to settle down and get married …"

She glared at Joël who explained that because he was in her catchment area, Géraldine had spent her first three years as a teacher trying to match him up with eligible single women.

"If we don't have enough children the local schools will close down, and who'll be the first to complain?" she said.

Evie thought it was just light-hearted banter until Géraldine began to ask her what she worked at and began to name companies in the area that she might consider forwarding her CV to. Then Céline took pity on Evie's panicked look and changed the subject. But the subject was the English who were buying up all the houses in the area, so it wasn't long before Géraldine managed to get in a plug for how property was rising so rapidly in price, and it was no surprise really because it was such a good place to bring up children …

"She's incorrigible, sorry!" Joël apologised later. It turned out that Géraldine was his cousin. Or rather step-cousin. "But she means well. She grew up in the city and always thought she'd end up teaching there. So when she got this job, and realised what country schools were like, she got a bit evangelical on the subject."

They were back at Monique's and someone had opened yet another bottle of wine. It was just the four of them now – Monique, Evie, Joël and Laurent – and all they seemed able to talk about was the other lunch guests.

Suddenly, after exchanging a look with Laurent who nodded, Joël told Evie and Monique about what the police had discovered in Tom's hotel room and the knives they had found in the woods.

"He wanted to kill me," Monique said in an amazingly calm voice.

"You can't be sure of that!" Evie cried out. But a look from Laurent silenced her and she realised he was right. There was no use pretending that Tom's death was some awful fluke accident. He had come to kill Monique, and he'd been stopped from killing her by being hit by a truck.

"You should come and see where he was hiding," Joël said to Monique. He knew she hadn't been near the woods since it happened. "It's not far from here. Just past that stretch of pine trees, but in a hide amongst the oaks. It's not far from where you used to go mushroom-picking. Do you know where I mean? Up near where they found those stone-age flints last year." He got to his feet. "Come on, let's go now."

Evie could see what Joël was doing. He was listing all the things Monique loved about the woods. All the things that made them familiar, that she had learnt about them in the past five years. They were her woods, not Tom's, and Joël's outstretched hand was inviting her to reclaim them.

"I'm not sure …" she said, looking to Laurent and Evie for support, but they remained silent. So Monique stood up and followed Joël, but neatly sidestepped the hand he was holding out.

Laurent and Evie were left alone. She stood up and began to gather up the glasses, taking them into the kitchen. Instead of putting them in the dishwasher, she rinsed them under the tap and began to polish them by hand. Laurent followed her but didn't say anything – he just watched her. She knew she was only doing it to keep busy, but it seemed desperately important to get each glass to a gleaming shine, so she rubbed and polished until the cotton squeaked. Finally she folded the teacloth carefully and hung it from the handle on the oven door. Then she leaned with her back against the cooker and gazed at Laurent, who looked as if he had a speech prepared.

"You got the letter I sent," he said quietly. "Was it before my e-mail or after it?"

She said nothing, but the look on her face gave him his answer.

"I'm sorry, Evie ... I wish ..."

"At least it let me know what your first opinion of me was."

They stood a few feet apart and Evie willed him with all her soul to say something to make it better. She didn't want to keep him at arm's length. She didn't even hold his mistrust against him any more. Her answering machine had confirmed that he had been phoning her every few minutes while she was in Killarney and his letter was in the post. She understood what had been going on in his head, but if she gave in too easily, it would deny him the right to try and justify himself.

"You have to understand how I felt ... I thought Alex was suffering from brain damage, and then when I discovered he wasn't ... I was feeling so guilty ..."

"We all felt guilty, Laurent. We all screwed up to some degree or another. But you were the only one who took the first opportunity you could to deflect some of your lousy feelings in another direction."

"I was the one who called Alex, Evie. I was the one who placed him there. And it was my idea to flush Tom out of the woods ..."

Evie shook her head slightly. She didn't want to go over the details of that morning again. But Laurent ignored her.

"He'd have gone after you too," he said. "Tom would have, if he'd made it to the house. He'd have hurt you too. There was no doubt in my mind and I was afraid for you.

When I phoned Alex to tell him to go down to the house, I wasn't worried about the danger I was putting him in. I didn't give a single thought as to what on earth he was going to do against Tom in the state he was in. I just wanted to put someone, anyone, between you and that madman. That morning I chose to put Alex at risk in order to save you so when I found that letter ... it was almost like I had to choose again. It was only for a few seconds, Evie, only for a few minutes at most ..."

"It's okay, Laurent," Evie said.

"It's not okay. I know it's not ... you haven't forgiven me ... I can see it in your face, in the way you're standing there ... how you've been all day. So stiff and uncomfortable, you wish you were anywhere else in the world right now rather than here with me ..."

It was so far from the truth that Evie had to silence him. She stepped towards him and kissed him in a way that told him she wanted much more. She needed to prove she was still alive amidst all the talk of death. And she needed to show Laurent that she felt the same about him as she had three months ago, and that if their situations were reversed she'd have done the same for him.

She explored the inside of his mouth with her tongue and his mouth moulded itself to hers.

Then she put her hands on his waist and pulled him closer, fitting her hips into the hollows below his. Laurent put a hand to the back of her head and guided her to the other end of the room, until he fell backwards onto the sofa. She straddled him and pulled at his shirt. In less than ten seconds they were both naked and it was all over in less than a minute.

"Come upstairs," Evie ordered, gathering up her clothes. She was afraid Monique and Joël might come back, but she wasn't ready to let go of Laurent yet. She was gone before he had a chance to object.

"Evie … we can't … you know we shouldn't do this …" he said as he came into the bedroom and saw her waiting for him in bed. He had pulled on his shorts for modesty's sake but given that he was carrying the rest of his clothes rather than wearing them, his protest sounded somewhat lame.

"Shh," Evie said. "And come here." She pulled back the covers to reveal that she hadn't put any of her clothes back on.

Laurent groaned half-heartedly, but joined her. "Seriously, Evie. We can't do this, you know that …"

♡　　♡　　♡

An hour or more had passed and Joël and Monique still weren't back. Evie and Laurent had made love a second time, slowly this time, and Evie was lying in his arms, now absolutely sure that this was where she wanted to be. This was a man she knew she could trust. Sometimes he acted too fast, without thinking, but behind those actions was an unshakeable loyalty to the people he loved. At the moment, Evie knew that she had to share that loyalty with Alex, but one day Alex would get better. He would no longer need Laurent, and then

Evie would have this wonderful, gentle man to herself. And even if she had to share him, Evie knew Laurent's heart was big enough for as many people as he wanted to love.

"Evie, you know we can't go on with this," Laurent repeated, more urgently now. "This was a really bad idea."

"What are you going on about?" Evie said lazily, sure he was about to complain about their living in different countries and the practicalities of long-distance love affairs.

"I think Alex still loves you," Laurent told her.

"What do you mean? Did he tell you? How could you have discussed me like that?" Although it felt silly, Evie pulled up the sheet to cover her breasts. Because she suddenly felt exposed, as if Laurent had invited Alex into the room with them.

"I never … well, not exactly. And he didn't say he was still in love with you, but …"

"But what?"

In a skilful movement that Evie suspected required a fair amount of practice, Laurent got out of bed, and although he had been naked only seconds ago under the sheets, now he was wearing boxer shorts.

"He never got over you, Evie. He thought you'd run off on him. And he …" Laurent hesitated. "Well, it's probably not too strong to say he hated you. But I don't think he stopped loving you either. So when Sharon goes to see him and tells him what really happened …"

"Hang on a moment, Laurent. Let me get this

straight. You think Alex, 'your good friend Alex', loves me, so you don't want to sleep with me again? You don't want to – what's the term – 'shit on your own doorstep'?"

Moments earlier she had been thinking in terms of this being the man she wanted to spend the rest of her life with. But now it was important to her that she reduce what had happened between them to nothing more than sex.

"Oh, God, it's not that … I …" He sat at the edge of the bed and put his head in his hands. "Please try to understand, Evie. We're friends, me and Alex. We've become good friends. But it's more than that – you know it is. I called him that morning, and because of me he ended up in hospital. His eyes … his face …"

Evie hugged her knees and waited for Laurent to say something else, but he didn't. He kept his head in his hands, and for all she knew he could have had his eyes closed.

"But, Laurent, we just … and the first time …" she avoided saying "the time in Alex's house", "it meant something. At least it did to me. And I'm sure it did to you too. Please don't tell me it didn't."

"Please, Evie … this isn't helping. I can't …"

Evie felt her anger build up, and not just at being rejected. She couldn't believe how her world had changed in the space of a minute. "You feel responsible for Alex's accident, so to make it up to him, you're 'giving' me to him. Is that it? Well, I'm not yours to *give*. To your 'friend' or anyone else. I can't believe you'd even think like that."

Laurent said nothing, so Evie continued.

"You took care of Alex in hospital. You solved the mystery of the little woman who dumped him all those years ago, and you hope he'll get a second chance with her. Tell me this, Laurent – sleeping with me today – what was that about?"

"Evie, I couldn't help it … I …"

But she didn't want to hear it. She was afraid it would hurt too much.

"I suppose if you slept with me today, and still walked away from me for his sake, it would be more of a gift. More of a sacrifice? It would go further towards salving your conscience. Is that it, Laurent? Or were you were just checking out the merchandise and you decided I wasn't really worth putting up a fight for?"

She tried to find the most hurtful, dishonourable accusations to throw at him, hoping he would be driven to defend himself, but knowing in her heart that he wouldn't.

"Evie, please …"

"Get out, Laurent."

Laurent looked at her for the longest time, as if he was trying to decide whether he should say something else. Evie prayed he would. For him to say anything, anything at all, would be better than this feeling of total emptiness.

Eventually he picked his jeans off the floor and pulled them up his legs. Evie had to bite her lip to stop herself from crying out, from begging him to stay, to reconsider.

"Alex is a good man, Evie. Twice the man I'll ever be. He'll be a lot better for you than I could ever be. Don't blame him for this," Laurent began when he was fully dressed.

"This isn't a courtroom, Laurent, and I'm not a child in the middle of a custody battle. I'm all grown up now, and I get to choose for myself."

"Alex is Holly's father, Evie …"

"Don't drag Holly into this," she warned. "This is between us."

"And Alex," he reminded her. "Just remember, Evie, it only took him a couple of minutes to get himself and his crutches into that car and down the road that morning. And it wasn't Monique he was rushing to protect. Do you know that when he woke up out of that coma, yours was the first name he said? It wasn't one of his kids, nor his ex-wife he called out for, but you, Evie."

Evie held her hands over her ears. "I don't want to hear about Alex. Your wonderful friend Alex! Just leave, Laurent! Just go. Get out that door and get the fuck out of my life!"

"Alex is a good man, Evie," Laurent said one last time as he left.

"But I don't love him," she moaned at the closed door. "I love …"

For a second Laurent's footsteps faltered, then he walked resolutely downstairs and slammed the front door behind him.

♡   ♡   ♡

Joël had left by the time Evie recovered enough to

come downstairs. From Monique's guarded expression, Evie guessed she must have returned in time to hear the end of her "discussion" with Laurent.

"I don't want to talk about it!" she warned Monique. "I just can't believe … oh, forget it!"

"Are you in love with him?" Monique asked.

"With Laurent?" Evie shrugged. "No! I don't know. I don't care. It doesn't matter."

"Come on, let's go for a walk," Monique suggested. "Only a few more weeks and it'll be too dark to walk through the woods at this time of the evening, and I've wasted most of the summer by not going near them."

"How did your walk with Joël go?" Evie asked.

"Okay," Monique answered, but she couldn't look Evie in the eye. "It went okay. The woods haven't changed and there's nothing for me to be afraid of there."

"And Joël?" Evie asked, sensing that he was deliberately being left out of the conversation.

Monique pursed her lips and shook her head in warning. "I didn't press you on the subject of Laurent, remember?"

Chapter 29

The following morning over breakfast, Monique surprised Evie by asking her what her plans were about allowing Alex access to Holly.

"I still have to introduce them to each other," Evie protested. "I haven't got anywhere close to thinking about 'access'. Yikes, 'access' sounds so legal, so formal. I hope to God we don't get to a stage where we're talking about 'access'."

"Sorry, I'm jumping head of myself here a bit ..." Monique had a look of fierce concentration, and Evie had a horrible feeling that she'd put a lot more thought into this than Evie had herself. "What I meant to say was, that with Alex living in France, and you in Ireland, you've got to think of the logistics of the whole visiting thing ..." She paused, then added quickly: "Unless of course you're thinking of moving over here yourself?"

"What?" Evie raised an eyebrow carefully. Monique had a nasty habit of reading her thoughts before they were even fully formed.

"I saw the way you were listening to Géraldine talk about schools yesterday. Even though you were pretending it was all a big joke. You must have thought about it, even semi-seriously if you won't admit to seriously. And you have to have given some thought to how often you're going to let him see her. Especially now that you know it wasn't his fault he lost her in the first place."

Monique was right of course. Evie *should* give some serious thought to this. But with so many unknowns, she didn't even know where to start.

"You know you're welcome to stay here any time you like ..." Monique was obviously building up to something.

"But?" Evie felt that there was a "but" coming.

"Well, I just heard that Antoine's thinking of selling his mother's old house – no, wait!" Monique laughed at Evie's wildly flapping hands. "His brother isn't that keen on selling yet, so I suggested to Antoine that he might want to rent it out instead. Just to get his brother used to the idea of someone else living there. It's been empty for ages. She lived with Antoine from the time she had her first stroke eight or nine years ago until she died last year."

"I'm not sure I –"

"Just let me finish, woman! It's a tiny place, and it

hasn't really been done up. So the rent would be negligible. I just thought that if you're going to be coming over fairly often … well, if you had your own place, it would make it easier for you to refuse an invitation to stay in Alex's. If that's what you wanted to do, of course …"

"I hadn't even thought of that!" As usual, Monique was several steps ahead of her friend. It was all very well to think that she could stay with Monique as often as she liked, but once Alex extended an invitation to stay at his place it would be very hard to refuse. And even harder to explain to Holly why they were staying with Monique rather than with New Daddy. Who had a swimming-pool.

The question was, of course, did she want to stay with Alex or did she want to keep her independence? Sharon's e-mail had opened a can of worms Evie hadn't even begun to untangle. In some ways she longed for the time when Alex was still the bad guy. It was so much easier to imagine what the future might bring. And any "access" she allowed Alex made her into Lady Bountiful.

"How are you holding up, anyway?" Evie asked Monique, eager to take the spotlight off herself. "We've never really talked about it."

Monique shrugged. "Not too bad, I guess. But I miss him …"

Evie tried to hide her gasp of horror by turning it into a sympathetic sigh. But it didn't fool Monique who looked at her wryly.

"I suppose I don't really miss Tom, but the idea of

Tom. The Tom from years ago, the one I fell in love with originally. I don't know where that Tom went. Maybe he disappeared into his own head because of whatever happened in the army. I know he went through a lot – a couple of really tough tours that he wouldn't talk about. But if I'm honest, Tom changed a long time ago, and I just held on to the hope he'd change back. Or rather that I'd change him back."

"What do you mean he changed?"

"He got more controlling … The more independent I got, the more paranoid he got. He had to know what I was doing all the time, who I was meeting. And the way he was reading all my e-mails, although I didn't know about it at the time." Monique shivered as she thought yet again of all he had been privy to. No wonder he had seemed so "sensitive" to her worries and knew what was going on in her head. By confiding different things to different people, you can feel as if you're the only person to have the whole picture, to really know the whole you. But Tom had effectively violated Monique's sense of privacy and "eavesdropped" on far too many of her inner thoughts. It didn't help that so much of Monique's communication was by e-mail. "But I can't remember it happening, so I suppose he changed slowly …"

"And you miss him …?"

"While he was alive there was always the hope he'd change back …"

"Wait, Monique," Evie interrupted. "Are you trying to tell me that right up to …" She wasn't sure how to put it. "Right up to the end … you'd have taken him back?"

Monique nodded. "I don't honestly know. But I think that deep inside there was always the hope that whatever had happened to him ... was ... I dunno ... curable?"

"And now he's dead, that hope's gone?"

Monique nodded again.

"I'm sorry, Monique ... I had no idea ..."

Evie's mother had told her that Monique was probably grieving for Tom, but she hadn't been able to imagine it. Now she was some way towards understanding.

"It's not necessarily a bad thing," Monique continued quickly. "That he's gone, I mean. Not dead, of course, but gone out of my life for good. As long as he was ... around ..." Evie sensed that she nearly said "alive". "As long as he was around, I was never going to be able to let go of him completely. I think he reminded me too much of my dad."

"Your dad?"

"My real father. Remember he died during my first year at college? He had liver cancer, and when he found out about it, he contacted me. I was nearly seventeen at the time, and I hadn't seen him since he left us when I was three. He was managing to stay off drink – he had to, if he was ever going to be considered for a new liver. But it was too late for him – he never got a transplant. But during that year I got to know him."

"And you think he was like Tom? Was Tom really drinking that heavily?"

"No, that's not exactly what I meant ... How can I explain it? My father was bitter about Mum. Although it

300

was he who left, he felt she hadn't put enough effort into 'saving him'. And although I didn't agree with him, when Tom put me in the same position …"

"You couldn't walk away from Tom because you felt it was your duty to 'save' him?"

"Does that sound crazy?"

Evie shook her head. "Do you still think like that?"

"No. To be honest, I'm not even sure I ever did. Not in so many words. But while he was still there … I guess I felt there was something I could do, that I should do… to stop him going off the deep end. I just had to discover what it was!"

Evie couldn't make out if Monique was facing her guilt for not doing enough for Tom or relieved that there was nothing else she could do, but either way, she was optimistic about her future.

Chapter 30

Evie spent the flight home worrying about the prospect of talking to Alex. By now Sharon must have spoken to him and he knew the truth. She wondered how on earth either of them could open the conversation they would need to have. As she picked up Holly and spun her round before giving her a cuddle in Dublin Airport, she wondered how on earth she was going to tell Alex he had missed nearly four years of doing that. And so she longed to talk to him but was dreading it.

"Alex started phoning the day you left," Marian said as they walked together to the airport car park. "There were about six missed calls on your phone when I went over to collect Holly's swimming things on Saturday morning, and the phone rang when I was there too. I answered it – I thought I'd better, to put him out of his misery. I told him when you'd be home, so he's bound to call again fairly soon."

Sure enough, the phone rang the moment Evie walked through the door. She looked around frantically at her mother — she wasn't ready for this. Not with Holly hanging out of her.

"You need milk and bread — I'll take Holly to the shops with me," Marian whispered as Evie's hand hovered over the receiver.

"Hello … oh, Alex … hi …" Evie felt like a teenager taking her first phone call from the school heartthrob. Outside she heard Holly protest at the sudden change in plans, then give in graciously to the offer of a comic.

Five minutes to walk to the shops, Evie calculated, however long Marian could delay her there and five minutes back. The clock was ticking.

"I'm sorry, Evie. I found out about what Sharon did," Alex blurted out. "I'm really, really sorry. I don't know what else to say. Is there anything I can say to make it less awful? I'm so sorry, Evie. I should have known you wouldn't have … Oh, God, Evie, I'm so, so, sorry."

"Hang on a minute, Alex. Slow down, I can hardly hear you, you're talking so fast. And anyway, it wasn't your fault."

"But it was more my fault than … she was my wife … it was me she was trying to hurt! And the way she fired you … and she made it look like you'd taken the money …"

"You thought I'd stolen that money from you?" Evie asked him.

"No, of course not … well … but I mean you saw the

letter … didn't you?"

"Yes, of course, sorry." This was too hard to do over the phone. She needed to be able to see his face.

Alex had obviously had the same thought

"I'm coming to Dublin," he said.

"When?"

"I'm booked on a flight coming in tomorrow."

"Oh." And then: "Tomorrow?"

There was silence on both ends of the phone. Then Alex added: "Sorry, I should have checked with you first. But I'm only staying one night. I've booked a hotel. I was hoping we could have dinner together. Just to talk. About … well, I don't know, but I feel that somehow we need to talk. I need to be back in Bristol on Tuesday for a hospital appointment. It was the only chance I had to come … I've loads of appointments … Look, I can cancel if you like… I knew I should have checked with you first …"

"Stop!" Evie interrupted. "It's alright. It's fine. Dinner's fine." Dinner was perfect actually; it was public, it was safe. There was no opportunity for emotional scenes. Alex would never make a scene in public. "You mentioned hospital appointments … I'm just surprised you're able to travel. How are you? I'm sorry I haven't been in touch …"

"I know, it's alright, things were complicated …"

You have no idea how complicated, Evie thought.

"But I'm fine. I mean, considering. My eyesight's almost back to normal in the good eye. The physio's pleased with the progress I've made getting walking again. The fractures in my legs have all healed, my hip's

… sorry, I'm sure you don't want an inventory. How are you? How's Monique?"

He didn't mention the bad eye, Evie noticed. Or the scarring.

"I'm fine. Monique's doing great. She's recovering well from the shock."

"Good, good," Alex interrupted. He sounded uncomfortable suddenly. "Listen, do you trust me to sort out dinner, or is there somewhere you'd like to –"

"That's fine," Evie said quickly. "You choose, the hotel will recommend somewhere. You can let me know tomorrow. I have your mobile number so I'll text you my work number and I'll sort out a baby-sitter …" She hesitated.

"Great, I won't keep you out late, I promise."

Suddenly Evie wanted to be off the phone. Holly and Marian would reappear any moment, and it would be hard not to mention Holly again if she was babbling noisily in the background.

"I'd better …"

"I'll let you go so …"

They both had spoken at once and laughed shyly.

"Tomorrow, then. I'll call you. Will I collect you in a taxi?"

"No!" Evie said. "It's fine. I'll make my own way. Just give me a time and a place. City centre or south side would suit me best."

"Okay, so."

"Bye."

"Bye."

"See you tomorrow."

"Right."

Evie was still holding the dead phone when her mother returned, one eyebrow raised in a silent question.

"He's coming to Dublin. Tomorrow. We're meeting for dinner."

Marian tried to hide her surprise. "Do you want me to collect Holly from playschool?"

"No, I'll collect her. Don't worry. And I haven't asked Tori to baby-sit for ages. So I really should give her a call."

Using her teenage baby-sitter would mean that Evie could come home without facing a hundred questions about her evening.

Marian looked momentarily hurt, but she smiled quickly to hide it. "Okay. But fill me in as soon as you can, won't you?"

♡   ♡   ♡

Evie had taken the bus into town and had allowed herself time for delays, so she decided to kill some time in St Stephen's Green. She wandered among people rushing home late from work, others just enjoying the evening sun and others, dressed up, obviously having a walk before dinner like herself. She looked at a man feeding the remains of a sandwich to the ducks. Two of the ducks hopped out of the water to investigate the empty paper bag in his hand, and the baby in the buggy he was pushing screeched with pleasure and delight. Alex had missed all that with Holly. Although she still loved to feed ducks, she was much too "sophisticated" now to show such glee and surprise in public.

He had booked a table in Bleu on Dawson Street, and Evie approached the restaurant from the other side of the street. She was deliberately about ten minutes late, and she could see Alex seated at a table by the window. He was obviously uncomfortable to have been placed there, and although he had chosen to sit with his back to the window, in the few moments she was crossing the road, Evie saw him put a hand to the back of his neck twice, as if he felt someone looking at him.

He stood up when he heard her introduce herself at the desk, and despite what he had said on the phone, he didn't seem totally at ease on his feet. He walked towards her stiffly and greeted her halfway to the table. He laid his a hand on her arm and kissed her quickly on one cheek. Then he led her the rest of the way, dismissing the maitre d', and pulled out her chair for her.

Evie didn't know whether to look into his face or not. The bad eye was covered in surgical tape and some kind of soft dressing. The good eye was very bloodshot but otherwise normal. Another dressing covered most of his cheek from just above his lip to where it met the eye dressing, so she had no idea what the scar underneath would look like. She decided to look into his face as normal and concentrate on his good eye.

They looked at each other awkwardly for a few seconds, unsure of what to say. A waiter appeared and hovered at the table.

"Are you driving, Evie?" Alex asked, before turning to him. When she answered that she had taken the bus and would be getting a taxi home, he nodded and the waiter left. He returned a few seconds later with an ice bucket on a stand and two glasses. The wine waiter came up behind him with a bottle of champagne.

"Oh, Alex …" Evie was about to protest.

"I thought the occasion called for it?"

He seemed so unsure of himself that all Evie could do was smile and feign delight.

A discreet pop, hardly a drop spilled and suddenly they were alone again, facing each other across the table.

"A toast!" Alex insisted, holding up his glass.

Evie raised hers too and held it touching his, waiting to see what he was going to propose.

"To finding each other after all these years. To the truth. To being able to forget the past?"

"I'll drink to that!" Evie agreed. "But I'd like to add – to you. To your continuing recovery and putting the accident behind you."

She hoped mentioning the accident might force them both to acknowledge his injuries, but he just looked down and sipped his drink in silence.

Before Evie had a chance to wonder what to say next, the waiter took their orders, then Alex was asking after Monique, and soon they were chatting easily. She brought him up to date, though she was surprised how much he already knew. He explained that Laurent had been keeping him informed.

Then Evie asked him was it true he planned to go

ahead with his move to France, and he nodded.

"As soon as I can. I still have to come back and forth for some appointments, but I intend to be out of the UK by the fifteenth of September at the latest. That's the day Sharon's getting married."

Now that Sharon had been mentioned, it was as though she had joined them and hung about near their table like a huge green gooseberry.

Fortunately, at just that moment their main courses were served and distracted them long enough to banish Alex's ex-wife. Evie let him lead the conversation, bringing her up to date with his life, mainly because that gave her an excuse to postpone bringing up the subject of Holly. Last night she had liked the idea of a restaurant – now she felt it was too public and that everyone was over-aware of them anyway because of the dressings on Alex's face.

Alex refused the offer of dessert, so Evie did too, despite his protests.

"And it's too hot for coffee. Let's go for a walk, and maybe we can get an ice-cream later," she suggested instead.

"Good idea!" he agreed and signalled the waiter again.

Out on the street, however, Evie realised that a walk was not a good idea. Before they had gone even a hundred yards Alex slowed to a painfully slow pace and was limping.

"It's not actually that sore," he reassured her. "But apparently I had quite a lot of muscle wasting ..."

Evie looked around helplessly for somewhere they

could sit down. Alex hailed a taxi.

"I've got a suite in the hotel. It's got a lovely living room and even a balcony. We can order anything we like off the room-service menu."

Evie didn't argue, although Alex's hotel suite was not where she had imagined spending her evening. But she still hadn't told him about Holly, and she wasn't going home until she had. At least in a hotel they would get some privacy.

"That's better!"

The suite, when they reached it, was actually a medium-sized apartment. Evie's eyes opened wide at the luxury as she looked around. Tall windows looked out over a leafy park, and one of them opened onto a small balcony on which a breakfast table and two chairs were arranged. Heavy doors opened onto what Evie assumed were the bedroom and bathroom, and there was a small kitchen recessed into an alcove.

"I have coffee, if you'd like it. Or tea ... Earl Grey, English Breakfast, Lapsang ... Oh and here are some fruit teas ... and biscuits ..." Alex was rooting through the cupboards like an excited child. He was much more relaxed now that he was away from public scrutiny and Evie wondered had he chosen to stay here, with everything on hand, to avoid having to venture out in public, or even down to the hotel dining room. She wondered if dinner had been a huge ordeal for him.

"There's beer in the fridge," he continued with the inventory, "and water, wine, more champagne …"

"Water sounds great. Sparkling if they have it."

"I'm going to have a beer." Alex expertly flicked the top off the glass beer bottle and drank straight from it, emptying half before he sat down opposite Evie. He put his hand to the dressing on his cheek and pressed against it, then rubbed it.

"Does it hurt?" she asked.

"Which bit?" he grunted. "Both legs hurt now after walking on them, my shoulder where …"

"Your face."

He hesitated. It was obvious that he didn't like talking about it. "Yes, the bad eye is … oh, shit … I don't know what all the secrecy is. There *is* no bad eye. It's gone. They had to remove it."

Evie tried to conceal her shock.

"In time I'll get an artificial, plastic eye, but I have to wait for the wound to heal and the implant they put in the back of my socket to settle." He was embarrassed but seemed glad to have the subject out in the open. "And yes, it hurts, but I'm on so many painkillers that I'm okay. The real killer is the scar on my face though. It itches like crazy. Apparently that's a good sign, it means it's healing well, but at the moment …" He pressed his hand to it again.

"When does the dressing come off?"

"The dressing?" Alex looked wary.

"When does it come off?"

"I … that is …"

Evie had heard Laurent talking about it to his mother

at Monique's lunch. About how Alex could take the dressing off now, in fact it needed to be exposed for a few hours each day, but that he preferred to keep it covered. She needed to see it before she went home tonight, otherwise it would keep her awake all night wondering about it.

"May I?" She reached forward and put one hand to the tape running below his nose. It was one of those papery tapes, which hardly sticks at all, which is why she guessed it was mainly cosmetic.

Alex didn't move, so she took his silence as assent. She peeled the tape back carefully and lifted the dressing. It came away completely clean, because the skin underneath had healed over.

But what she saw didn't look like skin she was used to seeing. Along the centre, where the washing-line pole had cut, was a deep purple gash. It was shiny, as though stretched tight. Rising towards the edge of the scar, the tissue became paler red, but it never quite matched the colour of the unharmed skin. The dressing over his eye was still in place. Evie looked at it questioningly but Alex shook his head.

She laid her hand along the length of the scar, and to her surprise it felt warm and soft. She wasn't sure what she had expected. Perhaps something cold and slimy, or smooth and hard. Or maybe even dry and scaly like snakeskin. In fact, it was more natural to the touch than it was to look at.

There were tears flowing out of Alex's good eye now and Evie tried to imagine what was happening in the sightless cavern on the other side. Was it too filling up with salty water?

She began to stroke his face like a child's. "It's okay, Alex, it's okay," she repeated over and over until at last he put his head on her shoulder and wept. She wasn't to know that this was the first time he'd cried since coming out of his coma.

And as they sat there, and as she held him in her arms, Evie knew that Laurent was right. If Alex still loved her, she would have to do her best to rediscover her love for him. And if she couldn't, then she could leave him for any other man on earth besides the Frenchman who had sent him to this. Her sadness only lasted an instant, then it was replaced by gentle resignation.

"Thanks," Alex said at last, reaching into his pocket for a hankie.

Evie wasn't sure what she had done to help, but she felt that she had just experienced one of the most intimate moments of her life.

"Listen, Alex, there's something I need to tell you."

Suddenly she wished she hadn't touched him and that he hadn't cried in front of her. She was afraid that exposing himself like that put him at a disadvantage. He might hate her for what she was about to tell him.

"What is it?"

"When I left Bristol that time …"

"Yes?"

"I …" Evie hated the way Alex was staring so intently at her. Especially as it was only one eye, a bloodshot eye at that.

"Go on, Evie, it's okay," he encouraged.

"I was pregnant."

"Your daughter, Holly. She's mine?"

Evie nodded. She tried to read his face, but he had learnt to keep his emotions hidden. She wished she knew if he was stunned, angry or disbelieving … or had so much happened to him in the past few months that nothing surprised him any more?

"She looks like you," she said.

She stood up and went to her handbag, which she had left by the door. She took out a photo album and handed it to him.

Then she went and stood by the window, leaving him in privacy to leaf his way through Holly's first four years. It was a collection of the best of the pictures; she had been putting them together, for this exact purpose, since her daughter was born. She was struggling hard to contain her own emotions, because she felt that this was Alex's time. His time to discover Holly. And although it wasn't Evie's fault that they had split, it had been her decision not to tell him he had another daughter. She was afraid he'd hold it against her, and he was entitled to. For no matter what Evie told herself, she realised that a tiny part of her had been punishing Alex for leaving her. He didn't know what he was missing at the time, which made the punishment less cruel, but nonetheless, Evie had to acknowledge that her motives in keeping Holly from him hadn't been entirely pure. And the more delightful Holly became with each passing day, the stronger she felt in her recovery from his betrayal.

She didn't join him again until she heard a sob-like gasp of breath. Then she crossed the room and looked over his shoulder. He had returned to the first picture, a picture Marian had taken in Holles Street Hospital within minutes of Holly's birth. In it, Evie was exhausted but elated, and Holly's face was screwed up in angry concentration as the midwife tried to put her to Evie's breast. Alex was stroking his thumb across the plastic protecting the photo as though he could bridge time and let his daughter know she was welcome from the moment of her birth.

"She's beautiful," he croaked. "You're both so bloody beautiful. I missed you so much, Evie, I hated you for leaving, but ..."

"It's in the past, remember?" she interrupted. "It doesn't matter any more." She was afraid of where this conversation might lead and she still didn't know how she felt about him. "We have to go forward now – you have to meet Holly. You have to meet your daughter."

The tension between them slowly evaporated as they made plans. Alex agreed their first meeting had to be special. And he wanted it to be in France.

"Are you sure ...?" Evie was uneasy – he hadn't been back since the accident. "Would you not prefer to be on more familiar territory ... I could bring her to Bristol."

"No," he insisted vehemently. "My home's in Ste Anne now. And I couldn't bear to bring her to Bristol yet. Too many memories. And my other kids are there. I know I have to tell them, but I want to keep Holly to myself for a while."

Chapter 31

Two weeks later, Evie and Holly arrived in Bergerac airport and Evie tried not to look too nervous as she collected their bags.

"Is that my daddy?" Holly whispered, pointing to the stern-faced man checking passports.

"No, darling. We'll drive to Monique's," Evie reminded her for what felt like the hundredth time, "and then we'll walk up to another house near hers, and you'll meet your daddy there."

Evie had thought it best to warn Holly in advance of what was coming, but she hoped she wasn't going to point to every man she met now that they were on French soil and ask was that her daddy. She had taken the fact that she was going to meet Alex for the first time very calmly. The fact that he lived in another country and that he and Evie had "lost" each other seemed to satisfy her curiosity as to why they hadn't met until now. She had looked a little worried at the concept of people "losing" each other until Evie reassured her that mummies never "lost" their bestest, favouritest girls in the whole wide world.

Evie had a key but Monique was already at home by the time they arrived.

"I finished a bit early – I was showing a property near here and it wasn't worth going back to the office," she said when Evie said she hoped she wasn't missing work on their account. "Hi gorgeous," she scooped Holly into her arms. "Are you looking forward to your little holiday?"

"It's not a real holiday," Holly explained seriously. "I've come to France to meet my daddy. I hope you don't mind, Monique, but you're not my only France person now."

"I'll have to think about that ..." Monique sat the little girl on the edge of the kitchen counter and spoke seriously. "Let me see. Will you still visit me every time you come to France?"

Holly looked at her mother for confirmation and then nodded solemnly.

"And will you still be my favourite godchild? And will I still be your favourite godmother?"

"Of course," Holly said with mock world-weariness. "You're my *only* godmother."

"Well, in that case," Monique smiled, "I *don't* mind that I'm not your only France person any more!"

"My daddy's called Alex, and he has a swimming-pool," Holly explained. "He has other children, but they live in England with their mummy. Like I live in Ireland with my mummy. And I don't think they've been in the swimming-pool, so I'll be the first." She held out her arms to be lifted down off the counter and ran outside to check that the swing was still attached to a low branch of an oak tree at the end of the garden.

"You're going to have a busy weekend," Monique predicted, looking after Holly as she ran up the garden. "I bet you'll be glad to get back to work and only have to answer questions about the Internet, the algorithms of search engines and why a particular client's rank has dropped after the latest Google re-jig."

"I know," Evie groaned. "You wouldn't believe some of the questions she's come up with. She asked Mum would she have to be a granny for Alex's other kids!"

"Mmm," Monique laughed. "I can almost see those little brain-cogwheels turning from here."

The next morning, Friday, Evie got up at the same time as Monique who was getting ready for work. Mainly because Holly was jumping up and down on her stomach and asking was it Daddy Day yet. She had told Alex she would drop in mid-morning, when it was warm enough to swim, because the swimming-pool seemed like a good icebreaker.

"Eat something," Monique ordered as Evie sipped on her second mug of coffee.

"Ugh!" Evie wrinkled her nose in distaste. "I'm not sure if I'll ever be able to eat anything ever again. I swear – I'm more nervous than I was on the first morning of the Leaving Cert. Or the day I did my driving test. Or before my first job interview –"

"Okay, I get the idea. You're nervous. Here, have a croissant anyway."

"My first real job interview was with Alex's company. He interviewed me, along with Mike, the head of the Internet section. And Alex's wife ... Sharon."

"Stop thinking about it," Monique insisted. "And if you don't want to eat that croissant, then pull it to bits and play with it. It'll give you something to do with your hands. If you look at your watch one more time – stop it – you'll wear it out!"

"Finished!" Holly yelled triumphantly from the other end of the room, where she had been working on a jigsaw. "Can I get dressed now?" She was still in her pyjamas, as Evie was determined to keep her pink cotton dress clean, at least until they got to Alex's.

"Why don't you take her for a walk?" Monique suggested. "I'm off to work in a minute, and you're going to drive each other demented. You've another two hours to kill."

"I don't want to tire her," Evie explained. Holly tired was not a pleasant sight. Definitely not a good first impression.

"Then ring Alex and go up early. He's probably up there looking out the window for you already. He's only been in France three days and he's already phoned me about ten times to ask if there's anything he could help me with to get ready for the two of you."

Evie grimaced when she heard this and remembered what Monique had said two weeks ago about renting Antoine's mother's place. And she was right. Depending on how today went, Evie would definitely have to think about where to stay when she visited France. There was no way Alex was going to wait long before suggesting that she and Holly stay with him. He was probably rehearsing it already: the huge house all to himself, the pool on hand for Holly to swim in, being able to leave some of her things there permanently … Whatever about Holly having a small collection of toys and maybe clothes in Alex's, there was no way Evie could contemplate it. You didn't leave things at a man's house unless …

"Monique," Evie said quickly as her friend kissed Holly goodbye, "Antoine hasn't done anything about finding a tenant yet, has he?"

♡　　♡　　♡

In the end, after spending as long as she could getting ready, Evie rang Alex to check if they could come early. He answered on the first ring.

The last time Evie had walked from Monique's to Alex's house she had been with Laurent. This journey was slower, and whereas she and Laurent hadn't said a word until they came to the bottom of the drive, Holly couldn't stop talking.

"Maybe I can take Alex to Mimi's shop some day," she said hopefully as they passed it. (Holly loved shops, of all kinds, so long as they stocked chocolate, ice cream or toys. Mimi's little shop in Ste Anne qualified on all counts.) "Do you think he knows his way to the shop? Or will I have to show him where it is? I bet I know it better than he does. I've been there at least seventy-eight times." (Seventy-eight being Holly's latest "big" number – best translated as infinity.)

"Do you think he knows about the ducks on the lake? Do you think he'd like to feed them? Will I tell him about the tadpoles and the frog jelly we found there? He might be afraid, but I'd hold his hand.

"Does his house have a wood, like Monique's does? Does he have a garden? Does he have swings? I don't mind if he doesn't have swings because he has a pool. Did you remember to bring my armbands?"

Suddenly though, Holly went quiet. They were turning into the driveway, and she guessed that the house at the top must be their destination. She took a firm hold of Evie's hand, and whereas she had been skipping ahead all the way through the village, now she fell back half a step behind her mother.

The front door opened before they were halfway up the drive and Alex stopped on the doorstep. Evie was relieved to see that he had removed the larger dressing, the one that ran from his lip to his brow. It left his scar exposed, although he still had a smaller dressing in his eye socket. He obviously remembered the fascination plasters of all kinds held for young children. A scar, although shocking at first glance, would soon be beyond notice, whereas there were a million questions to be answered about a plaster. Evie had decided not to warn Holly about the scar – mainly because she wasn't sure how to. If she'd implied it was something that Holly needed to be pre-warned about, Holly would build it up into a huge thing before she met her father. So Evie had said simply that Alex had been in a car crash and left it at that. When Holly asked did he get a "bump", Evie said he had but she didn't know where.

But now Evie wished she had said something. She was worried what Holly might say, and Alex was sensitive about it. But no sooner had she thought that, than she realised that Holly spontaneous would probably be charming. Whereas Holly rehearsed was likely to say completely the wrong thing.

These musings brought Evie and Holly to the top of the drive. Holly had slowed right down and was now almost dragging backwards. Alex was staring so intently at her that it was as though he was trying to memorise her. As though she was about to be whipped away and he would have to pass a test on her.

"Hi, Alex!" Evie tried to break off his scrutiny; she could feel Holly's nerves zapping up her arm.

"Evie, hi!" He looked away, with difficulty, for as long as it took to greet her. "And this is … let me guess … Holly?"

"Why is he guessing, Mummy? Didn't you tell him my name?"

Alex laughed out loud. "Serve me right for being patronising! Yes, darling. Your mummy did tell me. I just forget sometimes. Do you ever forget things?"

Holly looked up at Evie, who nodded her reassurance.

"Sometimes," the little girl shrugged. "But *I* didn't forget *your* name. You're Alex. And you're my daddy."

"Wow!"

The word dealt Alex a body blow. It was a few seconds before he caught enough breath back to agree with her.

"That's right. I'm Alex. And I *am* your daddy. And I'm very, *very* happy to be meeting you at long last."

"You'll have to be more careful in future," Holly warned him primly.

"Careful?"

"You lost Mummy, and I'm much smaller."

Alex laughed again. "If I promise to be very, very careful, will you come inside?"

"Is your swimming-pool inside? I have new swimming togs. Brand new. They're pink. I've never, ever worn them before. Not even to swim club."

"Well, the swimming pool isn't inside, but you have to go through the house to get to it. Do you want to come and see it?"

Holly looked up to her mother one more time for reassurance, then reached up and took the hand Alex was offering. As they walked into the hall, Evie heard Holly tell her father that she hoped the "ouch" on his face would get better soon.

♡   ♡   ♡

"And to think I was nervous," Evie laughed a while later, as she and Alex sipped orange juice and Holly spread a choc-ice all over a sun-lounger. (She would have to re-educate Alex on the type of ice creams suitable for small girls. Magnums might be delicious, but only a small fraction of them ever found their way inside a small girl.)

"*You* were nervous?" Alex looked at her in disbelief. "I haven't slept in three nights with the nerves. What did you have to be nervous about? She already adores you, that much is obvious. And you know every last thing about her."

Evie wanted to tell him that it wasn't a competition, that no one would be measuring how fast or how well his relationship with Holly developed, but she was afraid it would sound condescending. Instead she said: "You've far more experience as a parent than I have. Surely you remember what the 'first' time at anything is like? The first time at the supermarket – you're afraid they'll scream and draw everyone's attention. The first day at playschool – you're worried they'll be off in the corner like Johnny No-Friends. The first time in the swimming-pool without swimmies – you keep looking for that bulge in their togs. And I'm sure I – or rather now, *we*, will have plenty of more 'firsts' to get nervous about."

It was the right thing to say. From the moment Evie deferred to his experience as a parent, Alex began to relax. And when she referred to the two of them as "we" he began to positively beam.

"Hey, talking of swimming," he pointed at the pool, "I hope you brought your togs too!"

"Of course." Evie stood up and was about to lead the way to the changing room when she remembered that Alex had never shown her where it was. It wouldn't be a good time to let him know that she and Laurent had made extensive use of it in June. So she asked him coyly if she and Holly could use one of the bedrooms to change in, then showed full appreciation as he opened the door beside the pool for them.

"We won't be more than a couple of minutes. Then you can go in," Evie promised as Holly disappeared inside.

Alex shook his head. "No, I can't …" He lifted his hand towards his face.

Evie had almost stopped noticing his eye.

"You used to love swimming," Evie said carefully, thinking back to the thirty or forty lengths he used to put in before work every morning. She wondered was he worried about having to change a damp dressing in front of them, or was he genuinely not supposed to swim.

"I know and I'll get back to it. But the wound in there is very prone to infection – I have to be careful not to get it wet …"

"Come on, Mummy!" An impatient voice called from inside the changing room. "Do my buttons!"

"*Un*do my buttons *please*, Mummy," Evie corrected fondly, and then she went in to obey orders.

♡   ♡   ♡

Alex went back and sat down under the sun-umbrella while he waited for them. He couldn't believe how "normally" Evie was behaving. He felt a sense of anti-climax. He didn't know what he had been expecting, and he knew that the hours they had spent together so far had been amazing, special, unbelievable, but somehow the whole morning had lacked drama. Maybe it was because Holly was so young and so accepting of what the world threw at her. Maybe it was because at least two of the children in her playgroup had "daddies who lived in different houses" to quote Evie quoting Holly. But from the moment they were born, Alex had been at the very centre of his first three children's universes, whereas Holly seemed to regard him merely as an interesting newcomer. He sighed. It would take time, he supposed, and at least he had time. In the past few days his anger at his ex-wife had dissipated somewhat. She had no idea what she had set in motion with those letters. And Alex had come so close to losing everything that it wasn't hard to be grateful for second chances.

He pressed against the dressing in his eye to relieve an itch. He hadn't been completely honest with Evie. He could remove his dressing. But whatever about the scar on his face, Alex couldn't bear the sight of the gaping void in his skull that used to house his eye. And so he couldn't bear the thought of exposing it to anyone else, at least until he had the plastic replacement in place.

♡   ♡   ♡

"I think Alex is nice," Holly whispered seriously and studied her mother for a sign of approval. When she smiled Holly went on: "And I like his pool. And his house. *And* his telly." Monique only had French channels, and no DVD player, so although Holly enjoyed watching French cartoons on a Saturday morning, she missed her favourite programmes and being able to play her DVDs. "Alex said I could come and watch his DVD. Will you come too? Why has Alex got a hole where his eye is? I thought it was a plaster on a bump, but then the plaster would stick out, not in."

That would teach Evie to assume anything about Holly, she thought. They were both changed, and Holly was about to go out to the pool, so Evie had to think fast. What would Alex prefer her to say? Act ignorant, or explain and break the ice? And should she tell Holly not to say anything and risk having it all build up inside until it exploded in the most inappropriate and insensitive way?

"Come here, sweetheart," Evie said. "Your hair bobbins are crooked. I'll straighten them up for you before you go out again."

While she brushed Holly's hair and re-tied her pigtails, Evie explained carefully that Alex had damaged his eye in the accident (she was careful not to say "lost" – Holly would be certain to chide him again over his carelessness). "So he has a hole there for now, but when it gets better he'll get a pretend eye."

"Wow! Cool!"

Either Holly sensed that Alex didn't want to discuss his eye yet, or she needed to think about it a bit more before raising the subject, but the swim was uneventful apart from plenty of showing off on Holly's part, and even, as her courage built up, a few splashes aimed in her new daddy's direction. Then they had lunch together and Holly looked exhausted so Evie suggested they go back to Monique's so she could have a nap.

"She could sleep here," Alex suggested. "Maybe on the couch in the living room ..." He looked over his shoulder to the room and Holly, following his gaze, realised it was the room with the big television screen.

"Or I could watch a DVD! What DVDs do you have?"

Holly was outgrowing her afternoon nap so Evie had taken to letting her watch a cartoon or film for a half an hour or so after lunch like she did in playschool. If she was really tired, she'd fall asleep in front of it.

Alex looked panicked. This was his first big test – his choice of DVDs. "Why don't you come and see?"

Evie let them go, and Holly, as soon as she was sure that she would be able to reach Evie easily through the French doors from the living room, trotted after Alex to examine his collection.

"Phew!" He wiped his brow theatrically as he re-emerged. "I passed!"

"What's she watching?" Evie asked, not because she was worried his choice was inappropriate, but because Alex wanted to be told how clever he was to have chosen the right film.

"It was a toss up between *Finding Nemo* and *The Little Mermaid*."

"Good choices! Which won?"

"*The Little Mermaid*."

"She's more tired than she looks." Holly had chosen a film she had watched so often that she could recite most of the lines. The reassurance of repetition was a wonderful balm for exhaustion. "She'll be asleep within ten minutes."

Evie stood up to clear the table, but Alex reached out and touched her arm.

"Leave it. I can do it later. I want to talk to you."

Evie sat down again. They sat in silence for a few minutes until they were sure that Holly was engrossed in her film, then Alex told Evie he had set up a bank account for her so that he could deposit money into it easily.

"For Holly and you, expenses, whatever." He reddened. He was used to letting his solicitor deal with things like this. But Evie hadn't asked him for anything, and he suspected she had no intention of doing so.

She didn't answer. She hadn't thought this far ahead, but his offer stung. It was still so soon, and he was presenting it as a *fait accompli* rather than as an issue up for discussion.

"Alex, I didn't … that wasn't why …"

"Evie, I know. Please don't make this more difficult. Look, I set up an investment account for each of my children as soon as they were born. Holly'll get the same.

It'll go towards education, the deposit on a house, a business start up – whatever they need. It's for when they're older. This is different. This is for day-to-day stuff. It's no more than Sharon gets for each of the others …"

"Alex, I really don't think –" She didn't want to be compared to Sharon and she couldn't believe he'd be so insensitive as to bring up his ex-wife in a context like this.

"Please, Evie, she's my daughter too."

So you don't need to buy a share in her, she wanted to say. "We're not short of anything, Alex …"

"Look, Evie, if you don't want to spend it, then don't. It'll sit there and accumulate and Holly can add it onto the other account when she's old enough. But to be honest, it would probably be more useful to you both now, as it's a current account so the interest is non-existent."

"Let me think about it," Evie said at last. All her instincts told her to turn it down, to keep her independence and not give Alex any financial power over them, but could she do that? Could she turn down Alex's money and then worry the next time she had to bring Holly to see a consultant for her asthma?

"Okay. But I know that just coming to France this weekend involved you in extra cost. I can't expect you to foot that. And it wouldn't be reasonable to expect you to have to call me up for the money or tickets any time you wanted to bring Holly to visit me."

"You could come to Dublin occasionally. I'm sure Holly would love to show you her home." But Evie knew he was right, no matter how uncomfortable it made her feel.

"I will come to Dublin, of course. Soon." Alex sensed she was thawing and decided not to push things any further.

Chapter 32

The next day, Evie and Holly weren't going up to Alex's until the afternoon, because he had a designer coming to look at the two rooms he hadn't decorated yet and at the huge attic space which Laurent was converting to a studio for him.

"So, do you want to look at Antoine's mother's place?" Monique asked over breakfast. She had got hold of the key when she went down to the shop for bread, and waved it in front of Evie now.

"Definitely. In fact, I don't even need to look at it. I'll take it no matter what it's like."

She had explained to Monique the previous evening about how she felt she was losing her independence.

"I think you're overreacting," Monique said carefully. "Of course he's going to want to help out financially. It's not a macho masculine thing, or about control, it's just basic decency. It's a pity more men don't feel the same way."

"We've managed fine up to now without him."

Monique didn't argue. She knew Evie was honest enough to come to the fair conclusion herself.

"Okay, fair enough, you don't have to say it." Evie proved Monique right. "He didn't have much choice in the matter up to now. But it's hard to get used to someone else being involved. I suppose I have to consult him about major decisions to do with Holly now too?"

"And you wouldn't have done that if he hadn't offered to help out financially?"

"Of course I would, he's her father and now that I know …" Evie realised what Monique was up to and batted her friend playfully across the head. "Okay, I give up. Just stop trying to tie me up in moral knots!"

♡   ♡   ♡

The house looked tiny from the outside. It was on the turning off Ste Anne's main street, just past Antoine's café. In fact it was about halfway between Alex and Monique's houses, which made it ideal for Evie, because it was easily visible from the main road so Alex and Monique would pass it every day and would be able to keep an eye on it for her when she wasn't there. It was separated from the small side street by a tidily laid out little yard with two large empty flower urns and several concrete window-boxes. A high stone wall enclosing a side garden hid the side and back of the house.

Monique opened the front door. "Try to see past the dust and cobwebs. The place hasn't been in lived in for years."

Despite that, someone had obviously looked after it. The front door led into a cool, tiled hallway, off which Evie saw three recently painted wooden doors. The first door led into a small, beamed living room with a chimney and cast-iron stove insert.

"Antoine assures me the stove works fine. He lit a few fires in here every winter and had the chimney cleaned regularly to reassure his mother that she could move back in whenever she felt ready to."

Evie pictured the old lady pottering about her house, wishing she had the confidence to live on her own, then wandering sadly back to her son's house behind the café.

The kitchen and a small bathroom took up the rest of the ground floor. The kitchen was a reasonable size – the table by the back window would seat six at a squeeze although it really needed to be pushed against the wall to allow you to move at all – but the facilities were basic – a hob and no oven, just a gaping space where it should have been. The fridge was also missing.

"Obviously Antoine would put those back in if he got a tenant," Monique promised. "But don't expect the latest in luxury. They'd be clean and safe – I'd make sure of that – but cheap. And probably second hand."

"That wouldn't be a problem."

Evie liked the feel of the place. It was small enough that she could imagine herself and Holly walking in the door and feeling at home straight away, and similarly being able to walk out the door without having too much to do before a flight home to Dublin.

As she thought about it, she got a buzz of excitement. And a surreal feeling. What on earth was she doing here? This was crazy. She wasn't a second-home type of person.

"Let's look upstairs."

The two bedrooms under the roof were small. One fit a double bed, but with very little room to spare, the other barely fit a single. But the landing held a huge, elegant mahogany armoire that would provide all the storage Evie could possibly need.

She looked out the window.

"You can use the garden of course," Monique was saying. "And there's room to park a car – those gates at the back lead onto a laneway. Antoine uses those barns for storage, so he will need to get in and out occasionally, but he'll make sure they're locked and safe for Holly to be around."

"The garden" consisted of a small patch of yellowing grass and a terrace under a tangle of vines and ivy growing on a rickety-looking trellis. It wasn't clear from above, but Evie imagined she saw bunches of purple grapes hanging down in front of the back door.

"It's bound to cost me way too much," she mumbled, not wanting to build her hopes up. She loved the place. She could just imagine sitting on that little terrace with a big bowl (it would have to be a bowl if she were over here regularly) of café au lait, tapping away at her computer, while keeping an eye on Holly.

Then Monique told her the rent, and she sighed. Even with Alex's money …

"No, sweetheart, that's per month, not per week."

And Evie's mouth fell open as she totted it up. "No way! That means the yearly rent is about what you'd pay for a *month* for a house that size in some parts of Dublin!"

"But this isn't Dublin. And anyway, Antoine wants a fairly 'informal' agreement. Really just from month to month. Cash. No contract. So if he suddenly decides to sell …"

"Will he?"

"Not in the short term, if he feels the place is being lived in and paying for itself. And it'll be a while before he can afford to build somewhere else for storage. So no, in the short term, say a couple of years anyway, it's yours."

"Let me think about it," Evie said as they went downstairs again and locked up. "Come on, let's go back to the house and rescue Joël."

Joël had "dropped by" Monique's on the way to check on one of his vineyards and offered to play with Holly while they looked at the house. He had seemed surprised to see Evie and asked her if Laurent knew she was in France. Then he looked embarrassed that he had even revealed that his friend might be interested in the information and changed the subject before Evie could even answer.

"Do you want me to ask Joël not to mention seeing you?" Monique asked now as they walked back to the house. "I know you didn't want to go around saying hello to everyone on such a short trip."

"No, it's alright. As long as he knows why I'm over. I presume it's general knowledge now about Alex and Holly?"

"Kind of. Village mentality," Monique explained with a grimace. But then she smiled fondly and Evie guessed she was coming to appreciate the closeness of their little community.

"So have you seen much of Joël?" she asked.

"Don't, Evie. Please," Monique begged. "It's too soon."

"I'm not trying to match-make. I was just genuinely interested."

"It's got kind of difficult."

They were nearly back at the house and from the road they could hear Holly's shrieks of delight. No doubt she had persuaded Joël to push her on the swing.

"Come on," Evie said decisively. "They sound happy enough – they'll survive for another few minutes."

She led the way to a small stone bench at the edge of the road. It was beside a cracked concrete shelter, out of place in the picturesque scene. Rumour had it that it was once a bus-stop, but no one had seen any bus other than the school bus go through the village in living memory.

In the shade of a fig-tree, whose fruit was just beginning to turn purple in the September sun, Evie let Monique talk.

"Ever since the accident, Joël's been … I don't know how to describe it … attentive, might be the best word. He just drops by occasionally to say hi. Sometimes he points out some job on the house that might need to be done – spraying the drive was a recent one – and offers to do it. And I keep turning down his help. Sometimes I've even made an excuse and rushed out, saying I have a property to show or that I have to meet a client. And he must know it's not true, especially on a Saturday – I hardly ever do Saturdays any more."

"Why? Do you not feel comfortable around him any more? I thought you were good friends?"

"We were. We are, I hope, still. But …"

Monique went quiet and Evie could see that she couldn't fully understand herself what had happened between her and Joël so she decided to help her tease it out.

"Before …" Evie waved her hand in the general direction of the house and where the crash had taken place, to avoid actually referring to Tom's death, "did you think that things might have developed further between you and Joël?"

Monique nodded dumbly.

"And how did you feel about that? Were you glad? Do you think you could have been happy with Joël?"

"I'm not sure how I felt … I didn't feel 'free' of Tom, free to get involved with someone else. So I suppose any hint that Joël was falling for me was … I won't say unwelcome … but maybe scary would be the best word."

"You were scared of Tom?"

"No, strangely enough, though I don't expect you to understand that. More scared of myself. Of having to take a decision. Scared of taking the wrong decision.

Afraid of 'leading Joël on' and then letting him down."

"And now?"

Monique looked confused. "What do you mean?"

"How do you feel now about the idea of something further developing between you and Joël?"

"I can't think like that … it's too soon …"

"Oh come on, Monique! That's crap!"

"What?"

"You ended it with Tom well over a year ago. *You* ended it. If he hadn't come after you, if you hadn't seen him at all in the intervening time … Suppose you heard that he'd been hit by a bus in Bristol, can you imagine letting that stand in the way of your happiness with someone else?"

"Well, I suppose not, but that's different. That would be an accident … I'd have been sad, of course, but I wouldn't have felt …"

"Felt what, Monique?" Evie asked as her friend came to a strangled stop. "Felt responsible, isn't that it? You feel responsible for Tom's death and too guilty to be happy yourself."

"Maybe … I don't know," she said at last. "I don't know if you're right or wrong. It's too much to take in at the moment. But I still don't know what to do about Joël."

"Nothing, for the moment. Just accept his friendship. But don't turn him away because you think you don't deserve a shot at happiness."

"You make it sound so bloody simple!" Monique groaned wearily. "So, Mrs Psychologist of the Year, turn your gaze on yourself for a moment and tell me – are you going to take Antoine's house? And does that mean that there's definitely no chance of you and Alex getting together 'for the sake of the children'?"

♡ ♡ ♡

Holly was glad to see them but when it looked like that meant Joël would be leaving, she suggested that they might want to go out again, because she was playing "pony" (Holly being the rider and Joël the unfortunate four-legged creature) and Mummy or Monique just weren't as good at it.

Joël refused their offer of coffee, but when he heard that Evie would be out for the afternoon, he asked Monique would she like to come and look at a field of vines he was thinking of buying. He issued the invitation in a tone that sounded practised, and his face had almost composed itself into a "that's alright maybe some other time" expression, when to his surprise Monique accepted. It threw him for a moment, and his glance darted between the two women in confusion, before he broke into a wide grin and promised to pick up Monique at half two.

"That poor boy," Evie scolded after he was gone. "He reminded me of a puppy so used to being kicked that he didn't know what to do with chocolate when he was given it."

"Stop it!" Monique begged. "I feel guilty enough about him already. And I hope you weren't comparing me to chocolate – his reward for being so patient."

"You're only going to see a field of vines. No one said anything about rewards. For good boys or otherwise."

"Hmm …" Monique sounded cynical. "Anyway, I'd better go and look up some of my wine books. Don't want to mix up my Merlot and my Cabernets this afternoon."

"The lengths women go to, to impress a man!" Evie complained.

They were both grinning at the banter. Could they possibly be getting back to normal?

♡   ♡   ♡

Evie decided that afternoon that she was going to take Antoine's mother's little house. The more time she spent with Alex, the more she began to believe that they had a chance of regaining what they had had before. But the one thing she didn't want to happen was for her and Alex to "fall" into a relationship because of their shared love of Holly.

"When will you be over next?" Alex asked towards the end of the afternoon. Evie and Holly had to catch an early flight out in the morning, so they would be saying goodbye after an early dinner.

"I don't know. I didn't want to plan too far ahead … tempt fate or anything." It sounded ridiculous now, but Evie had been so worried about this first meeting that she hadn't been able to think beyond it. "Why don't you come to Dublin?"

As soon as she said it, and saw Alex's eyes light up, Evie regretted her invitation. She didn't want to take things too fast.

"You could meet Mum," she said quickly. "Actually, you might be able to stay with her ... I'm afraid my house is too ..."

"I'll stay in a hotel. The same one as last time. I think you said that was only a few minutes away from your house?"

"By car ... but will you be able to drive?" Because of his eye, he still had to pass a medical to get his licence back.

"Not yet. But they have taxis in Dublin, don't they?" He sounded prickly.

"Of course. Sorry."

They were sitting down to a dinner of pizza, fizzy orange and red wine when the phone rang. Alex took the call on the portable in the kitchen.

"Laurent! I was expecting to hear from you. You got the plans back from the designer? She's good, isn't she? What do you think? No, it's not a bad time. Hang on, I'll just go into the study to check that ... Yes, Evie and Holly are here ... What?"

Evie's stomach contracted at the thought of Laurent on the other end of the phone. It was impossible to sit here and not remember how he had taken champagne from that fridge ... had led her out that door, down the corridor to the bedroom ...

She heard Alex laugh and say, "Fabulous, Laurent, you have no idea ..." and then he closed the door of the study behind him.

Evie forced herself to think instead of the weekend of Monique's birthday. Of Laurent walking out of her bedroom. Of her shouting at him to get out of her life. But, to her disappointment, it didn't make her feel as bitter towards him as it should have.

"It's been great, Laurent. You have no idea. Holly is an absolute dream. And getting together with Evie again. Sorting out all that mess in the past. I owe you so much – you've made me a very happy man. I hope one day I can repay … What was that? Oh yes, sorry. I was getting carried away there. The plans."

Alex listened as Laurent proposed some changes to the studio to take the designer's ideas into account. The movers, in their ruthless efficiency, had unpacked boxes up there, and Alex had seen part-finished wooden sculptures laid out randomly on the workbench. He didn't know if he would ever be able to finish those pieces. They looked so different since the accident. The consultant had explained that losing one eye would affect his three-dimensional vision, that without the so-called binocular effect, Alex would find it hard to judge distance. But Alex knew it was more than that. Shadow, light and dark had all been altered. And his way of looking at things. Instead of seeing his carving as live pieces of wood yielding up their secrets to his chisels, now he felt it would be like conducting an autopsy on dead trunks, hewn from felled trees.

Laurent was still talking and Alex tried to tune in.

He wondered would any architect, would Laurent in particular, always pay so much attention to the finishing details of a client's home. Surely architects were more involved in the big picture – the walls and windows, light and shade. Should he not have handed the project over completely to the interior designer by now? That reminded Alex that he hadn't seen an invoice from Laurent since he bought the house. He would have to chase that up. Maybe he'd phone that girl in Laurent's practice some time when he knew Laurent wasn't going to be there. He didn't want Laurent working for free. Not out of friendship, and especially not out of pity or some kind of misplaced guilt.

If anything, it was Alex who should feel guilty. He had a good idea how Laurent felt about Evie, and he thought he knew why he was standing back. Alex hated himself for using what had happened as an excuse to treat a friend so shabbily, but he believed his love for Evie gave him the prior claim, and the saying "all is fair in love and war" had persisted for a reason. He had decided that, with the hand fate had dealt him so far, he had earned the right not to be too squeamish when it came to making use of any advantage he had.

He agreed with a few more of Laurent's suggestions and made small talk, but what he was really looking for was an opportunity to drop Evie back into the conversation. Not to twist the knife, of course, but to stake his claim.

Chapter 33

Holly was asleep and Evie had finished packing for an early flight the next day. She and Monique were having a last glass of wine before going to bed. The windows to the garden were open and Evie could see bats swoop across the garden to mop up the last of the evening's insects.

"How did it go with Joël this afternoon?" she asked.

"Good, it went well. I enjoyed it."

Evie was glad to see a contented smile settle on her friend's face.

"And I think he'd be mad not to buy those vines." Monique started to talk about soil and aspect, comparing the vines on offer to what Joël already owned. "And they're in the Pécharmant area as well, so he can alter the proportions of grape in his good vintage without having to rip out any of his own established vines."

"You've become quite the expert, in an afternoon," Evie teased.

Monique went quiet. "To be honest," she confessed at last, "I've been interested in wine … making wine, not just drinking it … for quite a while. I've absorbed more than I realised. Even Joël was impressed."

"You look happy."

"I am, I think. It wasn't Joël, although he helped. It was realising that I can be good at something in my own right. That I can decide to do something different and make it work."

"So you're going to buy a vineyard." Evie moved the wine bottle away from Monique in an exaggerated gesture, pretending she didn't trust its influence.

"No, I'm not going to buy a vineyard! That was just an example. I knew nothing about wine when I came to France, and today Joël said I knew as much as some of the people who grow grapes for a living. But I'm not sure I want to work in an estate agent's forever. I want to work for myself."

"What will you do?"

"Landscape gardening!"

Monique waved her arm towards her own garden outside the window. Evie had always taken it for granted, but now that she appraised Monique's half acre, she realised that over the past five years, her friend had made a huge number of changes. Some things had lasted, other plants or borders had survived a season only to be ripped out to make room for something else. Monique had been training herself in landscape gardening by trial and error and experimentation. Her bookshelves were full of books on the subject.

"But is there a market for it round here?" Evie asked sceptically. All she had seen were tidy plots with flowers and vegetables growing side-by-side or well-tended lawns dotted with shrubs or trees. She couldn't see their owners shelling out for Monique's expertise.

"Foreigners," Monique explained simply. "Second homes. I know I can't make a living out of it, but I could do it part-time. At first anyway. I'd have to start in my free time to see if I could build up a clientele. And there's a good course I can sign up to ..."

Evie knew Monique had never been afraid of hard work, but she was worried.

"You won't be working yourself too hard?"

"I reckon I put in at least five to ten hours a week on my own garden, just as a hobby. If I divert some of that time ... Anyway, it's just a thought. I haven't got my heart set on it or anything. If nothing comes of it, at least I'll have had fun having a good nose around other people's gardens. But how about you, how are you going to manage the next few months? Travelling to and from France just for weekends won't be much fun. Any chance you could work some weekends in Ireland and then come over for four or five days at a stretch?"

"No, I wouldn't want to do that. It wouldn't be fair on Holly. We'd end up with hardly any time together, just the two of us."

"So maybe you might go back to being self-employed? Pick your own working hours?"

"I don't know … I like the security of a pay cheque …"

But an idea was beginning to form in the back of Evie's head.

"How easy would it be to get broadband in Antoine's place?" she asked.

"I can't imagine it would be too hard – I have it here. Why?"

"Maybe I could 'tele-work' occasionally. From here in France. Once Holly's got to know Alex better. Then if she's spending time with him, I could be working."

"Find out in work if you can do it, and then you can use my connection here. No point in shelling out for a broadband line until you know you need it."

Monique emptied her glass and got up to get ready for bed.

"But be careful of making too many plans, Evie …"

"What do you mean?"

"The way you said 'if Holly's spending time with Alex' … it sounded like you see yourselves spending separate time with Holly."

"I never said that!"

Monique smiled. "There's nothing wrong with that. There's no law saying that you and Alex have to get together just because you have a daughter together. On the other hand, if you make concrete plans, and tell him about them, it might send out the wrong signal."

And Evie had no idea what signal she wanted to send Alex.

♡　　♡　　♡

At first Evie's boss hated the idea of her tele-working. Not because he didn't like the idea of her working away from the office – he knew Evie well enough to know that he'd more than get value for money from her – but he could see this as the start of the rot. It was only a short step from there to her going out on her own again, and he really didn't want to lose her. When he heard that she planned to do some of her tele-work from France, however, and he heard why, he relaxed. After all, if she was commuting back and forth regularly to the Dordogne, she was hardly going to find a huge amount of time to set up her own business again. And if the worst happened, and she moved over there permanently, he reckoned he could probably keep her on the basis that he would be able to pay her far more than she'd ever be able to earn in France. So without sounding too positive, he gave Evie a trial period of six months to see how they both managed the new arrangement.

Next Evie had to break the news to her mother. Marian was thrilled to hear that it had gone so well with Alex, but not so thrilled that Evie planned to spend so much time in France.

"Won't you be sending him the wrong signal, love? I mean this is about Holly, not about you and Alex. Not that there's anything wrong with you and Alex but …"

Why was everyone so bloody concerned about the signals she was sending Alex all of a sudden, Evie wondered. She was an adult – surely she was old enough to know her own mind. So she told her mum about the house she would be renting, to keep her independence, and that seemed to worry Marian all the more.

"Poor Holly won't know whether she's coming or going. And what will happen when she starts school? She can't go missing days like that all the time."

"She won't start school for another year, Mum. And by then we'll be in a better position to judge …"

"To judge what?" Marian asked when Evie left the sentence hanging. "Whether you want to live in France? While I think it would be great to live there, and Holly would love that little school in the village, if you move to France it has to be for the right reasons."

"I know that, Mum."

"And what about Laurent?"

Evie's eyes opened wide in surprise. "What about him?"

"I don't know …" Marian wouldn't look directly at her daughter.

"Have you and Céline been talking about me?" Evie knew all about her mother's e-mail correspondence, and she knew that the two women spoke on the phone at least once a week. It was a friendship that had come right out of the blue. As far as Evie was concerned, the two women seemed to have nothing in common. "Seriously, Mum, has Céline said anything about Laurent?"

"Have I ever meddled in your love life?" Marian asked, getting up to empty the teapot – her signal that she considered the conversation closed. She liked what she had seen of Laurent and she admired the way he had stood by Alex after the accident. He was also younger than Alex, and he had never been married, so he came without baggage. If she were a betting woman, Marian would have given Laurent much better odds when it came to providing her with more grandchildren.

It was true, Marian had never meddled in her daughter's love life, but just implying that there might be a love life to meddle in wasn't *actually* meddling, was it?

Chapter 34

Monique sank gratefully into a hot bath. She couldn't remember ever being so physically exhausted – she'd certainly sleep well tonight and that was a pleasant thought. It was getting harder to think up ways of tiring herself out just so that she could sleep.

But before she could sleep, Monique was going to a grape harvesters' supper with Joël. She had spent the day in the vineyards with him. Two of his regular pickers had been involved in a tractor accident while working on another property, so when the weather forecast predicted a heavy storm, Joël's friends and family rallied round to help get in the last of the grapes for his Premium Cuvée. Several hours of backbreaking work had only just got the harvest in ahead of a heavy rainstorm, and Monique felt a unique sense of achievement as she had stood, soaked to the skin, in Joël's *chais* and watched the grapes being crushed.

Joël had been surprised to see her when she arrived with Laurent. He hadn't thought of calling her, he admitted, assuming she would be too busy with work. But Laurent had just dropped in on his mother in the office when he took the call on his mobile, so Monique had offered to come along as well. Céline waved her out the door without a second's hesitation – this was wine country; selling houses could wait.

Joël was clearly glad to see Monique, and not just because she was an extra pair of hands. Although he was run off his feet all day, driving a tractor and supervising the crushing of the grapes, he kept an eye on her, checking she was alright. Then he insisted on driving her home himself.

Although it was only a fifteen-minute drive, and they had hardly spoken a word the whole way, Monique felt that in their silence they had achieved a new level of closeness, and to her surprise she was completely comfortable with it. It wasn't that they had become more intimate; it was more a shared sense of victory over the elements and an appreciation of the physical exhaustion it had brought.

♡   ♡   ♡

The cosy little restaurant was nearly empty when they arrived, apart from their rowdy group of harvesters who occupied a long table down one side of the room.

Everyone looked up with friendly curiosity when she arrived with Joël, and she couldn't help thinking they had probably been talking about her. But although six months ago the prospect of being talked about would have horrified and embarrassed her, now she felt she was with friends, and she had nothing to hide from them. Laurent stood up to make room for her on the long cushioned window seat and Joël, after greeting all his workers and ordering more wine, sat down opposite her with a smile.

Monique hadn't enjoyed an evening this much in years. Although she was tired, she was also totally relaxed. She wasn't worried what any of these people thought of her. They had all seen her work hard all day and although her baskets may not have filled up as fast as the more experienced amongst them, they respected how fast she learnt and the fact that she hadn't given up until the last bunch was in. And none of them, apart from Laurent and Joël, had ever met Tom, so they weren't judging her in relation to him. And more importantly, Monique realised, she wasn't judging herself. She wasn't measuring her every action wondering was she giving a "wrong impression". She wasn't looking at herself and trying to see herself through other people's eyes. She wasn't asking how she fit into this group. She was just being herself and living in the moment. And she couldn't remember ever doing that before. She had tried to be the person Tom wanted (always falling ever so slightly short) for so long that he had gradually sapped her confidence and left her with no idea of who she really was.

Suddenly she realised, as if for the first time, that he was really gone, and she had no choice now but to find out who she was and who she could be. It was a terrifying but exhilarating prospect.

"Thanks for tonight, I really enjoyed it," Monique told Joël as he dropped her home.

"I'm the one who should be thanking you. You and all the others. Without you I'd never have got the grapes in before this storm." The rain had started again and was hammering a tattoo on the top of the car.

"I enjoyed it, seriously. It was fun. Hard work, but fun."

"Hmm, I'm not sure you'd think that if you had to spend your whole year doing it!"

"Why not? You seem to," Monique challenged. "You're never so happy than when you've spent a day in the vineyards, pruning, tying in vines, weeding between the rows. Whereas you're like a bear with a sore head when you have to spend a day in the office, filling in forms and doing paperwork."

Joël laughed. "I didn't realise I was that transparent! But yes, paperwork is the bane of my life. A day devoted to the red tape of winemaking makes me wonder is it all worthwhile. I'm sure I could get a respectable job with half the hours and twice the money."

"So why don't you?" Monique teased.

Joël looked indignant, then noticed Monique's impish grin, barely visible in the glow from the dashboard display. He grinned back in silence.

"Thank you," she said again, quietly this time so he

had to strain to hear her.

"For what?" he asked gently, knowing that it wasn't just about tonight.

She wasn't sure how to put it but she knew it was important to try. "For being there for me, through it all. And for understanding when I didn't want you there and not holding it against me."

Their eyes met then and they looked at each other without saying anything. The only noise was the tinny rattle of rain on the top of the car.

Joël reached out and tucked a strand of hair behind Monique's ear, then continued to hold her face in his hand.

"I'm good at waiting," he said.

And Monique knew it was a promise for the future as much as an explanation of what had gone before.

♡   ♡   ♡

Two days later, Monique was on the phone to Evie. They were settling the last details before Evie took over the "tenancy" of Antoine's mother's house. There were very few formalities to organise. The arrangement was 'entr' amis', between friends, and Evie would pay Antoine in cash every two months. She wasn't going to bother connecting the phone and the electricity was still in Antoine's name so there was nothing to draw the attention of the tax man. Which was how Antoine preferred it, and it suited Evie because it kept the rent low.

"Laurent was asking after you," Monique said, after they had got business out of the way.

"When did you see him?" Evie tried to ignore the sudden somersaults in her stomach.

"The other night. A few of us went out together." Monique hadn't mentioned the harvesting supper because she wasn't yet ready for an interrogation on the subject of Joël. Any time she thought of him it gave her a lovely warm feeling and she wanted to keep it to herself for the moment.

"What did he want to know?" Evie asked, hoping she sounded casual. "He was talking to Alex the other day, so I'd have thought he'd be up to date with most of my news."

If she sounded sarcastic it was because she was hurt that he hadn't made any effort to contact her, despite knowing she had been in France, and surely knowing that she had plans to return regularly. She might have told him to stay the hell out of her life, but surely he had enough cop-on to know that she hadn't meant him to obey her to the letter?

"He asked how you were," Monique said, "and then he seemed just happy to chat about you. About the day we spent in St Émilion together. He asked had Holly fully recovered from her asthma. Things like that."

They must have been talking about her for quite a few minutes, Evie realised. She was just a casual subject of conversation to him. Something he and Monique had in common. On the day of Monique's birthday he had made it sound like he was making some big sacrifice in refusing to pursue their relationship, and yet he had managed to get over her without a second thought.

"I'd better go, Holly's calling me," she lied.

She couldn't stay on the phone. It wouldn't be hard for Monique to guess from her tone of voice or silences how hurt she was. And she was furious with herself for not getting over him as quickly and not being able to talk about him with the same apparent ease.

Chapter 35

The next time Evie came to France, she stayed in her new little pied-à-terre in Ste Anne. She was childishly excited arriving in her rented car, stuffed to the gills with duvets, pillows, towels and kitchen things. For once in their lives she and Holly had used up their entire luggage allowance, and although Evie had weighed each bag several times before leaving the house in Dublin, she held her breath in the airport as the digital numbers rose alarmingly high when the bags were loaded onto the belt.

Monique had given the house a good clean and an oven and fridge had been installed since Evie's last visit. There was a stack of firewood in a basket by the living-room stove and electric storage heaters had taken the chill off the stone walls.

Evie was surprised at the change in the area. The hot

Indian summer of her last trip had given way to a gloriously coloured autumn with a distinct nip in the air. She had only rarely visited Monique at this time of year. As the property business cooled off with the weather, Monique usually jetted off somewhere warm. And by the time she came back, Evie was usually saving for Christmas. This year, however, Monique was staying where she was, Alex was keen to see Holly and the money in the account he'd set up hadn't been touched. So Evie swallowed her pride, booked flights and took out cash for the trip.

Alex had been to Dublin for a long weekend as promised, but although his stay had been a success (they had celebrated Holly's fourth birthday in style), Evie had a feeling that she would be making the trip more often than he would.

For one thing, Evie hated bringing Holly to a hotel to meet her father. And while the time they had spent at home had been fun, there were just too many reminders there of the years he had missed.

If Evie could have got it all out of the way in one go she would have said: "Here are the photo albums and here's Holly's baby book. She took her first step, there, just where you're standing. And that table, the one I've moved over out of the way beside the sofa – that's the one she fell against and split her lip. We spent hours in casualty over that one – can you see the remains of the scar? No, well, if you know where to look …"

But no matter how much she told him about Holly's first years, there would always be something she left out.

Holly would refer to an event as occurring before or after her room was painted pink. Or Evie would go looking for the second of a matching pair of hairclips, only to remember that it had been lost that amazing day at the kids' art day at the National Museum when Holly won a rosette for her collage ... And each time a detail like this rose to the surface, Alex frowned, and his face closed over so she couldn't tell if he was feeling anger or regret.

They would be in France for five days this time and it was Evie's first chance to try working from home – away. Her laptop was safely charging in her bedroom, out of Holly's reach, and she had set up a table by the living-room window to work on later. Although now that she looked out the window, Evie wondered if she'd have to move herself into the kitchen for discipline's sake. Every time she stared out the window at Holly exploring her new garden, she spotted something else that caught her attention. Those withering leaves, succumbing to the first severe frost of the previous night, looked like peony. She would need to stack some sticks or straw on that bed if she wanted good flowers next spring. And what were those little velvety sprouts appearing under the sycamore now that it had starting shedding its leaves? Could they be cyclamen?

With difficulty, Evie dragged herself away from the window when she heard her mobile phone. It was Alex, checking that she was settling in and asking was it okay for him to call down.

He had Sophie with him for a few days – it was her mid-term. The two half-sisters would meet for the first time later that afternoon.

When Alex did appear, Holly threw herself at him with delight, and Evie looked on fondly as she showed her dad round the house, but more importantly, round "her" garden. He hadn't seen the house yet – Monique said he had offered to help her with anything that needed to be bought, or sorted out, but he had stopped short of actually coming in. Evie was grateful – it seemed to indicate an understanding that she needed her own separate, private "space"; into which Alex would only come by invitation.

He had had his new acrylic eye fitted since the last time she saw him and Evie was amazed at how realistic it looked. It matched his good eye perfectly, right down to a few thin red veins visible in the white. She thought it would stay staring ahead all the time, but it actually moved the same direction as his seeing eye and within a few minutes she had stopped noticing it at all.

"Sophie's really looking forward to meeting Holly. And you, of course. She doesn't really remember you from before."

"How much does she know about … you know, what happened between us?"

"Everything."

Evie was surprised, but Alex explained. "Sharon told her. She reckoned it was easier to get the whole thing out in the open. The boys don't know the full story yet, but they will in time."

"Are they jealous at all of Holly?" Evie finally asked the question that had bothered her since finding Alex again. He was effectively retired now and well off. It would be impossible for his older children not to compare their childhoods with the amount of time and money he would be free to spend on Holly.

"I don't think so. But I can't be certain," he admitted honestly. "Sharon's been doing her best and trying to keep me up to date with anything they say. She says that if anything they feel sorry for Holly. And Sharon's worried that she may have made Sophie feel slightly guilty – she explained that one of her motives for splitting us up was to protect them."

Evie wondered how he could be so willing to trust Sharon's advice and input. But then the children lived with her and had probably long ago learnt to hide any sign of discontent from the father who so obviously adored them. Also Alex seemed to have been able to put his bitterness towards Sharon behind him much more quickly that Evie would be able to.

♡   ♡   ♡

"Hi, Holly, I'm Sophie."

The teenager sensibly stayed sitting on a cushion on the floor where she was reading a magazine rather than getting up to greet her half-sister.

Suddenly all Holly's confidence and excitement vanished, and she clung nervously to Evie's legs. Meeting a sister for the first time seemed to be a much more intimidating prospect than meeting a new daddy. Evie guessed that a father was an adult, easy to categorise, place in a box, whereas a sister … shouldn't a sister be another child? Holly had very little experience of teenagers. Her baby-sitter was nineteen, and that was adult in Holly's eyes. Sophie was sixteen, and although to Evie she looked like a young woman already, long-legged and confident, to Holly she clearly fell into some new category. Not to be trusted until it was understood.

Holly continued to peep out from behind her mother while Evie asked Sophie about her flight, how school was going and how her brothers were. Then they moved to the couch and while Alex fussed about with cushions, he asked Holly would she like an ice cream or a drink and pointed out the window at where the pool was covered over for the winter.

But Holly only had eyes for Sophie.

"Do you like Barbie dolls?" Sophie asked suddenly as though she had only just thought of it.

Holly nodded solemnly.

"I *love* Barbie," Sophie confessed *sotto voce*. "I know I'm too old, but I still have *all* my old Barbies from when I was your age. And I even …" she dropped her voice to a whisper so that Holly had to slip off the couch and creep nearer to hear, "I even have Barbie pyjamas."

Holly's mouth dropped open in surprise. "So do I!" she squeaked. "They're pink!"

"Really?" Sophie suppressed a smile. "I don't believe it – mine are pink too. Same-same! Pink's my favourite colour."

"Mine too!" Holly's eyes filled with adoration. "Same-same!" She hunkered down beside her sister then.

"What are you reading," she asked, pointing at the magazine.

"Just something I bought in the airport. Do you want to see my room?"

Holly hesitated and looked at Evie.

"You could help me arrange my stuff. My make-up and things – I'm moving some of it over so that I can have a French room here, a bit like my English room at home."

"I have a French room too," Holly told her shyly.

"Can I see it some time?" Sophie asked.

"Uhn, hmn," Holly agreed.

The teenager stood up and walked towards the door without looking back. Holly followed her after a moment's hesitation and Evie and Alex were silent until they heard the two girls chattering away on the other side of the house.

"She wants to be a primary school teacher when she leaves school," Alex said proudly.

"She'll be bloody good at it," Evie predicted with confidence.

"I'm glad they seemed to have hit it off so well," Alex said smiling. He came and sat on the couch beside Evie. He took her hand almost absent-mindedly and squeezed it. "It could have been really difficult if they didn't."

Evie didn't say anything. She just squeezed his hand back before getting up to go into the kitchen for a drink of water.

"I'm doing up a bedroom for the boys too," Alex said

later that night. They were in Evie's and she had just finished putting Holly to bed. "Sophie's coming to IKEA with me tomorrow to pick furniture for them – the boys don't trust me to do it on my own!"

"That's nice," Evie said lamely, afraid of what was coming.

"I'd like to do a bedroom up –"

"Holly's French bedroom's here," Evie said firmly. "Upstairs."

Alex looked hurt.

"She's too young, Alex. It would be too confusing. Three bedrooms, in three different houses? Come on! How could any four-year-old cope with that?"

"I just don't want her to feel left out," Alex protested. "The others will all have a room in my house."

"We'll think about it again when she's old enough to worry about things like that," Evie promised firmly. "But for now let's let her get used to having a father, two brothers and a sister who all live in a different country. Let's not go assuming she's going to get jealous before she's even met the boys."

"They'll be over next weekend …"

"No, Alex, I can't make it again next week. I'm sorry, but we talked about this already. Anyway, it's probably best that we take things one step at a time. Holly and Sophie are getting on great."

"Sophie always wanted a baby sister." Alex decided to let the subject of meeting his sons drop. "She was always asking me and Sharon when we were going to have another baby …"

"Pity she never got to see Holly as a baby," Evie couldn't help remarking.

"Nor did I," Alex reminded her.

"Sorry."

"I'm sorry too," he said. "Look, I know things are difficult at the moment, but let's look forward, not back, okay. I'm really glad you're here. And I'm glad you've got this place. So you can come as often as you like."

Alex stepped so close to Evie that she could feel the heat of his body. A shiver ran through her as, out of nowhere, she remembered the last time they had made love. It was the night before he went to Turkey, and she was complaining that it would be a week until he could hold her again. He was trying to persuade her to come with him, and she was using work as an excuse not to. Not so convincing when he was her boss.

As he held her in his arms that night, he had talked seductively, painting a picture of some Eastern hotel where they could hide away for a few days, make love on a warm beach and feed each other cheese and olives at dusk. He teased and caressed her to the point where she would have agreed to anything and she said she'd think about it, before they finally came together again. After that night how could she possibly have believed the letter that had supposedly come from him? But she managed to persuade herself over time that he just wanted to bring her to Turkey to break it off far away from home. Maybe even give her a last glorious week to remember him by. Whereas when he got his letter, he must have thought she was plotting her escape even as they lay together.

How could she have been such a fool? The missed opportunities hurt her almost physically now, as they rushed into the present and forced her to think of what might have been. If only she had confronted him in a rage; if she had demanded that he do the decent thing and break it off with her face to face, like a man. Then the whole story would have come to light at the time, rather than taking five years. And the only reason she hadn't been able to face confronting him, although she didn't know it at the time, was because she was pregnant and hormonal, and feeling desperately emotional and vulnerable.

"You're right, Alex," she said, placing her hand gently on his cheek. "We need to look forward. Looking back is far too painful."

And that was when she leaned forward and kissed him.

♡   ♡   ♡

Monique sat reading a book on shrubs. Laurent had introduced her to one of his clients who wanted to re-landscape the area around a new swimming-pool now that the diggers had left. The hard landscaping had already been done by the pool company, because to build the pool they had to blast into underlying bed-rock. Now it was up to Monique to decide where to place borders and containers, and what to plant in them. Having spoken to a few pool experts, Monique realised that it wasn't enough to consider the usual light, shade, soil and moisture requirements of the plant – she also had to take into account what time of year her chosen specimens would shed. Leaves, blossom or pollen could all cause no end of work and irritation in the form of clogged filters and cloudy pool water.

It was a challenge, but one Monique relished. All the more so, because the site she was working on was on her way to work, so she would be able to drive past it each morning and watch the progress of the garden throughout the next year.

She crossed another plant off her list – a Ceanothus or Californian lilac. It was ideal in terms of soil and aspect, it was evergreen and for three or four months in summer it would be covered in tiny blue flowers. But then she imagined millions of tiny blue petals floating on the matching blue water. Compromise was needed, Monique realised, frowning. Then she cheered up as she remembered Joël was coming over. He had promised to bring over his father's collection of pool enthusiasts' magazines. Monique had no particular interest in the technology of keeping the water clean, but she was dying to see all the photos of readers' pools to get inspiration from the planting around them.

♡   ♡   ♡

Evie let her lips settle against Alex's and mould themselves to his. Then she pulled back for a moment.

She was about to say something, but he just put his finger to her mouth.

"Ssh, please. Don't say anything."

He stood there, like that, not moving, and stared into her eyes for what felt like an eternity. He must have liked what he saw there, because he smiled.

All the time, Evie could feel a pulse in her lips where his finger was pressing against them. It was one of the most erotic sensations she had ever experienced.

Her lips parted. Alex's finger moved away from her mouth and followed the line of her jaw, then down her neck stopping at the collar of her blouse. He lifted his other hand to the back of her neck and pulled her towards him.

As they kissed, bruising their mouths off each other, it wasn't enough for her so she put her arms up, tangling her fingers in his hair to pull him even closer. Then she began to kiss his neck, then his throat and the triangle of flesh where his shirt parted to reveal his chest.

"Oh, God, Evie," he managed to groan before she returned her attention to his mouth.

He was pulling at the back of her shirt and freed it from the waistband of her jeans. Then with both hands he explored the skin of her back. She was kissing his face and she froze for a second at the unfamiliar feel of the scar on his cheek, then all sensations fused together and all she knew was that this was Alex. Every bit of skin touching hers was familiar, and her body longed to be able to hold him forever.

"Mummy!"

The plaintive call from upstairs made them jump apart. Evie tucked her blouse into her waistband and

Alex buttoned up the front of his shirt. Neither of them was able to look at the other.

"What is it, sweetheart?" Evie looked up to see Holly standing at the top of the stairs rubbing her eyes. If she had taken even three steps down, she would have seen them together.

"Will you take me to the toilet, Mummy?"

"Of course, darling." It was one of the disadvantages of having a downstairs bathroom.

Evie went up to bring Holly down and saw Alex slip quietly into the living room.

♡   ♡   ♡

With Joël's help, and by flicking through the pile of magazines he had brought, Monique compiled a list of plants she thought might be suitable for her project. She checked some of their qualities on her favourite Internet sites, and all she had to do now was hope the local nursery would stock at least some of them.

Joël had gone outside to get some more wood for the fire.

"You really will have to put in a stove, you know," he scolded when he came back with a heavy basketful. "Most of that heat is going straight up the chimney and heating the sky."

"Bossy boots!"

"Seriously, you could heat the whole house with the amount of wood you get through each winter. And heat your water."

"But I like an open fire," Monique complained, pouting. "It's cosier than one of those fitted glass stoves."

"I never had you down as the romantic type, Monique," Joël teased. "I thought you were a practical girl at heart."

"There's a lot you don't know about me," she retorted with a snort. Then more quietly: "In fact, there's a lot I don't know about myself. And it's about time I started learning."

Then she got embarrassed and began to fuss about the kitchen.

"It's okay, you know," Joël said gently, coming up behind her.

"What is?" Monique turned around quickly to find him only inches from her.

"Revealing things about yourself. I'm not going to judge you."

She stared at him for a few seconds, then, feeling terribly tired, she leaned her head against his chest. He put his arms around her and she felt so comfortable in his embrace. At home.

"It's not other people's judgement I worry most about any more," she confessed at last. "It's my own. I've made such a mess of my life up to now, and it's bloody uncomfortable looking back."

"Then don't."

"What?" Monique jerked her body back, almost colliding with Joël's chin on the way.

"Don't look back. You can't change it. I've seen you have some really happy times in the past few weeks and they've always been when you're living in the present. Like that time in the vineyard. Or when you were grubbing around in my garden, advising me on what to plant. Or that mad time you agreed to come to the 70s night in Bergerac with me."

"You're right, I suppose," Monique agreed reluctantly. "But it's hard not to look back and wish I'd made different choices. Or beat myself up over where I made mistakes."

Then she stood back from Joël, before taking both his hands in hers. She looked solemnly at him.

"There's something else about all those times I've been happy. Those times in the past few weeks. Something you don't seem to have noticed."

"What?" Joël's heart was beating faster.

"You were there."

And finally Monique gave in to the desire that had been building slowly within her until she could deny it no longer. She leaned forward and pressed her lips against his.

It felt strange at first. It was so long – years and years – since she was a teenager in fact – that she had kissed anyone other than Tom.

Joël's mouth was gentler, more yielding, and yet more insistent. It was softer. He kissed her back more actively than she could ever remember Tom kissing her.

And there the comparisons ended. Joël put a hand behind her head, supporting her as he explored her face, her eyes and her neck with his mouth. Monique put her arms around him to feel the heat of his body, the shape of him. Suddenly he was the only man on earth she had ever wanted, and she wondered how she could have waited this long for him.

Chapter 36

The next day, Sophie had taken Holly for a walk in the woods to look for fairies while Evie worked at her little desk in her house in Ste Anne. She hadn't seen Alex since he left at the small hours of the morning. Sophie said he had some business to attend to – he had cancelled their trip to IKEA and had caught the train into Bergerac. Evie couldn't help wondering if he was avoiding her after last night, but she hadn't time to dwell on it because she had to get this piece of work finished and then she could use Monique's computer to send it back to Ireland.

She had called in earlier that morning to pick up keys, before Monique went to work, and saw Joël's car outside. There had been a heavy dew, but the gravel under the car was dry, so Evie made sure Monique realised she had Holly with her before she opened the door.

Joël was in the kitchen, fortunately fully dressed, making coffee. Monique grinned sheepishly at Evie and Holly went to help herself to a yoghurt.

"Hey, Holly!" her mother objected. "Ask Monique first before you go raiding her fridge."

"She's fine." Monique smiled. "But wouldn't you prefer some pancakes, Holly? Joël's making some."

The yoghurt was shoved back into the fridge and suddenly Joël was Holly's new best friend.

"I'm glad," Evie whispered to Monique, glancing in Joël's direction. "About time too."

Monique just grinned goofily and Evie wished she could feel the same about her night with Alex. But then she reminded herself that he wasn't as new to her as Joël was to Monique; indeed her awakening memories of the Alex she had loved before made sleeping with him last night eerily strange. Like sleeping with a stranger, but one you've dreamed about for years and years and years until he's almost real and yet nothing like you imagined.

"Pancakes?" Evie said to Joël. "Not the most French of breakfasts."

"Something I learned in my time in California," Joël told her. "I was supposed to be studying modern wine-making techniques." He slid two pancakes, each the size of a small fried egg and dotted with deep purple splodges, onto a plate for Holly. "The best blueberry pancakes this side of the Atlantic," he promised with a French-accented American drawl, making Holly laugh.

They all ate breakfast together until Joël got up to leave. Monique walked him to the door and spent a long time saying goodbye.

"I think they're kissing," Holly murmured through a mouthful of pancake. "Does that mean Joël's Monique's boyfriend now?"

"I guess it does, sweetheart," Evie answered.

"Cool," Holly approved. "I like Joël."

♡   ♡   ♡

Evie finished her rewrites on a client's website, saved them and copied the file onto a CD. She had promised Sophie she would be up at the house by lunchtime so it gave her just under an hour to send this off to Ireland. But as she was going out the front door, she found Alex outside about to come in.

Hell, she thought to herself. Then out loud she said: "Alex, hi. Do you want to walk up to Monique's with me? I need to get this sent off before lunch. Holly's with Sophie – I'm meeting them up in your house in a few minutes."

"I know, I spoke to Sophie on the phone. But I was hoping to catch you here. We need to talk."

Double hell, Evie thought. She was holding her computer disk in one hand and Monique's keys in the other. Alex looked like he hadn't slept all night. And given that it was barely after one when he left her, he must have been doing some worrying.

"Come in," Evie said, trying not to sound too reluctant. "This can wait." She put the disk back down beside her laptop. "Coffee?"

"Please."

Alex went to the French window and looked out while Evie filled the jug and spooned coffee into the filter of the machine. She took her time getting out mugs, spoons and a jug. Partly because she was suddenly all thumbs, and partly because in unpacking everything when she arrived, she had just shoved things into any space she could find.

The machine began to splutter suddenly, making them both jump and look at each other guiltily. Then they laughed, breaking the tension.

Alex walked across the room and took Evie's face in his hands and kissed her.

"I've wanted to do that all night," he said.

Evie couldn't help responding, although in her head she wasn't at all sure what was happening.

"This isn't so straightforward, Alex," she protested gently when they finally pulled apart. She pushed him away gently. "There's Holly to think of now. And Sophie. And your two boys."

"I know. That's what I wanted to talk to you about."

Evie said nothing else until she had poured the coffee. "Will we take these outside?" she asked, handing Alex his mug.

He agreed, noting that she had automatically added milk, just a tiny drop, the way he liked it.

Although it was far from hot, the terrace was a sun-trap and completely sheltered so it was quite pleasant. Also, it was potentially overlooked from upstairs over the café, so they were unlikely to get into any more romantic clinches.

"I spent the morning walking around Bergerac. I needed to be alone, to think," Alex said, confirming Evie's suspicion that his trip was to avoid her. "And I think I came to a decision."

"About what?" Evie asked, bristling slightly. He had always made the decisions, but when she was younger it had never bothered her. She was so besotted with him then that if he'd said he was thinking of emigrating to the moon, she'd have gone to pick a space suit.

"About us. About what happened last night. About where we go from here."

"Ok … ay?" Evie tried to smile. "Do I get to hear it?" Or do I get a say in it, she felt like adding.

"Sorry! Of course." Alex stood up and began to walk back and forward across the patio. "We need to take things more slowly, Evie."

"We do?"

"Yes. You were right what you said about Holly, and Sophie, and the boys. It's not just us any more."

It wasn't "just us" five years ago either, Evie couldn't help thinking to herself.

"And I've got a lot to get used to …" He waved his hand in the direction of his face. "And you and Holly have to get used to having me and my kids around. Hell, you're virtually going to be a stepmum."

Evie nearly choked on her coffee, but Alex didn't seem to notice.

"All in all, I think it's much too much pressure to put on you all at once," he concluded. "I'd rather you took your time. When we get together, I want to know all the obstacles are out of the way …"

When, Evie thought, what happened to *if*?

Alex stopped walking, stood in the middle of the patio and looked pleadingly at Evie. "You hate me, don't you, for saying all that? You think I'm wrong. I knew it. I knew I should never have kissed you last night and then …"

"No!" Evie jumped to her feet. "You're right. I was going to say the same myself."

"You were?" Alex looked at her warily. Then he smiled knowingly. "Good. I'm glad we agree. Let's take things slowly."

Evie nodded helplessly, then remembered her errand with the computer.

"I've really got to go up to Monique's … work …" She stepped back inside the house and picked up the computer disk, holding it to her chest like a shield.

"You can send that from my computer, silly. I have broadband too. And a much more up-to-date computer than Monique's," he assured her. "Come on, we'll go and join the two girls for lunch."

"Right, so."

Evie followed Alex through the village, wondering why she suddenly felt so confused.

Hang on, she remembered suddenly with a burst of silent indignation. Last night *I* was the one who kissed *you*! You didn't rush *me* into anything!

Chapter 37

Christmas, or rather where Holly (and by extension Evie) was going to spend it, proved to be the first real bone of contention between them. Alex's ex-wife Sharon was pregnant and having a very rough time of it, so she had gratefully agreed to let the kids spend Christmas in France. So of course Alex wanted Holly (and Evie) there too.

"Come on, Evie," he pleaded irritably when he was in Dublin at the end of November. "Holly loved the boys when they finally met, and they adored her. Surely they should all be together on Christmas Day? Christmas *is* about children after all."

Like an ostrich with its head in the sand, Evie had avoided thinking about Christmas. And having got to the end of November without the subject coming up, she had assumed that she would just stay in Dublin where she and Holly had built up their own little Christmas routine. Holly slept in Evie's bed on Christmas Eve (she wasn't afraid of Santa, but the elves were another matter altogether – she didn't get what they were about at all), and then they woke up together and went downstairs to see what they might find beside the chimney. Then they went to Granny Marian's for Christmas dinner. And this Christmas, with Evie's brother in New Zealand, Marian would be on her own if Evie was away.

"Why doesn't your mum come to France too?" Alex asked when Evie raised her as an objection to his happy-families scheme.

But Evie avoided giving him an answer that weekend and Alex went home, if not in a huff, then with his nose seriously out of joint. It wasn't that Evie didn't want Holly to spend Christmas with Alex, or even that she didn't want to have to share her Christmas, it was more that this was their "first" Christmas, and she was afraid that if she agreed too easily to this one, it would set a precedent. And, although it was true that they had all got along fine the weekend the boys were over, Evie just wasn't ready to play happy families with them just yet.

In the end, Monique came to the rescue.

"I can't face going home to Bristol, so Mum and Dad are coming here. Joël's father is away skiing, so we're spending Christmas together. Why don't you come over to your own place with your mum and split your day between there, Alex's place and us? Morning in your house, dinner with Alex and join us later – I don't know, for mince pies and tea or something."

It was the perfect solution. She would get her Christmas morning with Holly. Alex would get his big family Christmas day. And Holly and Evie would escape before they were welded irretrievably into the Ryder family circle. (Evie was still worried about forcing Holly on the two boys. Irritation with a younger sister could easily turn to jealousy and dislike. And that wouldn't make any of their lives easier.)

"Monique, you're a genius. I can't thank you enough!"

"Glad to be of service. Besides, I have something I want to ask you when you're over."

"Why can't you ask me now?" Evie wanted to know.

"I want to wait ... and ask you in person."

"That sounds ominous ..."

"It's not, I promise. Will you stay at least until the New Year, by the way? New Year's Eve in France is much nicer than in Ireland or England."

Evie grinned at Monique's sudden change of subject.

♡ ♡ ♡

The remaining weeks up to Christmas passed in a blur. Evie was up to her neck in work and was quite jealous of Alex who claimed to be only *thinking* about getting back to any kind of productive work. He and Céline had been to see an accountant and a notaire and were in the process of drawing up a partnership agreement for a future property venture.

Finally the day before Christmas Eve arrived. Evie was up at six because she still hadn't finished packing. She had bought presents for Sophie and the boys but although she was happy with the beaded silk wrap she bought Sophie, she was having a major crisis of confidence about the boys' presents (PlayStation games), so she wanted to leave herself with extra time in the airport. She also had to remember to leave a letter to Santa in the fireplace to tell him that Holly would be in France. (Backup for the letter posted to the North Pole and for the wooden sign saying "*Stop here, Santa*" that they were bringing with them to plant in the garden in Ste Ann.)

Finally she was ready, so she woke Holly, phoned Marian to say they were on their way and finished packing the car.

Dublin airport was bedlam. Evie dropped off Marian, Holly and the bags and was diverted to a long-term parking space so far from the terminal building that she might as well have left the car at home. She fought her way through the crowds, very glad that she was flying direct to Bordeaux and wouldn't have to face this all over again in Stansted. By the time the three of them had checked in and cleared security, there was no time for shopping. James and Alan would just have to make do with their PlayStation games, Evie realised with relief. One decision less to make.

Monique was collecting Evie, Holly and Marian from Bordeaux because Alex's kids were flying into Bergerac. Evie didn't like to admit it, but it was a relief. Although

Alex had been given the go-ahead to drive, Evie wasn't convinced his sense of distance could be trusted. And instead of becoming a more cautious driver since his accident, he now drove like a maniac, as though to prove that it hadn't scared him.

"So," Evie asked quietly, while she and Monique were loading the back of the car, "what was it you wanted to ask me? You've got me here in person now! I'm dying to know what all the secrecy is about."

Monique smiled smugly. "I'm afraid you'll just have to put up with the secrecy a little bit longer, sweetie."

"Am I allowed guess?"

"And spoil my surprise, you brat? Not a chance. Get into that car before the others wonder what we're talking about."

As they drove to Ste Anne, Monique and Holly gabbled about Santa Claus, St Nicholas and what French children got for Christmas. But soon the early start took its toll and the little girl nodded off. Marian asked Monique how Céline was. The two women had planned a trip into Bordeaux between Christmas and the New Year for the sales, and Marian was almost a little nervous. She had only spoken to Céline a few times in June, and since then their friendship had developed entirely by e-mail and phone.

"Céline's dying to see you," Monique told her. "In fact, she'll be at my house for drinks, so you'll see her this evening."

"Drinks this evening?" Evie hesitated. "I'm not sure …"

"You're coming!" Monique told her firmly. "It's all

arranged. And it took so much arranging that if you dare to try unpick my plans, I'll kill you. Alex is going to leave his crew with Sophie for a few hours and call in; you and Marian and Holly are coming. Joël is coming. His father is popping in quickly before he sets off for the Pyrenees. Some other friends are coming, Céline's coming ..."

"I give in!" Evie grinned – those definitely sounded like the kind of plans involving an "announcement".

"Oh, and Laurent's coming," Monique said quickly.

If she was expected to react, Evie missed her opportunity completely. She was too busy praying they weren't going to leave the road as Monique took a corner far too fast. Suddenly she wished they had taken the motorway.

"Is there any chance you could call down a little early this evening?" Monique asked her discreetly as they were unpacking the car later. "You don't need to bring Holly, maybe your mum could walk down with her later, but I'd like to get a chance to talk to you on your own ..."

Evie agreed readily and wished Monique would just come out and announce whatever it was she wanted to announce!

Laurent was late. He had promised Joël half eight at the latest. It was half eight now and he was two miles from Ste Anne and not moving in its general direction. Instead, he was across the valley standing on the side of the road looking down at the village. It was at times like this he wished he still smoked, so he could light up and justify standing here at least until he'd finished his cigarette. He counted the windows to work out which house was Monique's.

She'd be there by now, Laurent knew. Evie would. She'd be there looking at her watch, wondering when Monique and Joël were going to kick off proceedings so that she could celebrate with them and then get Holly off to bed. Laurent knew what they had all been called together for. Joël had asked him to be best man. And Monique had no sisters, so Evie would no doubt be chief bridesmaid. And so Laurent would spend the day "squiring" the woman he wanted to marry himself.

That was the first time he'd said it – Evie was the woman he wanted to marry. He never thought he'd want to get married, and yet the only thing that would make him happy would be for her to stand in front of Madame Le Maire with him and promise to love him forever.

And it wasn't going to happen.

And what killed Laurent was that he could have made it happen. He could have slipped in and stolen Evie right out from under Alex's nose and she'd never even have known what hit her.

Sometimes … often, Laurent wished he had.

♡ ♡ ♡

There was a strange tension in Monique's house, Marian noticed, as she sat beside Céline and chatted. And the tension built the longer they had to wait for Laurent. By now it was clear that Holly was the only one in the room who had no idea why they were all gathered. And if the nervous grins were anything to go by, the news of Joël and Monique's pending nuptials would prove welcome news to their friends. Evie had obviously been told when she came down earlier, but she had refused to divulge the details to Marian.

"You'll have to wait like everyone else," she grinned happily and Marian couldn't help wondering if and when Evie would ever get married. Although she liked Alex, Marian really couldn't see him and Evie doing the whole happy-ever-after thing together. Evie needed a man with more spark to him than Alex, and she needed someone who would allow her own spark to burn. And Marian hoped Evie would settle down with someone who wanted more children.

Alex doted on Holly, and he adored his older children – but although she knew she was wrong purely from an age point of view, Marian saw him as belonging more to her own generation than Evie's. He'd already served his time on nappies and late nights. Marian wouldn't willingly go back there again, and she wasn't convinced Alex would want to either.

Evie and Alex might have worked out if they'd stayed together five years ago, she believed. In raising Holly and maybe other children together they would have helped each other grow stronger through the hard times and have built memories to cherish in the good times. But Evie had raised Holly on her own whereas Alex had led … Marian wasn't sure how to put it, when suddenly the word "pampered" popped into her head. Yes, Marian thought, Alex had led a pampered life while Evie had struggled in Dublin. He had worked hard, there was no doubting that. He had earned his luxuries the hard way and he had earned the right to take some time off now and take things easier. But for the past few years he had done it all on his own terms. Another person's happiness had rarely been the first thing he woke up thinking about in the morning or the last thing he thought about as he fell asleep. It was a difficult joy to appreciate, and the longer you lived without it, the harder it was to get back. And apart from that, Marian believed that living alone aged you faster than living with children. So instead of narrowing with the passing years, she was convinced that the age gap between Evie and Alex was even wider than it had been before.

♡ ♡ ♡

"What's keeping Laurent, do you think?" Marian asked Céline. It hadn't escaped her notice that the Frenchwoman jumped every time she heard a car and she had been watching Evie like a hawk all night.

"I'm sure he's on his way. He'd have phoned if he was seriously delayed," Céline answered in a distracted way. Then suddenly she brought her head closer to Marian's as the noise in the room increased, offering her the chance to talk privately. "Is there anything between Alex and Evie?" she asked. "More than just having to work out the problems of sharing parenting from different countries, I mean. Is there a romance between them?"

Marian smiled; sometimes Céline's English was so quaint.

"I'm not sure," she answered carefully. She didn't know what the other woman's agenda was.

"It's just that any time I talk to Alex," Céline continued, "I get the distinct impression that he and Evie are ... well ... lovers. But I never get that impression from Evie ..."

They both looked over, then as quickly turned their heads away so as not to be caught staring.

"You get the impression?" Marian asked.

"Well, to be honest, Alex *gives* me the impression. Deliberately, I think. Without actually saying anything. But there is no doubt in my mind that Alex wants me to believe that he and Evie are lovers, and yet ..."

"If they are, she hasn't told me," Marian said quietly. She looked at her daughter discreetly. Evie looked uncomfortable. She was standing in a small knot of people by the big open fire, talking a mixture of French and English, and Alex was hanging on her every word.

"But why do you think Alex wants you to believe that they're ... em ... lovers?" Marian asked carefully. Now that she looked at the two of them together, she could see what Céline meant. He never took his eyes off her. He made the most of every excuse to touch her – putting a hand on her arm to draw her attention to something, touching her shoulder as he removed a hair and threw it in the fire, brushing her hand as he took her glass to refill it. And yet Marian hadn't noticed him behave like this before. On the occasions she met him in Dublin, he was almost careless of the impression he made. More intent on pleasing Marian, Holly or Evie's friends than Evie herself. "I mean, why you do think he wants *you* in particular to believe it?" Though she had already guessed the answer.

"Because of whose mother I am," Céline said simply.

And just then, Laurent arrived.

♡ ♡ ♡

Laurent had brought a half case of champagne with him as a gift, so when he kissed Monique in greeting, and handed it to her, there was no more need to pretend that they were all gathered for a friendly pre-Christmas drink.

Monique and Joël made their announcement, everyone cheered and Joël's father cracked open several more bottles of champagne.

Then Monique tapped on her glass again.

"The thing is …" she began. "The thing is, now that we have you all here together – and, boy, did it take some planning – we'd actually like to get married as soon as possible. I hope I won't shock you all when I tell you that we've organised it for March, and I hope you'll all join us to celebrate it!"

There was more excited cheering and Holly was beside herself with delight. She was to be a flower girl, and Monique's mother promised her the prettiest pink dress she had ever seen.

"And a crown, Mummy!" the little girl breathed excitedly for the tenth time. "A real crown!"

The first four or five times Evie had tried to explain what a tiara was, but a crown was just easier.

Evie was happy for Monique. She and Joël were as perfect for each other as any couple Evie had ever known. Not only were they obviously in love, but they shared so many interests and enthusiasms that Evie found herself wondering how on earth she had ever believed Monique could have married Tom. He had merely tolerated Monique's interest in wine, gardening and the countryside as if they were a phase he expected her to grow out of once she got down to the serious business of being a wife.

But no matter how hard she tried, Evie couldn't stop her mind wandering onto her own plans for the future. Because earlier that evening, Céline had offered her a job.

"I need someone else in the agency. I'm getting busier and Monique wants to cut her hours back a bit," Céline explained. "I wouldn't need you full-time, not at first, but eight to ten days a month – you could fit them around your other commitments. It would be mainly office-based work, like writing English versions of the sales brochures and updating our website. But if this project with Alex gets off the ground, I need to be flexible and I need to be able to produce web brochures quickly and organise e-mail campaigns with very little notice. What do you think?"

On paper the job was ideal for Evie. With even a small amount of work in France, she could afford to move over here. Her boss had reluctantly agreed that Evie working from "home" worked fine, but there just wasn't enough distance work to keep her going full-time. However, if she lived full-time in France with a few days' work a week, she could rent out the house in Dublin, cut down on childcare costs … As Evie did the maths, she realised her decision was already made. In fact she had probably made her decision the first time she had seen Holly throw herself happily at Alex after an absence of a few weeks. She had just been waiting for a way of making it feasible.

♡   ♡   ♡

Monique had known for some time that Céline was planning to offer Evie a job. But she'd also hoped that it could wait a bit longer. Monique wasn't sure that Evie moving to France right now would be such a good idea. Much as Monique would love to have her nearby, she wasn't sure how it would affect Evie's relationship with Alex. Monique would be willing to bet that if Evie moved to France, Alex would want to get married. He wasn't the kind of man who would find it acceptable to have his daughter and her mother living down the road without at least attempting to regularise the situation. And if Alex proposed, Monique suspected Evie would say yes; but she wasn't convinced it wouldn't just be because she didn't want to say no.

♡   ♡   ♡

Céline watched the way Laurent and Evie avoided each other all evening. Although neither actually looked directly at the other, Céline was fairly sure that each of them knew exactly where the other was every second. Otherwise there was no way they could have so skilfully choreographed their avoidance strategy. She had given up asking Laurent about Evie. At first her questions had angered him, now they just seemed to send him into longer and deeper bouts of depression. It was obvious he was in love with her, but it wasn't until Alex had returned to France and Céline saw the state he was in that she fully understood why Laurent had taken such a back seat with Evie. In some ways she admired her son. He had never before shown himself to have such honourable tendencies. To sacrifice his own chance at happiness for the sake of a friend. Or a debt. But at other times she just wanted to scream at him that she wasn't getting any younger and when the hell was he planning on providing her with grandchildren? She planned to be a glamorous granny, and that was harder to pull off on a Zimmer-frame.

♡   ♡   ♡

Suddenly Evie found herself beside Laurent. She wasn't quite sure how it had happened – one moment she was talking to Géraldine the schoolteacher, then they were joined by Céline with a reluctant Laurent in tow and, within seconds, Céline had removed Géraldine to show her something in the kitchen.

But no sooner had Laurent opened his mouth in a polite greeting, than Alex was at her side again. Suddenly

Evie realised that her avoiding Laurent all night had been made a lot easier by Alex's constantly steering her away from the Frenchman. And although she had no particular desire to talk to Laurent, neither did she want to be told who she could associate with.

So out of sheer contrariness, she beamed at Laurent, knocked back her drink and waved her empty glass within inches of Alex's nose. Eventually manners prevented him from ignoring it any longer and he went to look for a bottle that hadn't been drained yet.

"You've got him well trained," Laurent said cynically as they watched the other man retreat. "It didn't take long for you to decide what you wanted from him."

Considering the state he'd been in last time they met, Evie couldn't believe her ears.

"I'm sorry, Laurent, but what did I do to you to make you talk to me like that?"

Evie knew she was flushed but the noise level had risen, so nobody noticed her raising her voice. For a second Laurent's glacial expression softened, and she thought she could see remorse. But then his face went blank.

"I apologise, Evie." He performed a mock bow, inclining his body forward about one inch from the hips. "I didn't mean to offend you. You know I would never intentionally be rude to someone who means so much to a friend like Alex."

Polite though it sounded, it was like a slap in the face. He didn't see her as a person any more, she realised. Just as an extension of Alex. The bastard. He had more or less said that he didn't give a toss what she felt, but he wouldn't dream of insulting the woman, the *possession*, of a friend.

Evie's instinct was to slap him hard across the face. Hit him on the chest with her fists, or scrape her nails across his cheeks. She wanted to hurt him and shake him out of his smug complacency. She wanted to remind him what her skin felt like, but this time she wanted him to remember it beyond the next morning. Her hands tingled as she clenched them in tight fists by her sides.

But before she could react in any way, Laurent surprised her by leaning forward to say quietly: "I thought we could be friends, Evie. But you were the one who told me to 'get the fuck out of your life'!" Then he was gone, across the room to talk to Joël.

Leaving Evie open-mouthed in his wake.

She almost didn't notice Alex coming back without a drink but with a tired and sulky-looking Holly in tow.

"She's exhausted," he said. "We should take her home."

He was right, it was time to get her to bed, but it bothered Evie that Alex was the one to make the decision. And she felt small-minded in her suspicion that Alex was using Holly as a way to get her away from Laurent.

"I've already checked with Marian, and she said she'll stay a while longer," Alex said, when she seemed to hesitate. He held open her coat patiently. "And Céline promised to see her home safely. So I'll take you and Holly home now."

♡   ♡   ♡

"What do you think that was all about?" Monique asked Joël after they had waved Alex, Evie and Holly goodbye.

"What do you mean?"

"I know Laurent's your best friend, but I'm nearly your wife, so stop bullshitting me. I saw you watch Evie and Laurent together with just as much interest as I did."

"And like you, *chérie*, I was trying to figure out what was going on."

"Laurent hasn't said anything to you? You know he's been avoiding Evie like the plague since my birthday? And yet, whenever he meets me on my own, he always asks after her. And he sounds like he really cares – he's not just being polite. I know they had a row, but ..." Monique hesitated, not sure how far she should confide Evie's secrets.

"He's said nothing to me – in fact I don't think I'm being oversensitive to say he's been avoiding me," Joël said, sensing her reluctance to say anything else. "When we were children, if Laurent hurt himself, or if he was upset by something, we never saw him cry." He put his arms around Monique from behind and rested his chin on her head. They took a few minutes out from their party to enjoy the stillness of the winter night and the millions of stars in the sky. "He would run away and hide, and none of us ever knew where to find him. He wouldn't let us near him. Sometimes he was gone for hours until finally he would emerge when he was ready. He was usually in a bad mood and he often took it out on the rest of us – he could be especially spiteful to anyone who'd seen him when he was down."

"Is there anything we should do?" Evie asked.

"I wouldn't advise it," Joël warned. "He'll work things out in his own time. One thing about Laurent is that he's scrupulously fair. When he sorts himself out, he'll make it up with anyone he upset."

As they went back inside the house, they didn't see Laurent slip around to where his car was parked and leave quietly.

Chapter 38

On Christmas morning, when Evie saw the trouble Alex had gone to decorating the house, she was glad they'd come to France. Holly's excitement rose to fever pitch from the moment she saw hundreds of fairy-lights twinkling all over the bare wintry branches of trees on the lawn. Inside, Alex had decorated two huge trees on either side of the fireplace and there was enough spray-on snow to make the windows look like the house was deep in a heavy snowdrift. There were decorations and Christmas ornaments everywhere they looked, and Evie had to duck under a garland when she and Holly arrived to join the others in the living room. Sophie had entered enthusiastically into the Christmas spirit and even James and Alan seemed willing to put aside teenage bah-humbuggedness when they saw Holly's delight.

"I think Santa got lost," Alex said when he had finished tickling her in greeting.

"No, he didn't! No, he didn't!" Holly jumped up and down excitedly with relief. Santa getting lost had been a real worry despite all the precautions. "He brought me a huge teddy, and a baby-doll who really cries and weeeeeees! And a pair of rollerblades – pink rollerblades, just like Alan's. But they're pink! So they're not really like Alan's, but they are rollerblades! So I'll be able to go rollerblading with Alan!" Holly already hero-worshipped her new half brother.

"Well, you'll never guess what," Alex finally got a word in when his daughter stopped for breath, "I think despite all that, Santa did get lost, a little bit. Because when we woke up this morning there was a present by our chimney and I only know one little girl called Holly …"

Evie opened her mouth in protest. They had agreed – one Santa Claus! Her mother fired her a warning look not to say anything, so she bit off her words.

Alex led Holly over to the biggest box in the room. Her eyes shot open.

"For me?" The box was nearly as tall as her and wrapped in sparkly pink paper.

"Well, let me see … oh, I don't have my glasses – can you help me here, Sophie, what does that say?"

Sophie screwed her eyes up and read out, "H-O-L-L-Y! Anyone know what that spells?"

"Holly!" the little girl screamed. "That spells Holly! That must be for me!"

"You promised," Evie complained when Alex finally

joined her and gave her a Christmas kiss. But she was finding it hard to begrudge Alex the joy it was clearly giving him to see both his daughters rip shiny pink paper off the big box.

"I know, love, but it was for Sophie, really." He laid an arm casually across her shoulder but dropped it when he saw Andrew's head shoot up in surprise.

"A Barbie bike?" Evie laughed as the last scrap of paper fell away. "It looks a bit small for Sophie, to be perfectly honest."

"Very funny!" Alex cuffed her arm and led her into the kitchen to get drinks for everyone. "But seriously, Sharon had a scan last week and she's expecting a boy. Sophie didn't let on she was disappointed, but I know she was hoping for a girl. Sharon's unlikely to have another child – this pregnancy's proving a nightmare and she was told it should be her last – so Holly's the only sister Sophie's going to get." He shrugged and looked over at Sophie who was pulling her delighted little half sister round the room.

"Well, glad to know we're useful for something," Evie muttered under her breath, but it was hard to begrudge either girl the pleasure they were getting from the little pink bike.

She filed away till later Alex's statement that "Holly was the only sister that Sophie was going to get". Somehow she didn't remember ever having discussed that with him.

They had dinner with Alex and then walked down through the village. Nearly every house had some kind of decoration outside. Some had trees decorated with boxes, wrapped to look like presents in shiny coloured paper. Others had lights on window frames or balconies. Even window boxes were pressed into service with angels or stars pushed on sticks into their lifeless winter soil.

But once they arrived at Monique's all they could do there was admire the mince tarts her mother had made, because they had eaten so much turkey and roast potatoes that none of them thought they would ever eat again.

"Are you going to accept Céline's offer?" Monique asked Evie when she got her on her own for a few minutes.

"Was it your idea?"

"Céline is very much in charge of her own business, but she did ask me if I thought you'd be interested …" Monique trailed off, not wanting to admit her reservations about how soon Céline had gone ahead with the offer.

"Yes, I'm going to take it. I think so, anyway. I'll have to check out the details when we go home. But it's too good an opportunity to miss. It means I can move to France. Which I think is what I've been trying to work out a way of doing since … well, forever probably, but more specifically since I realised Alex would be living here, and he wanted to be involved in Holly's life."

"What does Alex think?"

"I haven't told him."

"Will you discuss it with him before taking a decision?"

Evie was surprised at Monique's question, but when she thought about it, it made sense. Any decision about moving would affect Holly. But, if she were to consult Alex, he might think that he was being asked permission for a major change to her life rather than being consulted as a matter of courtesy about a change to Holly's.

"I don't know," she hesitated.

"You don't have to …" Monique was glad to see Evie retain her independence. "I was only asking because, well … Holly …"

"I know what you mean," Evie said quickly. "And I'll think about it."

"And how do you think your mum will react?" Monique asked.

Evie went quiet. It was the one thing that she had worried about since Céline's offer had turned her dream of moving to France into reality. And she had avoided mentioning it, getting the feeling that it might put something of a damper on Christmas.

"I think she'd be happy for me … and for Holly," she said carefully. "But she'd miss Holly."

"She can always come over to stay."

"I know, but it's not the same as having Holly come around to her house."

"Oh well," Monique said, grinning. "If you all move in with Alex she can always take over your place and Holly can keep her bedroom there."

She'd meant it as a joke, but Monique could see from her thoughtful expression that Evie didn't think she was joking.

♡   ♡   ♡

"So, Monique," Marian asked when they joined the others, "what are your plans wedding-wise? Are French weddings very different from English and Irish ones?"

Monique noticed that no one imagined for an instant that she'd be getting married in Bristol.

"They're similar in some ways, different in others, and I'll be doing a combination of both really," she began to explain. The legal ceremony would be in the local Mairie and performed by the mayor. Then there would be a church wedding. "And then we'll have dinner and a reception in the Château de Beaulac, which is handy, because any guests from England, or Ireland, can stay there overnight."

"And where will you go on honeymoon?" Evie wanted to know.

"Somewhere warm!" Monique said threateningly to Joël, who laughed.

"It's already booked," he told them, "but I haven't told Monique."

"I'm getting worried though. He says I don't need any injections and most places hot enough at that time of year need injections."

"I've already told you, darling, you don't need any injections for glacier-climbing in Norway."

"You need bloody good life insurance though," Monique warned him. "I could be a very rich widow if you made that spectacularly bad a choice of honeymoon destination."

Chapter 39

Once Evie started planning her transfer to France, everything began to move even faster than she expected. Her boss, Jamie, grumbled but accepted the move as inevitable and agreed to keep her on part-time as an e-worker. Especially when Evie told him that there were plenty of small businesses run by English and Irish people in the Dordogne and that she would be perfectly placed to tender for their Internet business.

Someone at work had a cousin moving back to Ireland, and he agreed to rent Evie's house for the first year at least. He hadn't much furniture, so Evie could leave hers, and pretend her move was on a "trial basis" only.

Marian had expected Evie's announcement, and made her promise to phone often and buy a sofa-bed for the living room.

"You and Holly can't be expected to share a bed all the time I expect to spend in France!"

The only person who showed any ambivalence at all to her decision was Alex. He came to Dublin towards the end of January to see Holly because Evie was so busy she couldn't make the trip to France.

"That house is very small, Evie," he protested when she said she had no plans to look for anywhere else. "Where's Holly going to do her homework, bring her friends ..."

"She's four, Alex!"

"Well, in time she'll –"

"Have homework and want to bring friends home, I know. But the house is big enough for the moment."

She didn't want to tell him that she was reluctant to sell her Dublin house because she could smell burnt bridges. Nor did she want to speculate about what the future might bring.

"Besides, Holly won't only have one house – she can always bring friends up to your place too. And once the weather gets warm, I'd imagine your pool will be more popular than my back garden!"

Alex grinned. "Aha! So you're really looking for cheap baby-sitting? You should have said!" He was obviously pleased with the idea of a house full of his daughter's classmates. "And will you have enough room to work from home? Although I suppose you'll be with Céline a couple of days a week, and you could always set up an office in my studio ..." He frowned.

Evie knew he still hadn't gone back to sculpture, and although he hadn't said anything, she knew it bothered him. Sometimes she saw him look longingly towards the stairs to the attic studio and suddenly his hands would get restless.

"No, Alex," she said firmly. "That's your studio, for you to sculpt in whenever you're ready to get back to it." She was afraid that by offering it to her he was making an excuse never to try again. "One of these days you're going to get the urge to make something, and you have to have it ready and waiting for you. If I monopolised a corner of it you'd be afraid to come up and disturb me."

Evie didn't like to add that she didn't like to move in, even to such a small part of his house, unless she knew exactly where their relationship was going. She was worried what Holly might read into it.

♡   ♡   ♡

Two weeks before she was officially due to move, Evie was in France for the weekend. She was sorting through some of the hundreds of things she needed to do, and she was trying to organise Monique's hen night. Monique claimed that she didn't want a fuss, but Evie insisted that if she wasn't going to come to Dublin, dress in a nun's costume, get drunk and be stripped naked and handcuffed to a lamp-post in Temple Bar, Evie would have to make sure she at least got a drunken night out in Bergerac.

"Although I'm warning you, you're missing out on a

cultural institution … you could have been able to tell your grandchildren 'I had my hen night in Temple Bar'… and they'd be as impressed as if you'd fought lions in the Colosseum."

"I've been to Temple Bar," Monique replied grimly. "So give me the lions any day."

"Spoilsport!"

So Evie was left with the task of organising a night out in Bergerac and she wasn't sure where to begin. She consulted some of Monique's French friends and she consulted Céline. And soon a plan of some sorts began to come together. Drinks followed by dinner in a restaurant in the old town, near the old river-port. Then a night-club, more drinks and back to Monique's for a giant girlie sleepover.

♡   ♡   ♡

"So are you looking forward to coming over here to live, finally?" Céline asked. They were in her office, and Evie was sitting at the desk she would be sharing with Monique. She had a mountain of tax, insurance and health forms to fill out before she finally took up employment in France and she was working her way through them with occasional assistance from Céline.

"Can't wait to make the final break!" Evie answered.

At the moment every day in Dublin was just so busy that she sometimes wondered when she found time to sleep. She had to have the house redecorated for her tenants. She had to move her clothes to France and some of her furniture to her mother's. She needed to enrol Holly in school in Ste Anne and she had found a French student in Ireland to teach her some of the language so that her first day in school wouldn't be too strange.

"And you plan to stay living in that tiny little house you're renting in Ste Anne?" Céline asked.

"Yes." Evie was getting tired of justifying the decision. "It makes sense to go on renting, at least until I decide what to do about my house in Dublin. I have a tenant sorted out for a year and …"

"I suppose you're wise not to make any decisions until Alex …" Céline paused and her pause was loaded with meaning.

Evie had a feeling it was a question rather than a statement. "Until Alex what, Céline?" she asked innocently.

"Well, until … you know …" Céline frowned, as if she were annoyed with Evie for not recognising that she was trying to be subtle.

Evie just waited for her to finish her sentence.

"Until Alex proposes, I suppose I mean. Surely it's no secret that that's what he intends ultimately? You, Holly and Alex all together again as one big happy family?"

"If it is, he hasn't told me," Evie said. She was afraid she might have sounded more aggressive than she meant to, so she bent down her head and concentrated on filling in her tax forms. A minute or so later, however, she ran into another language problem and needed Céline's help. When she looked up to ask her, she was surprised to see that the other woman was still looking across the room at her – now with a slightly puzzled expression on her face.

"So Alex really hasn't spoken to you about the future?" Céline asked after they had finally finished Evie's tax forms. "He's happy to just let things move along as they are and not formalise your relationship?"

"There's nothing to formalise, Céline."

"Oh, I'm sorry, I must have misunderstood ..." Céline's expression of polite apology looked too perfect to be genuine.

"Céline, has Alex been saying something?"

"To me? Of course not. Why would he talk to me about your future together if he hasn't even spoken to you? Alex and I are just business partners after all ..." Céline's smile was wide enough and insincere enough to make it quite clear to Evie that she wasn't being told the whole truth, and that she was supposed to work it out for herself. "So how is Marian?" Céline asked, suddenly changing the subject in a way that unnerved Evie. "I think she is looking forward to coming to visit, but sad to have you moving so far away ..."

Evie spoke for a few minutes about her mother and knew that out of politeness she should now ask after Laurent, whom she hadn't seen since the night of Monique's engagement party. But Céline didn't wait to be asked.

"Laurent is thinking of moving to Carcassone," she told Evie. "His firm are setting up a new office there, and they want him to go."

"I thought Laurent was determined to stay in the

Dordogne. Isn't that why he accepted the job with this firm in the first place?" Evie had heard that he had been offered a number of jobs, some with very prestigious Parisian architectural practices.

"Yes, well …" Céline sighed dramatically. "He loves the area of course, but maybe there's less to keep him here now …"

Evie couldn't be sure, but she had a feeling that this was directly connected to Céline's earlier comments about her future with Alex.

"What's changed?" she asked innocently.

"Oh, you know …" Céline waved her hand around vaguely, unscrewed the lid off a bottle of mineral water on her desk and took a few quick sips. She left a long enough pause to indicate that "oh, you know" was all the answer Evie was going to get to her question. Then she said: "Alex must be *so* looking forward to having you move over. To see more of Holly, I mean. I know he misses her when you're away."

"Yes, he does." Evie noticed the immediate reintroduction of Alex into the conversation just after avoiding the question about why Laurent was thinking of leaving. "He complains that she's changed a bit every time he sees her …"

♡   ♡   ♡

Later that day Evie and Monique were moving some of Antoine's stores around in the barn nearest the house, so that Evie would have some extra storage space.

411

Monique had promised a barbecue as a moving-in present and Alex was buying them some garden furniture, so she needed somewhere to put them for the winter.

"I feel that I'm in the middle of some complex game, all about me, and that I'm the only one who doesn't know the rules," Evie complained as they stopped for a drink of water. Holly was outside on a swing Antoine had attached to the chestnut tree at the other side of the little garden.

"Oh, aren't we full of ourselves? A game all about you, no less!" Monique teased.

"Seriously, Monique, every time I come to France, I get the feeling that people have been talking and making decisions in my absence and no one's going to tell me what's happening." She told her how Céline seemed to be fishing for information earlier and how she had carefully dropped her own little bits of information into the conversation.

To her surprise, Monique went quiet. It was almost a guilty silence.

"Monique? What have you not been telling me?"

Monique took a mouthful from her water bottle and dabbed at her mouth with her fingers. "Nothing … at least …"

"What?"

"Well, I suppose I kind of assumed you and Alex were going to get engaged too. I even thought Alex was holding off until after Joël and I got married, so as not to 'steal our thunder' so to speak."

Evie was speechless.

"I didn't say anything to you," Monique continued, "because you didn't say anything to me. And I thought you wanted to keep it quiet. But this means absolutely nothing to you, does it? You have no plans along those lines at all?"

Evie shook her head dumbly.

Holly skipped into the barn and asked if she could "help", so Monique gave her a small box of paper napkins and told her to put it carefully on the pile in the corner. Then she gave her another and then another. It was enough to curb her enthusiasm.

"I'll go back on the swing now. When are we going up to Daddy's?"

"Later, love. For dinner," Evie answered weakly. And as soon as Holly was out of earshot again, she asked: "Monique, did Alex actually say something to you about us getting engaged?"

Monique tried to remember. She looked puzzled. "Do you know, I can't remember? Now that I think about it, I don't think he ever mentioned the word 'engagement', or even 'marry'. It was just a general impression I got from him. He was always referring to 'we' meaning the two of you. How Holly must be looking forward to having 'us' together. And then he'd add quickly, as if he'd slipped up, 'together in the same country of course'. I'll ask Joël if he can remember Alex saying anything more concrete, because he was dead certain you two were going to be making an announcement fairly soon ..."

"Joël?" Evie asked, as she felt pieces clicking together

in her head. "But Joël and Alex were never particularly close – it was always Alex and Laurent who looked like being the better friends."

"That's true, I never thought of that. But Joël's definitely seen a fair bit of Alex in the past few months. They seem to run into each other a fair bit in Lalinde Market. And Alex has been up to the vineyard a few times to buy wine …"

"Monique …" Evie hesitated. "You don't think Alex has *deliberately* been trying to give you and Joël the impression that things have got more serious between me and him?"

"Deliberately? Why on earth … oh!"

Evie finally filled Monique in on the full details of what had happened between her and Laurent on the day of her birthday party.

"So Alex may have guessed that Laurent is 'standing back', and he wants him to stay out of the way so that he can take things at his own pace? Have you spoken to Laurent?"

"No, not really." To Evie's surprise she couldn't tell her friend about Christmas Eve, because once she got over her anger at the way he treated her that night, all that was left was a deep sense of hurt. And of loss.

"But Alex sees a lot of Laurent and may guess that he's still –"

"We don't know that he ever was, Monique," Evie cut in. She didn't want to hear her say "in love", because she couldn't bear to think about him like that.

They moved boxes for a while longer and then they

went inside. Monique was about to go home when she asked Evie: "When Alex asks you to marry him – what will you say?"

"Let's wait till he asks, okay?" Evie said quickly.

Monique noticed that she didn't say she hadn't considered it. Nor did she protest at Monique's use of "when" rather than "if".

Chapter 40

Evie pulled the door closed with a loud click and walked halfway down the path to look back at the house which had been her home for the past five years. And Holly's home for her whole life.

It's not permanent, she reminded herself as she blinked back a few tears. If things don't work out in France, I can always come back. The house will still be here. I haven't completely given up my job; Holly can still get into school …

Then she mentally rapped herself on the knuckles and resolved to look forward not back.

Holly was in a lather of excitement. They had booked a large taxi-van, because Evie had sold her car and Marian's small one wasn't big enough to bring them and all their possessions to the airport.

Evie picked up her last bag, and the taxi-driver came up the path to take it from her.

"Is this really the last one?" he complained jokingly. "You look like you're emigrating!"

"We are!" Evie laughed back. "We're emigrating to France!"

Marian looked shocked as she said it, and Evie remembered too late about her brother in New Zealand. To her mother's generation, the word "emigrate" had such negative connotations that she was sorry she'd joked about it.

"You can't emigrate to France!" the young driver protested. "It's too near. You can commute from France. A guy I work with does … not in this job, in my other job, in the hospital, as a night porter …" Evie hoped he hadn't come straight off his shift into the taxi. "No, this guy I work with couldn't get a job at home in France. He works in maintenance here, but he's a plumber at home, and all the Poles have come in and taken all their jobs. So the poor bugger had to leave his wife and kids behind and come here to get a job. Still, he goes home every weekend or they come here …" He pulled out into traffic. "Of course it will be like that here soon. No jobs, I mean, with the foreigners under-pricing us. You couldn't live on what they charge for a job. A mate of mine, a carpenter, put in a reasonable quote there recently …"

Evie and Marian smiled at each other. They were both glad they had drawn a talkative taxi-driver for the drive to the airport. That awkward time between leaving Evie's house and getting to the airport, the time during which they were leaving home rather than on their way to France, would pass much more easily to the sound of a gabby cabby.

"And my uncle," he went on, "now that's really a scandal. Twenty-eight years, experience as a carpenter and cabinetmaker he had. Come back from the States two years ago – he had to come back 'cos he never got the green card and they're a lot more fussy about red tape since 9/11. Anyway, here's my Uncle Paudi, twenty-eight years' experience in New York, working with some of the best crews in the U S of A – he helped build the bloody World Trade Centre – and not one of the ones that fell down, mind you – do you think he could get a job when he come back to his own country? The country where he was born and bred? Could he? Not a chance. All those Poles and Lithuanians on the building sites …"

Now Evie and Marian were stifling hysterical giggles. This guy could do stand-up. Except he was the genuine article, and he really didn't see the irony.

"Well, enjoy France!" he told them as he unloaded their bags at the airport. "Never really could see the point of France myself, to be honest. Not enough sun. And a lot of it looks quite like Ireland, so I'm told. Give me the Costa del Sol any day. My girlfriend's father has a place down there, so we get to go for free …"

Evie could see his lips still moving in the rear-view mirror as he pulled away.

418

This is the last time I'll have to be picked up from the airport in France, Evie thought with a shiver of excitement, as Alex waved to them in Bordeaux. In future I'll have my own car and I'll be able to leave it in the airport, because I'll be travelling in the opposite direction …

"Marian!" Alex protested as he picked up one suitcase after another labelled with her name in large writing in black laundry pen. "How many outfits do you need for one wedding?"

"I lent Evie some of my bags," Marian explained. "It's handy because they'll be coming home empty with me … except that we all know what has to happen to empty bags."

"You told me you were coming to help me settle in!" Evie yelped in protest. "Not to spend the fortnight shopping!"

"Did I?" Marian asked innocently. "Do you mean I forgot to tell you about Céline's and my plan to go to Bordeaux to shop, visit a beauty spa and spend the night? Oh well, I'll tell you now so … it's the night of Monique's hen night!"

"Yes, and Sophie and I are going to baby-sit. Holly's going to spend her first night at the house." Alex beamed with pleasure, leaving Evie to wonder just how pally he had got with her mother to have been arranging things behind her back.

"It's time she spent a night there," Marian said without any apology later, when Evie challenged her about it. "She'll be living down the road from her own father and will never have spent a night in his house.

What will she say to her friends? And what will *their* parents think? That you don't trust Alex?"

"I just don't understand … Alex never told me he wanted to have her stay over …" Evie conveniently forgot his desire to decorate a room for her.

"Because you never offered, you big silly. When Céline suggested an alternative night away for us 'real' hens rather than cramp the style of you spring chickens, I rang Alex to see if he could baby-sit. And if you stop and think about it for a few minutes instead of getting all indignant, it's the easiest way of getting over the barrier of her 'first' night with him! It's not an issue between you and him, he's just doing me a favour. After the first time she spends a night there, it'll be much easier to arrange other nights."

"But Holly's only –"

"She'll sleep the night in Sophie's room on a pullout bed and she'll love it!" Marian was talking in her "don't mess with me" tone, so Evie stopped arguing. Besides, deep down, she knew her mother was right.

Chapter 41

Three days later, Holly had her first day in school. Evie was stunned at the length of the French school day. She was expected to drop off her baby at a quarter to nine and not arrive to collect her till half four.

She felt silly having a huge lump in her throat as she waved Holly goodbye on the first morning, because the rest of the children in her class were well into their second term and their parents were totally blasé about leaving them.

"I'll put her sitting beside Naomi for the first few days," Géraldine promised. "Naomi's mother is English so she speaks it at home. But don't worry, Holly will be speaking French like a native before the end of the school year. The lessons you got her in Ireland really seem to have paid off."

Evie gulped and nodded. She was afraid to open her mouth in case the sob building up inside burst its way out.

She fled from the school and almost didn't hear someone calling her name.

Joël was walking along the other side of the road with Laurent.

"Shit!" Evie muttered under her breath, but she crossed anyway to say hello.

"First day?" Joël nodded towards the school building.

Evie could only nod and pull a fake grin.

"She'll be fine," Joël promised, and his kind reassurance was all that was needed to let Evie's sob escape.

"Oh, come on!" He put an arm around her shoulder. "Laurent and I were just going to get a coffee in Antoine's. We had my bachelor night last night, and the coffee I make at home just isn't strong enough. My head is calling out for Antoine's unique blend of Costa-Rican beans and Dordogne tar."

Evie tried to think of some polite excuse to escape, but before she had managed to, she was sitting at a window table in Antoine's with Laurent, while Joël went to the bar to order the coffees and gossip with Antoine's wife Lucie.

"Did you have a good night?" Evie asked Laurent, desperate to dispel the heavy silence between them.

"Yes," he grunted.

Evie wished she were anywhere else in the world. Or more specifically she wished she could just get up, go home and bawl her eyes out with guilt for abandoning her baby to the mercy of strangers. Foreign strangers at that.

"Holly will be fine," Laurent said, guessing how she was feeling. "You couldn't find a better teacher than Géraldine to start school with. And the language won't be a problem for her – kids learn fast. Besides, Holly's going to make loads of friends. She's like her mother."

"Thanks." Evie acknowledged the only friendly words Laurent had spoken to her in months.

"Does Holly like making things?" Laurent asked then, surprising Evie completely with his change of subject.

"Yes, she …"

"I mean – would she enjoy modelling-clay?"

"Well, yes, of course. She loves play-dough, and she made a little clay pot at playschool so …"

"Good."

Laurent explained that he had bought a big lump of modelling clay for Holly as a "moving in" present.

"I'll give it to her in Alex's place so he'll have to show her what to do with it. It's a huge lump, so he'll probably realise that the best place to do it is in the studio …"

"That's clever …" Evie had been wondering how she could persuade Alex to try sculpting again. Teaching Holly would be an irresistible temptation for him. And a new medium might stop him from comparing his new work to what he did before. She managed to smile at Laurent and he smiled back. She wondered if they were beginning to call a truce. "And thanks, in advance … for Holly's 'present'."

423

"You're welcome."

Joël rejoined them. "We just missed Alex," he said. "Apparently he left about ten minutes earlier than usual or we would have seen him."

"Ten minutes earlier than usual?" Evie repeated. "What do you mean?"

"Antoine's started setting his watch by our resident Englishman," Joël explained with an indulgent smile. "Every morning Alex goes down to Mimi to buy the paper at precisely eight thirty – the *Telegraph*, she gets it in specially for him – then he comes into Antoine's, orders a coffee, *un grand* no less. He always sits at the same table, outside on the terrace, no matter how cold it is …"

"Even if it's raining?" Evie asked with disbelief.

"No, if it's raining he stays inside – he may be English but …" Joël laughed. "Then at nine fifteen he folds his paper, drains the last drops from his cup, spends a few minutes just watching the world go by, calls for his bill, pays and walks home."

"Every morning? Always the same?"

"Yes, except Saturday – Mimi doesn't open till nine, so that pushes Alex along by half an hour, and on Sunday Antoine doesn't open, so I presume Alex has to have his coffee at home."

"You look surprised, Evie," Laurent said ironically. "Is Joël revealing a side of Alex you've never seen?"

She flushed. "I knew he was a creature of habit but … well, I suppose I always assumed it was because of work."

The time Evie and Alex had worked together and the

history that went with it was too uncomfortable a subject for them to pursue and they began to talk about the wedding instead. "I'm trusting you to look after Monique for me at the weekend!" Joël warned. "Laurent delivered me home in one piece this morning, so you'd better do the same after Monique's hen night!"

"Don't worry. Monique insisted on a fairly quiet hen night. I don't think she's planning on getting up to too much mischief," Evie laughed.

"It's not Monique I'm worried about," Joël said dramatically. "It's that crowd of college friends of yours coming over from England!"

Outside the café, Evie kissed Joël goodbye and then turned awkwardly towards Laurent.

"I'm walking up your way," he said. "I left the car at Alex's last night."

Alex had been invited along on Joël's stag night and he had joined the others for the meal but had cried off going to a night-club and for drinks later. His French was improving, but it wouldn't stand up to much alcohol intake, and the others had a tendency to forget their English as they drank.

The pavement was very narrow through the village, and after a couple of paces walking uncomfortably close, Laurent stepped onto the road to walk beside Evie. By the time they reached her turning they still hadn't exchanged a word.

"Well, I'd better …"

"Do you want to …?"

They both spoke at once and Laurent held out his

hand in an "after you" gesture.

"I was just wondering if you'd like to come up? Have a look around?" Even as she said it, Evie knew it was a lousy idea. She waited while Laurent formulated some kind of a polite excuse. Or maybe he wouldn't bother being polite now that Joël wasn't around.

"Yes, please. I'd like to."

"That's alright, I … oh! Okay – this way." He'd caught her completely off-guard by accepting.

She dropped her keys while she was trying to open the door and they both bent down at once to pick them up. Evie felt herself go red when Laurent got to them first and handed them back to her.

Get real, girl, she told herself as she fumbled with the lock. Her fingers felt like they were made of Plasticine.

"And this is more or less it," she said, as she finished showing Laurent the living room. "There are two small bedrooms upstairs …" *but there's no way I'm showing you those*. "Would you like a drink, another coffee or anything?"

"No, I should be getting off …"

"Okay. And, Laurent, thanks again for the modelling clay. It's a brilliant idea. You've really got inside Alex's head, haven't you?"

"I don't know about that … but …"

He turned to leave but Evie could have sworn she heard him mumble something like "but he's certainly got inside mine".

"What was that, Laurent?"

"Nothing, I was talking to myself."

426

"Okay – bye so …"

"Bye …" But he turned back from the door. "Evie?"

"Laurent?"

There was so much electricity between them that Evie almost expected her hair to crackle with static.

"Nothing … I mean … Look, we can be friends, can't we, Evie? Even though you and Alex …?"

"What?"

She had meant it as "me and Alex … what?" but he must have understood it as "What!!!" in the indignant sense of "What the hell are you talking about after the way you treated me?" because he just muttered "Sorry" and left without closing the door behind him.

But at least, Evie consoled herself, he had made the first move to banish the ill-feeling between them. She hummed happily as she wandered about the room moving and rearranging things, as she made the changes needed to transform her little house from holiday home to "Home Sweet Home".

Chapter 42

When school finished that day, Evie and Alex collected Holly together. She was a tiny bit tearful with relief at seeing them, but within seconds she was chattering happily about her new *"amis"*. They walked together through the village and when they were almost at Alex's house, he told Holly he had a surprise for her.

"Laurent left a moving-in present for you," he told the delighted little girl. "But I'm not going to tell you what it is until we get home."

Evie chafed at his use of the word "home" to Holly when he was referring to his house but told herself she was being irrational. Holly had two homes, and maybe one day she would have only one, and it might just be the house Alex was referring to …

"I'll head back to the house, while you two get to

grips with Laurent's present," Evie said as they arrived back at Alex's. "I'll come back later for dinner," she added when she saw Alex's tiny frown. "I'll just get in the way while you're working on … you know …"

"About seven?" Alex said stiffly, and Evie wondered what she had done wrong this time.

"Seven's fine," she answered, thinking he had probably hoped to palm off the clay project on her. "I'll see you then. Bye, sweetheart."

She kissed Holly and walked down the drive briskly. She heard her daughter chattering happily with Alex and thanked heaven children were so adaptable. She would never have believed, when she first found Alex again, that introducing him into Holly's life could have been so un-traumatic. But Holly really liked Alex. It was probably too soon to say that she loved him, but Evie knew that it was just a matter of time before their bond was just as strong as any father-daughter bond.

And what about her – did she love Alex? The simple answer was yes, she believed. But it was a slower burning love than last time around. When they were together before, she hadn't been able to stop thinking about him. Time spent apart, and fortunately there wasn't too much of it because of work, was agony. Whereas now, when she was apart from Alex, she could sometimes go for days without thinking about him. But then she would see him and the wreck of his face made her heart stop at the thought of what he had gone through for her. At how much he must have loved her to get into the car at such speed that morning to be her knight in shining armour.

And how he must still love her to be able to forgive the injuries he had sustained on her behalf. It felt good to be loved that much, if a little suffocating, and why on earth would anyone want to walk away from a love like that?

She didn't find it strange that she didn't have the same passion for him as she remembered, because she suspected that her fiercest passion was now reserved for Holly. And that was how it should be. If, in the middle of the night, she suddenly remembered how Laurent had made her knees go weak and how for weeks on end she hadn't been able to stop thinking about him, by morning she was usually able to drive the memory from her mind. And now that it looked as if they were going to be able to be friends, maybe Laurent wouldn't find it necessary to relocate to Carcassone and out of her life.

♡   ♡   ♡

"You knew about the modelling clay?" Alex said later that evening as Evie helped him pack the dishwasher after dinner.

Alex's question sounded like an accusation, and even if it hadn't, Evie would have felt defensive. She and Laurent had conspired to get Alex back into his studio, and she knew that Alex hated to be manipulated.

"Yes," she mumbled, turning away from him. "He mentioned something about it … Holly seemed to have enjoyed it anyway …"

"When did you see Laurent?" Alex asked. "You never mentioned it."

"Should I have?" Evie's defensiveness disappeared, to be replaced with a sense of indignation at his tone.

"Well … I mean …" Now Alex was on the defensive. "Of course it's not that you should have … I mean … I was just surprised, that's all. He's a friend, you were talking to him and you didn't think to mention it …"

Evie realised that the subject of Laurent was going to be an awkward one between them for some time. She wondered how aware Alex was of the dynamics of the relationship between the three of them and what would happen if he discovered the full truth.

She moved to defuse the situation.

"It was this morning," Evie smiled casually. Then she looked towards the next room where Holly was watching a DVD and lowered her voice. Partly so that Holly wouldn't hear and partly to generate a feeling of "conspiracy" between herself and Alex. "Joël saw me outside the school – I was in bits after dropping herself off – and he brought me for a coffee. Laurent came too."

"I knew you should have let me come with you to the school." Alex's tone was part reproachful, part sympathetic. "I knew what you'd be like."

"I just thought it would be easier … you know … for Holly to only have to say goodbye to one person." Evie didn't explain that she never had any intention of sharing Holly's first day at school with Alex. This shared parenting thing was all very well in theory, but there were some lone parent intimacies Evie intended to guard jealously for as long as she could.

They continued clearing the kitchen like a "real"

couple, Holly came in to ask for some more ice cream and their awkwardness dissipated slowly like mist on a sunny morning. But Evie couldn't help asking herself if there would ever be a time when they could go for a whole day without at least some awkwardness creeping in. At the moment, life with Alex was hard work – he was so prickly and Evie felt it was her responsibility to put him at ease all the time. And she wasn't even "with" Alex in the full sense of the word.

He walked them home soon after that and came in and made coffee while Evie put Holly to bed. When she came back downstairs, she was surprised to find that he had taken out her good wineglasses as well as the coffee things, was in the process of lighting candles around the living room and had added a few more logs to the stove in the fireplace. He was clearly settling in for a long evening.

"I thought we'd celebrate Holly's first day at school," Alex said when he heard her come in. "And I have something to ask you …"

He looked so nervous that Evie's heart stopped for a moment. Then it began to pound heavily, no doubt to supply blood to the butterflies cavorting in her stomach.

"Mnhh?" was all she managed to mumble as her legs turned to jelly and she sank onto the sofa.

"Back in a tick …"

In his own nervousness, Alex seemed totally unaware of Evie's nerves.

She remembered what Céline and Monique had said and wondered if Alex was just about to "pop the question".

What the hell was she supposed to say?

Evie knew she had about two minutes to figure it out while he was in the kitchen getting the wine (or champagne?) and coffee.

Of course she'd say yes … wouldn't she? Oh, God, no, she couldn't!

"I'd like to book us a holiday," Alex said when he finally joined her.

There was no sign of champagne, no little black box hidden behind the wine bottle (a bottle he'd found already opened in the fridge) and clearly no intention on Alex's part of proposing a long and loving life together. Although Evie's overwhelming feeling was one of relief, she also felt a stab of – not quite disappointment – but frustration. Frustration at being kept hanging on while he made up his mind.

"A holiday for you, me and Holly," Alex explained as he poured coffee. "Maybe during the school holidays at Easter?"

"Well, yes … I suppose so …" Evie mumbled, unable to think quickly of a reason why not. "Where were you thinking of?" She'd worry later about the logistics of whether Alex planned for them to have separate rooms "for Holly's sake". "Somewhere nice and hot, I hope!"

"Actually," Alex blushed faintly as he said it, "actually I was thinking of Turkey. The holiday we missed out on five years ago. The one I sent you the surprise tickets for?"

"Did that hotel have a kids' club?" Evie teased. "It wouldn't have been an issue when you were booking back then!"

"Oh! I never thought of that," Alex said seriously. "Gosh, I'd better check before I make any booking, hadn't I? A kids' club …" he seemed to be making a mental note, "and what exactly would that entail?"

"The brochure will explain it," Evie said wearily, wondering when exactly Alex had lost his sense of humour.

Chapter 43

"Were you disappointed?" Monique asked the next day when Evie was telling her the story. They were in the airport waiting for the rest of the hen party to arrive from England.

"That he didn't ask me to marry him? Are you joking? You have no idea what kind of a fright I got when I thought he was about to!"

Suddenly Evie seemed to realise that this wasn't how she should be talking about Alex so she tried to row backwards somewhat.

"Of course, I don't mean a fright as such … that is …"

"Evie, this is me – Monique. Tell me what you're really thinking. Do you want to marry Alex?"

"No! I mean … well, you know what I mean …"

Monique shook her head silently, forcing Evie to go on.

"We're back together, and that's enough for the moment …"

"But …?" Monique prompted when Evie went into a daze for about the tenth time since they had started the conversation.

"But …" Evie waved her hands around in frustration, "I don't know where I stand with him. We slept together …" She noticed Monique's raised eyebrows and added quickly, "Just the once, and then we agreed to take things more slowly … you know, not to confuse Holly or anything…"

"You kept *that* very quiet," Monique said sulkily.

"I was going to tell you but …"

Evie wasn't sure why she hadn't told Monique. Possibly because there was so little to tell and probably because she was afraid of the question she knew Monique was getting ready to ask. The sulky look had passed in an instant and Monique's face was lit with an air of gossipy mischief.

"Was it good?"

"What?" Evie pretended not to understand even though she had predicted the question only seconds before.

"When you slept with Alex. Was it good? The sex? Did he make your knees go weak and your –"

"Stop it, Monique!" Evie interrupted. She certainly didn't need a list of what she should have experienced. "It wasn't like that … you know …" She was about to say something like "homely" or "comfortable" but she didn't think her friend would be impressed.

"No, I don't know what you mean, I'm afraid," Monique said somewhat smugly. "Joël is –"

Evie held her hands up in a restraining gesture she hoped would be interpreted as "too much information". "It was just …" she tried in vain to explain, "it was just … different from before, that's all."

"Different good or different bad?"

"Just different!"

"You're not in love with him, are you?" Monique finally put it into words for her.

"No, I guess not," Evie agreed.

She realised she was kidding herself if she thought their relationship was ever going to proceed further than it had. She just didn't feel that way about Alex any more. She loved him, but not passionately. It was more like the love she had for her brother or for Monique. She loved him because he had given her Holly. Because he had loved her once, and because he loved Holly nearly as much as she did herself, but she didn't love him in the way she needed to love a man she was willing to spend the rest of her life with. And she wasn't prepared to marry a man who had said, no matter how indirectly on Christmas morning, that he had no intention of having more children.

To her surprise, it felt good to finally make her decision. She had given it her best shot, but it hadn't worked out. It would have been good if the two of them had ended up together, for Holly's sake. And, Evie couldn't help thinking, it would have shown Sharon, once and for all, how wrong she had been to split them up in the first place. But Holly was not a good enough reason to get married. And Sharon was an even worse one.

♡   ♡   ♡

Soon their two cars, Monique's "bug" and Evie's second-hand Renault, were filled to overflowing with giggling girls. Evie was delighted at how, despite the years that had passed since college, they fell back into their old routines. Between them they had quite a collection of life experiences – nine girls had collectively gone through five marriages (one of them could lay claim to two), two divorces, one commitment ceremony in Amsterdam (to be upgraded to a gay wedding as soon as English law allowed). There had been three broken engagements (including Monique's) and they had a total of seven children between them (twins to the lesbian couple). And yet as soon as they stepped out of their planes in Bergerac Airport they looked like the most carefree bunch in the world – clearly intent on having the weekend of their lives. Or maybe, Evie thought, they were determined to banish the spectre of the last time they had all seen each other – at, or about the time of, Tom's funeral last summer.

Unbelievably, they all fit into Monique's house. They would sleep here tonight and tomorrow night for the hen, and then move to the château for the wedding. But wedding outfits had to be hung, make-up had to be checked and hair had to be practised so the rest of the day was spent transforming Monique's home into a space resembling a cross between an upmarket department store and a circus tent. But as the evening progressed, and food delivery containers, wine bottles and beer cans began to pile up, Evie thought the place began to look more like the campsite at a rock concert and she was glad to escape at around ten to her own house for tonight at least.

"I have to get up in the morning to get Holly to school and to call into the office," she laughed as one of the others tried to block the door in protest at her departure. "Someone has to do a bit of work if Madame here," she pointed at Monique who obligingly raised her glass in acknowledgement, "insists on taking three weeks off just to get married and go on honeymoon. There'll be plenty of chances to get me plastered tomorrow," she promised, crossing her fingers behind her back. "Holly's going to her dad's so I won't have to go home."

Evie retreated then and wondered had she imagined a sense of "strangeness" in the others' reaction to her. For as long as they'd known her Evie had been a wild partygoer, then a single mum. Now she was talking of dropping off her daughter with a responsible dad tomorrow and retreating early to bed herself tonight.

Oh well, she thought, we've all changed. They've all just left their responsibilities behind for the weekend. Maybe they're just feeling guilty!

And for the first time, she was glad to have Alex to leave Holly with. He was her dad, so if Evie wasn't around, then it was right that he was next in line to mind her. To Evie's surprise she suddenly felt very grown up.

And she was even more surprised that it wasn't an unpleasant or scary feeling. She liked the feeling of being "settled" or "sorted". And she loved the security of knowing that Holly had someone to fall back on if anything should happen to her.

♡   ♡   ♡

Marian was packing for her own "girls' day" with Céline when Evie got home. Holly was asleep hours ago, exhausted by all the new things she had to take in at her new school.

"So …" Marian asked when she finally decided that her little overnight bag was appropriately packed for the kind of hotel she thought Céline would pick, "are you nervous about tomorrow?"

"The hen night? You bet – I'm terrified that Monique will need a lot more than twenty-four hours to recover from whatever they plan to do her. You'd want to see that lot. But I'm looking forward to it too!" Evie laughed.

"Not the hen night," Marian said. "I meant are you nervous about your first time manning the office on your own? When Céline and I head off to Bordeaux in the morning?"

"I wasn't, no. Not until you asked me," Evie answered grimly. She had conveniently forgotten that she was covering until lunchtime tomorrow and then they would be closing the agency for the weekend in honour of Monique's wedding. "Why? Do you think I should be nervous?"

"Well, no, of course not ..." Marian looked as if she would happily swallow her shoe if it meant successfully retrieving her foot from her mouth. "I just thought ..."

Evie began to think too.

Her mother was right of course. In all the fuss and excitement of the past few weeks, it had never occurred to Evie that she might run into problems. What if someone spoke a particularly idiomatic French to her? What if there was a sudden problem with a contract that was going through and she had to deal with lawyers? What if a client came in with a huge budget and Evie scared him or her away through not appearing to know the business well enough? Suddenly there seemed to be so much that could go wrong that she couldn't believe Céline had decided to leave her business in the hands of a complete novice for four whole hours. But then Evie remembered that Céline would be at the end of one phone and Monique at the end of another and she began to relax somewhat. She had a feeling she wasn't going to sleep too well though, so when Marian said goodnight she decided to stay up and reread one of the books Céline had lent her about the business of buying and selling a property in France.

She jumped when her mobile phone rang.

She picked it up quickly so it wouldn't wake Holly or her mother and noted with annoyance that it was after half eleven. She didn't recognise the number that came up so it took her a couple of seconds to recover when she heard Laurent's voice.

"I'll be on site just down the road from the agency

tomorrow morning," he was saying and she prayed silently he wasn't about to say that he was available "if she needed any help". Whatever confidence she might have kidded herself into having would vanish if she thought Céline had asked him to keep an eye on her. "I promised I'd put together an idea of the work to be done on a couple of the agency's properties," he was saying. "So I was hoping to pick up the keys. But my mother just told me you'll be looking after the office tomorrow …" He hesitated, and Evie realised that he hadn't known till just now that Céline wouldn't be at work. She sighed with relief that her new boss had confidence in her.

"I'm closing up at lunchtime, Laurent," she told him in a business-like tone. "So if you could come in before then. If you want tell me which places, I could get the keys out for you. Does Céline allow you to keep the keys out over the weekend? Because you know we won't be opening again until Monday?"

"I could come in early," he offered. "And get the keys back to you by lunchtime?"

"That's fine. Give me a list and I'll have them ready for you."

They discussed the three properties casually for a few minutes, then there was a moment's awkwardness as they concluded the "business" side of their conversation, and Evie wondered if she should just say goodbye.

"Look, I'm sorry, Evie," Laurent said abruptly, "about the last time we talked. I mean the way I stormed off like that. I may have misunderstood you."

"I think we should try to be friends, Laurent," Evie

said gently. "I'd like to be your friend anyway."

There was silence at the other end of the phone.

"Holly loved the modelling clay," Evie said. "And Alex spent time with her in the studio. I saw the start of a model of some sort of bird of prey, and there's no way Holly could have made it, so Alex –"

"Yes, he told me," Laurent interrupted. He didn't seem to want to talk about Alex. "I'll see you tomorrow, Evie. When I pick up the keys. Just after ten alright by you?"

"Yes, that's fine," Evie managed weakly just before he hung up.

Obviously Laurent's definition of friendship didn't include much small talk, Evie realised with regret. Maybe he was only making the effort for Alex's sake.

♡   ♡   ♡

But the next day, Laurent surprised her.

He came to pick up the keys as arranged, but later, just as she was closing the office for the weekend, Laurent pulled up outside and came in, leaving his car's hazard lights flashing.

"I'm just about to go for lunch," he said as he handed her the keys. "Do you want to join me?"

Evie wasn't sure she did, but she couldn't think of a polite excuse not to, so a short time later she found herself tearing a piece of French bread into dozens of small pieces as she sat across from Laurent. They had both just given their orders and he was talking to the waitress in fast, fluent French which Evie could have understood if she made the effort, but she just allowed her mind to drift lazily as she studied Laurent's animated face.

It was a shame, she couldn't help thinking, that they had met when they had. Or rather that they had got together, however briefly, when they had. Although there was no point in regrets, Evie wished she'd paid more attention to him years ago when they'd met for the first time. If they'd connected then …

Suddenly she realised he was talking to her.

"You said yesterday that you wanted us to be friends – does that mean you don't hate me any more?" he asked.

"I never …"

He waved away her denial as an irrelevance. "You thought I was rejecting you. No matter what my reason was – if you'd done that to me I'd have hated you. The way I felt about you, there were no half measures: it was either love or hate."

He said "the way he felt", Evie noticed with a stab of disappointment. Did his use of the past tense imply his feelings had changed?

"And now?" she asked, not sure what she was hoping to hear.

"Now you are back with Alex, and I hope you can forgive me, and that you can understand why –"

"No, I didn't mean that," she interrupted impatiently. "You said 'the way I *felt* about you'. Does that mean you don't –"

"Don't, Evie," Laurent warned. "There's no point.

You love Alex, he loves you. You know there's no way I'm going to get between you. *No matter what happens*. Let's just get on with our meal and chat. Let's talk about Monique's wedding like good friends."

Evie stared straight into his eyes, until he broke away and began a careful examination of the tablecloth between them. But those few seconds' study gave her the answer to the question he had refused to address. There was no point in telling Laurent she had decided she and Alex would never make it as a couple, because Laurent would never accept her rejection of Alex. Because he would always know that he was partly the reason for it.

The knowledge filled her with the most soul-shattering despair.

Chapter 44

She didn't have a chance to dwell on her despair. The afternoon passed in a blur of activity. Evie had to get a "sleepover" bag ready for Holly to take to Alex's. She had to phone the restaurant in Bergerac to confirm their booking and she had to take two of her English classmates shopping to buy drink and nibbles for before and after their night out. She had to collect Holly from school, bring her home to change and have something to eat, and spend some time with her before walking up to Alex's to meet him and Sophie there. And she needed to press Holly's flower-girl dress for Sunday, because she wasn't sure what kind of state she was going to be in tomorrow.

So when she finally reached Monique's house for a pre-dinner glass of champagne, she could quite happily have skipped the night's revelry and slipped quietly into bed.

"Knock that back and have another glass!" Monique ordered, when Evie held her hand over her glass as the bottle went round for the third or fourth time. "The taxis will be here in a moment, and these ..." she waved about two half-full bottles of champagne, "will be flat by the time we get home later tonight."

"Much, much, *much* later!" came the chorus. Then: "Down the hatch, down the hatch, down the *hatch*!" And magically, Monique's two half-full bottles, and another full one, were emptied in the few minutes it took the taxis to arrive.

♡   ♡   ♡

The meal was superb, but rather rushed as most of the group regarded the food merely as soakage for the main business of the night. Evie and Monique grinned apologetically at Louis, the owner of the restaurant, when they arrived, but he had been pre-warned and ushered the group quickly into a small private back room and closed the door firmly behind them. Monique was a regular at Les Trois Epées, and although she had hesitated before allowing Evie book her hen night into one of her favourite spots, she knew that if Louis ever discovered that she had gone elsewhere, he would never forgive her.

And the meal was a huge success – not least because by the time they had left the establishment, the entire staff had been made promise to join them in a night-club later when their shift finished. At one point Monique thought even Louis's patience would reach its limit as the whole hen party invaded the kitchen just at the busiest time of the night and insisted that the chefs lay down their tools for a photo opportunity. But Louis took it in his stride and cleared the kitchen quickly by suggesting the girls might like to help out – and he pointed to a huge pile of langoustines that needed to be deveined before cooking.

In the nightclub there were long discussions as to who was "getting" each member of the restaurant staff when they arrived. Monique, they all decided, was exempt because of her soon-to-be-married status – although Sandra, gay, and therefore "left out" as the staff were all male, wondered if Monique, who was getting married to one man for the rest of her life, ought not have "first choice". "Just to make sure you're absolutely and totally sure you're doing the right thing, sweetheart!"

"Ah, but Sandra, I'm already totally and absolutely sure. I've never been more sure of anything in my whole life," Monique assured her with a sweet, if slightly crooked, smile.

There was a chorus of "aaah's" followed by theatrical sticking of fingers down throats and simulated retching.

Monique's French friends declared themselves exempt on the grounds of being on home territory, too close to their husbands and boyfriends.

Sarah, unmarried, unattached and single "for longer than I care to remember" was putting in a serious bid for the hunky head chef. She'd heard from Monique that he was not long out of a long-term relationship and therefore on the market again. She was staying a week in France "on a man-hunt" she declared as she was despairing of ever finding a man in the circles she moved in back in Bristol. "All gay, married or knife-wielding psychopaths!" she announced sweepingly, drunkenly oblivious to the uncomfortable glances directed anywhere but in Monique's direction at her reference to knife-wielding psychos.

Mandy and Stella, both recently and still very happily married, said they'd settle for someone to dance with, so they were allocated waiters Jean Marie and Jean Luc, both gay, and a couple Monique assured them were divine dancers.

"Jean Marie and Jean Luc, a couple?" Stella giggled. "You've got to be joking! How did two guys with names like that get together?"

The other two marrieds, Toni and Gemma, both with babies under two, got out so rarely that they were making the most of their freedom, and by now they were far too drunk for anyone to seriously contemplate matching them up with anyone except perhaps the toilet attendant.

"I'm the chief bridesmaid – I've got to look after Monique," Evie protested when the girls' attention turned to her. "Don't try matching me up with anyone because I take my duties very seriously."

"I can look after Monique for you," Sandra offered magnanimously. "So if you happen to see anything you fancy – feel free to indulge. After all, you're the only one here who has a totally empty house to retreat to. I have to admire your planning by the way. Shipping your mother and your daughter out the same night …"

"Oh, very well," Evie said, playing along. "If I must … let me see … François! Yes, that's it – I pick François." She was referring to the wine waiter who was still in training in college in Bordeaux and just worked Friday and Saturday nights in Les Trois Epées. He was a nephew of Antoine's and Evie knew him from seeing him in the village café long before he worked here.

"Cradle-snatcher, cradle-snatcher!" the others sang, when they remembered who François was.

"Oooh, I forgot about him," Sarah complained. "Maybe I want to change my mind!"

"Too late!" Evie said firmly. "He's mine!" To her this was a game, but Sarah was rather serious about her plans for later on tonight and Evie didn't want her landlord on her doorstep asking what her man-eating friend had done to his innocent nephew.

By the time the restaurant staff appeared, however, it was clear that all bets were off.

"He's just toooo sulky!" Sarah complained of the chef, Marc, who was obviously still not quite over his long-term girlfriend. Of course the fact that Sarah's French was limited and Marc's English almost non-existent didn't help. François the baby-faced wine waiter, on the other hand, spoke reasonably good English, and his summers in Brighton learning the language had also been spent perfecting English chat-up lines. He and Sarah got on like a house on fire and Evie, having taken one admiring look at the way he honed in immediately on his most likely prospect for a "score", decided that he was more than old enough to look after himself.

She was exhausted by now and offered to mind the drinks and coats while the others got up to dance; so for a merciful few moments she found herself on her own until Marc, the "sulky" chef, came to keep her company.

"I hope you don't think I was being rude to your friend," he apologised, speaking heavily accented English – better English, Evie noticed, than he had managed with Sarah. "I just wasn't …"

"It's alright. I understand," Evie reassured him. To her surprise she slipped unselfconsciously into French as she was clearly more comfortable in French than Marc was in English. "And don't worry, she'll probably have forgotten you by the morning."

"Forgotten by the morning?" Marc put his hand to his chest dramatically. "I'm wounded. It's a good thing she's not my type."

"So what is your type?" Evie asked, just out of a desire to chat and be polite rather than to really know. Under any other circumstances, he would probably have been her type, her ideal type even, if he'd been a bit older. Tall, dark and brooding but with his hair cut hygienically short as befitted the head chef in a kitchen as well-managed as Louis'. And Evie had always had a thing for men who could cook well. Not that she had encountered too many of them.

"My ideal woman …" Marc said, smiling mysteriously, "that would be telling!" He looked Evie up and down slowly, not offensively, but sexily appraising and added: "Besides, I'm in the middle of re-defining my type. I intend to conduct a series of controlled research projects to determine exactly what my type is. In fact I'm recruiting research assistants at the moment."

The way he looked at her made Evie shiver deliciously. It was a long time since she'd been flirted with so obviously. Not since …

Then she remembered the afternoon she and Monique had spent in St Émilion and how Laurent had flirted with her. How that had ended up. And what she had seen in his eyes earlier today.

I'll be a long time dead, she thought, knocking back the remains of a flat glass of sparkling wine. There's no way I can marry Alex, and as for Laurent …

To hell with it! I could sit here and mope or I could do something to get my life back on track … and there are a lot worse ways to jump-start my new life than a one-nighter with someone as cute as Marc. She gave him one of her most seductive looks and leaned across the space between them, steadying herself by placing a hand on his thigh. She squeezed harder than strictly necessary just to keep her balance. Then she whispered in his ear over the sound of the booming music: "What kind of research were you hoping to carry out?"

The poor man looked as if he'd just swallowed a live bumblebee, and then just as the others came back to sit down, he caught Evie's eye and said cautiously, "You English, I never know when you're joking?"

"Aah, but I'm Irish," Evie informed him sternly

without cracking the faintest trace of a smile. "And the Irish don't joke about important things like research." She moved her hand further up his thigh. "In fact we're world leaders when it comes to research. Hadn't you heard?"

"Of course ... the Celtic Tiger," Marc replied with a grin. "And the Irish, do they make good research assistants, would you say?"

"Excellent ones," Evie promised, reaching down to get her handbag.

Chapter 45

On the morning of Monique's wedding, Evie woke with a start, wondered why she was feeling so anxious and darted to the window to throw back the shutters and check on the weather. Some of her nerves vanished as she saw a blue sky with just a few cotton-wool clouds floating lazily across it.

"Holly," she shook the little bundle in the bed beside her, "it's time to get up. It's Monique's wedding day."

Holly turned over grumpily, half sat up and rubbed her eyes. Then her mother's words penetrated her sleep-numbed mind and she cast off drowsiness in the way only an excited child can pull off. "The wedding!" she called out excitedly, jumping up and down on the bed on her knees. "Will I go and get my dress?"

"Breakfast, bath, hair and *then* dress," Evie insisted,

then called out to her mother. "Mum, it's half seven, you asked me to call you!"

The three of them met downstairs in the kitchen. Holly's excitement was contagious and Marian noticed that Evie ate hardly anything, which was unusual for her. In an attempt to calm the atmosphere down a bit, she began to tell Evie and Holly all about her day in Bordeaux.

"The hotel was gorgeous," she told Evie. "An old merchant's house, down near the old wine quarter. It was full of antique furniture. The bathroom in my room even had an old wooden washstand with a porcelain bowl. With modern plumbing, though," she added when she saw Evie's eyebrows raised in surprise – Marian was well known to love her creature comforts. "And the beauty salon, well, I really should call it a spa, it was the last word in luxury …"

Evie only half listened to the rest of her mother's story. She had heard some of it last night when Céline dropped Marian home, but her distraction was caused more by nerves than boredom. She was nervous for Holly with her starring role in today's ceremony. She was nervous for Monique – never having got married herself, she couldn't understand how Monique seemed so calm. She was nervous about the reception. There was to be no "top table" at which she and Holly would be expected to sit with Monique – instead the relatively small wedding party (by Irish standards) would sit at tables divided along the lines of family and friends. Monique and Joël's families would sit with the bride and groom; some of the

English crowd had had their partners join them so they took up a large table, which meant Marian, Evie and Holly would be sitting with Céline, Laurent and Alex. For Evie this promised to be beyond awkward, and yet she would have to put on the performance of her life to keep her mother and Céline from any suspicion.

She owed it to Alex to talk to him properly, but there was no way she was doing that until after the wedding. She didn't want to throw a shadow over the day. Monique suspected something was up but she didn't have the full facts, and Evie had managed to avoid being alone with her so she couldn't ask straight out. She had avoided all the other members of Friday's hen party since leaving the night-club without them in the early hours of Saturday morning.

The ceremony in the Mairie, or Town Hall, was to be followed by a wedding in the church where Joël's parents had exchanged their vows well over a quarter century before. It was a small sandstone church, isolated in the middle of the fields, with only a few houses scattered around the fourteenth-century château to indicate that it had ever served any parishioners. Now the church was only used on feast days so Joël and some friends had cleaned it up the day before, and this morning the women on the church committee had filled it with local flowers.

They shared cars from the Mairie to the château, parked in the grounds and walked to the church. Once again, as they made their way down a road so little used that grass grew along the centre of the tarmac, Evie gave thanks for the good weather.

Although by now, under French law, the couple were already married, Joël led the party with his father and Laurent, while Monique took up the rear, on her father's arm. Evie and Holly walked with Monique's mother while the rest of the wedding guests filled the space between the front and back of the procession.

This is what I want, Evie thought, holding Holly's hand tightly as they walked. If I ever get married, and that's beginning to look more doubtful, this is the kind of wedding I want. No fancy hotels, no wedding cars or big crowds. Just a few close friends and family strolling through the budding vineyards and sprouting sunflower fields to the church.

The ceremony was short and friendly. The curé, who had christened Joël, knew just enough English to haltingly translate the French marriage ceremony as he went along, and soon he was releasing the bride into the groom's care, and the procession made its way back out of the church again into the sunshine – this time with Joël and Monique leading the way.

They assembled for photos. Monique was wearing a simple ivory silk dress, with an asymmetric hem just below the knee. The only adornment in her hair was a sprig of creamy freesias and she wore her hair softly curled and framing her face.

Evie rearranged one of the curls and handed Holly back her little bouquet of flowers for the photo. Joël put his arm around his new wife's shoulder, Monique held

Holly close to her, Evie and Laurent took their places beside the happy couple and all the guests began to snap happily.

It wasn't until they sat down to dinner that Evie realised she hadn't spoken to Alex all day. She had been so busy with Monique that it hadn't occurred to her to seek him out, but she suddenly realised that he hadn't even come up to her so they could share their pride in how gorgeous Holly looked. He would have told Holly herself, Evie hoped – he had carried her on his shoulders back from the church when she complained that her shoes pinched – but he hadn't come anywhere near Evie. She knew they were coming close to a showdown, but she was determined not to let it spoil Monique's day.

Fortunately the table was big enough and the conversation lively enough that Evie and Alex's lack of conversation seemed to go unnoticed, but by the time dessert had been eaten and coffee served, Evie knew she wasn't imagining things and that it wasn't just her guilty conscience that led her to believe he was avoiding talking to her. The mild relief she felt that she could stop pretending did very little to calm her nerves.

So when, after just an hour of dancing, Alex offered to drive her home with Holly who was beginning to look exhausted, Evie knew she had no choice but to accept his offer.

They were silent all the way back to the village. The only voice in the car was Holly's as she relived "the best day of my life" in sleepy tones.

"Will you put Holly to bed for me?" Evie asked,

knowing that Alex needed an "excuse" to stay, but guessing that he'd feel uncomfortable on his own downstairs. As if he were lying in wait for her. "I want to change out of these shoes …"

Evie opened a bottle of wine. Not because she wanted something to drink – although through nerves she had hardly eaten or drunk anything all day – but she needed to take the edge off the confrontation that was to come, and there was a social "niceness" about stemmed wine glasses that could never be achieved with a cup of tea.

♡   ♡   ♡

Alex accepted the glass of wine she offered him when he came back downstairs, but he put it beside the fire without a word and just stood there until Evie had taken her seat again.

"I was in Antoine's yesterday morning," he said, almost conversationally.

"Were you?"

"Yes, it's part of my routine in the mornings. Just because you're not working doesn't mean you shouldn't have a routine, I always say."

Evie said nothing. There was no point. Alex had obviously rehearsed this and she wasn't about to screw it up for him. But she couldn't help asking herself why she hadn't noticed how old Alex sounded. Had she been loyally blinding herself to his faults? He seemed to have aged twenty years, not five, since they split up.

"On my way down to Mimi's shop to get the

newspaper to read over coffee," he continued, "I happened to notice a car parked outside your house. It wasn't a car I recognised, so I assumed it was one of Monique's friends. I thought maybe her house had been too small to take the whole group of you after all and that you'd hosted the overflow."

He paused, as if waiting for her to confirm this. But she said nothing, and he almost smiled, as if congratulating her for not falling into his trap.

"Imagine my surprise then, when from my table on Antoine's terrace, I happened to see that same car stop at the end of your road, to pull onto the main road. It was no further from me than you are now, Evie." He glared at her from where he was standing on the other side of the room.

"Were you planning to tell me there was someone else, Evie?" Alex asked when it was clear that Evie wasn't going to say anything at all.

"Someone else?"

"Don't try to lie to me, Evie. I saw him. Clearly. The driver of the car that had been parked in your front yard."

"I wasn't denying anything, Alex, but by saying 'someone else', in that offended tone, you're implying that we made some kind of commitment to each other ..."

"But I thought ..." He stopped and looked at her. Now he looked confused and bewildered rather than wounded and self-righteous. "The past few months ... I mean ... did they mean nothing to you?"

"They meant a great deal to me, Alex. I've got the

father of my child back."

"And that's all I am to you – the father of your child?"

"You never gave me any indication you wanted to be anything else, Alex!"

"For God's sake, Evie! What did you want? A marriage proposal?" When she didn't answer he looked sadly at her. "I was going to propose, you know. In Turkey."

"And now you've changed your mind?"

"No, I mean five years ago. When I sent you those tickets. Originally I had been waiting until my divorce came through, but I was afraid of losing you to someone else, so I thought I'd ask you to marry me and we could wait together for the divorce. But ..." He had started pacing up and down Evie's small living room and suddenly he stopped as her last words sunk in. "You thought I meant I was going to ask you to marry me *this* time in Turkey! And you just asked me if I've changed my mind!"

Evie said nothing. She just let him work his thoughts through to their conclusion.

"You had another man here, Evie!"

"We hadn't made any commitment to each other, Alex."

"But he was here," he waved his hand about in frustration, "in this house! And you imagine I could still marry you?"

"I wasn't a nun in the years we were apart, Alex. And I don't expect you were celibate either."

"That means nothing!"

"Saturday could mean nothing if you wanted it to … if you loved me, if you really wanted to marry me . . ."

Alex sat down. Defeated. He put his head between his hands.

"Something's happened to you, Evie. The Evie I was in love with five years ago wouldn't have done something like that."

"But I'm not the same Evie. And you're not the same Alex. And it was foolish of both of us to think we were. We've been 'together', for want of a better word, for nearly nine months. And you're still not in love enough with me to want to commit to me. Isn't that the truth?"

"Evie, you slept with another man!"

"Oh for God's sake, Alex! This isn't about sex, and you know it isn't. You didn't want to marry me last week, before this happened. You don't want to make a commitment to me, because you're not in love with me. This 'other man' crap is just giving you the excuse you need to come out with it and admit it to yourself."

"But I do love you, Evie!"

"And I love you. But we're not in love."

"So what's been going on between us for the past year then?"

"Guilt!"

Alex stood up and the colour drained from his face. His scar stood out lividly red against the pallor. A blood vessel throbbed in his forehead.

"So it's not enough to betray me!" he snarled. "You have to humiliate me into the bargain. You're saying that the past few months, everything we've shared, has been because you've felt 'guilty'? About this?" He pointed to his face.

"The accident happened, Alex. I'm truly sorry it did, but I don't feel guilty about it. And I certainly wouldn't have … Anyway, I was talking about your guilt."

"What do *I* have to feel guilty about?"

"For believing that letter. For leaving me on my own with Holly for nearly four years. For not falling back in love with me like before. That's what you feel worst about, isn't it, Alex? You thought you'd found me and that you'd been given a chance to make up for the past – to give me back what Sharon took from us. But you can't."

Alex sat down again and stared at Evie. How could he admit she was right? The past few months had been exactly what she said, an attempt to make up for those missing years.

"But you …" he tried one last time to get them back onto an even footing, "you believed your letter too."

Evie nodded silently. She didn't want to point out the obvious: that she had been the one without any power in the situation. The employee losing her job as well as the man she loved. And the letter she received showed Alex to be a man returning to his wife – there was some nobility there. Whereas the letter Evie was supposed to have sent, the one Alex believed in, portrayed her as a scheming blackmailer. Ultimately, Evie knew that was what would always come between them. That was his real betrayal.

"The past happened, Alex. Shit happens! But I'm not prepared to build my whole future on it," she said then.

"And you don't want a future that includes me?"

"Yes, I do. But not as a couple. As parents."

"I suppose that's not such a bad basis for a relationship."

"It's probably one of the best. It's just a shame we didn't recognise it straight away."

"You'll stay in France?"

Evie nodded. They were silent for a few moments, then Alex stood up to leave.

"Just one question, Evie," he said, standing in front of her.

"What?"

"That man, on Saturday. Was that deliberate?"

"What do you mean?"

"Did you go out to sleep with someone deliberately?" Alex asked. "Was I supposed to find out? Was it to drive me away or to make me realise that I didn't really love you enough?"

"Does it matter?" Evie asked in reply

"No," he shrugged. "I suppose not. The result's the same."

In time, Evie knew, he would probably come to realise that his precise morning timetable was the subject of fond amusement amongst the villagers, and he might work out how she had pulled it off. How she had managed to kick Marc out at a time she knew Alex couldn't fail to see him. But hopefully by then it really wouldn't matter.

They stared at each other. There was so much to say, so much to work out and organise, but instinctively they both knew that this was not the time.

"I suppose I'd better say goodnight then, Evie," he said instead. "Is Holly going to school tomorrow? Or do you think she'll be too tired?"

"I think she'd want to go to school if it meant sleep-walking. She's dying to tell everyone about the wedding."

"Can I bring her to school, then? Pick her up at about, quarter to nine?"

"She'd love that," Evie smiled.

Chapter 46

Late one evening a couple of days later, after a series of phone calls, Evie was standing outside the imposing building that housed Laurent's architectural office. She pressed the buzzer and Laurent answered.

"Evie!"

She wondered how he knew it was her, then realised that there was a little lens above the buzzer and that it must be a camera security system.

"Can I come up? I know it's after closing but …"

"Yes, sorry." He buzzed her in.

When she reached the office, he was apologetic. "Look, sorry to be … but I'm expecting someone. My mother said she was sending someone over from the agency. Someone who wants me to look at some plans …"

"*Ta-da!*" Evie produced a folder from behind her back.

"Oh, she didn't tell me it was you!"

"I asked her not to." Although she hadn't explained anything to Céline, the other woman had been more than happy to fall in with her subterfuge, and Evie wondered how much she had guessed.

Evie placed the folder on the table and opened it.

"I'm thinking of buying Antoine's house, the house I'm renting at the moment, and I want your opinion. It's not really big enough for me and Holly in the long term so I'd need to extend or maybe convert one of these barns ..." She explained her plans, pencilling in ideas over the rough plan of the house she had brought with her, ignoring Laurent's cold silence.

"Evie," he said at last, "if you want me to ask one of my colleagues to look at this ..."

"No, Laurent. I want *you* to look at it."

"I'm not sure that's a good idea ..."

"Why not, Laurent? Everyone knows you're the best in the region, and I never settle for anything less than perfect."

"Come on, Evie ... don't play games with me, we've talked about this ... And besides, is it wise to invest so much money into a property that you might not be living in permanently? What does Alex have to say to all this?"

"Alex and I have agreed that there's no future for us together."

Laurent's face was guarded. "What have you done to him, Evie? Have you broken it off with him?"

"No, Laurent. Alex ended it actually. He realised that he wasn't ready to make a commitment to me. And that he never would be. He was in love with someone he let escape five years ago, and even then he probably didn't love her or trust her enough to go looking for her."

"What happened?"

Evie told him about Monique's hen night and how Alex had seen Marc, the head chef from Les Trois Epées, leave her house early the next morning. And how it had forced him to realise that he could never marry her.

"But he hadn't already asked you to marry him?" Laurent checked.

"No."

"And you hadn't made any commitment to each other. Beyond sharing Holly?"

"No."

"And how about unspoken commitment ... I mean could he have assumed ... was there anything implied ..."

He looked so awkward that Evie was tempted to force him to articulate what he meant. But she was too impatient, so after a couple of seconds she put him out of his agony.

"We weren't 'a couple', if that's what you mean. We weren't even sleeping together, Laurent. Apart from one time back in –"

"Enough! I don't need the details," he said holding up his hands. But his radiant grin of relief told Evie that he'd heard what he needed to.

"Were you testing him, Evie?" Laurent asked then.

She shrugged.

"He's a fool." Laurent's grin grew wider.

"What do you mean?"

"He let you go a second time, and just because of something like that …"

He reached out and put one hand on Evie's hip and when she didn't move away he pulled her towards him. Their lips met, gently at first, and then she pressed herself against him. She wanted more of him. The waiting, the longing, the uncertainty of the past year boiled up inside her and threatened to explode.

"Is there anyone here …?" Evie asked breathlessly.

"The building's empty," Laurent told her as they lowered themselves to the floor.

For a moment, Evie was glad of the thick-pile of the rug in front of Laurent's desk as it brushed the bare skin of her back. But then she was aware of nothing except the man holding her, undressing her, stroking her. Who wanted her as much she wanted him.

"This Marc," Laurent asked when it was over, when they had taken as much pleasure from each other as they had to give and were lying wrapped around each other on the rug. "The chef from Les Trois Epées – I can't really remember what he looks like. Is he big?"

Evie studied Laurent for a moment, then answered with a sparkle in her eye: "He's about your size, why?"

"In case I have to fight him for you."

"You wouldn't fight Alex for me!" she reminded him with a pout.

"But in the end, he gave you up without a fight. Twice. So he doesn't deserve you."

"And what makes you think *you* deserve me, Laurent?" Evie asked. "You were prepared to give me up too, to sacrifice me to your idea of nobility, to your loyalty to your friend."

"To be perfectly honest, I don't deserve you. Not for an instant," he admitted happily. "But you chose me, so I swear I'll spend the rest of my life trying to deserve you."

"Good answer!" Evie conceded reluctantly. "Okay, here's another question. How do you know I chose you? How do you know I haven't just come running to you because Alex rejected me?"

"I don't know. And even if that were the case, I wouldn't care. I've loved you ... it sounds trite to say 'as long as I've known you' ... but it's true. But how do I know you chose me? Because you make decisions and you make things happen. It's one of the things, one of the many, many things, I love about you. And because of what happened with Marc."

"What do you mean?"

"You weren't just testing Alex, were you? You were proving to me that he didn't really love you. Not enough."

"So you think I slept with Marc to release you from your promise. The one you made to yourself, that you'd stand back and let Alex have me?"

"Am I wrong?"

Evie shook her head.

"And it doesn't bother you?" she asked nervously. Apart from hurting Alex, it was the one fear that had almost led her to back down from her mad plan on Monique's hen night.

470

"What doesn't bother me?" Laurent asked with his eyes gleaming. "That you slept with another man, or that you'd stop at nothing to prove to me that Alex didn't love you enough? To 'release me' from the promise I'd made myself?"

"I guess that answers my question ..."

Laurent kissed her to silence her, then pulled back and examined her face. He was grinning wildly, as if he couldn't believe that she was actually in his arms, with him. That she'd taken such a huge gamble to win him.

"Do I get to ask a question now?" he asked.

"Ask away," Evie told him coquettishly. "I might not answer though. I have to keep up some aura of mystery after all ..."

"You'll answer this one!" Laurent threatened. "I won't let you go until you do." He wrapped his arms even more tightly around her.

"Oooh, I'm sooo scared ..." Evie giggled with delight when he tickled her. Then she watched him turn serious and she tried to match his mood.

"Will you marry me, Evie?" Laurent whispered.

"I thought you'd never ask ..."

THE END

Direct to your home!

If you enjoyed this book why not visit our website:

www.poolbeg.com

and get another book delivered straight to your home or to a friend's home!

www.poolbeg.com

All orders are despatched within 24 hours.